T0278440

# DAYS of EIGHT

Michael
Pallamary

Days of Eight

Michael Pallamary

ISBN (Print Edition): 979-8-35092-793-1

ISBN (eBook Edition): 979-8-35092-794-8

This book is dedicated to the neighborhood of Dorchester and all of its parishes, priests, poolrooms, packies, parks, playgrounds, police, beaches, bridges, buses, bars, beers, bowling alleys, schools, subways, streets, synagogues, steps, three-deckers, trains, trucks, trolleys, tonics, tracks, teachers, nuns, corner stores, gas tanks, hoodsies, and everyone lucky enough to grow up in this beautiful slice of heaven.

It is also dedicated to my family, friends, and enemies. You all know who you are.

"I didn't kill anybody."

— Billy McDermott

This story is set in 1968 in Dorchester, Massachusetts, a predominantly Irish, blue-collar community in Boston, when racism, homophobia, bigotry, and anti-Semitism were prevalent and made up much of the cultural elements of the community. The story, names, characters, and incidents portrayed are fictitious. No identification with actual persons (living or deceased) and products is intended or should be inferred.

The events that provide the backdrop for this novel occurred more than half a century ago when the country went through unprecedented turmoil and tremendous pain. It was the year Martin Luther King Jr. and Robert Kennedy were assassinated, and nearly seventeen thousand lives were lost in an unforgivable war, in a foreign land, on the other side of the world.

In order to pen a novel of this sort, one must remain faithful to the story and avoid watering it down with contemporaneous conventions and cultural niceties. To do so diminishes the narrative and robs the work of the power and pain found in the spoken word. I must therefore ask for the reader's tolerance for my use of offensive language. It does not reflect my views or those of my family.

Michael Pallamary
San Diego, CA
July 2023

# PROLOGUE

The number of United States Servicemen that served in the Vietnam War stands at 2,594,000, of which 1,736,000 were US Army, 391,000 were US Marines, 293,000 were US Airmen, and 174,000 were US Sailors. In total, 58,220 American soldiers died in the Vietnam War, of which 76 percent were from lower middle/working-class neighborhoods like Dorchester. The number of soldiers recorded as MIA (Missing in Action) stands at 2,338; 25 percent were draftees. They accounted for 30.4 percent of these deaths. Caucasians account for 88.4 percent of the men who served in Vietnam, while 10.6 percent were black. Seventy-five thousand men were classified as "severely disabled," 23,214 were classified as "100 percent disabled," and 5,283 were lost. The average age of the Vietnam soldier was nineteen.

---

*"Focusing on the world of working-class of Boston . . . He compares the sacrifices of poor and working-class neighborhoods with the rarity of wartime casualties in the "fancy suburbs" beyond the city limits, in places such as Milton, Lexington, and Wellesley. If three wounded veterans "wasn't bad" for a street corner in Dorchester, such concentrated pain was . . . unimaginable in a wealthy subdivision. "You'd be lucky to find three Vietnam veterans in one of these rich neighborhoods, never mind three who got wounded."*

*"Those who fought and died in Vietnam were overwhelmingly drawn from the bottom half of the American social structure . . . The three affluent towns of Milton, Lexington, and Wellesley had a combined wartime population of about a hundred thousand, roughly equal to that of Dorchester. However while those suburbs suffered a total of eleven war deaths, Dorchester lost forty-two . . . In other words, boys who grew up in Dorchester were four times more likely to die in Vietnam than those raised in the fancy suburbs."*

– *Working-Class War, American Combat Soldiers & Vietnam*
Christian G. Appy

The war in Vietnam ended on April 30, 1975.

There are 80 names on the Vietnam War Memorial in Dorchester. Others remain Missing in Action.

A letter to Mother.

*Now that death is constantly near,*
*'Tis being dead I no longer fear.*
*Nor am I worried of failure or scorn*
*But of what kind of man this war has born.*
*And what of the men with hair so long*
*Who burn their draft cards and chant their songs?*
*They are men with spines so weak*
*Who haven't been here, but choose to speak?*
*I know, I've been here, so I can say*
*They're a sad excuse for a man today!*
(Author unknown)

—Lance Corporal William (Billy) P. Dunn, Vietnam, OFD
Dorchester, MA, 1970

# 1

## AUTUMN 1967

The knuckled fist came out of nowhere and landed on the Click's nose, snapping his black-rimmed glasses and cutting a gash in his cheek. The chino-clad kid went down like a sack of potatoes as warm blood filled his mouth, causing him to gag. He flayed about, searching for something to hold on to, struggling to get to his feet as the screeching train wound toward Fields Corner. When the car pitched, he fell, and his head bounced off the corner of a rigid car seat. The piss-colored lights flickered as the rails rattled a morbid rhythm accompanying the carnage. The last thing he remembered was the silhouettes of three-deckers peering onto the subway tracks. The heel of a size ten boot landed on his jaw, splitting his lower lip open and giving his blood a new course to gurgle down. The leather-clad Rat, hair greased to the gills, planted another kick to the kid's head as if he was punting for the Patriots. "You fuckin' pussy!" he shouted, looking around for an audience. "YOU FUCKIN' PUSSY!" Louder. Another kick and more teeth popped out. At the other end of the car, one of the Rats bent a second Click over the side of a bench seat, laughing as he stretched him apart, tossing his loafers to the other end of the car.

Two of the Rats looked like a distorted version of Laurel and Hardy, while the other looked like an oily rag with two legs. The would-be Laurel had a thin face with close-set eyes and a stringy crop of hair pasted onto his head. Hardy was plump and greasy, held in place with baggy cuffed dungarees and a black leather jacket, like a gift-wrapped garbage bag. The oil rag had black eyes, black hair, and a black leather jacket that matched his beady little eyes.

Laurel jerked the Click's arm through the rail, pulling it until it was out of its socket. At the other end of the bench, Hardy punched the other kid in the ribs, listening for cracking bones.

At the far end of the car, Bridie McSweeney pulled her youngest son, Frankie, close to her side, already aching from her period. If she squeezed him any tighter, his eyeballs would pop. She and Frankie had just seen a Disney movie about a little boy and a horse, and they'd been talking about it on the ride home, and now, he wanted one. "I'll feed him, Ma. I promise I will . . . I'm gonna name him Nightwind," he said as he rubbed his face, itchy from his mother's woolen jacket. Her chest tightened every time a punch landed, and her breathing grew shallower. She prayed, but it did no good. The Lord had failed to purchase a token on the Red Line tonight. The howling that had filled the car was replaced with weeping, whimpers, and wind. A sharp breeze found its way through the rubber-lined doors; the station was close.

"Spread out!" the obvious leader, Tony screamed. "As soon as the doors open, run like a motherfucker!"

He looked at Bridie and wiped his mouth on the sleeve of his leather jacket while hanging on to the large metal handles, rocking back and forth. She tried to look away but couldn't; his eyes sucked the breath out of her. The wheels bayed, and the lights flickered as the train entered the station. Four Boston cops and a half dozen MBTA cops were on the platform, waiting.

"Fuckin' faggots," Tony muttered, wiping his mouth again.

Pug-nosed Hardy twitched as the train pulled in. "Oh man, we're fucked! Where'd all those cops come from?"

"Motherfucker," whistled Laurel.

Everyone looked at Tony. He kept wiping tiny beads of sweat from his face. The other two moved closer to him, fidgeting like boiling crabs. Bridie loosened her grip on her son as soon as the train stopped. Frankie peered around her back, trying to figure out if anyone was dead. When the doors opened, they startled Bridie. A blast of cool air filled the train. The T-cops went straight for the Rats, while the Boston cops watched from the sidelines.

Tony yelled again: "Fuckin' faggots!" as he windmilled toward the T-cops. His first two shots landed, but that was it; the fight was over. One of the cops, a younger one, took him down after clubbing him behind his knees. A short, overweight cop, sporting a tight military cut and huffing and puffing, clipped the smallest of the trio across the ribs, cracking them with his club. The last Rat put his hands up, surrendering. As soon as he lifted his arms, another cop whacked him across his lower back, sending him to the concrete deck, writhing in pain.

"They're all yours," the short cop wheezed. The Boston cops grabbed the kids by the collar and dragged them into a waiting wagon. Another cop stepped into the car. Bridie recognized him. She'd seen him around the neighborhood. He nodded at her and spoke. "Are you okay?"

She nodded, too stunned to speak.

"And the boy?"

"He's fine, thank you."

"You should leave," the officer said. "Would you like me to walk you out?"

"No, we'll be fine. Thank you."

She released her grip on Frankie while keeping him close to her. The pallor left her face. Her sky-blue eyes and soft Irish skin recovered their Celtic beauty. A small band of freckles spread like shamrocks across her cheeks. She stepped outside. The cool night air filled her lungs. She reached for Frankie as he tried to squirm away. He wanted to see what was going on back in the subway car. She glanced at him, and he quit tugging and fidgeting. He could see she was serious.

Several cops paused to look at her, something she had experienced many times and had never gotten used to. She remembered the first time as if it were yesterday. She was twelve. On her first day back at school, the older boys in the upper classes looked at her differently. It had continued ever since.

Bridie and Frankie walked out onto the concrete platform, spotted with gum, grease, spit, and urine. Another gust of cold air blew through the station, bringing the sounds of running engines, people talking, and a police radio chattering away. They shuffled through a crowd of gawking rubberneckers. Frankie turned to watch the paddy wagons start up while Bridie tugged him behind her. She pulled her neck down into the depths of her woolen coat and lifted her shoulders until her collar touched her ears, reminding her of Thomas's chin. She hadn't seen him for over five years, *devoted* as he was, *for better or worse,* having left when Frankie was six, Danny was twelve, and Chrissy fourteen. It was early fall, an Indian summer evening, a Saturday when he went to buy a pack of Camels and never returned. Another chilly breeze worked its way through her collar and down her neck, carrying the memory away on the whisp of the evening chill. She fought with the thick wooden turnstile as the rusty iron gate clicked, letting them through.

"C'mon honey," she said as they began the long, slow descent down the sloped concrete ramp that led to Geneva Avenue, past the concrete walls that reeked of piss, alcohol, and vomit. Frankie curled his fingers around the sleeve of his mother's coat as they weaved around broken beer bottles and other street debris, listening to the cooing of pigeons perched together on dark metal rafters, trying to stay warm.

They turned right when they reached the sidewalk and walked for several blocks, crossing over before passing Gavin's, with its thick green door and jade-painted windows, stuffed at the end of a long, three-story brick building, a structure topped with two floors of apartments filled with tenants used to the unwanted noises that erupted at two in the morning after the bar had closed, a place filled with men who had reached their peak in life—a steady union job, a wife who stayed home and cleaned and cooked, a couple of kids, and an apartment in a nearby three-decker.

Bridie remembered how Thomas had sat at the bar with its nicotine-stained shades casting a pitiful haze of light from dim bulbs that struggled to illuminate the long, dark mahogany bar stained with tears and a week's wages of spilled drinks, wondering how often her husband, beer in hand, eating a pickled egg, had watched her walk home with her arms full of groceries, only to complain about how much she spent to feed their family.

Another cold blast of wind greeted them at Westville Street, where, on the other corner, a group of kids was hanging in the entryway to Charlie's Central Spa, shadow-shrouded figures illuminated by the dull glow of cigarettes. They continued past a row of two-story duplexes and houses, neatly lined up like shipping crates in an old warehouse. Frankie tugged his mother's coat when their home was in sight. "What time is it, Ma?"

Bridie glanced at her watch. "Nine thirty-five," she said, pleased that the words came out clearly.

"Can I stay up, Ma? Can I? Can I?"

"We'll see," she said as they trudged up the long wooden stairs to the third-floor apartment. "We'll see."

"I want a horse. I'll take care of him, I promise, I will, I will."

# 2

Danny got up early for a Saturday. As soon as he did, Frankie sat up, wiped his nose, and started blabbering. "You shoulda seen it, Danny, you shoulda seen it! There was blood everywhere! They beat these Clicks up really bad! I saw the whole thing! And then the cops came and beat the Rats up! There were three of 'em! Me and Ma were there. We watched the whole thing. We did."

Danny rubbed his eyes and scratched his head. "Huh?"

"There was a fight on the train when me and Ma were coming home."

"A fight? What time did it happen?"

"I dunno, it was after the movies. It was kinda late."

"Did you know any of them?" Danny asked, yawning and stretching his arms.

"Naw, I ain't never seen any of 'em before. You shoulda seen it. The cops were waiting at the station; they beat the crap out of the Rats."

"Hmm. Hey, I'm gonna get some breakfast. You hungry?"

"Yeah. I think we got some Cocoa Puffs."

They both took a leak, went into the kitchen, and filled a couple of bowls with cereal and enough milk for everything to soak in. They carried them into the parlor and sat them on the coffee table. Danny turned the TV on and fiddled with the crumpled strips of aluminum foil clinging to the rabbit ears antenna until the static stopped and the picture was clear. After the third episode of *The Three Stooges*, Frankie burped, farted, and got up to get more cereal. Danny followed, putting his bowl in the sink and then going to the bathroom, where he closed the door and studied himself in the mirror, rubbing the stubble that peppered his cheeks. He removed his father's razor, crusted with shaving soap, picturing his father shaving a thick mat of whiskers from his face. He ran the un-bladed shaver along his chin, listening for the sounds of scraping stubble. After a few more passes, he returned the rusted implement to the same place, hoping his mother wouldn't notice it had been moved.

He returned to watch a little more television while the sun soon made its way out from behind the early morning clouds. He stretched his legs until they basked in the morning light, and when they were warm, he got up and went into his bedroom. He rifled through a pile of soiled clothes until he found a pair of dungarees. After sniffing them, he put them on, slid a T-shirt over his head, draped his Saint Christopher medal over his neck, and said a *Hail Mary*. He stuffed his arms through his sweatshirt and caught the scent of fresh coffee, something his mother made to entice Mrs. Feeney to come up so they could share the latest gossip. Marion, her neighbor, a chain-smoking, overweight nurse twice divorced, lived on the first floor with her frail mother, Kathleen, a seventy-two-year-old alcoholic who liked cheap scotch, nightgowns, and forty-ounce bottles of malt liquor.

"Morning, Ma," Danny said as he shuffled into the kitchen.

"Good morning, honey. Did you get something to eat?"

"Yeah. Me and Frankie had some cereal."

"Any plans for today?" she asked as she stirred some sugar into her cup.

"Naw, nothing really. I'm gonna hang out with the kids."

She nodded agreeably in response.

"I'm gonna go. I'll be back later."

"Are you gonna be warm enough?"

"Yeah, no problem," he said. "See you in a while."

"Okay."

Danny took the stairs two at a time down to the front porch, onto the sidewalk, and headed to Four Corners, crossing the street at Abe's Pool Room, where greasy-haired guys in leather jackets and white T-shirts leaned against tall plate-glass windows painted over with black paint. The crew nodded and parted when Danny entered.

"Just looking around," Danny said, nodding at Abe, who looked up from his dog-eared racing pages and nodded back. His desk was next to an old Coke machine that rumbled like a '57 Chevy needing a tune-up. Eight drink-stained pool tables were crammed into a long, narrow building like a dresser drawer. A long wooden bench, carved with the names and initials of every guy in Dorchester, sat alongside a foul-smelling restroom wherein the stains in the toilets matched those on the walls and ceiling. None of the kids were there, so he left, went outside, and strolled past the corner drug store into the deli. A row of white-and-blue Naugahyde booths and Formica-topped tables trimmed in strips of stainless steel ran along the left side of the high-ceilinged dining room. A Seeburg jukebox anchored the back of the restaurant. To his right, a long counter with a row of spinning seats sat in front of a stainless-steel grill and a pair of stoves, where the owner made breakfast, lunch, and dinner, splattering the walls with grease and oil, thickly layered from years of cooking.

"Can I have a bag of chips?" Danny asked the waitress, a thin blond wearing a grease-and coffee-stained apron.

She grabbed a bag from the counter. "That'll be ten cents."

He handed her a dime, thanked her, and left. He passed Sullivan's, a three-desk real estate office that always smelled of alcohol whenever a lease was signed or a house was sold. When he reached the Mount Bowdoin Y, he leaped up the wide, granite stairs and went through the large oak doors into the front office.

"Morning, Carl," Danny said.

"Morning. You staying out of trouble?" Carl replied.

"Me?" Danny responded, lifting his hands in the air.

"No, the other guy."

Danny laughed, paid the twenty-five cents entrance fee, and strolled through the foyer into the gym, past some little kids playing squash. He took the stairs two at a time to the boy's room in the basement; none of the kids were around. After taking a leak, he headed upstairs to the second floor, where "Leader of The Pack" wafted through the hallway. He heard some female voices, but couldn't place them. He caught his reflection in the window. He leaned forward, licked his hand, and patted his cowlick until it lay flat.

"Hey," Danny said, sticking his thumbs in his belt loops—something he'd seen Paul Newman do once in a movie—as he entered the "Teen Room." A jukebox sat in the corner. Several card tables and some magazines were scattered about. The place was full of girls, all of whom turned and stopped talking. Danny locked eyes with Becky Morrison, something he hadn't planned. She was a tall, leggy blonde wearing a cherry red, high-collared sweater matching the color of her lips. A pair of false pearl earrings shimmered in her lobes. Her slacks, black as the ace of spades, looked like they had been painted on. She sliced him in half with her stare.

"Hi, Danny. How are you doing?" Patty asked in a pleasanter exchange.

"Um, good. What-are-you-up-to?" he replied, sounding as if he had a mouth full of rubber bands.

Unlike Becky, who dressed like a magazine model, Patty McNulty was Irish-pretty, freckled, blue-eyed, and light-haired. Patty wore a light blue sweater, jeans, saddle shoes, and white socks. Her hair, blending blonde streaks with red hints, flowed across her shoulders, complementing her freckles.

Becky was sitting next to Katie Campbell. Everyone called her Kat. She wore a pink skintight sweater that hugged her chest as tightly as her spandex slacks hugged her hips and ass. Her dark silky hair was tied in a ponytail with a matching pink bow. A pair of black pumps accented her slender ankles. "Hi, Danny," Kat said, making the greeting sound like a solicitation.

"Um, hi." Danny felt his mouth dry up. "You girls seen any of the kids?"

"Like who?" Patty replied.

Becky stood up, drawing everyone's attention, fluffed her hair, leaned forward, and breathed on the window overlooking the church next door. She drew a little heart with her finger, stepped back, and admired her work. Danny waited a second before speaking.

"You know, the kids. Bugsy, Mooch, Charley, Mikey, and Billy."

"I haven't seen them," Patty said. Becky coughed loud enough so everyone would notice her. She drew another heart, larger than the first one.

"Um, okay," Danny said, shaking his head and turning to leave.

"G'bye," Kat said in a syrupy voice. Danny felt a pulse in his stomach and another, lower, thicker one between his thighs.

"Bye-bye," Patty added cheerfully.

Becky paid no attention to Danny; she started up again, "So I told her, for the second time, she shouldn't call him. It's not the first time like I said . . . *blah, blah, blah*." Danny left the room, went downstairs, pushed the front door open, and glanced across the street at half a dozen black kids hanging out on the corner. He lit a cigarette, and they stared at him. He stared back just as hard. They yelled something he couldn't make out. Danny took another drag on his cigarette and flicked the snipe in their direction. They shouted again, something he couldn't make out. He gave them the finger and walked past Levine's funeral home to Mother's Rest, nestled at the top of a gently rolling hill. A long row of splintered benches ran parallel to the sidewalk. Danny leaped onto the first bench and jumped from one to the other until he reached the last one, where he stopped and stared across the park, admiring the three-story homes that lined the streets as they marched out toward the bay. He walked down the concrete steps to Claybourne Street, circled the block until he returned to the Y, and went downstairs again. The craft room was filled with little kids making what he thought were animals out of newspaper and plaster of Paris. A tall, lanky man with horn-rimmed glasses and an acne problem was teaching a group of little kids how to bowl in the two lanes tucked against the far wall.

Danny turned when he heard the rumbling of bigger kids barrelling down the stairs, banging and bouncing off each other. His best friend, Bugsy Mulrey, a tall Irish kid with a chiseled face and reddish hair, led the unruly pack. He wore a blue windbreaker over a gray sweater and neatly creased dungarees.

"Hey! Douchebag! What's going on?" Bugsy yelled.

The bowling teacher yelled at Bugsy. "Hey! There're kids here."

"Fuck you," Bugsy yelled back.

The teacher shook his head and stared at Bugsy before continuing the lessons.

"So, what've you been up to?" Bugsy asked.

"Nothing much. You guys been upstairs?"

"Yeah," Billy replied, wiping his nose on his sleeve.

"The girls still up there?" Danny asked.

"Yeah. Becky, Kat, and Patty," Billy replied.

"I saw them earlier."

"I could eat a mile of that Becky's shit," Mikey said.

"You can eat some of my shit if you want," Fitzy said. Mikey rolled his eyes. The other kids shook their heads and looked at each other. The kids called him "Fathead." His head looked like a mop-topped pumpkin, and his nose was fat and wide. His teeth, green and yellow, were separated by a gap large enough to stick a cigarette in.

"Let's go downstairs," Bugsy said. Everyone followed. He tried to open the door at the bottom of the stairwell, but it was locked. "Fuck," he muttered.

"Get outta the way," Fitzy bellowed in a constantly irritating voice. He pulled out a ring full of keys and thumbed through them, sticking them in and out of the lock, stopping when he found one that worked. "Open sesame," Fitzy said, swinging the door open.

"Where'd you get all those fucking keys?" Mikey asked.

"Found 'em."

"Stole 'em," Danny said.

Fitzy shouldered his way in and flipped the lights, illuminating the room. He walked over to the rear door. A pair of wires ran from a metal plate on the door to a small box mounted above the threshold. He walked over to a nearby closet and grabbed a coat hanger from a wood dowel. He twisted one end onto a wire on the box and the other to another wire on the door and pushed the door open, flooding the room with the morning light and chilly air. A rickety wooden stairway led to the rear of the property. The kids stepped outside. Danny lit a cigarette and stared through a small grove of maple trees, void of leaves, at a row of weathered three-deckers that lined the street below. Frozen sheets and towels bounced back and forth from clotheslines strung across the porches. When he came back in, the kids were rummaging through the desks and closets, pulling things out and stuffing them into their pockets.

"So, what are you doing tonight?" Bugsy asked when he saw Danny.

"I don't know. I was thinking of hanging out and drinking some beers."

"Hey, can you shut that fuckin' door?" Billy yelled, wrapping his arms around himself. "It's fuckin' cold out."

"What are you, a fuckin' pussy?" Fitzy responded, brushing up against Danny before stepping outside, unzipping his jacket, and leaning against the snow-dusted railing. Danny said nothing while Bugsy stared at Fitzy just long enough for him to know he was watching. "You kids want to go upstairs and play some cards?" Bugsy asked.

They responded in unison, *Sure, Yeah,* or *Sounds good.*

"I'm gonna grab some lunch. I'll meet you kids later," Danny said. "Is that gonna hold up?" he asked, looking at the jury-rigged wire system.

"Of course, it will. What do you think? I'm a fuckin' amateur?" Fitzy replied.

"No, just an asshole," Danny said.

"What did you say?" Fitzy asked.

"Nothing," Danny said. "Nothing. See you kids later." He swung the door open and jumped to the frozen ground below.

"What did he say?" Fitzy asked Bugsy.

"Nothing. Not a fucking thing."

# 3

Danny woke up, covered in sweat, banging his hand against the wall. It was a dream; a barking dog, again. Danny ran his fingers across the scar on his chin. It was a warm Sunday morning, humid like most summer days. He and his friends were playing half-ball in the gas station parking lot across the street. Charley Evans hit the halved pimple ball, almost good enough to be a home run. Danny ran and leaped to catch it but wasn't fast enough. He landed on his side as the ball sailed over his head, slamming into the brick apartment wall across the street. His best friend Bugsy Mulrey hollered, "Danny! Get up! Get up!" Danny turned and found himself staring at a mangy-looking dog, snarling and snapping at him. His eyes widened. He froze and pissed his pants.

"DANNY!"

The dog came closer.

"Get up! Get up! Danny, get up!"

Bugsy and Charley both shouted and threw rocks at the raging beast. Danny scrambled backward as fast as he could. The dog leaped at him and bit him on the jaw, drawing blood and leaving a gash on his chin. He screamed louder as the dog continued snapping at him. Suddenly, his father appeared out of nowhere. He grabbed the mongrel by its back legs and yanked it so fast that its jaw bounced off the sidewalk. His father, a thick-muscled man, kicked it, sending it high into the air. As soon as it landed, he grabbed it by its rear legs and threw it against the base of a low granite retaining wall. Blood flowed from its mouth and eyes; shattered teeth lay strewn across the sidewalk. Danny placed his hand across his bleeding chin and watched his father stomp on the dog's neck, sending blood and fur all over the sidewalk.

Bridie ran across the street, screaming while Thomas calmly picked Danny up, saying nothing as he carried him across the street. A small crowd of wide-eyed neighbors parted, letting them pass as they walked back to their apartment. Still in shock, Danny stared at the dark tattoos on his father's arm, a marine emblem: an eagle, globe, anchor, and the letters *USMC*. His father stopped when he placed his son on the parlor couch, saying nothing and leaving the room. Bridie came into the room. "Hold this on your face," she said, handing Danny a small towel. He sat up and pressed his face into the cloth, shaking as he cried. "I'll be right back; keep pressing it." She returned a few moments later with their first-floor neighbor, Marion Feeney.

"Get a cold compress," Mrs. Feeney barked. "Make sure it's clean. I gotta grab a few things."

Bridie retrieved a clean hand cloth while Mrs. Feeney returned with a small leather medical bag. She unrolled a hand towel on the coffee table and laid the contents out, carefully arranging everything in its place. The wound was raw but clean. "Get me some ice and some rubbing alcohol," Mrs. Feeney said to Bridie, who left to retrieve the items. Mrs. Feeney propped Danny up. "You'll need to sit still for a few minutes so I can fix you up." Danny, wide-eyed, nodded. She took the compress from him, refolded it, and placed it against his chin. "Press it as hard as you can. We have to stop the bleeding." Danny wiped a new stream of tears from his cheeks and complied.

Mrs. Feeney, meanwhile, lit a cigarette and fumbled around with her tools. "Are you pressing hard?" she asked. He nodded, glancing nervously from her to the things on the table—a long thin knife, a funny-looking needle, scissors, and a small cup filled with green-colored fluid.

Bridie returned to the room with a small bowl of ice and a half-filled bottle of Canadian Club. "I don't have any rubbing alcohol," Bridie said, lifting the bottle.

"So, what happened?" she asked Danny, puffing and wheezing on her cigarette as ashes fell on Danny's lap.

"I . . . I was playing half-ball with the other kids across the street. And . . . and this big dog came out of nowhere, and he bit me, here on the face."

Mrs. Feeney nodded. She pressed the cloth against his face for a minute before removing it. "This is gonna hurt, so you're gonna have to be strong, okay?" Danny looked over to his mother; she nodded, reassuring him.

"Where's Dad?" he asked between sobs and sniffles.

Bridie glanced at Mrs. Feeney and then at Danny. "He had to take care of something."

"Is he okay?" Danny asked, peering up at his mother.

"I think so, honey."

Mrs. Feeney picked up the large curved needle and threaded it from a small roll with black thread. "Ready?" she asked, curling her words around her cigarette. She opened the bottle of CC and tipped it with the cloth held against the top until it was soaked. She dabbed the wound and held Danny by the head as she wiped the blood away and snubbed her cigarette out. "Here, hold his head, honey," she said to Bridie. "He can't move around; he's got to be perfectly still."

As soon as Bridie complied, Mrs. Feeney stuck the needle in Danny's chin, and as soon as she did, he howled and jerked his head. "You gotta hold him tighter," she said to Bridie. Danny continued crying and wincing every time Mrs. Feeney stuck the needle in. Seven stitches later, they were done. Bridie let him go, rolling her arms from exhaustion. Mrs. Feeney lit another cigarette and handed the cloth back to Danny. "Hold it against your face. Hard."

Danny wiped some tears away and nodded.

"Can I get you a cup of coffee?" Bridie asked Mrs. Feeney.

"How about some of that CC?"

"Sure, of course," Bridie said. "Let's go in the kitchen."

# 4

Bridie got up early to cook her Thanksgiving turkey along with a month's worth of mashed potatoes; a week's worth of string beans, stuffing, cranberry sauce, and rolls; and a year's worth of canned corn. Chrissy helped with the gravy, while Frankie stayed out of the way, watching cartoons in the parlor. Danny woke up and followed the scents to the kitchen. "What time's suppah?" he asked, looking at everything being prepared.

"Same time as usual," his mother replied. "Two o'clock."

"Okay. I'm gonna go out for a while."

"Where're you going?"

"To the Rest. It's the annual Toilet Bowl game."

"Okay. Don't be late," Bridie said.

"I won't."

"Are the front stairs clean?" Bridie asked.

"Yup."

"Good! The Smiths are coming by for pie and coffee after dinner."

"Oh," Danny said, doing his best to sound happy. Bob and Charlene Smith worked at the corner drugstore. Bob was a tall, bespectacled man with a hairline that seemed to vanish by the hour. He had a deep scar across his left hand, one he'd gotten in the war. If you waited long enough, he'd tell you all about it. Charlene was short, plump, and permanently plastered with a layer of makeup that stood out like the pitcher's mound at Fenway Park. Her breasts and stomach moved before the rest of her. It's not that Danny didn't like the Smiths; "They're nice people," his mother always said. He just wasn't used to that much *nice*. It was as if he was supposed to go to church or at least genuflect whenever she mentioned them.

"I gotta go," he said. "I'm late."

He walked toward the park and inhaled the scent of burning leaves. The saccharine smell came and went as he passed through the neighborhood and by an occasional pile of smoking leaves stacked in the gutter. When he reached the Rest, the game was in full swing. The goal lines were marked with jackets, cans, branches, beers, sticks, and rocks. The girls were huddled on several benches, watching the game. The guys were on another bench, smoking and drinking beer and liquor out of brown-bagged bottles. As soon as Bugsy saw Danny, he waved and yelled. "Get in, even it up! Charley, you get in too!"

One of the girls tossed Charley a small rag to tie on his ankle, similar to the one the other kids on his team had on theirs.

Danny ran out to the field. "Play in the backfield, next to Mikey," Bugsy said. "If I get the ball, I'll toss it to you. You can outrun those fat motherfuckers."

"Is it one or two-hand touch?" Danny asked.

"Two," Bugsy replied.

Danny crouched down and watched as the ball spun toward Bugsy. Danny's heart pounded when Bugsy caught it and shovel-pitched it to him. Danny pulled it into his stomach and ran along the sidelines, chased by the kids on the other team. He had to get by three more kids to score. Suddenly, Fitzy grabbed him by his belt and shoved him down the slope. While Danny rolled down the hill, Fitzy stood above and taunted him. "Nice run!" he yelled.

Bugsy ran over to Fitzy and shoved him. "ASSHOLE! It's two-handed touch," he spat.

"That's all I did. I only used two hands."

"You're an asshole."

"C'mon, man, it's just a fuckin' game. He's a fuckin' pussy."

Bugsy pushed Fitzy again, shutting him up. He then turned his attention to Danny, who had climbed back up the hill. "You okay?" Bugsy asked.

"Yeah, I'm fine."

"C'mon, let's finish the game," Fitzy said as he trotted back onto the field, grousing, "Fuckin' pussy."

"Are you sure you're okay?"

"Yeah, I banged up my knees," Danny said, lifting his pant legs to reveal blood dripping down his shins.

"You oughta take a break," Bugsy said. "That looks kinda nasty."

"I'm okay," Danny said.

A couple of the other kids asked the same. "You sure you're okay?"

"Yeah. Why's he gotta be such an asshole?"

"He's got a small dick," Bugsy replied.

"He's a fucking douchebag," Danny said.

"Yeah, I know. I was about ready to whack the motherfucker." Bugsy glanced over to Fitzy. "I didn't because it's Thanksgiving and all. He's trying to impress the girls. C'mon, I'll help you."

"Naw, I'm okay," Danny said.

Patty met him midway across the field. "Are you okay?" she asked.

"Yeah, I just scraped my knees."

"God, what's with that jerk?" Patty said. "Why's he gotta be such an idiot?"

"Bugsy said he was trying to impress you."

"ME!"

"I'm kidding."

"I hope so!"

"He said all of the girls."

"Gross!"

"I don't know. I guess it makes him feel good," Danny said.

"C'mon, sit down," Patty said, lifting his arm over her shoulder to help him walk.

"I'm okay," he said, pulling away, hoping Fitzy hadn't seen them. "I can make it."

"I know," she said.

Danny sat down, stretched his legs out, and closed his eyes, listening to the kids call the teams into formation.

"Hey! Want a cold beer?"

He looked up to see Patty offering him a can of Schlitz.

"Thanks!" He took a long swig, pulled his pant legs up, leaned over, and started picking the dirt and rocks out of the open wounds.

"That looks like it hurts."

"A little bit." He took another swig and rolled the can sideways across his thigh.

"Leave it alone," Patty said, gently slapping his hand. "Here, let me help you."

She grabbed one of the team rags from a basket on the other bunch, dunked it in a small cooler, returned, crouched down, and dabbed his knees.

"That's okay, you don't have to do that. I'll get it."

"Don't be silly. I don't mind doing it."

His teammates hollered; they'd scored a touchdown. Bugsy came over and passed a half-pint of brandy to Danny. "Thanks," Danny said, swilling back a mouthful. "How're you feeling?" Bugsy asked.

"I'm okay. My knees are a little fucked up."

"Of course, they are. You spend so much time on them." Patty giggled. "They don't look too bad to me. I think Fitzy's right—you're a fucking pussy," Bugsy said.

"Take a Dudley."

"I'll be right back," Patty said. "I'm gonna get a couple more rags."

"You didn't hurt your dick or nothing, did you?" Bugsy said. Danny laughed so hard that he spat his beer out.

"What's so funny?" Patty asked.

"Nothing. Nothing," Danny replied.

She looked at Bugsy, who smiled back like an altar boy. "I'll catch you in a bit," he said.

Patty placed one of the rags on the bench and started cleaning his knees. "So, what were you two talking about?"

"That piece of shit Fitzy."

"Oh," she said, content with the answer.

"Bugsy thinks he's an asshole."

"Doesn't everyone?"

"I guess."

She folded the cloth, end over end, and scrubbed harder.

"Ouch!" Danny yelped.

"I'm sorry. You got a lot of dirt in there. You don't want to get an infection."

Danny bent over to look. "I guess."

Patty continued picking dirt and small pebbles from his knees, and although it was painful, he smiled and laughed. He wasn't going to give Fitzy the satisfaction of knowing how much it hurt. When she was done, she folded the rags in half and handed them to him. "Here, hold these on your knees. I'll get you another beer."

"Thanks," Danny said.

They both sipped a beer while watching the game, occasionally brushing hands and knees against each other. Billy and Mikey walked over when the first half ended. "I'm gonna sit with the girls," Patty said.

"You okay?" Mikey asked.

"Yeah. I fucked up my knees," Danny said.

"No, you didn't. That asshole Fitzy did," Billy said. "You can't let him get away with that shit."

"He ain't worth it," Danny said.

"What'ya mean?" Mikey asked.

"I ain't gonna waste my time with that piece of shit. I think the real reason is he's got a small dick. He's seen my dick at the Y, and he's jealous," Danny said, grabbing his groin and tugging it. "I'm ready to play. I ain't gonna let that asshole fuck up my day."

"Sounds good," Billy said, clapping his hands. "We're down this end. We kick."

"Let me do it," Mikey said.

Once everyone was lined up, Mikey kicked the ball high in the air. Fitzy waved his arms and yelled, "I got it. I got it!" He caught the ball, tucked it into his ribs, and ran down the field, while the other kids formed a wedge around him. Bugsy ran alongside them, pacing himself with Fitzy, looking over to Charley, who was supposed to block for Fitzy. Instead, he slowed down just enough to let Bugsy through. As soon as there was enough room, Bugsy lowered his shoulders and drove into Fitzy, knocking him down and the ball out of his hands. Mikey picked it up and ran down the field unopposed. He spiked the ball and yelled, "Touchdown!" The girls got up, shouting: "Mikey! Mikey! Mikey!"

Fitzy was sprawled on the ground, moaning. His arms were bleeding, and his pants were torn. Bugsy grabbed two beers and walked to Danny, handing one to him. "You didn't have to do that; not for me anyway," Danny said.

"Yeah, I know," Bugsy said. "He needed a tune-up."

"It was a great shot."

"I coulda done worse, but I just wanted to get his attention."

"Yeah, ya did that."

Bugsy chuckled. "Fuck him."

Fitzy got up slowly, wobbling. Someone threw a rock in his direction, making him scowl as it bounced by. When he looked up, everyone was talking to someone else as if nothing had happened; there were no sympathizers. He limped back to one of the benches and sat alone.

"So, are you gonna meet us at the Y tonight?" Danny asked.

"Six, right?" asked Bugsy.

"Yup. Are the other kids coming?"

"I think so."

"Great. We oughta make a ton tonight."

"I hope so," Bugsy said.

Danny finished his beer and sat with Patty. "So, what are you doing this weekend?" she asked.

"Nothing much. Hanging out," Danny offered up with a shrug. "You?"

"My aunt and uncle are visiting; my mom made some plans for the weekend."

"That's cool. Hey, thanks for helping me. You're a good nurse."

Patty blushed. "You're welcome."

They watched a little more of the game. "I gotta head home," Danny said. "Maybe I'll see you over the weekend."

"That'd be nice," Patty said.

---

After filling his belly with turkey, mashed potatoes, green beans, and his grandmother's homemade cranberry sauce, Danny left, anxious to leave the house before the Smiths arrived. He hiked over to the rear porch of the Y and waited for Bugsy. When he did, Danny slid a thin piece of wood into the doorsill and popped it open.

"Let me make sure no one's upstairs," Danny said.

"Okay, let me know so I can switch the lights on," Bugsy said.

"All good," Danny yelled from the front office.

Bugsy threw the light switch, illuminating the gym. Danny joined him in the office. "What time are the other kids coming?" Danny asked.

"Six thirty," Bugsy replied.

"Okay. I'll get the basketballs."

Danny grabbed the keys from a hook beneath the counter and opened the tall metal ball locker. He took four basketballs out, placed them under the counter, locked the cabinet, and stepped outside, joining Bugsy for a smoke. Mikey and Billy showed up fifteen minutes later, carrying two brown-bagged bottles. "Everything set up?" Mikey asked.

"Yup. Just like last time. Danny and me are gonna run the front office. We'll collect all the money, and you guys walk around like you're checking things out. Now and then, fold your arms and stare at them, like Carl does," Bugsy said. "Act like a prick or something."

"Like we did before, 'member, Billy?" Mikey said.

"Of course. I ain't an idiot or nothing," Billy replied.

"I didn't say you were. Hey, let's see if there's anything worth swiping," Mikey said.

"That sounds good," Billy said.

Bugsy grabbed a *Sports Illustrated*, put the radio on, sat on a high stool behind the counter, and thumbed through the pages. Danny sat at the front office desk, removed some papers, put his feet up, and shuffled through them as if he were working. Ten minutes later, three black kids walked into the office.

"Can we get a court?" one of them asked.

"Yeah," Bugsy said, looking up from his magazine. "Fifty cents for the ball and twenty-five cents each to play. I'll need a dollar for a security deposit. I'll give it back when you return the ball. Everyone wearing sneakers?" Bugsy leaned over the counter and looked down.

Bugsy grabbed a ball and waited until the kids put the money on the counter before passing it over. Danny kept reading, looking up occasionally as if he was busy and as if he knew what he was reading. Over the next hour and a half, more black kids came in. Bugsy and Danny continued collecting money until Mikey walked into the office. "We can't fit any more of them spooks in there. The place is full."

"Get Billy and Mikey, will ya?" Bugsy said to Danny. "We gotta go. I'll meet you downstairs."

Danny stuffed the papers into the desk, walked out to the gym, and waved at Billy and Mikey. When they came over, he whispered, "Time to go."

Everyone met downstairs. They slipped out the back door and cut across Levine's and the Rest. They stopped at a phone booth on the corner next to the Kentucky Fried Kitchen. Bugsy dropped a dime in the slot and dialed. "Police Department. How can I help you?"

"Hello. This is Mr. O'Reilly. Um, Jim O'Reilly, from Algonquin Street. I just drove by the Mount Bowdoin Y, and the place is packed with a bunch of nig—um, colored kids. I thought the place was closed today. Something doesn't look right."

"Are you there now, sir?"

"No, I'm home. We got family over, you know, for the holidays and everything."

"I understand. How many of them are there?"

"I don't know. I didn't go in. There's a lot of them."

"Can I have your number?" the officer on the other line asked.

"Yeah, it's eight two five . . ." Bugsy hung up and laughed. "Let's head to the Rest to watch the shitshow."

By the time they reached the park, sirens were everywhere. Two paddy wagons and a couple of squad cars barreled by, blue lights spinning and sirens screaming. They pulled up in front of the Y, and a small army of cops piled out. A few minutes later, they started dragging the kids outside.

"We paid, man! We paid!" one kid hollered, waving his hands.

"I paid, man," said another.

And another: "I didn't do nothing wrong. I paid man, I paid. This ain't right. We paid the guys in the office."

"What guys? No one's in there," a tall sergeant said.

The cops stuffed the kids in the paddy wagons, kicking and screaming. "Shut the fuck up and get your black ass in there," the sergeant said. Twenty minutes later, the place was empty.

"Dumb fucking boneheads," Mikey said.

"I heard Mary Beth is having a party tomorrow night," Bugsy said, limping a cigarette from the corner of his mouth. "Her grandma's sick; her parents will be out of town."

"You going?" Danny said.

"Yeah, I was thinking about it."

"Nothing for nothing, but did she invite you?"

"Are you kidding? That cunt'd never invite me."

"Anyone else going?"

"I dunno; these mooks maybe."

"So, what're you doing tomorrow?"

"I gotta do some work at home. My ma's got a bunch of shit she wants me to do with the holidays coming."

"Yeah, my ma's been chasing me all week, too."

"I'm gonna head home. I want to get it out of the way," Danny said.

"I'll see you tomorrow night?"

"Sounds good."

# 5

Danny moved the things his mother had asked him to move, and he swept the steps out front. When he was done, he shuffled into the kitchen. "Did you get everything done?" Bridie asked.

"Yup. I even raked up out back," he said.

"Thank you. That was nice of you. Are you hungry?"

"Yeah, I could eat a horse."

She laughed. "I don't have any horses. How about a turkey sandwich and some potatoes? I have some leftover corn."

"Sounds great!"

"Why don't you wash up while I get suppah ready?"

"Sure."

"Oh, can you take the trash out first?"

"Sure," he said, glancing at Frankie, who'd somehow escaped that one.

Danny grabbed the trash bucket, lugged it downstairs, and dumped it into the garbage can. He sat on the back steps, lit a cigarette, and listened to the sounds of the neighborhood: sirens, barking dogs, kids laughing and screaming, a couple arguing next door, and cars wheeling by. He leaned back and closed his eyes. He was in Florida, drinking rum from a tall glass. Tall palms swayed in the wind. Patty and Becky were naked, swimming in a long blue pool; their breasts bounced every time they moved.

"C'mon in," Becky waved.

"The water's nice," Patty said.

Danny rolled his toes in his sneakers, imagining they were in the warm sand.

"DANNY!" his mother yelled from above.

He waved without looking up. "Coming, Ma." The girls turned and swam away.

Danny grabbed the trash bucket and jogged up the stairway. After washing his hands, he sat at the kitchen table across from Frankie. Bridie laid out a couple of pieces of bread and covered them with turkey, mayonnaise, and cranberry sauce. She scooped a large serving of potatoes and corn on his plate and placed it alongside a tall glass of cold milk. She poured herself a cup of tea and sat down. "So, how's school?" she said.

"Good," he mumbled in between a mouthful of food.

"How're your grades?"

Frankie slowed down, more interested in the answer than his meal.

"They're okay," Danny said.

"Have you met with your school counselor?"

Danny took a bite of his sandwich and slowly chewed it to death while Bridie sipped her tea and waited patiently.

"So have you?" she asked after he'd swallowed.

"Um, not in a while." He took another bite. Bridie sipped some more tea and glanced at Frankie, who stuffed his mouth to be safe.

"I've been real busy," Danny eventually said, the words sounding like a whisper.

"Doing what?"

"Stuff," he said.

"There's always going to be stuff. You're not getting any younger. You need to start thinking about your future."

"I know."

"You don't want to spend your life working under the table or packing ice cream at Seymour's, do you? You need a good education these days; it's not like the old days."

"Yeah, I know, Ma. It's just . . ."

"Just what?"

"It's just; I don't know."

"You're gonna be a man soon. You gotta start making choices; you need an education. And you," she said, turning to Frankie. "How are your grades?"

"Okay, I guess."

"'I guess.' I guess we'll see when I get your report card," Bridie replied. She looked at Danny until he took another bite of his sandwich. She finished her tea and got up.

"I'm done," Frankie said, belching. "I'm gonna watch some TV."

"Give me your dish," Bridie said.

"Sure, Ma."

"I'm going out, Ma," Danny said. He picked his dish up and placed it in the sink.

"Where?"

"Out."

"Out?"

"Yeah, out."

"Okay. Don't be too late."

"I won't."

Danny grabbed his favorite shirt and a pair of black pants. He stuck his head out into the hallway and yelled, "Hey, Ma! You got a safety pin?"

"In a minute," she responded over the din of dishes clattering in the sink. Danny walked into the kitchen, holding his pants by his side.

"Put them on, then. I'll get a couple of pins from my bedroom."

He changed and found his mother rummaging through a small wooden box in her bedroom.

"Let me see," she said. "Here, turn around. Hold them there." She tugged on his pants and stuck some pins in the back. "How's that feel?"

"Good."

"Turn around again." She tugged on his pants again. "That should be fine."

Danny looked at himself in the mirror and turned to look at his backside. "Thanks, Ma. I 'preciate it. I gotta go."

Danny returned to his room and grabbed his shoes, realizing he'd forgotten the right one had a small hole in it. "Shit," he muttered. He grabbed a pair of scissors from the kitchen pantry, grabbed a box of Cocoa Puffs, and cut the top off. He folded it several times and stuck it in the bottom of his shoe.

Several inches of snow had fallen outside, covering everything beneath a fluffy white blanket. When Danny approached Stan's Texaco, he threw a large snowball against the large plate-glass window, shocking the attendant, Artie, into looking up. Artie gave Danny the finger, and Danny flipped him back, causing them to laugh. Danny pulled his collar to his ears to fend off the harsh winds burning them. He stopped at Shur's corner store and banged his snow-covered shoes on the granite stoop. "Can I get a pack of Winstons?" he asked inside.

The potbellied clerk looked up from a dog-eared copy of the *Herald*. "Soft or hard pack?"

"Hard."

"Need any matches?" the clerk asked.

"Yeah," Danny replied.

"That'll be twenty-four cents."

Danny handed over three dimes and waited for his change. He stuffed the coins into his pocket, stepped outside, buried his head in his collar, and started walking. A snowplow made its first night pass, rumbling down Washington Street, burying everything parked in front of the curbs. When he reached the Rest, he tramped his way to the other end of the park, where he heard snow-muted voices rising from the lower end of the stairs. He could make out the soft glow of cigarettes and clouds of steam rising above a cluster of fuzzy silhouettes. He walked closer; it was a bunch of twelve- or thirteen-year-old kids smoking and passing around a couple of GIQs.

"Hey, Danny. What's going on?" Tommy O'Connor's little brother, Pinhead, asked, offering the bottle to Danny.

Danny shook his head. "Does your brother know you're out here?"

"I dunno. Ain't none of his fuckin' business."

"Keep out of trouble," Danny replied, continuing down the stairs. He turned and headed uphill toward the Lucy Stone School. When he was close enough to see the kids, he threw a couple of snowballs high in the air. When they landed, everyone started yelling, responding with a barrage of snowballs. Danny returned fire as he slid down the hill. "I thought you kids were at the Rest."

"Too windy up there," Billy said, passing Danny a bottle of Jack Daniel's. Danny took a swig and handed the bottle back to Billy.

"Want a beer?" Bugsy asked.

"Yeah, thanks!"

Bugsy pulled a frost-covered beer from a cardboard box jammed into the snow and passed it to Danny. "Any more beers left?" Fitzy asked, walking over.

"Naw, we're gonna have to make a buy," Bugsy said.

Danny pulled out a handful of change and gave it to Bugsy. After the other kids chipped in, they had enough for two cases of beer and a couple of jugs. "Anyone want to take a walk to the square?"

"I'll go," Danny said.

"Me too," Billy said.

"Anyone else?" Bugsy asked. Fitzy stuck his hands in his pockets and shuffled his feet.

Ten minutes later, the kids ran into Dodo, a grizzled old bayzo who'd been around for as long as anyone could remember. They made the deal: two cases of beer and three pints of JD, two for them and one for Dodo. When they were done, Danny passed a lit smoke to the old man, who remained speechless.

"Thanks," Dodo said with a green-toothed smile, showing those left in his head. Danny and Bugsy tossed a case on each shoulder, and Billy stuffed the bottles in his back pockets.

"Did you ever do it with Mary Beth?" Bugsy asked Danny.

"Naw. Came close. She gave me a hand job once."

"That's cool," Bugsy said. "She's got a great-looking ass, hasn't she?"

"Yeah, she has."

"Hey," Bugsy said crisply, nodding at a cop car headed toward them. He and Danny kick-dragged the beer behind a snowbank and continued walking. The cops glanced at them, and they, in turn, glanced back. After the car disappeared down the street, they backtracked, dragged the cases back out, and continued walking. When they reached the schoolyard, they started throwing snowballs at the other kids, lighting them up like a swarm of bees. After battling for a few minutes, the rest of the kids came over and lugged the cases to the stairs on Alpha Road. Half a case later, they were in front of Mary Beth's home. They climbed the broad wooden stairs to the front porch, tidily trimmed with hand-carved bulbs and stems hanging from a thick white fascia wrapped around the house. Everyone spread out and peered into the windows, thick with steam.

Fitzy strode past the kids to the front door and knocked. No one answered. He knocked again, louder and harder. He waited a moment, knocked, and kicked the door. A female voice yelled from inside, "Hey! Mary Beth! Someone's at the door." Mary Beth opened the door a minute later, carried by a blast of warm air and thick perfume.

"Hey, can we come in?" Fitzy said, poking his nose toward the warmth. She stared at him, blinking and speechless. "It's cold out," Fitzy said.

"How . . . how?" she stuttered. "What are you? I mean, how did you?" she went on, stamping her feet in exasperation. "No! It's a private party."

"Hi, Mary Beth," Bugsy said. Her eyes glazed over as soon as she saw him. "We heard you're having a party." A small crowd dressed in nice clothes, creased pants, and button-collared shirts gathered behind her. Mary Beth stepped outside and turned the doorknob behind her just as Mikey tossed his empty beer in the front yard and started pissing off the porch.

"Asshole!" Mary Beth yelled. "Get off my porch!" Mikey turned and waved his dick at her.

"Hey, dipshit, show a little class," Danny said, stepping forward. Mikey chuckled and turned around.

"I'm calling the police," Mary Beth said, fueled by a beet-red face.

"I'm sorry," Danny said. "He's been drinking."

"No kidding," she said, stomping and yelling again. "Get off my porch!"

"C'mon, Fitzy," Mikey said. Fitzy leaned over the railing, gagged a loogie, and spat it onto the front sidewalk.

"That's disgusting," Mary Beth said, nearly gagging.

Fitzy worked up another throatful of steaming snot. He rolled it around in his mouth and spat it out in the same spot.

"C'mon," Mikey said, passing a couple of beers to Fitzy. "Let's go."

Fitzy responded with a grunt. He and Mikey walked to the house next door, sat on the front stoop, and continued drinking.

"You can't stay there!" Mary Beth yelled.

"Fuck you," Fitzy said, chucking her the bird.

"Danny. Can't you do anything?" Mary Beth said.

"I wish I could. If I say anything, that'll just get 'em going. It's better to leave 'em alone."

"They're such assholes."

"What can I say?" Danny said. Mary Beth replied with a shake of her head. Danny leaned forward and whispered. "Can I use the can? I really gotta go."

"I gotta go, too," Billy said, hardly whispering.

"I have—" Mary Beth stuttered. "I have company, and . . ."

"C'mon, Mary Beth. You don't want us pissing in your yard, do you? We'll only be a minute," Billy said. "Promise."

"Okay, okay," Mary Beth replied, defeated. She looked at the other kids mulling around the front steps and spilling out to the sidewalk. "Make it quick."

Billy nudged his way forward, and Danny followed. Mary Beth pulled the door behind her as soon as they were inside. A stream of voices, laughing and chatting, came from the other rooms.

"Who are those kids?" Billy asked. "What parish are they from?"

"Saint Kevin's."

Bugsy nodded.

"Danny. Can you do me a favor?" Mary Beth said.

"Sure. What is it?"

"Can you ask the kids out front to leave? They're getting loud, and I don't want any trouble."

"Yeah, no problem."

"I'm gonna call the police if they don't leave."

"I understand," Danny said.

"I'm serious. I will if I have to."

Mary Beth turned at the sound of voices from the living room. "I'll be back in a minute. You two gotta finish up," she said, leaving the room.

As soon as she left, Danny opened the front door. "C'mon," he said, waving the kids in. Billy came out of the bathroom, and Danny went in. He took a quick piss and followed the voices to the kitchen. Mikey was sitting at the kitchen table, talking to a well-stacked blonde in a bright red sweater, sipping a red drink from a tall glass. He stopped chatting when he heard Billy yell, "FUCK YOU!" from the living room.

A voice Danny didn't recognize followed with, "FUCK *YOU*, ASSHOLE!"

Then, another "FUCK YOU!" rang out, followed by the sound of someone being slammed into a wall. Someone screamed; someone else was slammed into the wall.

"C'mon!" Danny shouted to Mikey, grabbing him by the arm. They stepped into the living room. Billy was slumped against the wall alongside the remains of a broken picture frame. Mary Beth was screaming and flapping her arms like she was trying to fly. Billy scrambled to get up but fell against the wall as one of the other kids kicked his legs out from under him.

Mikey tried to help Billy but was stopped by a pug-nosed kid wearing an oversized letterman's sweater couple. "Where're you going, asshole?" he asked, pushing Mikey into the kitchen and on the kitchen table, sending half a dozen beer bottles onto the floor. The kid started swinging. Mikey started to swing but was stopped when one of the other kids grabbed his arm, and another punched him in the stomach. Mikey gasped for air and braced for another punch when his arms were suddenly freed; it was Bugsy, tossing the other kids aside, grabbing them by the neck and shirt collars.

Danny grabbed the kid who had jumped Mikey and locked him up while Mikey worked him over, nailing shots in the stomach and sides. By now, everyone was fighting. The girls were screaming and running around the house, knocking chairs over, while the boys bounced off the walls, sending splintered furniture across the room. Mary Beth screamed again before collapsing and curling up like a newborn baby. Danny ran to her side. "C'mon," he said as he tugged on her arm. "You gotta get up. You're going to get hurt if you stay here." He pulled again, to no avail; she wouldn't move.

"Is she okay?" a tall brunette in a long skirt and flowery blouse asked. Danny looked up at her and half a dozen other girls, similarly dressed, leaning forward, peering over his shoulders.

"I think so. I don't think she's hurt or nothing," Danny said, looking around. "I wanted to make sure she didn't get hurt."

"That was nice of you," the brunette said.

Everyone froze when they heard Fitzy yelling. "You fuckin' pussies! Come back. I'll kick your ass!" Mary Beth let out another ear-piercing scream, startling everyone.

"Can you girls take care of her? I gotta see if I can get that asshole out of here."

"Yes," the brunette said.

Danny opened the door and stepped outside. "Did you see that stupid fucker?" Fitzy said. "I beat that asshole from wall to wall."

"My sister could have kicked his ass," Bugsy said.

"Hey, you guys. The cops are gonna be here. You guys ought to leave."

Fitzy started up again. "I gave him a real ass-kicking."

Danny stepped back inside and closed the door behind him.

"How is she?" he asked.

"Better. Lisa, get another cold towel," the brunette said, turning and talking to a blonde in a plaid skirt, one from one of the local parochial schools. Danny couldn't remember which one.

"I gotta go," Danny said. "Are you girls gonna be okay?"

"Yeah, thanks. What's your name?"

"Danny."

"Thanks, Danny," she said. He stepped onto the front porch just as Mikey yelled, "Cheese it, the cops!" Sirens were coming from every direction. The kids scooped up the beers while Fitzy picked up a rock and threw it through the front window of Mary Beth's house. When he caught up with the rest of the kids, Bugsy said, "What'd you do that for?" Fitzy shrugged and looked around at the other kids, none of whom acknowledged him.

Blue lights and sirens filled the neighborhood. "Let's meet at the Stone!" Danny said. The rest of the kids scattered in every direction. Danny and Bugsy stuffed their beers in the bushes, ran, and turned onto Alpha Road, where they slipped through an opening in the lathwork beneath the front porch of a house at the end of the street. After catching their breath, Bugsy leaned against the granite foundation and wiped some blood from his knuckles. Danny settled for a couple of pieces of wood.

"That little fucker had a hard head," Bugsy said.

Danny looked at Bugsy's hand. "Does it hurt?"

"Naw, it's okay."

"So, what's up with Fathead?" Danny asked. "Why'd he have to throw that rock through the window?"

"I dunno. He's such an asshole."

There were more sirens; the cops were getting closer. They listened and waited a minute before speaking. "Hey, can you get me some snow?" Bugsy asked, still nursing his hand.

Danny peered outside before clawing a handful of snow. "Did you see the tits on that blonde?" he asked, passing the ball of snow over. "The one with the red sweater?"

"Fuck, yeah, how could you miss her?"

"She looked familiar, like maybe she's a cheerleader or something?"

"I don't know, but I'll tell you, I'd give her something to cheer for," Bugsy said, rubbing the snow over his hand and drawing more blood.

"So, do you know any of those kids?" Danny asked.

"Yeah, I seen 'em around before—they're from Upham's Corner. I think that little fucker who was whacking Mikey is related to Tommy Sweeney, a cousin or something."

"Are you shitting me?"

"Naw, I'm serious, man," Bugsy said, sticking his head outside.

"How's it look?"

"Quiet." Bugsy stood up and brushed the dirt from his pants. Danny joined him. They stepped out onto the sidewalk. "If the cops see us, act cool, like we didn't do nothing," he said.

"Sounds good. Let's get the beers," Bugsy said.

Other than the sound of barking dogs and the wind finding its way through the branches of the leafless trees, it was quiet. When they reached Tremlett Street, they heard Mikey, Billy, and Fitzy coming down the hill, and as soon as they met, Fitzy started up again. "Did you see that big motherfucker I whacked?"

"I thought it was one of the girls," Bugsy responded.

# 6

Danny got up early. He didn't want to; he had to take a leak, but it was too cold, so he stayed beneath the covers flicking through a Superman comic until he couldn't hold it anymore. The windows were covered in frost so thick he couldn't see out. "I'm freezing," Frankie chattered, peering from beneath his blankets. "Can you ask Ma if she can turn the heat up?"

"You ask her," Danny said.

"C'mon. You're getting up, ain't ya?"

Frankie pulled the sheets over his head and curled up into a ball. Danny wrapped himself in his blanket, got up, tiptoed to the bathroom, and peed. He pulled the blanket tighter, walked down the hall to his mother's bedroom, and knocked on her door.

"What is it? Is everything okay?" his mother responded in a sleepy voice.

"Can I turn up the heat? Me and Frankie are freezing." He tiptoed around some more. "I can warm the place up so it won't be so cold when you and Chrissy get up." He waited a moment.

"Okay, but not too high. Just enough to warm it up, okay."

"Sure. Thanks, Ma."

Danny shuffled back to his bedroom and peeled his socks, stiff as cardboard, from the radiator. He opened the valve and waited until the pipes started to rattle before climbing back into bed. The radiator hissed and steamed for an hour, melting the frost from the windows. When he could see outside, he kicked his blanket to the floor and shuffled into the kitchen. Bridie was in front of the stove, bundled in her bathrobe, pouring hot water into a teacup. "Can I get you some hot cocoa and oatmeal, honey?"

"Yeah, that'd be great," he said, hugging himself. "Man, it's cold. My toes are like ice cubes.

"I know, honey. I know. The weatherman says it was down to ten degrees last night."

"What's it now?"

"Can't be much warmer." She looked out the window. "Maybe fifteen, twenty degrees."

Danny came alongside her and rubbed his hands above the hissing tea kettle. She leaned over and kissed him on the cheek. "Wash your hands, and I'll get everything ready."

He gave her a peck on the cheek, held his hands above the kettle a moment more, and went to the bathroom. When he returned, he walked over to the window, now moist, no longer frozen. He turned the valve until he heard the pipes rattle. He lifted a small bowl filled with water from below the metal regulator, emptied it in the sink, and returned it to the same spot.

"So, how was your night, honey?" Bridie asked.

"It was okay. Kinda quiet."

She stirred her tea. "Are you going to church?"

He pretended as if he hadn't heard her. Instead of answering, he went into the rear pantry and scratched some frost off the small window framed above the back porch. He looked at the flat-roofed buildings covered with thick snow. Streams of smoke puffed out of the chimneys, billowing away like old men in an Irish Pub. "Oatmeal's ready," Bridie called out.

Danny returned to the kitchen table and sat alongside the whistling radiator, opposite his mother and her cup of tea. "So, are you going to church?" she asked, in the same tone she'd used the first time.

He ate a mouthful of oatmeal and gave a gentle sigh. "Ma, I ain't been to church in a long time." If she was surprised, she didn't let on.

"You should go, honey; it's your duty. You've taken all the sacraments."

Danny stared out the window at a row of icicles hanging from the edge of the roof next door, glistening in the morning sun. "Can I ask you something?" he said.

"Of course."

"How come you don't go anymore?"

Bridie waited a moment before answering. "Well, honey, it's a little complicated." She paused again and then wrung her hands. "When your father was around, we used to go all the time. I grew up in the church; we both did."

"I know."

"We were good people, Danny. Good Catholics. Your father and I raised you and your sister to honor the sacraments."

"What about Frankie?"

She sipped her tea longer than usual. "We baptized your brother, *of course*."

"I know. I remember."

"After your father left, I . . . I didn't follow through with his first holy communion." Her voice quivered ever so slightly. "I lost faith in the church and stopped going."

Danny gave her a moment before speaking. "Why? What happened?"

"Well." Her voice grew tighter. "After your father left, it wasn't the same. I didn't feel comfortable going to church, not without him. I didn't know how I'd explain things to Father Driscoll." She took another sip of tea and looked out the window. "How's the oatmeal?" she chirped.

"Good, really good." Danny propped himself up and ate some more. "Can't you go to church after you separate? Isn't that what they call it?" He waited for her to say something. "Did you get divorced?"

"Heavens, no! You can't get a divorce in the Catholic Church. It's a union under God. You have to honor your marriage. It's one of the holy sacraments."

"How does that work when someone's husband leaves like Dad did? What're you supposed to do? What if he died?"

"There's not much you can do. I couldn't tell Father Driscoll he died; that'd be lying. What would I tell Father Driscoll if he asked where your father was? Mother of Jesus," she said, blessing herself.

"I didn't know they had rules for stuff like that."

"Mother Mary, the church has rules for everything."

"Can I ask you another question?"

"Of course," she replied.

"Why'd Dad leave?"

"I'm not sure. I wish I knew."

"Where'd he go?"

"I'm not sure. Florida, I think."

"Florida?"

"Yes. I ran into his brother Ricky. He told me he was in Florida, working on a fishing boat, or maybe it was a cruise ship. He wasn't very clear about it. He'd been drinking, and half of his words didn't make much sense."

"I don't remember him having a brother. So, he'd be my uncle?"

"Yes."

"Where's he live?"

"The last I heard, South Boston."

"Where?"

"Somewhere around L Street."

"Do you miss him?"

"Ricky?"

"Ricky? Heavens no! He was a worthless drunk. Still is."

"No, Dad—my father."

"I miss him for you kids. I wish he was here for you when you needed a father." Her eyes reddened. "After the war, he wasn't the same. He used to be so much fun. He didn't have a care in the world, not one. When he returned, I tried to make him happy but couldn't. I tried, honey; I did." She took her handkerchief out and ran it across her eyes.

"It ain't your fault, Ma."

"I know, but I should have tried harder."

"I know a lot of kids don't have a father. It's no big deal."

"It is a big deal to me," she said, reaching for his hand and holding it as she cried. He placed his other hand on top of hers and held it firmly.

"I remember he had a box of medals and other stuff from the war. And that time with the dog, remember?"

"Mother of Jesus. How could I ever forget something like that? All the neighbors were so kind. They brought food over and asked if they could do anything. We didn't know many of them then, but we knew them all by the end of the day."

"I don't remember any of that. All I remember is the dog biting me and getting stitches." He lifted his hand and touched his scar.

"You can't really see it anymore. When you smile, it disappears."

"Really?"

"Yes. You need to smile more. That was your father. He was always a man of action. Did you know he was in one of the war's most famous battles? He saved seven men. That's where he got all those medals; he earned every one of them."

"I didn't know that," Danny said.

"He didn't like to talk about the war. Your father was private about those things. He had his problems, and he loved you very much. You used to sit on his lap, and he'd rock you to sleep. He was so happy in those days."

"I don't get it. Didn't he like us?"

"Christ on the cross! He loved you kids! Oh, honey, where would you get an idea like that? He loved all of you. Mother of Jesus, don't ever talk like that again," she said, wiping a new stream of tears from her face. "He had a lot of problems after the war. I don't know what they were, but he changed. I'm gonna pour some more tea. Would you like any more cocoa?"

"I'm gonna use the bathroom. I'll be right back," he said. When he returned, she was smiling, and her teacup was full.

"He had a friend, Denny Doyle, who used to come around and visit. Denny was a nice man and handsome. Mary, Jesus, and Joseph, he was handsome. He could've married the prettiest girl in town. But he never got married. He lost an arm in the war—his left one," she said, tapping her elbow. "I think that bothered him, with the girls and all. Denny used to come by and visit all the time. They'd drink beer, watch baseball, and talk about all kinds of things. I never knew what about, but they'd stay up late, even after the games were over."

"That must have been nice for Dad and his friend."

"It was. Your father was always happy when Denny came around. He used to laugh back then."

She sipped her tea and continued. "Then, one day, Denny stopped coming around, and your father stopped watching his baseball games, and he stopped laughing. I asked him what was wrong, but he didn't want to talk about it. After that, he started drinking and staying out late. There were times he didn't come home at all. And then," she said with a sorrowful shake of her head, "he lost his job at Kirley Lumber. He got fired for missing work and coming in late. I didn't find out until later. They were good to him. They gave him a lot of chances."

"I heard Kirley's is a great place to work."

"It is. He was running the docks."

"I didn't know any of that stuff. How come you didn't tell me any of that before?"

"You were too young. I told your sister when she was your age. Someday I'll tell Frankie when he's old enough."

"I understand. I didn't realize how much stuff you went through."

"It is what it is, honey. It's in the past. You can't change it now. He had his good side, of course. Mother Mary, you should have seen him when we first met. He was tall and handsome and always well-dressed. His shirts were always clean, and he tucked them in, you know, like a real gentleman. And he always wore a coat and tie when we went out," she said wistfully. He got up, placed his bowl in the sink, and returned to the kitchen table.

"You still believe in God, don't you?" Danny asked.

"Yeah, of course, I do. Why do you ask?" She stirred her tea and stared at him.

"I don't know how to say it, Ma. I know how much you love the church, so don't get mad at me."

"Mad? What are you talking about? Why would I get mad?" she asked, with a tinge of anxiousness.

"I don't know, Ma. You mentioned church and everything, so I thought I'd ask, you know, about it. It's something I don't feel so good talking about."

"Don't be silly. You can talk about it with me."

"Promise not to get mad."

"I promise."

"Well, me and the kids, we heard some stories, and Ricky Fitzgerald; you remember Ricky, we went to the third grade together. He lives over near Ronan Park. He used to live on Dakota Street."

"Sure, I remember him."

"Do you remember he was an altar boy?"

She nodded. "I remember."

"Well, he told us that Father Kerrigan did some things with some of the altar boys." He paused to gauge his mother's reaction and continued. "Some of the little kids."

"What kind of things?" she asked.

"*Things.*"

"Things? What kind of things?"

He rotated his cup in the saucer, moving it around in small circles. "Things."

"Honey, I can't read your mind. Just come out and say it. What kind of things?"

Danny stared at his cup for a dozen decades before speaking. "*Bad things.*"

"Bad things? What do you mean?" she asked as her voice slipped an octave higher.

"Well, we heard that Father Kerrigan and a couple of the other priests like to"—Danny turned his cup again—"take showers with some of the altar boys."

"Showers?" Another octave.

"Yeah, and they wash them all over and play with their private parts when they're in the shower."

Bridie gasped like she was suffocating.

"And they stick the boys' penises in their mouths."

"What?" she stammered. "Where did you hear that? Mother of Christ, Danny, these are priests you're talking about. Priests! You should be ashamed of yourself!"

"But, Ma," Danny pleaded. "You told me you wouldn't get mad."

"This is different. Those boys are liars! I won't have any of it, Daniel, none of it! Suffering Jesus, Mary, and Joseph. None of it!"

"Ma, I ain't saying it's true or nothing. I heard it from some of the kids."

"You should be ashamed of yourself. You need to go to confession and absolve yourself."

"I'm sorry, Ma. I didn't mean to get you upset or nothing. I wouldn't do nothing to get you upset. I wouldn't. I wouldn't."

Bridie said nothing more. She placed her cup in the sink, left the kitchen, and went into her bedroom, pulling the door shut behind her.

# 7

Monday morning was the coldest it had been in a long time. Bridie got up early, put the heat on, and turned the radio on to WBZ. The police department issued another black ice warning—the third of the month. Anyone who could afford to stay home should, they said. Bridie always smiled when they said that; no one she knew could ever afford to stay home.

Danny and Frankie stumbled into the kitchen, barefoot and wrapped in blankets. Chrissy was sitting at the kitchen table, drinking tea. She didn't say anything to them, and they replied in mutual silence. They knew better than to talk to her so early in the morning.

"I'm making some oatmeal," Bridie announced. "You boys want some hot cocoa?"

"Yeah."

"Sure."

She glanced at them. "Put some clothes on. I don't want you dragging your blankets across the floor."

Danny returned to his room, grabbed his hardened dungarees from atop the radiator, and put them on. He put on a second pair of pants and two shirts. Frankie lay back down, bundled up in his blanket, and covered his head.

Danny ate silently with his mother and sister while they listened to the radio. The schools in the western part of the state were closed, and there were a lot of accidents on the expressway. After his second cup of cocoa and another oatmeal, Danny placed his empty cup and bowl in the sink. "I gotta go," he said.

"Are you warm enough?" Bridie asked, peering over her teacup.

"As warm as I'm gonna be."

"Goodbye, Chrissy," Danny said for his mother's benefit.

"Bye, bye," Chrissy responded, smiling for her mother's benefit, Danny figured.

A bitter blast of frigid wind greeted Danny when he stepped outside; his lungs burned when he inhaled. At Washington Street, he lit a smoke and leaned against a streetlight, watching the cars slide through the intersection, blasting horns at each other. He walked across the street to the bus stop, where a small crowd waited for the Ashmont bus. Danny got in line behind an old lady clad in a three-foot-thick jacket and deep brown hosiery that made her legs look like tree trunks. She hobbled up the stairs and shuffled to the middle of the bus, looking for a pair of open seats, side by side. He grabbed an overhead rail at the front of the bus and swung until he got off at Norfolk Street and headed down Peacevale Road. He daydreamed through his morning classes, waiting for the lunch bell. As soon as it rang, he, Bugsy, Mooch, and Billy ran outside and met in the parking lot. Mooch had talked his father into letting him borrow his car because of the cold. They piled in and drove to the McDonald's on Gallivan Boulevard, where a pimply-faced kid with breath that smelled like tuna fish took their orders.

After paying, they climbed into the car and jostled for their seats. Mooch grabbed a six-pack of beer from the trunk and got in. They sipped their tonics, tossed the rest out the window, refilled their cups with beer, ate, drank, and listened to the radio. When they were done, they threw their trash out the window and drove back to school. During the last break before final class, Mooch leaned into Danny and Bugsy and said, "You kids want to get out of here?"

"Sure. What about Billy?" Danny asked. "Who's he got for last period?"

"Fuck, I don't remember," Bugsy said.

"Howard," Mooch said.

"Howard? That guy's a prick. He'll never skip his class," Bugsy replied.

"Okay. I gotta pick up some shit for my old man," Mooch said.

"Then let's get the fuck outta here," Bugsy said.

# 8

When the final bell rang, Billy ran outside and shouldered through the wind and snow, looking for Mooch's car. He gave up and headed toward Norfolk Street through the tall wrought iron gate that led to the street below. He pulled his collar up and turned when he spotted the kids from Mary Beth's party. Some were in front of him, and some were behind. By the time he reached the sidewalk, they had surrounded him. The little shit from the party started mouthing off. "You're some tough guy, huh?" Billy turned to see how many kids there were.

"You're not so tough when your friends ain't around, are you?" said one of the kids, a short kid wearing a green scally cap on his head.

"Hit him, Marky, hit him," one of the other kids yelled.

"Yeah, hit the faggot fuck," another yelled from behind. Marky peeled his jacket off and hollered, "I call you out!" Billy lifted his arms up as the mouthy kid came swinging at him. His first punch glanced off Billy's forearm. Billy backed up against an old Ford Wagon, blocking the punches.

"I'm gonna kill you, you fucking fag!" Marky screamed, throwing more shots. One of the kids climbed on top of the Ford and yelled at Billy. As soon as Billy looked up, Marky punched him in the stomach, knocking the wind out of him. Billy keeled over and grabbed his stomach. After catching his breath, he looked around for Marky. The kid on the car kicked him in the face, sending him to the ground. Billy started gagging on a mouthful of blood while Marky strutted around like a rooster. One of the kids flicked a cigarette in Billy's face, and Marky slammed a trash can over his head. A girl started screaming, "STOP! STOP! You're going to kill him. STOP!" A police siren wailed.

"Let's get the fuck out of here! The cops are coming!" Marky yelled. He slammed the trash can again on Billy's head, knocking him out. A cop car pulled up. Two cops got out, took a few steps, stopped, and turned toward the small crowd around Billy.

"What happened?" the first cop, a stout man with a whiffle cut, asked the kids.

"I didn't see anything."

"I don't know anybody."

"I didn't do nothing."

"I don't know those kids."

Nobody knew anything. The cop shook his head and approached his partner, who was tending to Billy. He was a tall, good-looking Italian cop who looked like he belonged in the movies.

"Is he okay?" the whiffle cop asked.

"I can't tell. He's beaten up pretty badly."

"I'll call it in."

"What's your name?" the Italian cop asked, leaning over Billy. His name shield shone in the afternoon sun: *Lonardelli.*

The other cop spoke into the car radio. "This is Officer Johnson, car forty-five. I need an ambulance at Dorchester High."

"Which side?"

"Peacevale."

"How many are there?"

"One."

"Can you describe the victim?"

"White male, seventeen, eighteen years old. Multiple contusions to the head, semi-responsive, bleeding from the head. Could have a concussion."

"On the way," the voice rattled through the radio speaker.

"Ten-nine. We'll take him to the Carney." He grabbed the first aid box, placed it next to Lonardelli, removed a large gauze bandage, and carefully lifted Billy's head so Lonardelli could wrap it.

"Can you grab a blanket, Tom?" Lonardelli asked.

Officer Johnson returned with a thick, woolen blanket. Lonardelli placed it under Billy's head and shone his flashlight in Billy's eyes while Johnson tried to squeeze some information out of the kids still hanging around, but the crowd knew less and less.

Billy's eyes flickered. He slowly lifted his arm and tried to touch his head, but Lonardelli stopped him. "Leave it alone, kid. You got a bad cut. I got an ambulance coming. You can't move, okay." He placed his fingers on Billy's wrist and checked his pulse. The ambulance barreled around the corner a minute later, spraying red lights on everything. Two white-clad orderlies got out, went to the back door, and pulled a stretcher out. They placed it on the ground next to Billy. They put a collar on his neck, lifted him onto the stretcher, carried him into the ambulance, and left.

---

As soon as Danny opened the front door, Frankie yelled, "Danny! Danny! Did you hear about Billy? Didja? Didja?"

"Whoa, slow down. What're you talking about? Hear what?"

"Billy! Billy!"

"What about him?"

Frankie told the whole story, as best he remembered, as best he'd heard, somewhere near the truth and some made up. "He ain't dead or nothing. He ain't!" His words came out so fast that they stumbled over each other and bounced around on the floor.

"Okay, okay. Thanks."

Danny picked up the phone and dialed the operator. "Can I have the Carney Hospital?" The line clicked. "Can I help you?" the voice on the other end replied.

"Do you have a patient, Billy Buckley? I mean William . . . William Buckley."

"Who is this?" the voice asked.

"Tommy. Um, Tommy Buckley."

"Are you a member of the family?"

"Yes, I'm his brother," Danny replied.

"Mr. Buckley is in room five-oh-two."

"How's he doing?"

"He has a concussion and a severe contusion to the head. And he has some facial abrasions along with a fractured jaw. He needed some stitches."

"Thanks," Danny said. "What time are you open till?"

"Visiting hours close at eight."

"Okay. Thanks," Danny replied, hanging up and turning to his brother. "Frankie, if any of the kids call, tell 'em I went to the Carney and tell 'em what happened. And don't tell Ma nothing. If she asks, tell her I went out. Don't tell her nothing else, okay?"

"But, but—" Frankie stuttered.

"No buts, Frankie. Don't screw it up. Don't say nothing. I'm not fucking around!"

"Okay," Frankie said. "But—"

"Don't fuck with me," Danny said. He ran downstairs and headed straight to the Y. "Hey Carl, do you mind if I take a quick look around? I want to see if any of the kids are here." Carl nodded, *okay.*

Danny ran upstairs, but the place was empty. He retraced his steps and jogged through the gym before heading downstairs to the locker rooms. None of the kids were there, either. He headed back upstairs and ran into Bugsy, strolling through the front door.

"Did you hear about Billy?" Bugsy asked.

"Yeah," Danny replied. "I heard he's all fucked up."

"I heard that too. I'm headed over to the Carney."

"Me too. Let's go."

"Did you hear how many kids there were?" Bugsy asked as they hopped down the front stairs.

"A bunch. I heard he was alone."

"Must'a been the kids from Mary Beth's party."

"I'm sure."

"What a bunch of fuckin' pussies. Those cocksuckers'll pay. I can promise you that," Bugsy said. "I'm gonna bust some fuckin' heads." He grabbed a handful of snow, made a snowball, and threw it at a passing bus. It exploded when it hit a side window. A tall, gangly man with glasses stood up and leered at them. Bugsy ran after the bus, grabbing chunks of snow to make another snowball. He threw it at the same window, and when it hit, the tall guy leaned forward and gave Bugsy the finger. "Fuck you!" Bugsy yelled, chucking him the bird back. "C'mon, let's hop a car," Bugsy said.

They ran across the street and chased a Ford Fairlane down a few blocks later, pacing with the slow-moving car. They grabbed the bumper and wedged their feet into the snow, arching their backs and leaning back on their heels. The vehicle pulled them down the street until they let go at Codman Square, where they skidded to a stop. They grabbed another car and continued hopping until they reached Gallivan Boulevard, where the street had been plowed, and they had to start walking.

They bantered as they walked past squat duplexes that gave way to stately three-deckers behind small white picket fences. When they reached the corner, the street was covered with snow. They ran out and hopped a new Ford as it puttered by, and as soon as they grabbed it, the driver hit the brakes, sending the vehicle into a long slow skid. Bugsy and Danny pushed off as the car continued sliding. Bugsy made a large snowball and threw it high in the air. It landed on the vehicle's roof, thumping and leaving a large ugly dent. The car stopped sliding when it hit a soot-covered snowbank. Bugsy ran over to the driver's side and banged on the window.

"Get out, you fucking faggot!"

Danny walked around to the other side of the car and leered into the passenger side window.

"You got a problem, asshole?" Bugsy yelled, banging the window again. The driver glared at him and then at Danny. "Asshole!" Bugsy screamed as he pulled on the door handle. The driver jammed the car into low gear, sending the wheels spinning and the vehicle fishtailing back into the street. Bugsy threw a chunk of ice at the car, making another thud and leaving another dent. "Fucking fag!"

"That faggot must be from Milton." A few minutes later, they walked into the brown-marbled hospital lobby. A large, sour-faced woman sat at the reception desk, shuffling stacks of papers as if she was dealing cards. "Act like you know where you're going," Bugsy muttered as they passed by the front desk, turning left, where they stopped in front of a row of wood-paneled elevators. Danny punched the button for the fifth floor, and they got in. The car stopped on the third floor. A large-breasted candy striper with curly blonde hair got in. Bugsy stared at the badge pinned to her chest. "Nancy? Is that an Irish name?" he asked, peeking down at her chest. She pulled the buttons of her blouse together, stepped over to the corner of the elevator, and cemented herself against the wall. "Jeez," Bugsy muttered. "What's your fucking problem?"

She stayed there until Bugsy and Danny got off on the fifth floor, where they found themselves staring at a beehive-headed nurse looking up from behind a pair of reading glasses perched on the tip of her nose. A stack of dog-eared paperwork separated her from them.

"Can I help you?" she asked.

"I'm here to see my brother," Danny said.

"What's his name?"

"Billy—er, William Buckley. William James Buckley. He's in room five-oh-two."

"Buckley? We've been trying to get in touch with your mother. Is she with you?"

"No."

"Is she home?"

"Um, not yet. She works downtown, and she won't be home till six. They won't let her take any calls at work or nothing. I left her a note to call when she gets home."

"And who are you?" she asked Bugsy.

"He's my cousin. I mean, our cousin. Me and Billy's," Danny said.

"Don't stay too long. Your brother needs some rest."

"No problem," Danny said.

"Down the hall, third door on your left," she said, returning to her paperwork.

Billy's room reeked of alcohol, antiseptics, and other things that would be hard to scrub off. Billy was propped up, with a large bandage wrapped around his head and an IV in his arm. A tight mesh of stitches held the corner of his mouth together.

"Psst. Billy. You awake?" Bugsy whispered, leaning over. He waited a moment before trying again. "Psst."

"Maybe we ought to let him rest," Danny said.

Bugsy tugged on Billy's johnny. "Psst, Billy, wake up." Billy groaned and rolled his head to the side. "What time is it?" he mumbled, rolling his tongue across his lips.

"I dunno, five thirty, six," Danny replied. Billy touched the top of his head, stopping when he felt the bandages.

"So, what happened?" Danny asked.

Billy licked his lips again. "A bunch of kidz jumped me; they fucked me up," Billy replied. "My fucking head hurtz," he said, touching his bandages again.

"Was it the kids from Mary Beth's party?" Bugsy asked, leaning forward.

"Yeah, I think so. That little cocksucker, with the big mouth, waz there."

"We'll straighten this out when you get out," Bugsy said.

"Hey, I was talking to the nurse out there. She said your ma doesn't know nothing." Danny said. "If anybody asks, I'm your brother, and he's your cousin. That's how we got in."

Billy stared at them before replying. "The doctor said I have a concussion. It kinda messes with my head, understanding shit."

"Fuck, I'm sorry, man. How long are they gonna keep you here?" Danny asked.

"I don't know. My doctor's s'posed to come by in a little while."

"Do you want me to tell your ma what happened?" Danny asked.

"Yeah, that'd be cool."

"What do you want me to say?"

Billy stared at the ceiling. "I dunno, tell her I fell or something. Tell her I slipped leaving school. Tell her I banged my head."

"Okay. Anything else?"

"Naw."

"Did you recognize anyone else?" Danny asked.

"I dunno. It's hard to remember. But, hey guys, I'm getting tired, and my fucking head hurtz. I gotta take some medicine."

"How about the big ugly motherfucker?" Bugsy asked. "Remember him? He was wearing a blue jacket; he was in the kitchen when the fight started."

"I dunno. He coulda been there," Billy said, almost in a whisper.

"Get some rest," Danny said, patting Billy on his leg and glancing at Bugsy. "I'm gonna go see your ma."

"Don't worry about nothing," Bugsy said. "We'll get them motherfuckers."

# 9

Danny and Bugsy hopped a few cars until they parted at Ashmont Station. Bugsy went in one direction while Danny continued, jumping more cars until he got to Billy's apartment, where he trotted up the stairs and knocked on his door. Billy's mother let him, and Danny started to tell her what had happened, but he didn't get too far.

"I don't have time for this, Danny. I spoke to the police, and I know what happened."

"But . . ."

She interrupted him. "I'm disappointed in you." She stared at him until his eyes bled and his throat dried up.

"I'm sorry. I . . . I . . . Can I do anything?"

"I think you've done enough," she said sternly.

"I understand," he said as he turned and shuffled out the door.

---

The next day was even colder, so the kids stayed in school all day. They sat near the heaters in the corner of the lunch room, chasing the freshmen away with nothing more than a stare. "So, we gonna scope out Uppies this weekend?" Bugsy asked, chewing on a wilted ham and cheese sandwich.

"Sure," Mooch said. "How's Billy?"

"He's still messed up," Danny said. "The poor kid's still in the hospital. Those motherfuckers beat him over the head with a trash can; he's having headaches and stuff."

"Are you shitting me?" Mooch replied. "I didn't know that those motherfuckers . . ."

"Totally fucked him up," Danny said.

"Mooch, can you get a hotbox?" Bugsy said.

"Does a bear shit in the woods?" Mooch responded.

"A four-door," Bugsy added. "With a big trunk."

"Sure," Mooch replied.

"How does Thursday night sound?" Bugsy asked.

"Sounds good," Mooch replied.

"Eight o'clock?" Bugsy added.

"Works for me," Danny replied.

---

Everyone met at the bottom of Mother's Rest. Billy showed up even though he was supposed to be home, resting. As soon as Fitzy saw him, he asked, "How're you feeling since that little fucker kicked your ass?"

Billy laughed the first time, as did the other kids. After the third time, no one laughed. The fourth time, Bugsy stepped between Fitzy and Billy. "Here," Bugsy said, handing a bottle of CC to Billy. Billy smiled and drained a mouthful. Half ran down his chin. He fumbled in his pocket, took a pill, and popped it in his mouth.

"So, how're you feeling?" Bugsy asked, his back turned to Fitzy.

"Like shit," Billy mumbled.

"You don't look too bad," Danny said, coming alongside Bugsy.

"I think you look like shit," Bugsy said, putting his hand on Billy's shoulder. "You always do."

Billy laughed. "Don't worry. We're gonna get those motherfuckers," Bugsy said.

"I know you will, Bugsy. I know you will," Billy said. "Thankz," he added, slushing the words out.

"Yeah, payback's a bitch," said Mooch, nudging Fitzy aside. "Billy, we all want to get these motherfuckers, but we should wait until after Christmas. No sense fuckin' up the holidays. And besides, you gotta get better, right?"

"Yeah, yeah," Billy said, dribbling his words down his cheek. "Whenz Chrizmaz?"

"I think it's on a Monday. No, wait, it's a Tuesday," Danny said.

"Naw, you were right the first time. It's on a Monday," Bugsy said.

Billy sputtered again, "Yeah, thaz okay. I can wait. I ain't going nowhere."

"Hey guys," Charley, a squat fire-hydrant with blubbery skin and a whiffle, said. "I talked to my cousin Bobby, and he knows them faggots. He heard about what happened. Those punks were bragging and shit, telling everyone they kicked our asses."

"Oh yeah," Bugsy said, spitting. "Bobby's a Parksman, ain't he?"

"Yeah," Charley replied. "He said they're a bunch of lightweights. He and some friends have wanted to dance with those pricks for a long time. Bobby said they ganged up on a couple of Parksmen and fucked them up, just like they did with Billy. There were like ten of them or something."

"They aren't too fucking smart, are they?" Danny said.

"I'm gonna fuck them kids up. Billy!" Mooch said. "I'm gonna make that little shit suck your dick."

"What did ya say? Suck my dick?" Billy erupted in laughter, shaking so hard he fell on his ass. Bugsy laughed at him before giving him a hand and passing him the bottle. Billy winced when the whiskey dribbled out of the corner of his mouth.

He pulled another pill from his pocket and chased it with another swig before handing the bottle back to Bugsy.

"Don't you think you ought to slow down on them pills?" Danny said.

"Yeah, I guess," Billy replied. "My head hurtz like a motherfucker."

"Hey guys, we're out of beer. Anyone wanna make a run?" Bugsy said. The kids shuffled around, digging change out of their pockets. "How about you, Fitzy?"

"I'm broke," Fitzy said.

"You're always broke," Bugsy said. "You're a chintzy motherfucker. Why don't you get a fucking job?"

Fitzy stuck his hands in his pocket and shrugged. "I've been looking, but I can't find nothing."

"They're hiring at Seymour's," Bugsy said.

"Seymour's? I ain't gonna work down there. That place's a fucking shithole."

"What the fuck? You think you're gonna be the president of IBM or something?"

Fitzy bent his head and stuck his hands in his pockets.

"We got enough?" Bugsy asked, peering over Danny's shoulder.

"Yeah, plenty," Danny replied.

"We should get some Budweiser," Fitzy said.

Bugsy glanced at Fitzy; someone else muttered, "Asshole."

"Hey, can you help me carry the buy?" Danny asked.

"I can't," Fitzy said. "My legs are hurting."

Bugsy shook his head. "Who's going?" he asked, looking around.

"I am," Mikey replied, nodding.

"Anyone else?" Bugsy asked. He said to the other two a moment later, "Let's go."

The three lit a smoke and trudged down the street. A few blocks later, they heard voices calling from behind: Patty McNulty and Kat Campbell. Danny took one last drag, flicked his cigarette into the street, and stopped while Mikey and Bugsy continued walking. "Mind if we join ya?" Kat asked.

"It's a free country," Danny said, distracted by Patty's perfume.

"Hi," Danny said to Patty. "What's up?"

"Kat wanted to buy some cigarettes."

"Oh," Danny replied, nodding. They continued walking until they were alongside Mikey and Bugsy. "Hi, Bugsy," Kat said.

"Hi," he replied with as brief a response as he could cough up.

"How are you doing?" she asked Mikey.

"Fine," he said, flushed, stuffing his hands so deep in his pockets that his forearms disappeared.

Patty lagged behind, quietly motioning Danny to stop. "I'll catch up," she said to Kat, who continued dribbling on like a running toilet.

"So, Danny, what happened at Mary Beth's? I saw her, and she told me everything. I couldn't believe it! I've never seen her so mad in my whole life." Patty waited for a response, but Danny said nothing. A wave of disappointment washed across her face.

"They broke a lot of family heirlooms. They had to throw most of it out. Did you know their furniture and a lot of pictures came all the way from Ireland?"

"I didn't know that."

"Everything's ruined; she said it can't be replaced." They remained silent over the next block. Danny spoke up at last. "I don't know. Things got out of hand."

"Out of hand! Out of hand!"

"Can I tell you something?" he asked.

"What?"

"You look cute when you get mad." She started breathing harder, and her eyes glazed over until she gave up, gave in, and smiled. "Did you know that?" he asked.

"You're such a jerk."

"See, you just got prettier."

"I'm serious," she said.

"I am too." He reached out and touched her hand. She paused before holding his. "We didn't start it—the other kids did. I tried to stop it. Did you know that? We just wanted to use the bathroom, that's all. We weren't looking for trouble or nothing."

"Still, you shouldn't have been there," she said. "You weren't invited; it was a private party."

"I know."

"And who broke the stained-glass window?"

"Fitzy."

"That figures. What was he trying to prove?"

"I dunno, she never did nothing to him. Shit, he hardly knows her." Danny lit a smoke and continued talking. "I seen him do a lot of stupid things like that before. If he sees something nice that someone else has, he has to fuck it up. Remember when Marty O'Neil's dad got that new car, the Chevy Impala?"

"I do. It was blue, right?"

"That's the one. Fitzy keyed it right after he got it."

"What's wrong with him?"

"I dunno. I think because Marty's dad had a newer car than his mom."

"Are you serious?"

"Yeah, that's what I mean about him. If it ain't his and it's better, he's gonna ruin it."

"You should have stopped him."

"I didn't know he was gonna do it. No one did. He threw the rock before anyone knew what he was doing. I wish it didn't happen, but it did. The other kids didn't help things, you know. The kids from Uppies. They started it."

"It doesn't matter. It was her party."

"Yeah, I know," Danny said. "You're right." She squeezed his hand and pursed her lips tightly, saying nothing more until they met up with the other kids.

"We're gonna look for a buyer," Mikey said.

Kat started to say something, but Patty interrupted her: "C'mon, Kat, we gotta go." She grabbed the back of Kat's jacket and tugged it. "C'mon," she said.

Once they were out of earshot, Bugsy spoke. "Man, that chick doesn't know when to shut the fuck up."

"I don't know what to tell you," Danny said. "I heard she wants to have your baby."

"Yeah, she's got the hots for you," Mikey added, bumping his shoulder into Bugsy.

"Fuck you," Bugsy said, pushing Danny into the street and punching Mikey on his shoulder.

"I'm telling you, she wants your baby," Danny said.

"Take a Dudley."

"Blow me."

"Maybe the best way to shut her up is if I stick my dick in her mouth," Bugsy said.

"Why don't you quit fucking around and marry her?" Mikey said. "Get it over with."

"Fuck you."

They ranked each other until they reached the Town Field bleachers across from Supreme's, a large wood and concrete structure that could seat several thousand spectators. The dull orange glow of cigarettes hovered above the upper row of benches. At the top, some twenty-odd kids lounged on the benches or leaned against the back wall. Bobby Lyons, one of the eight Lyons brothers, was standing in the corner, a beer in one hand and a cigarette in the other.

"What's up, guys?" Bobby asked.

"Nothing much," Bugsy replied. "We need a buyer. Is Harry or JL around?"

"Yeah, Harry's at the Tavern."

"Do you think he'll make a buy for us?"

"I dunno. He might if he's not too fucked up or nothing. But you know he ain't gonna do it for free. The fucking prick charges *me*."

"What an asshole."

"No argument here."

"Fuck it. Let's do it."

"Cool."

They walked across the field to Dorchester Avenue and stopped below one of the many dim yellow street lights hovering over the sidewalk. "Why don't you kids wait here?" Bobby said.

"No problem."

Bobby crossed the street, opened the front door of the Town Field Tavern, and yelled, "Harry!" A minute later, he yelled again. "HARRY!" His brother stumbled out, towing a thick cloud of smoke behind him.

"Whaddya want?" Harry slurred.

"Can you make a buy?"

"It'll cost you."

Bobby waved at the kids, beckoning them to join him and his brother, two blonde-headed fire plugs, fixtures in Fields Corner.

"What do you need?" Harry splattered.

"A case of Gansetts," Bugsy said.

"You do, huh? How much you got?" Harry asked.

Bugsy stuck his hands in his pockets and fumbled around. "You ain't playing with your dick or nothing, are ya?" Harry asked, laughing. Bugsy pulled some crumpled bills and a handful of coins out of his pocket.

"I'm gonna need a pack of smokes," Harry said.

Danny pulled his Winstons out and offered one to Harry. Harry grabbed the pack, stuffed it in his pocket, and extended his hand toward Bugsy, palm up. Bugsy looked at Bobby before handing the money to Harry. Bobby responded with a shrug. Harry put the cash in his pocket, lit his smoke, and walked toward the packie.

"I'm sorry, guys," Bobby said. "He can be such an asshole."

"No shit," Danny said. "It ain't your fault."

"Yeah, I know. So, what have you kids been up to?" Bobby asked.

"Same old shit."

They continued chatting and smoking until Harry staggered out of the liquor store carrying a case of beer and a large brown bag. "Here," he said to Bugsy. He passed the bag to Danny. "Wait here till I get the other one." They waited until Harry came back. "Have fun," Harry said, handing the case to Danny. Harry went back to the bar, while Danny and the other kids went back to the park, crossing the street to the blare of car horns and yelling. They stopped at a large concrete picnic table, where Bugsy opened one of the beers and passed it to Danny, then to Mikey, Bobby, and himself. Danny took a swig and spat the beer out. "It's fucking warm!" he said, wiping his sleeve across his face.

"What an asshole," Bugsy said.

"Sorry, guys," Bobby muttered.

"It's no big deal. Your brother's a dick," Bugsy said, patting Bobby on the back. "We're good. It ain't your fault."

"You sure?"

"Yeah. Grab a couple for yourself."

"Thanks."

"It's cool. We're gonna head back."

Bobby stuffed a second beer in his back pocket and headed toward the muffled voices hovering above the bleachers.

# 10

The temperature dropped into the twenties a couple of days before Christmas, doing little to discourage the holiday crowds. They were everywhere—on the streets, in the stores, and in the packies, stacked with beer piled so high you couldn't see through the windows plastered with advertisements. Coins and cash flowed freely, money handed out by guilt-ridden parents and former boyfriends, filled with holiday spirits, mostly eighty proof. The cold didn't stop the kids either. They met at the upper end of the Marshall playground, where the retaining wall stopped the fierce winter winds.

When Danny arrived, Fitzy and Grunta were stuffing Jay Jay Johnson, a mentally challenged kid, into a large truck tire. As soon as he was placed, they rolled him down the stairs, hooting and hollering as he bounced across the upper schoolyard and crashed into the wrought iron fence at the far end of the playground. A minute later, Jay Jay stood up, limping and holding his arm. "Did I do good? Did I? Did I?" he yelled. "Did I?"

"What a dumb fuck," Fitzy said. "You owe me a dollar," he said, turning to Grunta. "He made it all the way."

"Who wants to make a run?" Misfit asked. Tall and Clark Gable good-looking, Misfit McNamara came from a family of six hard-drinking boys like their father, Knuckles, a big, boisterous man with cousins in every parish in Dorchester and some in Southie. Like his father and his father before him, Knuckles was a card-carrying member of the Longshoreman's Union.

"I'll go," Danny said.

"Anyone else?" Misfit bellowed. At six foot two inches, everyone listened when he spoke. "Come on, you cheap fucks!" Everyone handed whatever spare change they had to Danny, who counted it as fast as it came in. "How much we got?" Misfit asked.

"Gimme a minute," Danny said, tilting his hand toward a streetlight to see and mumbling as he counted. "Six dollars and fifteen cents!"

"Anyone else wanna go?" Misfit asked in a voice that made the hike seem like an adventure.

"I'll go," Bugsy said.

"Me too," said Charley.

"We'll be back," Misfit said. Danny, Bugsy, and Charley followed, shuffling through the snow, stepping in each other's paths. After finding a buyer, they headed back. "It's gonna be a long hike up that fucking hill," Danny said.

Charley opened one of the cases and passed some beers around.

"We got any money left?" Misfit asked.

"A little," Danny said, shuffling the coins in his pocket.

"Let's take a hack," Misfit said. "It shouldn't cost a lot."

"I'm in. Misfit and Charley, why don't you guys wait here? We'll get the hack," Bugsy said.

"No problem," replied Misfit.

Danny and Bugsy weaved their way through a stream of holiday shoppers. They stopped in front of McManus's to watch a plump waitress with no ankles press several scoops of ice cream into a large cone and hand it to a fat guy sitting on a stool stuffed halfway up his ass. Bugsy banged on the window, and when she turned, he mooned her. When they reached Dot Ave, Bugsy whistled a cab down. The driver tilted his head and pulled over in front of Yum Yum's.

"Hey," Danny said, poking his head inside the passenger's window. "Can you give us a ride?"

"Sure," the driver said. "Where ya going?"

"Around the corner. We gotta pick up a couple of friends. And then, we're going to Westville Street—the Marshall School," Danny said. "You know where it is?"

"Yeah," the driver replied, looking over to Bugsy, standing behind Danny. "How many of you are there?"

"Four, including me," Danny said.

The driver lifted his hands off the wheel. Danny noticed a tattoo; a bulldog wearing a rumpled cap above the letters *USMC*. "The marines, huh?" Danny asked.

"Yeah."

"Vietcong?" Danny asked.

The driver pulled his sleeves down and looked back at Danny. "Vietnam," he said. His tone ended the conversation.

Danny glanced at a dog-eared copy of *The Boston Globe* spread out on top of an army fatigue jacket. A large handgun rested on the edge of the seat.

"Okay, get in," the driver said, tapping the meter and covering the gun with his jacket. Danny leaned forward to look at the operator's license: Peter Godding.

"Peter, right?" Danny asked, sitting back.

"Yeah," Godding said, glancing at Danny through the mirror. Godding slipped the car into gear and headed out.

"They're just over there," Bugsy said, pointing at the truck delivery area where Misfit and Charley were cooling their heels.

"This is good," Danny said.

Godding pulled in, and Danny and Bugsy got out. Misfit and Charley lifted the bags and boxes out from behind a dumpster. Godding went to the back and opened the trunk. "Anyone over twenty-one?" he asked.

"My uncle is," Misfit said. "His car's broken down, and he asked me to pick this stuff up. He's got a tab at the packie."

"He does, huh?"

"Yeah, he called it in."

Godding closed the trunk. "Let's go. The meter's running."

Everyone climbed in. Godding stuffed his jacket between himself and the driver's side door, shoveling the paper and the gun beneath his seat before shifting into gear and turning onto Geneva Avenue. Danny pointed the route, waving his finger as they went. "Up here, you can take a right at Kingman Road."

They passed rows of homes lit with red, white, and blue holiday lights, all casting a cheerful array of colors on the snow-covered ground. They gave way to lines of three-deckers, neatly stacked like Dagwood sandwiches and all lit up for the holidays. Godding turned onto Kingman Road, a narrow, dim-lit street, unplowed and lined with snow-covered cars.

"Take another right on Westville," Danny said. "Then you can slow down; Yeah, here's good."

Godding pulled over and flicked the meter. "That'll be a buck thirty."

Danny stretched his legs out and pulled the money from his pocket, counting it while the other kids climbed out of the hack.

"Thanks," Godding said, stuffing the money in his shirt pocket. He and Danny got out and walked to the back of the taxi. Godding opened the trunk. Misfit whistled toward the schoolyard. The darkened alley suddenly came to life as a small crowd of kids emerged from the shadows.

"So, which one's the uncle?" Godding asked, putting a Camel in his mouth and watching the kids carry the beers back into the shadows.

"He musta gone to bed or something," Danny said.

"Yeah," Godding replied, lighting his cigarette, shutting the trunk, and walking to the front of the cab.

"Hey, wait a minute," Danny yelled, holding his finger up. He jogged over to Bugsy, grabbed a beer from one of the cases, and brought it back to Godding. "Thanks for the ride."

"No problem," Godding said. "Stay out of trouble."

"Me? I never get in trouble," Danny said.

"Yeah, right."

Godding got in, left, and Danny walked into the shadows. "Did you see that roscoe?" Misfit asked as soon as Danny reached him. "It looked like a thirty-eight."

"I think it was a forty-five. I got a good look at it," Danny said. The other kids drew closer. "Did you know that guy was in Vietnam, a marine? He had a cool-looking tattoo," he added, tapping his arm.

"I didn't see it," Bugsy said.

"Yeah, it was right here," Danny said, tapping again. "It was pretty cool." He turned to Billy. "So, how're ya feeling?"

"I'm fine, I'm fine," Billy mumbled. A small stream of drool ran down the corner of his mouth. "Fine as a motherfuckah!" he rattled on in his best Roxbury accent. "Fine, fine, fine. Fuck, I'm fine!"

"Ya know we're gonna get them, cocksuckers," Charley said, spitting so hard he could've drilled through a wall.

"I know, Charley, I know," Billy said. "I 'preciate it. You know I do."

"Well, me and some of the kids—Mooch, Mikey, Misfit—been talking, and we found out where those faggots hang out," Charley said. "They're from Upham's Corner. Mikey's cousin Ebby lives near them. Mikey's gone by a couple of times, and he seen 'em all, even that little piece of shit that jumped you after school."

Billy perked up. "So, what you kidz got in mind?"

"We're gonna kick the shit out of them motherfuckers," Bugsy said.

"When?" Billy drizzled.

"Soon. We're gonna do it at their corner," Charley said.

"Fucking cool," Billy said.

"We're gonna check 'em out tomorrow night," Charley said.

"You know, Charley," Bugsy said. "I don't mean to mess with your plans, but this is Christmas weekend. So, Christmas is what, Tuesday?"

"It's Monday," Charley said.

"I mean, it's Christmas, and I don't want to sound like a pussy or nothing, but my ma's invited everyone over tomorrow night. My cousins, uncles, and aunts, everyone. It's a big family night, and if I ain't home, my ma will be pissed," Bugsy said.

"So what? We owe these pricks. Look what they did to Billy! They won't be expecting us or nothing. We need to give them something to remember us by," Charley said, puffing out his chest.

Mooch came up alongside Charley and spoke after taking a swig from his bottle. "You know, Charley, I want to get those motherfuckers just as bad as you. We all do, but like Bugsy said, it's fucking Christmas. I'll bet you it's the same with those faggots. They might not even be around. Fuck, wouldn't it be a drag if we went down there and none of those assholes were out?" Mooch placed his arm on Billy's shoulder. "We're gonna get 'em." The rest of the kids nodded in agreement. "You know what I think?"

"What?"

"I think we need to make that little prick give you a blowjob. Make that little prick suck your dick."

Billy started laughing, shaking at first and then breaking into a high-pitched chortle that reached inside everyone's brain. Charley laughed so hard he cried. The other kids joined in as Billy heaved back and forth like a balloon caught in the wind.

"Here," Danny said, extending a bottle to Billy. "Take a swig of this. It'll put hair on your chest."

Billy lifted the bottle to his mouth and took a deep swallow. His eyes rolled back in his head. He blinked a couple of times and sputtered, "Yeah, a blowjob from that little shit!"

Fitzy came alongside Billy. "Hey," he said, loud enough to get everyone's attention, "speaking of blowjobs, I remember when Danny got his first blowjob. He ran home to tell his sister. 'Hey, I got my first blowjob today.' She asked him, 'How was it?' Danny said, 'it tasted kind of salty.'"

Fitzy slapped Billy on the back and started laughing. Billy bent his head down and stepped away.

"Well, you got part of the story right," Danny said calmly. "It wasn't my first blowjob. It was my second. Your mother gave me my first blowjob, and you know what? She never complained about the taste. She said it was sweet." It got so quiet you could hear the snow falling. "She told me I should drink orange juice to make it taste better. She said *your* cum tasted salty, like your little brother's."

Everybody exploded with laughter. Fitzy slammed his beer to the ground and ran straight at Danny, grabbing him by the shoulders and pushing him backward.

"Take that back, motherfucker," Fitzy barked, pushing Danny again.

"It was a joke, Fitzy. So, what's the matter—can't you take a joke?" Danny said.

Bugsy put his beer down and stepped between them, standing so close that Fitzy could feel the warmth of his breath. "He's right," Bugsy said. "You started it. What're you, a fucking baby? Can't you take it?"

Misfit strolled over from behind Fitzy and handed Danny and Fitzy a beer. "C'mon, guys, it's fucking Christmas. It was a joke. A fucking joke. Bugsy's right. You started it. If you want to talk about blowjobs, talk about Billy. He's the one getting the hummer."

Danny lifted his beer. "Here's to Billy's blowjob," he said, taking a swig, staring at Fitzy, and walking away, joining the other kids standing in front of a low granite wall where they'd set up a small bar. Fitzy glared back and started breathing harder, huffing and puffing but doing nothing more. He took a few steps back, lingering near the alley side.

"It's really important that we get them on their own corner," Charley said. "We gotta show them we ain't scared and that they can't fuck with us."

"Fuckin' right!" Bugsy yelled, lifting his beer. The other kids joined in, lifting their beers high in the air.

"We gotta shit in their front yard," Charley said.

"Yeah, shit in their front yard," Billy mushed. He took a sip from his bottle and stumbled over to Fitzy. "Why you gotta be such an azzhole?"

Fitzy started to say something but stopped when he realized everyone was watching and listening. "Danneez a good kid. Why you gotta give him so much shit?"

Fitzy took a swig of his beer and glanced at the other kids.

"So, you wanna scope the place out," Charley asked, walking over. "We don't need to start any shit or anything. Just check it out."

"Fuck yeah!" Billy said.

He looked over at Fitzy, nursing his beer. "What about you?"

Fitzy looked around at everyone. "Yeah, sounds like a good idea."

"Cool," Billy said.

# 11

The kids showed up in small groups. Mooch arrived a little after nine, driving a maroon-colored Impala. As soon as he pulled up, Danny and Bugsy got into the front seat while Charley, Mikey, and Billy got into the back, lugging a case of beer.

"Where's Fitzy?" Billy asked.

"I told him ten," Bugsy replied.

"Fuck him," Danny added.

"I get it," Billy said. "I get it."

Mooch hit the gas and turned, driving through the neighborhood, passing corner stores, bars, and packies lit up like Las Vegas, continuing until he reached the Strand Theater, where he stopped at a red light, waiting for a large-assed family, swilling tonics and popcorn, to waddle by. He took a right and drove by the Dublin House, packed to the gills with locals, some of whom'd been going at it since early morning; another day at the office.

He hated that place.

He hated the walls and floor, the crowd, the smell of cheap beer, cheap cigars, and cheap smokes, and the smell of piss in the doorway. He hated every seat, sign, sound, light, face, and voice he heard. But, mostly, he hated the sound of his father's voice when he yelled at him when he poked his head in the doorway.

"One more," his father would slur. "One more." Over and over and over again. "One more, one more."

"Go get your father," his mother would say, telling him his father was a drunk, drinking the rent and grocery money away. "You kids have bad teeth because your father won't pay for a dentist," she'd say. And she blamed Mooch. It was all his fault for not getting his father out of the bar.

Mooch squeezed the wheel harder and didn't notice he was driving through a red light. Cars came screeching to a halt, and horns blared.

"MOOCH! What the fuck're you doing?" Bugsy yelled, slapping the dashboard. "You trying to get us killed?"

Mooch looked up, turned to Bugsy, and pulled over. "I . . . I'm sorry. I was thinking about . . . I'm sorry. I got distracted."

"You okay?" Bugsy asked, glancing around at the other kids. "What were ya thinking about? Pussy, I hope, not dick."

"Yeah, yeah. I'm sorry . . ." Mooch said, shaking his head. "Never mind. I'm fine."

"You sure?" Danny asked, leaning over Bugsy. "Want me to drive?"

"No, I'm okay. I am," Mooch said, turning to the other kids. "You guys ready?"

"I was born ready," Charley said.

"Alright! Let's go," Mooch said, turning back into traffic and banging a U-ey. "And yeah, it was pussy. I was thinking about Fitzy's mother."

"That shit's all dried up," Bugsy said.

"Not according to Fitzy, it ain't," Danny said.

Everyone lost their breath laughing. "Pull over, Mooch, pull over! I'm gonna piss my pants!" Billy cried.

Mooch laughed as he stopped between a couple of parked cars. Billy jumped out and took a long, loud piss. "You fucking guys are gonna kill me," he said when he got back in.

Two blocks later, they spotted a small crowd of kids huddled in the darkened entryway of a brick apartment building. Others leaned against a couple of cars: A Chevy wagon and an old Ford Fairlane. "Recognize anyone?" Mooch asked Billy, staring out the window like he was on the Congo Cruise. Billy started bouncing up and down like he had to take a leak.

"There he iz! I saw him! I saw him. It's him, that little prick!"

Bugsy leaned over the back of his seat and grabbed Billy by his arm. "Hey man, you gotta be cool."

"It's him, it's him," Billy said. "Thaz him!"

"Yeah, that's him," Danny said. "The little prick. Looks like Dennis the Menace. Billy, you think your dick'll fit in his mouth?"

"How about up his ass?" Bugsy said.

Billy started laughing and wheezing, blowing snot out of his nose. He wiped it on his sleeve and kept laughing. Mooch continued down the street, fighting his laughter and doing his best to stay on the road. Danny and Billy twisted their necks to look out the rear window. Mooch banged another U-ey. "Which one?" Charley asked.

"Next to the little fucker," Billy said, pointing. "The middle one with the pea cap, alongside that tall ugly motherfucker. The one in front of the station wagon. He's the prick that cornered me so that little fucker could jack me up!"

Mooch rolled his window down and gave the kids the finger. The kid leaning on the station wagon yelled, "Fuck you!" and got in the car. Dennis the Menace got in the front seat, and half the kids got in the back. Everyone else piled into the Ford, and they all took off. Mooch put the car into neutral and revved the engine until it howled. Charley leaned out the window and threw a bottle at the station wagon, hitting the middle of the windshield and sending glass everywhere. The car screeched to a halt, and the Ford stopped, nearly rear-ending the station wagon.

"They gotta be pretty pissed," Danny said. "Not for nothing, but there's only six of us. There's like, what, a dozen of them maybe."

"Yeah, but they're a bunch of faggots," Mikey said, glancing back at the wagon.

"You guys are a bunch of fucking pussies," Charley said.

"Still, we oughta give them a little time to cool off," Danny replied.

"Okay, you fuckin' fags. Let's go for a ride," Mooch said.

"Where?" Bugsy asked.

"I dunno."

"We got enough beers?" Danny asked.

"I think so," Mikey answered.

They drove around South Boston, through the D Street projects, passing street corners covered with kids huddled together, smoking and drinking. After stopping at Castle Island to take a piss, they returned to Uppies. Mooch drove down the other end of the street, where the kids had been hanging out, a narrow road lined with three-deckers, crooked decks, and railings that looked like toothless old men smiling. As soon as Mooch drove up, the kids on the corner yelled and ran to the car. Mooch flipped them off, punched the pedal, and screeched past them through the intersection. One of the kids threw a bottle at the car—it skidded across the trunk, bounced off the hood, and landed on the street. Mooch started laughing. "Let's go by again!" he said. "Gimme a beer, will ya?" he said, waving his hand behind the seat, continuing until Mikey stuck a beer in it.

"Hey . . . um, I don't know about you kids, but I got a long day ahead of me. I got to help my ma get ready for Christmas. My grandma's staying with us," Danny said.

"Okay, we can split. I gotta grab some gas first," Mooch said. He weaved through traffic until he reached the Gulf Gas Station on Columbia Road, one of the few stations open late. "Danny, can you keep an eye on the pump? I gotta say hi to Vinny."

"Sure," Danny said, getting out and placing the hose in the tank. Everyone else got out and stretched.

"What time is it?" Bugsy asked.

Danny opened the front door and fiddled with the radio, stopping when he found a news station. "Twenty past ten," he said, stopping when the meter hit a dollar. A few minutes later, Mooch came out, carrying a small fuel can and a dirty rag. After filling the can, he placed it in the trunk.

"What's that for?" Bugsy asked.

"It's Christmas, ain't it?" Mooch said.

"Christmas?" Danny said.

"Christmas?" Charley parroted. "What the fuck're you talking about?"

"Yeah, Christmas," Mooch replied.

The confused kids looked at each other. "I gotta make one more stop," Mooch said.

"What for?" Danny asked.

"Billy."

"Me?" Billy said, surprised.

"Yeah, I got you a Christmas present."

"For me?" Billy replied, crunching his face in confusion.

"Yeah, for you."

"What the fuck're you talking about?" Charley asked.

"You'll see," Mooch said.

A few turns later, they ended up on Bakersfield Street, a couple of blocks from the street corner they had passed earlier. Mooch slowed and peered down every driveway, finally stopping when he spotted the Chevy wagon. He continued to the end of the street, turned, and pulled over.

"C'mon, Billy. Danny, keep the car running. Billy and me got a present for these fucks."

"We do?" Billy replied, twisting his head around.

"Yeah. We're gonna molly that fuckin' car," Mooch replied.

"We are?" Billy stuttered.

"You're fucking shitting me, right?" Charley said.

"What the fuck?" Danny asked, drawing the words out like a long rope.

Mooch laughed as he got out, opened the trunk, and tapped the rear window. "Mikey. Give me one of those empties, will ya?" Mooch removed the can from the trunk, filled the bottle with gas, and stuffed the oily rag into it. "C'mon, let's go," Mooch said to Billy as he closed the trunk.

Billy looked at the other kids. They responded with shrugs.

Mooch and Billy hustle-walked down the block and stopped across the street from the driveway. Mooch passed the bottle to Billy. "Hold this, will ya? Tilt it a little . . . yeah, like that," Mooch said. "There you go. Don't move."

Mooch snapped his lighter and lit the rag. A bright orange flame brought it to life. Mooch grabbed the bottle and took off in a slow trot across the street. When he reached the driveway, he threw the bottle at the car; it exploded when it hit the rear window, sending bright orange flames everywhere.

"Merry Chrizmaz, motherfuckerz!" Billy warbled.

"RUN, YOU CRAZY FUCK!" Mooch screamed. Billy stood like a statue, laughing like a two-legged hyena. "C'mon!" Mooch said, tugging on Billy's arm. "NOW!"

Lights started going on up and down the street. Mooch began to run, stumbling as he dragged Billy behind him. As soon as they got to the car, Mooch slid into the front seat, and Billy tumbled into the back seat, landing on Mikey's lap.

"FUCK! FUCK!" Billy screeched. "FUCK! FUCK, FUCK, FUCK."

Mooch hooted when he slammed the car into gear and took off. "We toasted that motherfucker!" he said, tilting his head at Billy, who was incapable of speaking as he was laughing so hard.

Mooch headed down Columbia Road and circled around Franklin Park. Every time they looked at each other, he and Billy started laughing, quickly infecting the other kids. Ten minutes later, Mooch said, "Let's go back and see what Santa delivered."

"Are you fuckin' nuts?" Danny replied.

"Yeah, nucking futs."

"I'm serious," Danny said.

"I wanna see," Charley said.

Mooch circled back around the block. The street was filled with people, fire engines, housewives in curlers, little kids in pajamas, and lots of cop cars. "Anyone want to get out?" he asked. No one answered.

"There're too many cops; it ain't worth it," Bugsy said.

Billy rolled his window down and hollered. "Merry Chrizmaz!"

"Let's get the fuck outta here," Danny said.

# 12

The sky was gray all week, trying to decide if it would let some snow through. By late Friday night, it had made up its mind. A cold cotton blanket covered everything. The boughs of the pines and firs hung heavy, while the oaks and maples stood bare, stripped of their leaves. Long, thin icicles hung from everything, shimmering like diamond jewelry, reminding Danny of the days when Santa Claus came, and there were presents everywhere; days when Christmas suppah lasted all week long, and people ran up and down the streets with their arms full of gifts, smiling from behind puffy pink cheeks. Still, Christmas bothered Danny. All year long, most people were assholes. Then, when Christmas arrived, they replaced "get fucked" and "go to hell" with "Merry Christmas" and "God Bless You." After the lights came down and the trees were tossed, everyone became an asshole again.

Danny's grandmother, Helen, arrived in the middle of the night with a trunk-load of gifts and a gallon of guilt for her daughter. She always bought the boys plenty of underwear, much to Bridie's relief. For as long as Danny could remember, she always brought him a new sweater. Sometimes the sweater was nice enough to wear, and other times it never made it out of the box it came in.

Danny got up early and ate three bowls of oatmeal. When he reached the Y, he found the kids drinking rum and Coke from wax cups in the locker room, passing around *The Boston Herald*. Mikey passed Danny a cup. Danny glanced at the front page over Mooch's shoulder at a picture of the burned-out station wagon wedged between a pair of blackened three-deckers. According to the article, no one was hurt. Four of the apartments were "uninhabitable."

"I wish I was there," Fitzy said. "You know I would've fucked up those kids."

"Gimme the sports page, will ya?" Mikey said. Mooch pulled the paper apart and handed the page to Mikey. Danny and Bugsy sat down, watching Fitzy make a bigger ass of himself as he got louder, bragging about how much stuff he was getting for Christmas, telling everyone that his Aunt Mitzie had married some rich guy from Connecticut. Mikey finally spoke up when he'd had enough. "Who gives a fuck? We get it! Your aunt gives good head. Big fucking deal. She sounds like your mother."

The room exploded in laughter. Danny laughed so hard he farted. Fitzy glared at Mikey.

"You feeling froggish?" Mikey snarled.

"Take it back," Fitzy blurted. "You can't rank my aunt."

"Yes, I can; I just did. And I ranked your mother."

"I call you out," Fitzy yelled, throwing his cup against the wall.

"You don't want to do that," Mikey said, putting his drink down. The other kids went silent. "Trust me," Mikey added.

Fitzy stepped toward Mikey and opened his mouth, about to say something, but stopped when he heard the clatter and chatter of several girls coming down the stairs. Everyone turned to watch Becky, Patty, and Kat sashay toward them, smiling and wiggling their hips. Mikey turned to Fitzy and spoke quietly, "Sit the fuck down. I don't want to embarrass you."

Fitzy glanced at the girls and glared at Mikey before going to the bench to make another drink. The girls sat at the other end, giggling and chatting. A few minutes later, Patty got up and walked over to Danny. "Hi," she said. Danny felt his heart shuffle a few beats. Her hair was tied up in a small bun held together by a wool headband. She wore a pink jacket trimmed with white fur that hugged her neck. She had on a pair of white boots and black winter leggings.

"Hi," he said, smiling.

"Do you have a minute?"

"Um, sure. What's up?" Danny replied as he pulled out his smokes and lit one. "Want one?"

"No, thanks."

"Can we take a walk?" she asked.

"Sure. Where to?"

"Outside," she said, tugging his hand. They strolled past the other kids, and one of the guys whistled. Patty blushed for a moment. After they went upstairs and stepped into the entryway, she asked, "How's everything going?"

"Good."

"You?"

"Okay. I'm kinda cold. I don't like this weather." He rubbed his hands together. "I wish I was someplace warm."

"Me too," she said, wrapping her arms around herself.

"C'mon," she said, stepping down onto the sidewalk. Danny followed, grabbed a handful of snow, packed it into a tight ball, and threw it at a street sign, clipping the corner. "Nice shot, Lonborg," she said. He made another and nailed it, rattling the metal like a big cymbal. Patty scooped up a handful of snow and made her own snowball; it fell apart as soon as she threw it.

"Nice shot," Danny said. She tossed a handful of snow at Danny. "Jerk," she said, laughing. She slipped her arm inside his and hugged herself into him. "What're your plans for Christmas?" she said.

"Eating!"

"Eating?"

"Yeah. My grandma's visiting. She loves to cook. Pies mostly."

"God, that sounds wonderful! What's your favorite pie?"

"Blueberry, but I like anything she makes. She's a great cook! What's your favorite?"

"Cherry."

"I love cherry too. Have you ever had cherry and blueberry pie?"

"No, but it sounds wonderful."

"It is; the best."

"Where's your grandma from?"

"Maine."

"Is she your dad's side or your ma's?

"Ma's."

"We were there for a vacation a couple of years ago. It's pretty. I wouldn't want to be there in the winter, though. It was September, and it was freezing at night."

"Yeah, that's Maine."

"What about your grandfather? Is he still alive?"

"Naw, he's been gone a long time. Ten years, or more, maybe."

"I'm sorry."

"It's no big deal. He was kinda old and everything. I didn't really know him."

"What did he die of?"

"Cancer."

"My Uncle Timmy died of cancer—lung cancer. I remember he smoked like a chimney."

"Same with my grandpa. I remember looking at his fingers when I was little. They were brown and yellow from where he held his cigarette." Danny squeezed her hand, let it go, and ran across the street, where he hid behind a parked car, and made a large fluffy snowball. He jumped up and lobbed it at her. It exploded on her arm and sent small chunks of snow everywhere. She grabbed a handful of snow and chased him, pelting him with the hastily made snowball. They battled until they were too close to throw anymore. A strong wind whistled up the street, dusting them with crisp light snow. They fell backward onto a small mound of snow. He brushed the powder from her face, and she, in turn, kissed him on the cheek, catching him by surprise.

"Let me brush you off," he said as he carefully ran his hands through her hair and across her collar. When he was done, she kissed him again and stood up. He joined her after dusting himself off.

"So, what was your best Christmas ever?" she asked, slipping her arm inside his. He was about to answer when she spoke again. "Best presents? Best holiday besides Christmas? Best Christmas dinner? Best time?"

"Whoa, whoa, that's a lot to think about. Let me think." He made another snowball and tossed it at a trash can. "The best Christmas presents involve my grandma—she always brings us stuff. And the best holiday would have to be Halloween."

"Best vacation?"

"Hmm. I ain't never been on vacation, not a real one anyway. We never went away except to my grandma's house in Maine."

"Well, that's a vacation, right?"

"Yeah, I s'pose."

Danny glanced at his three-decker as they passed it. Half a block further, Patty asked, "Don't you live around here?"

"Yeah, we passed my house, back there," he said, with a slight tilt of his head.

"Where?"

"On Bowdoin Street," he replied, too embarrassed to point it out to her. He tossed another snowball at her and then took off. She chased him, sliding and wobbling down the street. He slowed down so she could catch up, and as he did, she lost her balance. Danny caught her; they staggered backward, landed on a low, large snowbank, and stared at the sky.

"It's so pretty, isn't it?" she said, sticking her tongue out, catching some of the little snowflakes that landed around her. They lay there for a few minutes, flicking their tongues around, laughing and smiling at each other.

"I have to teach you how to make a snowball," he said.

"And I have to teach you how to throw."

"It's a deal! Danny said. He brushed her hair again. "I'm freezing."

"Me too," Patty replied.

"Let's take the steps."

They got up together and brushed themselves off. After shuffling through the snow and up the steps, they stopped at a corner bench. Danny grabbed his sleeve and wiped the snow off so they could sit down. Danny pulled his smokes out. "Want one?"

"No, thanks."

"Do you and your family go to midnight Mass?"

"Oh yes, for as long as I can remember. Everyone gets dressed up. My mom makes a ham suppah, mashed potatoes, green beans, and pies. And my dad makes the best hot cocoa. And the best part is he always has a present for my mom, usually jewelry. It's very sweet. Oh yeah, I forgot to tell you. At Thanksgiving, everyone puts their name in a bag. Whoever's name you pick, you have to get them a present. It's a lot of fun! My dad made the rules. You can't spend more than three dollars. He's made it really easy for everyone, you know, 'cause he gives us an extra allowance."

"Sounds really nice."

"It is."

The snow fell faster, and the flakes grew larger, covering the park in a blanket of snow. Patty leaned against Danny's shoulder. They watched a bunch of little kids laughing and dragging cardboard sheets behind them. "Hey, let's go for a ride," she said, grabbing him by his hand. "C'mon!"

"I thought you had to get home."

"I do," she said. "We have time for one ride."

"Okay," he said, smiling.

They stopped at a large maple tree at the crest of the hill, surrounded by large pieces of cardboard. Danny grabbed an old Sears and Roebuck refrigerator box and carried it over to the top of the slope. He sat down and curled the front edge of the cardboard toward him, rolling it up in his hands. Patty sat behind him and laced her legs around him. They took off and flew down the hill, laughing louder than anyone else in the park. When they reached the bottom, they slid onto a small snowbank. Danny rolled over and kissed her. After the kiss, she rolled on her back, catching more snowflakes.

# 13

Christmas day was the best day of the week, not because it was Christmas, but because newly fallen snow made the neighborhood look like a Currier and Ives lithograph hanging in a lace-curtained home in Milton. Frankie got up first. He entered the parlor and pulled the presents aside, knocking ornaments off the silver-tinseled tree. Bridie stuck her head into the hallway and yelled, "Frankie!"

"Little fuck," Danny mumbled when he heard his mother's voice. He pulled his sheets to the side and sat up. He looked at the frost on the windows, trying to figure out how cold it was. The thought made him want to go to the bathroom, so he did, quick-stepping across the hallway. When he finished, he went into the kitchen, where his mother and grandmother were talking about the wonders of Maine.

"The kids will love the country," his grandmother said. "The fresh air will be good for them. They can eat fresh vegetables right out of the ground! Can you imagine that?" Bridie listened patiently, tossing in an uh-huh every few minutes to be polite. "They don't call it the pine tree state for nothing," Helen said proudly.

"Yes, I know, Ma. It sounds wonderful."

"Good morning," Danny said.

"Morning," Bridie responded.

"Good morning, Danny," his grandmother said.

"Can I get you anything?" his mother said.

"No, I'm okay. I'm gonna make some hot chocolate."

"Use the milk. We have plenty," Bridie said. She and her mother continued conversing, while Danny hovered around the kitchen counter.

"And besides, you won't have to deal with all the coons and the spics. Jesus, honey, every time I come here, it gets worse. They're everywhere. Mother of Jesus, they don't belong here. We don't have any of them in Maine," Bridie's mother said.

"It's not that bad, Ma. The kids have a lot of friends, and the schools are good. They're city kids. I'm not sure how they'd do in Maine."

"I'm telling you, honey, they'll love it there," her mother insisted, continuing with her chamber of commerce pitch.

"Excuse me a minute," Bridie said. She got up and walked down the hall, hoping to coax Chrissy out of bed.

"I'm gonna drink my hot chocolate in my bedroom, Grandma. I'll be back." She nodded in response.

---

Ever since Chrissy had begun dating Henschel, the crown prince from Newton, her attitude had changed. The first time Danny's sister introduced Henschel to her family, she spoke in a voice reserved for weddings and coronations. "This is Robert James Henschel. He's from Newton," she said as if she was his press agent.

"Who gives a shit?" Danny replied. Danny figured everything Henschel wore was monogrammed—from his shirts to his handkerchiefs, underwear, diaper, and maybe even his toilet paper.

Chrissy and Henschel had met on one of those hot and humid days when everyone wanted to hang out at Filene's or Jordan Marsh, an air-conditioned place where you could wander around and no one would bother you. Henschel had impressed her as soon as she'd learned he was from Newton, where fresh milk was delivered every morning, everyone had two and three-car garages, and no one ever took a bus. Chrissy's love had deepened after learning that Henschel's father owned a Chevy dealership on Commonwealth Avenue. Her passion had blossomed when she'd seen his brand-new, cherry-red Corvette.

"Honey, it's Christmas," Bridie called out to Chrissy. "Grandma's here!" Danny listened to his mother while Chrissy mumbled something cranky and annoying. He heard snippets of their conversation and then the sound of his mother returning to the kitchen. Out of nowhere, Frankie suddenly bounded into the bedroom, hopping around like a grasshopper.

"Danny! C'mon, get up, get up! It's Christmas!" His hair was twisted like a Texas tumbleweed, and his pajamas were inside out.

"C'mon! C'mon!" Frankie said, tugging on Danny's bedspread, bouncing up and down like his legs were made of rubber. "Get up! It's Christmas! Get up!"

"You gotta go to the bathroom?" Danny asked.

Frankie squeezed his legs together and continued moving. "Um, yeah."

"Then go," Danny said, shaking his head. Frankie ran to the bathroom and took a quick leak, loud enough for everyone to hear. Bridie hollered from the kitchen. "Flush the toilet!" After he flushed, she yelled again. "Wash your hands."

Danny pulled a long-sleeve winter shirt from his dresser, dragged it over his head, put his dungarees on, and stepped into the hallway. His sister's door was closed as tight as a tomb; his grandmother's voice ebbed and flowed from the kitchen with the clinking sounds of dishes, cups, and silverware. The smell of bacon, muffins, and cocoa filled the hallway, reminding him of warm summer days when the scents from Baker's Chocolate filled the air. He took a deep breath and knocked on his sister's door—*shave and a haircut, two bits*—and waited. He knocked again. The springs on his sister's mattress creaked. Danny pried her door open. "Psst. Chrissy. It's Christmas, and everyone's up." He opened the door wider, letting more light in.

"Close the fucking door!" Chrissy snarled.

"Jesus Christ, Chrissy. Why do you have to be such a cunt? It's Christmas. Ma and Grandma made breakfast, and they're waiting for you. What's your fucking problem?"

"Get the fuck out!" Chrissy spat back like broken glass.

Danny swung her door open and flipped the light switch on, cleaning out the shadows. He strolled into the kitchen, where his grandmother, held together by a pair of meaty arms, was mixing a bowl of pancake batter. Her head wobbled back and forth like a ten-pound turkey. Thick rolls of pasty white skin fell from her jaw and disappeared into her neck behind a coffee-stained robe that cascaded to the floor like the tattered movie curtains at the Paramount. Her legs stuck out like giant sausages, bound by a pair of once-pink slippers stained with grease, grime, and everything else she had ever cooked. Danny kissed his mother on the cheek and turned to his grandmother. "Good morning, Grandma," he chirped.

Helen looked up and smiled. "Good morning, honey. I hope you're hungry. Your mother and I have been cooking up a storm."

"I am," Danny replied. He took a couple of steps toward the stove and leaned over. "It smells great."

"I made your favorite blueberry flapjacks," Bridie said. She was dressed in a bright green sweater and a red Christmas apron, adorned with felt silhouettes of green reindeers and a band of white-bearded elves. "Would you mind checking the cookies?"

"Sure, no problem."

"There's a mitt over there," she added before humming, "Rudolph the Red-Nosed Reindeer." The tune caught him off guard, reminding him of his father, something he hadn't expected. *Where was he? What was he doing? Who was he with? Was he opening presents? Was he married? Did he have children?* He fought to hold back the tears that filled his eyes, but they won; they came out.

"Is everything okay, honey?" Bridie asked, reaching for his hand.

"Yeah, I'm sorry, Ma, I . . . I . . ." he trailed off, unable to continue. Bridie filled a glass with water and handed it to him. He took a sip and closed his eyes. "Thanks," he said, wiping his eyes with his sleeve.

"Can I do anything?" she asked.

"No, I'm okay. I'm . . . I'm sorry. I was . . ."

"It's okay," she said, rubbing his arm. "It's okay."

Danny's grandmother looked up and was about to say something when Bridie daggered her with her eyes, sending Helen's head back into her mixing bowl. Danny wiped his face; walked to the window; and ran his fingers over the thin layer of frost, clearing enough to look outside.

After a few minutes, Bridie walked over to him and rubbed his arm again. "Honey, can you get your sister and brother? Let them know breakfast's ready."

"Sure, no problem."

"I hope you're hungry," she said in a voice that would cheer up a funeral.

"I am. I could eat a horse," Danny said, turning from the window, clear-eyed.

"I don't have a horse, but we have a lot of bacon and sausage," she laughingly replied.

"Sounds good." He went down the hall and popped his head into his sister's room. "Hey, Chrissy, Bobby's on the phone."

"Do you mean Robert?" she asked, suddenly alive, popping her head from beneath her covers. "What time is it?"

"Quarter past nine."

"Are you serious? Quarter past nine!" She wrapped her sheets around her and stood up. "I'm late!"

"What do you want me to tell him? You're taking a shit or something?"

"Get out! GET OUT!"

"I'll tell him you're on the rag."

"Jesus Christ, you're such an asshole! Get out of here!" She yelled louder. "GET OUT OF HERE!"

"Is everything okay?" Bridie called from the kitchen.

"Yeah, Chrissy's really excited about Christmas," Danny said.

"That's nice," Bridie responded, returning to the stove.

Danny left her door open, walked into the parlor, and turned the television off. "Breakfast's ready."

"But . . . but," Frankie replied as if he'd been kicked in the head.

"But, but, what? Ma's got breakfast ready, and I'm starved. Ma ain't gonna serve nothing until everyone's up." Danny looked around the room and saw the mess; most of the presents were open. "You gotta clean this mess up," he said, slapping Frankie across his head. "Clean this shit up before Ma comes in."

"Is everything all right?" Bridie yelled from the kitchen, raising her voice above the clinking of cups and saucers.

"Yeah, Ma," Danny yelled back, dead-staring Frankie. "We're just fooling around."

"Is your sister up?" she yelled.

"I dunno. I'll check," Danny hollered. He turned back to Frankie. "You better find all the cards and envelopes and put them back on the right presents. We don't need Ma getting upset. You know how she gets when Grandma's here." Danny kicked one of the torn-open boxes at Frankie. "I'm serious. Clean this shit up."

Frankie mumbled, a dying man's last breath, "Okay."

On his way back to the kitchen, Danny banged on Chrissy's door. She yelled something, but he didn't stick around to listen. He sat next to his grandmother. "What am I smelling?" he asked, lifting his head and poking his nose around like a hungry bloodhound.

"It's apple cobbler," she said proudly. "It's made out of Maine apples."

"It smells incredible."

"It's the apples. You could pick them right off the tree if you lived in Maine."

"Is everyone up?" Bridie asked, changing the conversation.

"Excuse me, Grandma. Frankie's up, and Chrissy's in the bathroom."

"Honey, would you help Grandma set the table?" Bridie asked.

"Yeah, of course."

"Let me clean up a little," his grandmother said. "I'll move this stuff over here, on the counter.

"Let me help you," Danny said, picking up some of the cups and boxes. When they were done, his grandmother wet a kitchen towel under the water and wiped the table top clean. Danny removed some dishes from the kitchen cabinet and placed them on the table while his grandmother arranged them. Bridie started humming again; *Jingle Bells*.

"Honey, can you get the extra chair from the back hallway?" Bridie said.

"Sure," Danny said.

He walked down and hall and banged on the bathroom door. "C'mon, I gotta go," he said, trying to irritate his sister. He shuffled into the parlor, where Frankie had done a good job cleaning up, much to his surprise. Danny strolled to the corner window, scraped some frost off, and surveyed the three-deckers lining the street. The only signs of life were the Christmas lights filling the windows of the nearby homes. "Okay, that's good," he said, turning to Frankie. "We better get in the kitchen before Ma gets mad at us."

# 14

When Chrissy figured out Danny had lied about the time and the phone call, her grandmother convinced her to stay home. "It's Christmas, honey. It only comes once a year." Of course, it helped that she had bought Chrissy several pairs of underwear, frilly bras, blouses, and two fancy perfume bottles from Jordan Marsh.

After breakfast, everyone sat around sipping hot cocoa or tea while going through the neatly wrapped presents, eventually figuring out who would get what. They ate their way through the day and watched all the TV specials. After the news, Bridie poured a cold glass of eggnog for everyone, topping hers and her mother's off with a healthy pour of ginger brandy. After the third drink, Helen started snoring like a freight train while Bridie dozed off quietly alongside her. Danny watched them for a few minutes, confident they were not getting up. He slipped into the kitchen and topped his eggnog off with brandy. After several refills, he joined his mother and grandmother in sawing logs.

---

Danny got up the next day sluggish; his mouth felt dry and fuzzy. The kitchen table was covered with every kind of breakfast imaginable: pancakes, scrambled eggs, sausages, bacon, ham, orange juice, milk, cereal, and a tall bottle of eggnog. Danny looked at the bottle and felt his stomach lurch sideways. "Danny, why don't you try on the pants Grandma got for you?" Bridie asked, peering over her cup of tea.

"Can I do it later? I'm tired."

"No, I want you to do it now. Grandma can take something back if it doesn't fit."

Helen looked up, smiled, and poured another spoonful of sugar into her teacup.

"And you too," Bridie said to Frankie, lingering behind his older brother, peeking around him, trying to hide. "Try on your underwear."

"But, Ma," Frankie groaned, sounding like he was choking on sawdust.

"And your socks. Put them on so we can see how they fit."

"But, Ma."

"No buts, young man. We don't have all day. Grandma spent a lot of money on you. Come here," Bridie said, handing him a pair of pants. "Put these on."

Frankie dragged the pants over his pajama bottoms. "Take your pajamas off so we can see how they fit. Go to your bedroom, and change. Take those pajamas off, and put on your new underwear. We don't have all day."

Danny watched everything from the pantry, leaning against the doorway, quietly sipping his cocoa. Frankie flopped back into the kitchen ten minutes later. "C'mon over here. Turn around. What do you think, Ma?" asked Bridie.

Helen reached over and tugged on the pants, pulling them up, down, and up again while slowly rotating Frankie. "They have to come up a little," she said, tugging at the bottom of the pants, folding them into small cuffs. "I can do it if you have a needle and some thread."

"I'll do it, Ma. I'll have plenty of time," Bridie said, looking over at Frankie, looking like he was stuck in a Vincent Price torture chamber.

Helen stood up and turned Frankie around one last time. "They need to be taken up just a little. Over here," she said, tugging at his waist. "Otherwise, they look fine."

"Can I go, Ma?"

"Yes. Take the pants off and bring them back."

Danny put his dirty dishes in the sink, quietly returned to his room, and put his pants on. He walked out into the kitchen and turned a couple of times. "These fit great," he said, spinning again and heading out before the women could say anything. After changing into his weathered dungies and putting his pea cap on, he popped his head into the kitchen. "I'm going out," he said.

"Where?" Bridie asked, her voice rising into a cusp.

"Out."

"Out where?"

"Out."

"Danny," she stammered.

"To the Corner."

"Before you go, thank Grandma for your presents."

"Thank you, Grandma," Danny said, smiling. "I'm wearing the long underwear you bought me."

"That's nice, honey," Helen said. "They'll keep you warm."

"I gotta go, Ma," Danny said.

---

The air was crisp, and the sidewalks were slippery. Danny semi-skidded down the street, turning now and then to shield himself from the wind and snow that gnawed at him. He stepped into a doorway to have a cigarette and take a break from the storm. When he was done, he pulled his collar up, jammed his hands in his pockets, and continued, leaning into the wind. As he neared the Corner, he saw a paddy wagon double-parked in front of Charlie's, flashing its blue lights, shoveling a couple of the kids into the back, bouncing them off the hard wooden seats. He crossed over to the other side and strolled as if he had somewhere important to go. He circled the block and came around the other way, where some of the kids were hanging out. Clouds of smoke and steam rose above their heads.

"What's up?" Bugsy asked when they were close enough to hear each other.

"Nothing much," Danny replied. "Was that Delaney?" he asked, referring to the cop supervising the bust.

"Yeah. He's with Rockhold. They've got a hard-on for Yaka and Roachie."

"Ever since they put Rockhold on a motorcycle, he's become a real prick," Danny said.

"No shit," Misfit added.

"So, what'd they bust 'em for?" Danny asked.

"B 'n' E. They broke into a couple of cars down at Bradlees."

"What a bunch of fucking idiots," Danny replied. "Why do they shit in their own backyard?"

"I dunno," Bugsy replied. "What're you up to?"

"I was thinking of going to the schoolyard," Danny said.

"Sounds good," Misfit replied. "There's too much heat down here."

"Has anyone seen Patty?" Danny asked as the kids started walking up the street, puffing on their smokes.

"I did. She and some of the girls were around earlier," Misfit said. "Becky, Kat, Maggie, and that chick from Codman Square, the blonde with the big tits. Shit!—what's her name?"

"Dianne?" suggested Headso.

"Yeah, that's it. Man, that chick's stacked. They call ger Double D. What's her fucking story?"

"I dunno," Danny shrugged.

"Well, she and Patty and the other girls split right after the cops showed up."

"Which way'd they go?" Danny asked, doing his best not to sound too curious.

"I'm not sure. They were talking about going to McManus's," Headso said.

"So, what are you kids doing tonight?" Danny asked.

"Same old shit. Different day; hanging out."

"You kids want to get some more beers?" Danny said.

Grunta gagged up a loogie and spat it into the street. "I'm broke, man. I spent what I had earlier. That asshole Rockhold poured all the opens down the gutter, and he and that other prick took everything else."

"At least you didn't get busted," Danny said. "I got you covered."

"Yeah, it coulda been worse."

"No kidding. A lot worse."

"So, you going bowling on New Year's Eve?" Grunta asked Danny. "Some of the kids were talking about going to Ten Pin."

"Who's going?"

"I ain't sure. I know it'd be better than standing around outside. It's too fucking cold out."

"No shit, Sherlock."

"Anyways, I'm thinking I might as well go. It don't make no sense to freeze."

Danny took his hat off, put some money in it, and passed it around. When they had enough to make a buy, Bugsy said, "We should all go. We'll freeze if we stand around here."

Danny said, "Let's play like the good shepherd and get the flock outta here."

They took off down the middle of the street, shuffling through the new-fallen snow. The sidewalks had not been shoveled, nor had the streets. A maroon Ford Fairlane followed them down the hill, a few yards behind them. The driver hit the horn, interrupting their conversation. Everyone stopped and stared at each other first and then at the driver. Headso walked back and flicked his cigarette at the car. It bounced off the windshield, sending sparks across the front of the hood. Grunta walked up to the front of the vehicle and pissed on the car, sending a cloud of noxious steam high in the air. The rest of the kids surrounded the car. After shaking his dick and pulling his fly up, Grunta walked to the driver's side and tapped the window. The driver, a young kid sporting a crew cut, a button-down shirt, a plaid tie, and a blue blazer, rolled the window down, an inch at best. "Can I help you?" he asked nervously, looking around at the kids circling his car.

"You're not in a rush, are you?" Misfit asked, wiping his nose on his sleeve and spitting on the hood.

"Um, no . . . no," the driver answered. "I don't want any trouble."

"Trouble? What do you mean trouble? What kind of trouble?" Misfit replied.

"I don't know. I mean . . ."

Misfit stared at the kid while lighting a cigarette. After it was lit, he walked over to the other kids, and they resumed their hike, staying in the middle of the street. The kids turned right at the intersection and continued walking; the car took a left and sped off.

"I didn't get enough shit for Christmas," Headso said.

"Me neither," Grunta said.

Headso started singing, "Santa Claus is Coming to Town." Grunta joined him. "We'll catch up with you kids later. We're going shopping," Headso said.

"Be careful, you fucking idiots. Remember what happened to the Yaka and Roachie," Misfit said.

Headso and Grunta responded by singing louder—"He knows if you are sleeping, he knows if you're awake . . ."

"Wait up," Fitzy yelled, separating himself from the bunch of kids to join Grunta and Headso.

The rest of the kids continued to the bleachers at Town Field, climbing to the last tier of seats, where they sat down. Five minutes later, they heard a car window being smashed and watched as Fitzy, Grunta, and Headso started yanking shopping bags and boxes from the back of a wood-sided Chevy station wagon.

After finishing their smokes, Bugsy, Misfit, and Danny headed over to Dorchester Ave, where they spotted Tommy Hennessey, a harmless old alkie, standing in front of Hi-Fi. Except for the day he was born at City Hospital, Tommy had spent his entire forty-nine years shuffling around the neighborhood, never leaving, not even to take a train. He was a fixture like a hydrant or an old street light. His head looked like a battered bowling ball covered with strands of wiry hair sticking out in a thousand different directions. His jacket had so many stains, it looked like a greasy map of Mexico. He smelled like a wet dog and a backed-up toilet rolled into one.

"Hey, Tommy, want a smoke?" Bugsy asked, lifting his cigarettes to him.

"Sure," Tommy said, smiling through a food-stained grin. Danny thought he spotted some pepperoni and tomato sauce. "You fuckin' kids are all right," Tommy said. "And I don't give a shit what they say about you." Everyone laughed; they always did. Tommy had one joke, but no one complained.

"Tommy, can you make a buy for us?" Danny asked.

"Sure. You got an extra smoke?"

"Yeah," Misfit said, offering his pack. "Take as many as you want."

Tommy fingered a couple of cigarettes, tucking one behind each ear, and stuck a third in his mouth. Bugsy lit it for him. "You fuckin' kids are all right. I don't give a shit what they say about you," he driveled. "What d'ya want?"

"We need a couple cases of beer and a couple of jugs," Danny replied.

"You fuckin' kids having a party or something?" Tommy asked.

"Yeah, in your mouth," Bugsy said. "Everyone's coming." Tommy coughed and laughed so hard that pea-colored snot shot out of his nose. His crotch darkened from pissing himself with laughter.

"Tha's a good one, you little shit. Ha, ha, ha. Tha's a good one." He wiped his nose on his sleeve, adding some more stains.

"We're just fuckin' with you, Tommy," Danny said. "You're a good shit."

"Everyone's coming. I get it. You fuckin' kids are all right, and I don't give a shit what they say about you." He stared across the street at something no one else could see. "So, what d'ya want?" he asked again.

"Two cases of Bud, a couple quarts of CC, and a pint," Bugsy said. "The pint's for you."

Tommy smiled through half a mouthful of discolored teeth. "Sure."

"Which way?" Danny asked.

"That way," Tommy replied, pointing down the street.

"We 'preciate you helping us, Tommy," Danny said.

Tommy took a drag on his cigarette, burning it down to the filter before flicking it into the street. "So, what have you been up to, Tommy?" Danny asked.

"Nothing much; same old shit."

Bugsy handed the money to Tommy. "We'll be around the corner," he said.

A few minutes later, Tommy came out, lugging a case of beer, straddling it on his stomach. The bottles were in bags on top of the case. As soon as Tommy saw Bugsy, he put the case down, and Bugsy carried it around the corner. "I got one more," Tommy said. He went in and returned with the other case of beer. Danny grabbed it and carried it around the corner. "I got you kids a good fuckin' deal," Tommy said, happily smiling as if he'd just given birth. "A really good one."

"Thanks," Danny said. "Here's a couple more smokes." Tommy stuck the cigarettes behind his ears. "You're good fuckin' kids," Tommy said. "I don't give a shit what they say about you."

"Me neither," Bugsy said, laughing.

"Tha's a good one," Tommy said. He took a long swig from his bottle.

"See ya," Danny said.

"You're a good fuckin' kid," Tommy said. He took another swig, stuffed the bottle in his jacket, and headed off. Danny grabbed one of the cases, and Bugsy grabbed the other. Misfit stuffed the bottles inside his coat. On the way back, they ran into Fitzy, Grunta, and Headso, standing alongside the stuff they had stolen. The bags were full of women's clothing—dresses, blouses, slacks, and fancy underwear.

"That doesn't look like your color," Bugsy said, picking up a pair of panties. "And they're not your size. You'll look good in them, though." Bugsy twirled them around and tossed them at Fitzy.

"Fuck you," Fitzy said.

"Fuck your mother. Everyone else does," Bugsy said. After the kids stopped laughing, Bugsy said, "What're you gonna do with all that shit?"

"I'm gonna take it all back. Me and Headso did it before. After we stole some stuff, we returned it to the store. I told them my grandma got it for my sister, and it didn't fit. Then when I couldn't find the right size, they gave me the money back. Once, I stole a suede jacket from Filene's; the fucking thing was too small. So, I took it back the next day and got one that fit me. It was brown colored, the same color as the hair on Danny's sister's pussy." Fitzy ran his finger under his nose. "And it kinda smelled the same."

Danny threw his beer at Fitzy and ran straight at him. Fitzy lifted his arms but wasn't quick enough. Danny nailed him on the side of his head, sending a small trail of blood down the side of Fitzy's face; they both went down hard; a minute later, they were back on their feet. Fitzy swung like a windmill, landing a couple on Danny's face. The next punch was better. It landed on Danny's nose and staggered him. They both tried to get their footing, but the street was too slippery. Bugsy grabbed Danny and locked his arms. Misfit did the same with Fitzy. Once Danny realized it was Bugsy, he quit struggling.

"It's over," Misfit said. Bugsy said nothing; he stared at Danny.

"You done?" Bugsy asked Fitzy.

"Yeah," he replied.

"Okay." Bugsy let Fitzy go, and as soon as he did, Fitzy sucker-punched Danny, sending him to the ground. Blood started flowing from the back of his head, discoloring the snow.

"You fuckin' pussy. You want a piece of me?" Fitzy yelled, standing over him. "You want a piece of me?" He kicked Danny in his ribs and yelled. "You fucking pussy! I'll kick your ass!" Danny looked up at the silhouette hovering above him. A second silhouette appeared. It was Bugsy; he had Fitzy in a headlock.

"It's over," Bugsy snarled, bending Fitzy over, onto his side.

"It's over when I say it's over!" Fitzy spat out.

Bugsy tightened his grasp until Fitzy's eyes bulged like ripened raspberries. Fitzy twisted around and yelled at Danny. "FUCK YOU!"

Danny sat up for a moment. He grabbed a handful of snow and pressed it against his head. Fitzy continued struggling while Bugsy tightened his arm around Fitzy's neck, pulling harder until Fitzy waved his arm, slowly at first and then frantically. Bugsy squeezed him one more time before loosening his grip.

Misfit handed Danny a smoke. "Thanks," Danny said. He took a drag, grabbed some snow, and wiped more blood off the back of his head. Fitzy got up and brushed the snow off his jacket. As soon as he was erect, Bugsy shoved him into the street, where he landed on his back. Fitzy sat up and stared at Bugsy. Bugsy took a couple of steps toward Fitzy.

"Unless you're feeling froggish, stay down," Bugsy said. "Or I'm gonna fuck you up."

Bugsy leered over him until Fitzy bent his head down.

"Fitzy," Grunta called out. As soon as Fitzy looked over, Grunta tossed him a beer. After drinking most of it in two guzzles, he glanced at Bugsy, who said nothing. Fitzy got up and started to pick up the boxes and the clothes. Headso came over and stuffed everything into the boxes. When they were done, they headed down the street, carrying the boxes. Danny and the other kids gathered the beer and alcohol and resumed the trek uphill.

"How's your head?" Bugsy asked Danny. "You alright?"

"Yeah. I was okay until that asshole sucker punched me."

"He's a fucking jerk. I was about to bury his ass."

"I saw that. You didn't have to do that for me."

"I know. I was looking for an excuse."

"I 'preciate it. I'm getting tired of his shit. I promise, his day is coming."

"Make sure I'm there when it happens."

"I will."

# 15

"Where are you going to stay tonight?" Bridie asked Chrissy, knowing she and Robert would be sleeping together but wanting to hear something else.

"The guys are going to get a room together, and me and Jerry's fiancée, Diane, will get our own room." Chrissy paused to ensure she didn't have to elaborate more than necessary. "We made the reservations last week," she added.

"That's nice," Bridie replied, convincing herself to be content with the answer. "You know, your father and I went to Times Square once. It was back in '47, or maybe in '48, just after the war. We took the train," she said wistfully. "It was such a beautiful ride. It was snowing, and people were singing. Mother of Mary, it was beautiful. Your father and I bought two bottles of champagne, and we ate the most incredible suppah. It was wonderful. A real romantic night."

"Sounds nice, Ma."

Bridie stopped and looked out the window. "But then your father screwed the whole thing up," she said like a balloon deflating. "He wasn't content with the champagne and had to get something stronger." Bridie spooned some more sugar into her cup. "When we got to New York, he couldn't wait to find a packie. He did and was plastered by the time we got to Times Square." She shook her head and drifted off again, "Your father . . ." She stopped and looked at Frankie, who was staring at her wide-eyed. Bridie wiped the corner of her eye with her soiled napkin.

"Frankie, you want some milk or something?" Danny said, tapping his brother on the arm. Frankie looked at his mother and then back at Danny, who tapped him harder.

"Um, no, I'm okay," Frankie said, still missing the point, not wanting to get poked again. "Where's Grandma?"

"She's resting, honey," replied Bridie, still dabbing her eyes.

Danny pulled his chair up close. "So, where are you and Robby staying?" Danny asked, knowing that if there was any way to redirect a conversation, it was to let Chrissy talk about Chrissy.

"It's Robert," she said coldly, snapping the "T" off. Danny rolled his eyes so far into the back of his head, that he was looking at his underwear.

"Um, okay. So where are you and *Robert* going?"

"*Well*, we're staying in Manhattan at a fancy place with room service and everything. *And* they have a small bar in the room. Can you imagine that?"

"Wow, that'll cost a bunch, I bet," Danny said, feigning interest for his mother's benefit.

"And romantic," Birdie chirped, stuffing her handkerchief in her sleeve.

"Oh, it will be!" Chrissy bubbled. Danny bit his tongue.

"So, what are your plans?" Bridie asked Danny. "Are you still seeing that girl? What's her name? Pam, no, Patty. That's it."

"Well, yeah, sort of. We're not going steady or nothing. We hang out together with all the other kids."

"Oh. I thought it was more serious."

"Naw. We're just friends."

"I see," she said, nodding.

"Anyways, me and a bunch of the kids are going to Ten Pin. They're gonna be open all night."

"Sounds like fun," Bridie said. "And you and me, young man," she said, turning to Frankie. "We're gonna stay up till midnight and look for your sister on television. Maybe we'll see her in Times Square." Bridie reached over and patted Chrissy's hand while Danny twirled his finger in a small circle, out of view of his mother. Chrissy glared at him, mouthing the word *asshole.*

"Well, I'm headed out," Danny said, standing up.

"Have fun!" Bridie said. "Don't stay out too late."

"I won't, Ma."

Danny jogged to the Corner, moving to stay warm. "So, I hear Mary O'Reilly's having a party," Mooch said as soon as Danny arrived.

Danny cupped his hands and blew on them. "Oh yeah? Sounds like a warm place to be. Better than the bowling alley."

"It will be," Bugsy said.

Danny was about to say something when he heard a car rumbling down the street. It was T-Bone Barrett, driving a '67 Caddy with the radio blaring. T-Bone pulled over and rolled the window down, and it disappeared into the door. "What's up?" Bugsy asked, sticking his head inside the car.

"Not much," T-Bone said. "What're you kids up to?"

"Freezing our fuckin' asses off," Bugsy said.

"Get in," T-Bone said.

"Where are you going?" Danny asked, hopping from one leg to the other.

"Who gives a fuck?" Bugsy replied.

"Savin Hill. Peewee McDermott's house," T-Bone said, inhaling a lungful of a Marlboro. "You know Peewee, doncha?" A few heads nodded. "His parents are away for the weekend."

"Savin Hill? Who's gonna be there?" Bugsy asked.

"I dunno, a buncha kids. From Saint William's, I think."

"How many can you fit?" Headso asked, peering inside the car.

"I dunno. Seven, eight, maybe. It's a fucking Caddy. If you don't mind sitting on someone's lap, nine, ten, maybe. Shit, I can fit a few more in the trunk. It's big enough to carry a horse."

"I'll go," Headso said. He pulled a six-pack out of a snow pile and climbed into the front seat. More kids followed, beers in hand until the car was packed. Danny, Bugsy, and Charley stayed outside with the others.

"You sure you kids don't want to get in? We can make more room," T-Bone said.

"Naw, we're good," Bugsy said.

"All right. I'll catch you fags later," T-Bone said. Danny made a small snowball and tossed it at the car. T-Bone put it in gear, jammed the gas pedal, and left a dark cloud of fumes behind, clouding the crisp winter air.

"What time is it?" Charley asked, hacking up a loogie.

"Quarter past eight," Misfit replied, admiring the face of the new watch his grandmother had given him for Christmas.

"You kids wanna do anything?" Charley asked, shivering in a thin windbreaker and a pair of sneakers. Danny paused, suddenly remembering the seventh grade when Charley's mother had been run over on Geneva Ave. She'd been crossing the street with an arm full of groceries. A fifteen-year-old kid in a hot box had run a red light and struck Charley's mother so hard her legs had snapped in half and her body had folded underneath the front bumper. Her head had rolled down the street, followed by a trail of bags, boxes, and cans. Charley would've gotten hit if he hadn't been dawdling behind her. He'd run into the street as soon as the car hit her, howling like someone had ripped his lungs out. "MAW! MAW!" he'd shouted, louder and louder, stopping cars, buses, and hearts. When the cops arrived, Charley had held what remained of his mother and the things she'd planned for supper. The cops had tried to calm Charley down without hurting him. They'd taken him to the Carney, where the ER doctors had pumped enough drugs in him to put him out for a few days. Whenever he came to, he'd wailed, "Maaaawwwww, Maaaaaawwwwww," a sound so painful half the nurses on the floor cried along with him.

A cold breeze found its way down Danny's collar. "Danny?" Bugsy said, punching him on the shoulder. "You okay?"

"Yeah, yeah, I'm sorry. I'm not interested in going to a party in Savin Hill."

"What do you wanna do then? It's fucking cold out," Bugsy replied. "I think my dick is gonna fall off."

"You kids wanna come over to my house?" Charley asked. "My old man's working a double." Charley looked over his shoulder at the other kids, half a dozen huddled in a circle. "I didn't wanna say anything before. There's too many kids."

"What about Mooch?" Bugsy asked.

"Yeah, okay," Charley said. Bugsy looked at Mooch, nodding until he got his attention. Mooch strolled over. "Hey, we're going to Charley's to watch the Bruins game. You interested?"

"Sounds good," Mooch said, flicking his cigarette away. He and Bugsy walked over to the snowbank, grabbed their beers, and strode back to Danny and Charley.

"You kids going to that party?" Misfit called.

"Naw, we're heading to Town Field," Danny replied.

Misfit looked at the other kids. "We're gonna stay here."

"No problem," Danny said, having figured that's what they would do. He, Bugsy, Charley, and Mooch took off. Halfway to Fields Corner, they turned at the sound of a car and saw a Ford Galaxy approaching them, horn blaring and headlights flickering. Bugsy yelled and pushed Charley and Danny into a snowbank. Mooch ran as fast as he could behind a parked car. The Ford screeched to a halt, and they saw the driver laughing. It was Bubbles Sampson.

"You fucking idiot! What the fuck are you doing?" Danny asked as he brushed the snow off himself.

"Just fuckin' with you kids," Bubbles said through a shit-eating grin.

"Nice ride. Where'd you boost it?" Bugsy asked.

"Downtown. The fuckin' doors were unlocked. Can you believe it? All I had to do was pop the ignition." He lifted a long screwdriver from the floor and waved it like a sword. "You kids need a ride?"

"Yeah, sure," Mooch said. Bubbles swung the passenger's door open.

"Where to?"

"Templeton Street," Charley replied.

Bubbles pumped the clutch and slammed the car into gear as soon as they were in. It slid sideways as it sloshed down the street. "We're going to my house," Charley said. "We're gonna watch the B's game," he added, trying not to sound too enthusiastic. He followed up even less enthusiastically with, "Wanna come?"

"Thanks, but I'm meeting my cousin Timmy. He stole a bunch of inspection stickers, and I gotta get 'em tonight."

"Is he still working over at that place in Somerville?" Danny asked.

"Yeah, that's where he got the stickers."

"I shoulda figured."

When they reached Charley's, everyone climbed out and shuffled through the slush to the granite stairs leading to Charley's brick apartment building. Bubbles waited until they hit the sidewalk before laying a thick patch of nose-burning rubber behind him. The kids took the steps two at a time up to the second floor, passing a couple of kids making out and tit grabbing in the hallway. Charley unlocked the door and flipped the lights on. The room flickered with cockroaches scurrying in every direction. The kids followed him into the kitchen and stopped alongside a chipped Formica table covered with plates, dishes, and bowls of half-eaten food, some rimmed with furry gray mold. They put most of the beers in the refrigerator, pushing aside open cans and twisted boxes of greasy Chinese food, and went into the living room, where a scraggly little Christmas tree sat in the corner, strung with a half-lit string of lights and a handful of chipped glass ornaments hanging from its thin, withered branches. Charley flipped the television on and fiddled with the foil-wrapped antenna until the picture came into focus.

"Hey, Charley," Bugsy said, rubbing his hands. "Can you put the heat on? It's colder than shit in here."

"Yeah, gimme a minute," Charley said, getting up and walking into the hallway.

"Goddamn it," the kids heard him mutter.

"Everything okay?" Danny yelled.

"Naw, I think the heater's broken again," Charley yelled.

"Hey, Charley," Danny bellowed. "You got any booze around here? I gotta shake this fuckin' cold outta me. I'm freezing my ass off."

"Yeah, that's a good idea," Bugsy yelled.

Charley returned to the kitchen, opened a cabinet, and removed a half-drained bottle of Canadian Club. He ran a glass under the faucet, filled it halfway with the liquor, and threw it down in one quick gulp. He put some water in the glass, filled the remaining half with the CC, returned to the parlor, and handed it to Danny. "Thanks," Danny said, tossing it down.

"What the fuck?" Mooch complained, lifting his shoulders.

"Yeah, what the fuck?" Bugsy said.

"Gimme a minute, you fucking homos," Charley said. "What's the score?"

"The Bruins are up by a goal."

Charley returned to the kitchen, made two more drinks, and handed them to the kids. He returned to the kitchen and filled the bottle with water until it looked the same as when he'd found it. He rejoined the kids and watched the Bruins lose three to two to the Rangers. Charley started flipping through the channels. The apartment door suddenly swung open, catching them by surprise. His stepmother, Judy, wobbled in, peeled her coat off, and tossed it toward the couch, revealing a tight-fitting sweater anchored by a dark wool skirt and long boots on a pair of lace-covered legs.

"Charley. What're you and your friendz doing?" she slurred, flapping her eyelashes like a French fan. The kids looked at her. Charley stared at his feet and said nothing. Judy shrugged, headed into the kitchen, and returned with a tall drink, stirring it with her finger. "So, who died?" she asked, flapping her eyelashes so hard the curtains almost fluttered. "It's like a fucking funeral in here," she said.

Danny swallowed and spoke. "We were watching the Bruins game, Mrs. Evans."

"You don't have to call me Mizziz Evanz. Call me Shudee. Everyone calls me Shudee," she said, waving her arm like she was painting the walls.

"Yes, ma'am, er . . . ah, Judy," Danny said, looking at Charley, waiting for him to say something. She sipped her drink and returned to the kitchen with one of the grease-stained Chinese food boxes. She plopped down in a floral-patterned reading chair and shoveled rice and brown-colored pork down her throat. She draped her leg over the arm of the chair, exposing a pair of red-trimmed garters.

"Charley, honey, will you do me a favor? Will you check the heat? It's cold in here," she said, rubbing her lifted thigh briskly.

Charley disappeared into the hall, adjusted the thermostat, and went to the bathroom. Judy was on the couch between Bugsy and Danny when he returned. "Whaz your name, honey?" she asked, turning to Danny and putting her hand on his knee.

"Daniel," he said nervously. "My friends call me Danny, ma'am."

She waved her finger in front of his face and tapped his nose several times. "Don't ma'am me," she said in a comically scolding voice. "The namez Shudee," she added, pausing to stick her finger in her mouth to remove a piece of pork from her teeth. "Charley," she said coquettishly. "Your friendz are real gentlemen." She patted Bugsy's thigh and left her hand there, holding a drink in the other hand.

"So, did you watch the game tonight?" Mooch asked between long, dry swallows.

"No. I hate football."

"Umm, no. It was hockey," Mooch replied, scrunching his forehead.

"I hate hockey too." She took another sip. "So," she slumped deeper into her chair, exposing her underwear. "I went to the Rover wiz my girlfriend, Arlene. We left, though. The place was too loud and crowded. Juz too crowded."

She rolled her legs around as if shifting gears and flipped one ankle on the other knee, revealing more of her panties as her skirt rode up. "You ever been to the Rover?" she asked, looking at Danny.

"Yeah, a few times," Danny said, as if he'd been there a million times.

Judy looked over at Charley, who was stoic and as quiet as a clam. "I hope I'm not dizturbing your little party, Charley."

Charley heaved his chest and let out a long, painful breath. "We aren't having a party. We were watching the Bruins game. It's over, and my friends are going home."

"Iz that right?" she asked, blinking, resetting. "Do you boyz have girlfriendz?" She got up, walked to the front window, pulled the curtains aside, and looked down the street. "You boyz mind if I have one of your beerz?"

"No problem," Bugsy said. As soon as she left the room, Mooch stood up. "I gotta go, guys. I gotta get up early."

Charley also stood up and, stretching his arms over his head and yawning, said, "Yeah, I gotta hit the rack."

"I'm about ready," Danny said.

"I'm gonna grab a beer for the road," Mooch said when Judy wiggled her way past him and nestled between Danny and Bugsy, knees to knees. She fluffed her hair like Ms. Clairol and leaned back. Her breasts pushed higher, and her blouse lifted, exposing her belly. She slid her boots off and propped her feet on the coffee table. Charley shook his head, got up, stuffed the Chinese food box and empty cans in the sports page, took the whole mess into the kitchen, and tossed it in the trash barrel.

"You kids want a beer for the road?" he called out from the kitchen.

"I'll have one," Mooch said.

Charley came out and handed one to Mooch.

"What about you guys?"

Danny and Bugsy glanced at each other and then over to Judy, rubbing her thighs as if she had an itch. Danny started to get up, but Judy stopped him, grabbing him by the belt and pulling him back onto the sofa.

"Charley, they can finish their beerz here. They don't have to leave yet," Judy said. She turned to Bugsy and whispered quietly, "You don't need to go. I can use some company."

Charley left and slammed his bedroom door behind him. The guys looked at each other and then at Judy. "I'm sorry, Mrs. Evans, but we gotta get going. It's getting kinda late, and we got a long walk," Danny said.

"Shudy. Call me Shudy," she said. "Don't be in such a rush. You can't be so bizee that you can't finish your beerz, right? And it's cold out, ain't it." She sat up and tugged the bottom of her skirt. "You fellowz like Guy Lombardo?"

"Guy who?" replied Bugsy.

"Guy Lombardo, the bandleader. He's the one who starts the new year at Timez Square on TV. He's famous."

"Oh yeah. My ma mentioned him," Danny said. "He's a band guy, right? Like Elvis or something."

"Elvis! He's not like Elvis. He's nothing like Elvis. For God's sake, no one's like Elvis. Jeez!" She sipped her beer and stretched her head back, exposing the top of her nipples as her breasts slid up from behind her bra.

"So, Danny, honey, where do you work?" Judy asked.

"Me? I don't have a job. I don't work," Danny said, trying not to stare at her breasts.

"Are you rich or something?" she asked, giggling.

"Well, yeah, of course," Danny said, blushing.

"You know I don't work or nothing, right? Charley's father doesn't want me to work. He expects me to sit around here all day and wash and clean and cook for him and fuck him at night. I used to do that when we first got married, but not anymore, the fat fuck. Now I blow him when he gets home. It's much quicker, and then he falls asleep."

Danny and Bugsy looked at each other wide-eyed.

"What the fuck am I s'posed to do? I got a life, right?" She lifted her head up and brushed her hair aside. "You boyz want another beer?"

"Sure," Bugsy said, stretching his legs out, using the chance to push his dick to the side. Danny answered with a quick nod, not sure what to say. Judy stumbled into the kitchen and bounced around, returning a few minutes later with more beers. She handed one to Bugsy and one to Danny. Judy started to wobble. Danny reached out to keep her from falling. She landed on his lap and slid around before getting up. When she did, she rearranged her bra and blouse, smiled, and made her way over to Bugsy. "So, what do you do, honey?" she asked.

"Me? Nothing," Bugsy replied, sipping his beer, struggling with a relentless hard-on.

"Nothing? Whaz *that* pay?"

"Nothing," Bugsy said, laughing.

"Aren't you still in school?"

"Me? Naw. I got tossed out."

"Were you a bad boy?'

"Yup. Still am."

"Hmm. I like bad boyz." She took a sip of her beer. "Charley's still in school, right?"

"He is, yeah."

"Did you get a spanking?"

The question made Danny blush. Bugsy stayed with it.

"Not yet."

"You must have been pretty bad."

"I was drinking in school and got caught."

"Drinking? Is that all?"

"And some fighting."

"Fighting? Are you a tough guy?"

"Naw, not really."

She took a sip of her drink. "Are you a party boy?"

"I've been known to tie one on," he grinned.

She walked over to the bay window, looked down the street, and turned. "Would you guyz like something stronger to drink?"

"Sure," Bugsy said.

"I don't know. It's getting late," Danny said, sitting up in his seat, trying to be more formal.

Judy glanced down the street and left the room. "C'mon, we gotta get the fuck outta here. This chick is fucked up."

"Yeah, but . . ." Bugsy stopped when Judy returned with the Canadian Club bottle and a couple of glasses. She filled them halfway, drank the first one, and handed the second to Bugsy. She refilled her glass, rimmed with a greasy layer of red lipstick, gave it to Danny, sat down, and rolled her legs around. "Where do you live?" she asked him.

"Four Corners."

"Do you have a girlfriend?" she asked.

Danny blushed. "Sort of, I guess."

"Whaz that mean, *sort of?*"

"I don't know. Sort of."

"Sort of? Sort of never around, like Charley's father. That kind of sort of?" She got up, returned to the window, and ran her finger over the glass, drawing small circles. Danny and Bugsy watched her, trying to figure out what she was doing. She sat, arched her back, and let her blouse slide up.

"I'm tired of waiting for him like this every night. I can't stay locked up here like a bird in a fuckin' cage. I can do my own things if I want." Judy refilled her glass and finger-swirled it.

"Um," Bugsy said. "Doesn't Mr. Evans, your husband, work for the phone company? That's a good job. He must make a lot of money. It's none of my business, but why does he work so much?"

"After Charley's mother got killed, he got stuck with a ton of bills. I don't know all the details or anything. I don't understand it; it's none of my business. That's what he tells me. So anyways, he's working another double. It's New Year's Eve, and he's working a goddamn double?"

"I'm sorry. It must be hard." Danny leaned over and tapped Bugsy on his knee. "We oughta get going. We got a long walk."

"One more for the road?" Judy asked.

"What the hell? One more won't hurt," Bugsy replied.

"Okay," Judy said, stumbling back to the kitchen.

"We gotta get going," Danny said. "She's all fucked up. It ain't good us staying here." He waited for Bugsy. "C'mon, man. That's Charlie's mother."

"No, she ain't. His mother's dead. She's his old man's wife, and that's different."

"No, it ain't."

"Nothing for nothing, but I'm gonna stick around," Bugsy replied.

Danny shook his head. Judy returned a minute later with a couple of beers. She handed them out.

"No, thanks. I gotta go. It was nice meeting you, Mrs. Ev—er, Judy," Danny said.

"Are you sure you can't stick around?"

"Yeah, I'm sure." Danny looked over to Bugsy, who'd kicked his shoes off and stretched out.

"You can find your way out, honey?" Judy said.

"Yeah, no problem."

As soon as Danny left, Judy turned the lights off, kneeled in front of Bugsy, pulled his pants down, and slipped her mouth over his stiffened penis.

# 16

Danny got up earlier than he wanted to after being awake most of the night, thinking about Bugsy and Charley's stepmother. He swore he'd never say anything, hoping Bugsy would do the same.

He put his slippers on, shuffled into the kitchen, rubbed the sleep from his eyes, and put the tea kettle on while watching his mother help his grandmother pack.

"You're up early," Bridie said, smiling, folding a newspaper around a small object.

"How do the slippers fit?" Helen asked.

"Great, Grandma. They fit perfectly, and they're really warm."

"I got them at L.L. Bean."

Danny nodded, not wanting her to know he didn't know the difference between L.L. Bean and a coffee bean.

"How'd you sleep?" Bridie asked.

"Okay, I guess," he replied, a response that raised more questions by the tone of his voice.

"Is everything all right?" she replied, busy wrapping and folding things.

"Yeah, everything's fine. I had a late night. Me, Mooch, and Bugsy watched the Bruins game over at Charley's." He grabbed a piece of bacon from a plate on the kitchen counter and nibbled on it.

"How'd they do?"

"The Bruins? They lost."

"That's too bad."

"We still got the Red Sox."

"That's true," she said.

"And the Patriots!"

"Them and the Celtics."

"One of them's gotta win."

"Oh, Danny! I have to tell you. Your brother was quite the reveler last night. He stayed up until nearly one o'clock."

"Really?" Danny responded as enthusiastically as possible. "What did you guys do?"

"We watched the celebration in Times Square. That Guy Lombardo and the Royal Canadians were wonderful. Heavens, he's such a handsome man. He reminds me of your grandfather, God rest his soul. We all went on the front porch when the ball dropped and banged some pots and pans. Remember when we used to do that when you and your sister were little? Everyone was out, even the Buckleys. God knows we made quite a racket."

"Glad you didn't get arrested," Danny said.

"Oh, Danny!" Helen replied. "We weren't *that* loud."

Danny wasn't sure if she was serious or joking. "Sorry. I missed it!" he said. "It sounds like fun."

"It was. It sure was," Helen said.

"Can I help with anything?" Danny asked, looking around and grabbing another piece of bacon.

"Yes," Helen replied, nodding toward a stack of boxes on a chair. "Would you mind taking those downstairs for me?"

"Sure, Grandma. Let me get dressed."

"Why don't you have some breakfast first?" Bridie said.

"Okay. Sounds good."

Danny returned to his room and put on a pair of pants and a long-sleeved shirt. He took a quick leak, returned to the kitchen, and sat down to a large plate covered with bacon, toast, home fries, eggs, a glass of orange juice, and a tall glass of milk. He covered the eggs with ketchup and chatted with his mother and grandmother about plans for the new year. When he was done, he put on his new winter jacket, which was more fashionable than expected. "Can I have your keys?" he asked.

"The doors are open."

"What? Grandma! This ain't Maine. You gotta lock things up around here!"

Bridie caught Danny's attention when she raised her eyebrows. He spoke again in a milder tone. "Sorry, Grandma, I didn't mean to be . . . it's just . . . you know, there's some bad kids around here. They'll steal any chance they get."

"That doesn't happen in Maine," his grandmother said, looking at Bridie. If Bridie heard her, she wasn't letting on. "The keys are over there, next to the cookies."

"Thanks," Danny said.

"And, if you don't mind, there's a couple more boxes down the hall, along with my suitcase. Would you mind bringing those down for me?"

"Not at all."

Danny picked the boxes up and headed down the hall to another stack of boxes and two large suitcases. He grabbed the boxes and clambered down the stairs, fumbling with the doorknob and pushing the door into the crisp morning wind. After wrestling with the frozen car door handles, he put the boxes in the back seat, got in, and started the engine. It coughed and sputtered a few times until it came to life, throwing a massive cloud of black smoke out the tailpipe. He rubbed his hands, leaned back, and stretched his legs, watching a couple of younger kids walk by. They crossed Greenbrier Street and returned down the other side, pretending they weren't looking at anything. Danny got out and watched them while cleaning the snow off the hood. A rumble suddenly shook his grandmother's car. He turned—it was Chrissy and her boyfriend pulling up in his Corvette. Henschel parked got out, and opened the door for her. Chrissy took her time getting out like she was royalty. Danny glanced at her and resumed brushing the snow off. She snarled at him and stormed up the front stairs.

Henschel walked around his car and wiped the rims of his tires with a monogrammed handkerchief. Danny returned to cleaning the snow off the roof, and before he knew it, Henschel was standing alongside him. "Hey," Henschel drawled, stuffing his handkerchief back in his pocket, "What's going on?"

"Nothing much," Danny said, not bothering to look at him.

"Your car?" Henschel asked.

"Naw, it's my grandma's," Danny said.

"Huh," Henschel sniffed. "Where's your car?"

"I don't have one," Danny replied.

"Why not?"

"I don't know. I'm okay with the T. It gets me everywhere I need to go."

"Don't you get cold? Just getting to the station, you gotta freeze your ass off."

Danny shrugged and continued brushing the snow off.

"I can get you a job at my father's dealership. We could use someone to prep the cars for sale. I can get you maybe twenty twenty-five cents over minimum wage. Heck, maybe you can wash *my* car. Wouldn't that be cool?" Henschel waited for a reply, something he wasn't going to get. "Here's the best part. You get to see all the new cars, and if you're lucky, you can move them around the lot. You might even get to drive a new 'Vette, just like mine," he added, glancing over to his car. "It's beautiful, ain't it?"

Danny clenched his fists and took a long, slow breath. "So, what did you kids do last night?" Danny asked.

"A kid's a goat, you *know* that, right?"

"Gee, I didn't." *Asshole.*

"Well, anyways, your sister and I are going to a catered party in West Roxbury. There's gonna be all kinds of food: champagne, steak, shrimp, and lobster. And there's gonna be a live band."

Danny leaned over the hood, reaching as far as he could, scrapping more snow. He strained himself, forcing out a rank-smelling fart. Henschel stepped back and, a minute later, continued talking. "Do you know Councilman Heinz? He's gonna be there."

*Big fucking deal.*

"Mayor White was supposed to come by but couldn't make it. He's skiing in Europe. He and my father are old classmates. They went to Harvard together."

*Who gives a fuck?* Danny thought.

"I bet a hundred dollars on the Hoosiers."

"Cool. You know she's gonna be a while, doncha?" Danny said.

"I know. That's why I'm gonna wait here. I figured we'd never leave if I went up with her. If I stay here, she'll hurry up, knowing I'm waiting. I learned that trick a while ago."

Danny nodded and returned to cleaning the car. Henschel strolled back to his 'Vette. "Yeah, this thing can blow anything out there away."

*Does your mother blow?* Danny wanted to ask. "So, what kind of engine's in there?"

Henschel popped the hood open, careful not to leave any fingerprints or spots. Danny thought about wiping some boogers on the hood but restrained himself. A chrome air filter sat atop a large, four-barrel carburetor, cleaner than his mother's best frying pan. Eight licorice-like wires radiated outward from the distributor, like a giant spider, into the spark plugs bolted into the sides of the engine.

"Nice, huh? It's a Rochester Quadrajet," Henschel said. "It sucks better than one of those Guinea whores from East Boston."

"How big are those tires?"

"Seven inches wide."

Danny grabbed his crotch. "Seven inches, huh?"

Henschel laughed.

"What's something like this cost?" Danny asked, instantly wishing he hadn't.

"Stock off the floor. Forty-seven hundred dollars. This one's loaded, of course."

*Of course.*

"It's got power steering. Heck, that's almost a hundred bucks right there. And the wheel covers, that's another sixty bucks." Henschel pulled his handkerchief out, bent down, and ran it over the rim, removing some dirt. "The tires, thirty bucks. And the stereo, it's the best on the market. That cost another two hundred dollars. And because it's so fast, it needs heavy-duty brakes to slow it down. They cost another four hundred dollars! As I said, it's loaded."

"Nice" was the best Danny was willing to offer. He looked up at his apartment. "I gotta go. I gotta get more of my grandma's stuff."

"No problem," Henschel said, leaning over and wiping something off that only he could see. "Where's she live?"

"Maine."

"Maine?" He shook his head." That's a long drive, isn't it?"

"It is," Danny replied. "It is." He got in his grandmother's car, shut it off, and returned to the front porch. He looked back at Henschel, now in the company of the two kids that had passed by earlier.

"That's a beautiful car," the shorter of the two said, hovering around. He wore a pea-green army coat and a thick wool cap pulled down over his ears. His friend, six inches taller and a little older, was thin, and his blond hair was close-cropped.

"What kind of car is it?" the taller kid asked.

"A Stingray," Henschel replied, looking for something to polish.

"I thought so! I ain't never seen a real Stingray up close or nothing. Can I see the inside?"

Henschel's face brightened—he might have had a hard-on. "Sure. I'll bet you didn't know it's the fastest car in the world. It can hit a hundred and seventy miles an hour."

"No kidding? That's as fast as a jet can go, ain't it?" the runt piped in.

"Not quite."

Danny sat down and lit a cigarette, watching and listening as snippets of the conversation listed toward him.

"Can I see what it looks like inside? I won't touch nothing, promise." The smaller kid pressed his face against the window. "I'll bet it looks like a jet inside, right?"

"Are your shoes clean?" Henschel asked, pulling his handkerchief out and wiping the greasy face print off the window.

"Yeah, mostly," the kid said, looking down at his feet.

"Here, come over to this side," Henschel said, looking at the kid's shoes. "Get in."

The runt climbed in, lowered himself into the leather seat, and hung his legs out the door. "Can you knock the snow off your boots?"

"Sure," he replied. After he'd finished doing so, Henschel looked them over. "Here, let me slide the seat forward."

The other kid stayed outside, sighting along the fenders like a long-distance sniper. "How big is the engine?" he asked.

"Four hundred and twenty-seven cubic inches. It's the biggest production engine on the market. It's got a four-barrel carburetor and a dual exhaust system. If it had wings, it'd fly."

"Wow!"

"Do you want to see?" Henschel asked, flipping the latch and opening the hood. The older kid crawled halfway across the motor to get a better look at things. "What's that?" he said as he pointed at one of the shiny parts of the engine.

"That's the exhaust manifold. And those pipes down there," Henschel said, pointing, "those are the exhaust pipes. And those red wires, they're distributor wires. They go to the spark plugs."

Henschel continued talking about the engine while the runt, peering over the dashboard every few seconds, rummaged under the floor mats. When Henschel's voice got louder, he popped the glove compartment open, removed a monogrammed wallet, and stuffed it inside his jacket. A couple of minutes later, Henschel came around to the side of the car. "What do you think?" he asked.

"Man, it's wicked cool."

Henschel looked back at the other kid. "Do you want to check it out?"

The two kids winked at each other. "Naw, I gotta be getting home."

"Me too," the runt said, stepping out to join his friend. Danny shook his head, flicked the stub of his cigarette, and went upstairs.

# 17

The rest of the week didn't pan out to anything worth discussing. USC won the Rose Bowl, and winter settled in. A nor'easter buried the city beneath a sheathing of ice and snow, perfect weather for skiing, skating, and drinking cheap liquor. As no one could afford to ski, the kids settled on drinking cheap alcohol and skating. Before entering the Neponset rink, they stopped and stuffed their bottles inside their underwear. Two plump girls collected the rental fees and passed out pairs of skates, some of which looked like they had been in use since the last World War. The kids sat on a row of long, wooden benches and put their skates on. As soon as Danny stuck his on, small rounded rivets pressed against the bottom of his feet. He pulled on his socks and wrestled with the jumble of knots and strings until he could lace up. He wobbled over to Bugsy and Mooch, themselves floundering on the ice. They were following a couple of girls, one dressed in a pink suit and the other in white. Billy and Mikey followed, flailing their arms and legs, slamming into anyone in the way. An official-sounding voice boomed from a mammoth speaker bolted above the entryway. "Please skate in a counter-clockwise direction. If this is your first time skating, please stay at the edge of the rink, along the wallboards. Be respectful of other skaters."

Danny laughed, watching the kids try to get back on their feet, knocking smaller kids down. He waited until the girls came by and pushed himself onto the ice as soon as they did. The girls turned and spun backward, lifting one leg over the other, balancing themselves on the tip of their skates, and glided across the ice. Danny shook his head and skated to the middle of the rink, where the rest of the kids were watching. The girls circled around them a few more times before making their way to the edge of the rink.

"So, did you talk to them?" Bugsy asked, out of breath.

"Of course," Danny replied. "I told them I played for the Bruins, and my dick was as long as a hockey stick."

"No, you didn't," Billy responded, blushing.

"Yes, I did. You saw my dick."

"No, I didn't."

"Yes, you did," Danny said. "I let you touch it once."

"No, you didn't. I never touched your dick," Billy replied, clearly flustered.

"Aw, I'm fucking with you, man."

"I know," Billy answered, confused.

The girls skated around a few more times before tiptoeing off the ice. "Fuck," Bugsy said, turning to Billy. "They must have smelled your breath."

"*No*, they didn't," Billy replied.

"I know. C'mon, let's go," Bugsy said.

After spotting an opening, they weaved through the crowd and shuffle-toed toward the girls. Bugsy sat down, pulled his bottle out, and took a quick swig. The girls giggled, got up, and clip-clocked to the bathroom.

"I told you it was your fucking breath," Bugsy said to Billy. Billy laughed, trying to figure out if it was a joke. They got louder, laughing. A tall MDC employee in a gray jacket with the name *Thomas* embroidered on the left side, above his pocket, his belt strained from his ample belly, swaggered toward them.

"Lose the jug," Danny muttered. Bugsy calmly bent forward and slipped the bottle into his pants cuff. Thomas folded his arms across his chest and leaned against a wooden column, carved and cut with the names and initials of every kid in Dorchester. The other kids wobbled over and glanced at Thomas as if he had done something wrong. Bugsy walked toward Thomas, stopped a few feet from him, arched his shoulders, and rolled his neck from side to side, bending until it cracked. The other kids looked back defiantly. Thomas took a deep breath, bowed his head, and quietly walked away. Bugsy walked back to the kids. "I'm gonna get a tonic. Anyone interested?"

Everyone muttered in agreement, joining Bugsy and walking to the snack bar. "Hey," Bugsy said, nudging Danny. "Check it out."

The girl in the pink outfit stood a few feet away, shifting her ass from side to side. "Can I have a ginger ale?" she said.

"I'll have one, too," her friend said. "Can I also have some Raisinets?"

"Sure," said the pimply-faced kid staffing the counter.

As soon as the kid turned, Danny grabbed a stack of wax cups and stuffed them inside his coat. In the meantime, the other kids ordered tonics, while the girls ass-wiggled their way back to their bench. Drinks in hand, Danny followed and sat across from them. "Cheers," he said, lifting his bottle in the air and causing the girls to giggle again.

The rest of the kids huddled in a small circle and poured some whiskey into the cups. The girls said something to each other and then got up and walked over. Danny nudged the other kids aside to make room for them. Danny patted the bench. "Here, sit down," he said.

The blonde in the white skating outfit waved her finger at them, adding a fake scolding voice. "You know, you can get in trouble for doing that."

"For doing what?" Billy replied, taking a sip from his drink. "This?" he said, lifting his cup up.

She waved her finger again in an exaggerated sweep of her hand.

"Not if no one tells," Billy said.

The girl in pink, shorter, with darker hair and brown eyes, smiled. "So, whatcha drinking?"

"Whiskey. What're you drinking?" Bugsy replied, glancing at her cup.

"Ginger ale," the blonde replied.

"Ginger ale? Shit, that sounds pretty boring," Mooch said, pulling his bottle out. "Here, let me see that." She looked at her friend before handing her cup over. Mooch poured half her tonic out, topped her cup with some of his whiskey, and returned it to her. She took a small sip and pursed her lips before passing the drink to her girlfriend. She chugged it down without blinking an eyelash, ending in a loud gulp. Bugsy leaned toward Danny. "I told you she swallows," he whispered.

Danny laughed so hard he nearly choked himself.

"What's so funny?" the blonde asked.

"Nothing," Danny replied. "I was thinking about something that happened this morning."

"So, where are you girls from?" Bugsy asked, rescuing Danny.

"Quincy," they said, at the same time, as if they'd rehearsed their response.

"Quincy? Whereabouts?"

"Wollaston."

"Wollaston? Nice place," Bugsy said with a nod.

"Yeah, it's a great beach," Danny added.

"Do you come here much? I ain't seen you two before," Mooch asked.

"Sometimes," the blonde said.

"Where'd you two learn to skate? You're really good," Danny said.

"Really? You think so?" the brunette replied, glowing like a Christmas lantern.

"Seriously, really good. I swear on my mother's grave," Danny said.

"I . . . I mean, we've had lessons, both of us," the blonde said, blushing.

"It shows. You girls look like professionals. I dunno, like Peggy Fleming or something," Bugsy said. "Doncha think?" he said, looking at Danny.

"Oh yeah, for sure."

"Really? Peggy Fleming? God, I love her," the blonde said.

"Who doesn't?" Billy added.

The blonde glanced at a mirror on the other side of the room and fluffed her hair. Danny wondered how girls did that: knew where every mirror in the room was.

"So, what're your names?" Bugsy asked.

"Jody," the brunette replied, her smile and teeth as perfect as a Crest toothpaste commercial.

"And you?" Bugsy asked, nodding at the blonde.

"Suzanne," she said, sitting up straight. "My friends call me Suzie."

"What should we call you?" Bugsy asked.

"Suzie."

"I'm Billy," Billy piped up, sticking his hand out, poking between Bugsy and the girls.

"Yeah, but his friends call him Dipshit," Bugsy said, slapping him on his head.

"No, they don't," Billy muttered.

"I was wondering, do you have enough to make another drink?" Jody asked, pulling her zipper down and revealing the crest of her cleavage.

"Yeah, sure," Billy said, lifting his bottle and filling her cup. She leaned back, thrust her chest out, and drained her drink like a cool glass of water. Her nipples, poking into her blouse, grew harder in the chilled air.

Bugsy got up and walked over to Headso, seated at the other end of the bench next to Misfit, who was tugging on his laces with a fancy metal hook made just for that purpose. "You got any liquor left?" Bugsy asked.

"Some," Headso replied tightly.

"How much?"

"Enough," Headso replied.

"Did you see the tits on the brunette?" Bugsy asked, glancing at her while lighting a cigarette. Headso mumbled something while he tightened his laces. Bugsy took a drag and blew a smoke ring toward the girls, framing them in the middle of the expanding circle before it dissipated.

Headso looked up and mumbled something.

"That chick's a fucking lush, and she wants a drink, and I'm all out."

Headso glanced at the girls and then back at Bugsy. "You owe me, fucker."

"Don't worry. I'll pay you back," Bugsy said as he stuffed the bottle into his back pocket. "I'll put you in my fucking will. Promise."

"Yeah, sure."

"I will."

Bugsy clanked his way back to the kids.

"So, where do you girls go to school?" Danny asked,

"Quincy High," Jody replied. "We're seniors."

"Us too," Danny said, lifting his eyebrows at Bugsy. "You girls want another drink?"

"I do," Jody replied.

"How about you?" Danny asked Suzie.

"Umm, sure, thanks. Can I have a ginger ale?"

"I'll get 'em," Billy said, smiling and lifting his chest above his ears.

Suzie leaned closer to Jody and said something only Jody heard. "I'm all right," Jody said. "I am," she stressed, shooing Suzie off with a flick of her hand. Suzie started to speak, but Jody interrupted her. "You've got to learn how to have fun," Jody said dismissively.

Bugsy watched them while leaning against a building column, a good vantage point to watch everyone waiting for Billy to return with the drinks. When Billy returned, he handed one drink to Suzie and one to Jody. Jody took a sip and passed her cup to Billy. He poured half her drink on the floor. Bugsy topped it with a slug of whiskey. Jody stuck her finger in the cup and swished it around before sliding her finger into her mouth like a popsicle on a hot summer day. Bugsy reached for Suzie's cup. She shook her head. *No.*

Danny, Mikey, and Billy continued talking mainly about the Olympics with Suzie. Bugsy lifted his drink to her, and she shook her head, *no*, every time he did.

After the fourth time, Suzie got up and walked over to Jody. "I'm gonna skate some more," Suzie said. Bugsy stared at Suzie while topping Jody's cup off, not bothering to ask, and she didn't bother to object. Suzie started to speak again but stopped when the kids walked over and introduced themselves.

"Hi, I'm Mooch."

"Mooch is queer," Bugsy said without missing a beat.

"Fuck you," Mooch replied.

Suzie raised her eyebrows.

"Actually," Mooch said. "I'm a lesbian. I like girls," a line that got Jody giggling some more, sending her breasts bouncing up and down like a pair of beach balls on Cape Cod. The rest of the kids quietly moved closer.

Bugsy rolled his head to his right, toward the other kids. "This is Misfit and Headso."

"Pleased to meet ya," Headso said, raising an invisible cigar as he bounced his eyebrows around like Groucho Marx. As soon as Suzie looked away, Headso popped his tongue in and out of his cheeks like a mouth full of dick. Bugsy mouthed the word *yup*. After taking a swig from his bottle, Mooch passed it to Bugsy, who topped Jody's cup off.

"Jody here's an excellent skater," Bugsy said. "She and her friend Suzie are from Quincy."

Mooch stood behind her, where she couldn't see him. He rolled his hand into a ball and mimicked jerking off. "Really? Quincy!"

"Yes," Jody said a bit conceitedly. "So, what's your real name?"

"Tommy."

She laughed and giggled like she was being tickled. "That's a funny name. Why do they call you that?"

"I dunno. My big brother gave it to me when I was little."

"Oh," she said, giggling again. "Does he have a nickname?"

"Yeah. We call him Dipshit."

"No, you don't!"

"I'm kidding. So, what's up with your girlfriend?" Misfit asked, looking over at Suzie.

"She's okay."

"Doesn't she like to party?"

"Sometimes. She's not feeling good today."

"What's wrong with her?"

"I don't know. Girl stuff, I think."

Bugsy leaned toward Mooch. "What're you driving?" he asked.

"An Impala; a '64."

"Where's it parked?"

"At the end of the lot. You can't miss it. It's maroon."

"Can you bring it out front?" Bugsy asked.

"Sure."

Bugsy leaned the other way toward Jody. "Want to take a walk?"

"Where?" she asked, turning her head with a look of curiosity.

"To my friend's car. It's warm. We can have a drink and listen to some music."

"Yeah, that sounds nice."

Bugsy looked down at her feet. "Where are your shoes?"

"I don't have any shooz. I'm wearing bootz."

He turned his head to listen better. "What did you say?"

"Bootz. You know. Bootz." She spun her finger in a circle, pointing at her feet. "With white fur around them. Bootz."

Bugsy looked at her, waving her finger around. "BOOTS? You mean BOOTS?" he said.

"Yeah. That'z what I said, silly. Bootz." She circled her pointed finger around her toes again.

Bugsy nodded. "Got it. I'll be right back. I'll get your boots. Wait here."

He took a quick look around and spotted them. After walking over and grabbing them, he returned and put them down in front of her. She leaned forward and fumbled with the laces on her skates. "Let me help you," Bugsy said, pulling her legs out and unlacing her skates.

Billy hovered behind Bugsy. "Need any help?"

Bugsy tugged her skates off and handed them to Billy. "Can you put these over there?" he said, pointing. "Next to those little kids. If her girlfriend comes over, tell her she went outside to get some air. Tell her she said she'll be back in fifteen minutes. Tell her she wanted to go for a walk."

"No problem," Billy said.

"You gotta make sure her girlfriend doesn't get nosy or nothing."

"Yeah, I get it."

"You gotta keep her the fuck away."

"Yeah, no problem," Billy said, staring at Jody's chest as it rose and fell when she breathed.

Bugsy turned to Mikey. "You too, you gotta watch out for her girlfriend. If she asks a lot of questions, you gotta distract her, keep her busy."

"Don't worry, I will," Mikey said. He stood up, looked around, and took a few steps toward the rink. "There she is. She's over there," he said, pointing.

"Don't point, idiot," Bugsy said. "I'm not blind; I see her."

Bugsy took his skates off and handed them to Mikey. "Can you get me my shoes?"

"Yeah. Sure. No problem. I'm gonna get mine too."

"Me too," Billy parroted.

"Can you get mine?" Danny asked.

After everyone had taken their skates off, Mikey scooped them up and returned them to the check-in counter, returning five minutes later with everything.

"You ready?" Bugsy asked, grabbing Jody by the arm and helping her up. "Danny, can you give us a hand?"

"Yeah," Danny said, grabbing her by the other arm and guiding her into the back seat. Bugsy sat beside her while Danny and Mooch got in the front seat. Danny started the car, put the heater on, and drove to the far end of the parking lot alongside a row of gray, leafless trees.

Bugsy pulled his bottle out, took a swig, and passed it to Jody. She took a slow swallow and handed the bottle back to Bugsy. He took another slug and put the bottle on the seat beside him. He slid his hand under Jody's shirt and started making out, sliding his tongue in and out of her mouth, like a snake. She started moving around and moaning. Bugsy pulled on her belt and zippers, unbuckled his belt, and pulled her spectacular skating pants off. He tugged so hard he ripped them, something she did not notice.

"No," she pleaded. "No, no," until it morphed into a long sigh; *oooh*. She lifted one foot in the air and rested it on the back of the front seat, nearly kicking Mooch in the head. Her leg slid to the side as she spread them both out, and the car started bouncing and rocking when Bugsy rolled on top of her, lifted her legs in the air, spread them apart, thrust himself in her, and started pumping. The sounds of groins slapping against each other drowned the radio out. Bugsy pumped and pushed as they moaned together. He lifted Jody's legs high, spread them further apart, and pumped so hard that the car rocked to his rhythm. A few thrusts later, he came and yelped.

He lay there for a few minutes before pressing himself up, rolling to his side, and sitting up. Danny rolled the window down to let the smell and moisture out. Bugsy grabbed his pants from the floor, opened the door, dangled his legs outside, and put his pants on. "You ready?" he asked Mooch.

"Fuck yeah!" Mooch yelled, swinging the door open, tripping on his feet, and getting out. He climbed in the back, yanked his pants off, not bothering to remove his shoes, slid in alongside Jody, and started thumbing her nipples and then licking them. She rolled her head to the side and moaned. Mooch pulled her legs apart, climbed on top of her, and jammed himself into her as hard and deep as he could.

She tried to fight him off, clumsily thrashing her arms, to no avail. He continued pumping and quickly blew his load.

"What was that, twenty seconds?" Bugsy asked, laughing.

"Fuck you," Mooch said, pulling away from her. "She loved it."

"Loved it? Shit, she doesn't even know you fucked her."

"Yes, she did," Mooch replied defensively.

"Yeah, sure, needle dick the bug fucker," Bugsy said. He turned to Danny. "Your turn. You're the winner if you can last more than twenty seconds."

"Naw, I'll pass. I don't do sloppy seconds." He looked at Jody. Her eyes were closed, her legs were spread apart, and her arms were propped wide as if she'd been crucified.

"Maybe she'll blow you," Bugsy said.

"Naw, I'm not *that* hard up."

There was a knock on the driver's side door. The windows were steamed up; they couldn't see who it was. Bugsy rolled the window down. It was Billy. "Can I come in?" he said.

"You got a note from your mother?"

"What?"

"I'm only fucking with you, man. Get in."

Billy pulled the back door open, and bare-assed, Mooch slid past him and stumbled outside. Billy, his pants wrapped around his ankles, crawled in on his knees and lifted himself up in front of Jody. He unzipped his pants, fingered her mouth open, pushed his swollen dick in, and started pumping. He grabbed her by the back of the head and pumped harder, forcing as much of his penis into her mouth as he could until he blew his load. As soon as he did, she gagged and vomited. Billy, victorious, did his best Tarzan scream and flexed his arms over his head, like Charles Atlas. Jody, gagging, tried to push him away. Billy backed up as she threw up on his legs before rolling onto her side and hugging her knees close to her chest.

"That fucking chick knows how to suck a dick; she loves it."

"You should get some," Bugsy said to Danny.

"Are you shitting me? She's a fucking mess. Look at her."

Bugsy shrugged.

"Fuck, if you ain't gonna get some more, I will," Billy said.

Danny shook his head. "I'm outta here."

"I'll join you," Mooch said.

"Me too," Bugsy added. Billy wiped the vomit off his legs, leaned over, and rubbed her tits.

---

"Where've you kids been?" Mikey asked as soon as he saw them.

Bugsy stuck his fingers under Mikey's nose. "Smell this."

Mikey pushed him away. "Asshole."

Bugsy laughed. "How 'bout you smell my dick?"

"No, thanks. Where's Billy?"

"Getting a blowjob."

"Are you shitting me?" Mikey replied.

"No, I'm serious. You shoulda seen him."

"Did you get laid?" he asked Bugsy.

"Does a bear shit in the woods?"

"What about you?" Mikey asked Danny.

Danny stuck his hands in his pocket and shook his head *no.*

"Me and Mooch both fucked her."

"We did; she wanted it bad," Mooch replied.

"Nothing for nothing, but she was too fucked up to stop you two," Danny said.

"You still shoulda nailed her," Bugsy said. "Did you see how big her snatch was? She's had a lot of dicks in there."

"Her friend's been looking all over for her," Mikey said.

"What did you tell her?" Bugsy asked.

"Nothing. Misfit told her she went for a walk or something."

"Did she buy it?"

"Fuck if I know."

"Where's everyone else?" Bugsy asked, looking around.

"Waiting for you guys. Everyone's ready to leave except Misfit. He said he's gonna stick around till the rink closes," Mikey replied.

"You shoulda seen, Billy. After me and Mooch fucked this chick, Billy gets in the back, and he worms himself, sideways, you know, like this, half crawling on his knees. So, he gets in front of her, pulls his dick out, and tries to get up high enough so he can stick it in her mouth. He's way up on his knees, and he's wobbling around. Man, it was funnier than shit," Bugsy said, squirming around, wiggling his hips, imitating Billy. "He almost broke his back trying to get it in her mouth. Anyways, once he got it in, he started jamming away like this," Bugsy said, holding his outstretched hands in front of him as if he was holding her head. "He grabs her head and shoves his dick in her mouth, face fucking her. So, when he blows his load, he does the Mister Universe thing," Bugsy said, lifting his arms and flexing his muscles over his head. "You should have seen it; it was fucking hilarious."

Danny lit a smoke. "We better check on Billy."

He and Bugsy walked back to the car. Billy was standing next to Jody, half-seated on the edge of the car seat, vomit everywhere.

"Is she okay?" Danny asked, studying her. Danny placed his hand on her shoulder, and she started with the dry heaves as soon as he did. "What the fuck did you do to her?"

"Nothing. She wanted to give me another blowjob," Billy said timidly.

"C'mon man, what'd you do?" Danny asked.

"Nothing. She wanted to suck my dick some more."

"Did she say that she wanted to blow you again?"

"Yeah, sort of." Danny waited. "Not really, I guess," Billy said.

Danny looked at her. She was rolling her head, and her mouth was open. Vomit ran down her cheeks and across her chest. "So what really happened?"

"I stuck my dick in her mouth, and she started gagging and puking everywhere. I thought she wanted it."

Bugsy started laughing, getting louder with each passing second. "You're a fucking idiot."

When he stopped, Danny turned to Bugsy. "What're we gonna do?"

"Me? Nothing," Bugsy replied. "Ask him," he said, looking at Billy.

"You guys fucked her too."

"Yeah, but she didn't puke when I fucked her," Bugsy said. "C'mon man, who gives a shit? She's a fucking pig." He flicked his cigarette onto the parking lot and turned.

"You leaving?" Billy asked.

"Yeah," Bugsy replied.

"What about the car?" Billy asked.

"What about it?"

"I dunno," Billy said.

Danny stared at Jody. Her underwear and pants were curled around one ankle and covered with vomit that had started to freeze. Her blouse was on the back seat, and her bra was on the car's floor. "Hey," Danny said, touching her shoulder and gently shaking her. "Are you okay? You oughta get inside. You're gonna freeze out here."

She nodded lethargically; Danny took it for a yes. "All right," he said. "C'mon, let me help you." He put his hand behind her back and lifted her. As soon as he did, she lurched forward and started dry heaving. Danny held her up to keep her from falling. After getting her back into the car, he climbed into the front seat, started the engine, turned the heater on, and slid the lever to its highest setting. He went in the back seat and wrapped her in her jacket; she curled up into a ball, and he left.

"Is everyone gone?" Danny asked Bugsy.

"I think so. Misfit's still skating around with that other chick."

"Does he know where her friend is?"

"Fuck if I know," Bugsy said.

"She's pretty messed up."

"So?"

"Don't you think we should tell her friend?"

"Fuck no. It ain't my problem."

Danny walked over to the rink, moving along the railing until he spotted Misfit. After getting his attention, Misfit skated over. "What's up?"

"The other chick's out back in Mooch's car. She's really fucked up. Her girlfriend ought to know."

"What happened?" Misfit asked.

"She got drunk. Really drunk."

"Uh-huh," Misfit replied, waiting for something more. "Is that all?"

"No, a couple of the other kids were fucking around with her."

"What do you mean fucking around?"

"You know, fucking around."

Misfit shook his head.

"I had nothing to do with it," Danny said. "Her girlfriend needs to know."

"Where is she?"

"Out back, at the end of the parking lot. You can't miss her."

"Is she alone?"

"I think so. The last time I saw her, she was."

"That's fucked up."

"Yeah, I know," Danny said. "I gotta go, man."

# 18

Danny jammed his hands into his pockets, buried his head deep between his shoulders, and leaned into the winter winds blowing off the Neponset River. He had given up trying to light a cigarette. When he came to Saint Anne's, at the top of the hill, he spotted a car pulled over on the side of the road, its flashers blinking, casting rays of bright red light on the surrounding mounds of snow. A middle-aged woman, dressed in *Sunday clothes*—as his mother would call them—was standing outside the car, looking anxiously down the street. Danny noticed the tire was flat. She took a few steps back when she saw him coming and stood alongside the front door.

"Hi," he said as he approached her, rubbing his hands together and blowing on them. "Do you need any help?"

"No, thank you. I'm fine," she said, her eyes flashing like the lights.

"You got a flat, huh?" Danny said, walking over to the rear of the car.

"Um, yes," she said. "I'm waiting for my husband. He'll be here any minute."

"You're in a pretty bad spot. You should move your car."

She looked at him and then down the hill fretfully.

"I can help if you'd like," Danny said, rubbing his hands.

"That's okay. My husband is on his way." An old Chevy pickup rumbled toward them and turned left. The driver laid on his horn and gave them the finger.

"Will it start?" Danny asked.

"I . . . I think so. It started making this horrible noise, so I had to stop."

"Why don't we try to get it out of the intersection, just to be safe? The people around here drive like maniacs. You could get hit here; I've seen it before."

"Are you sure?" she asked.

"It's no bother. Why don't we try to move it over there?" Danny said, pointing across the street.

"I don't want to put you out."

"You're not putting me out. This isn't a good place to be broken down. Why don't you try starting it up? I'll bet the noise you hear is the tire rubbing up underneath." Another car rambled around the corner. The driver laid on the horn and didn't let up until he was half a block away.

"Okay," she said. "Be careful; I don't want you getting hurt."

"I'll be all right," Danny said. "Why don't you get in? I'll let you know when it's safe to cross."

"Okay." She looked down the street again.

She got in the car, and after it sputtered to life, Danny tapped on the window. "You should put your headlights on." She looked up, hit the switch, and gave a small smile. He pointed to the lights on a corner pole. "When they turn green, take off slowly." As soon as the lights changed, she put the car into gear, and it took off, wobbling and making a lot of noise. She looked at him wide-eyed. "It's okay," he yelled. "The tire's hitting the fender. It won't hurt nothing as long as you go slow," he said, waving her through the intersection. When she pulled alongside the curb, he waved his hand across his throat *cut it.*

"My, that was frightening," she said.

"You did great."

"I don't know what I'd have done without you."

Danny shrugged. "You'd have been fine."

"I'm not sure about that."

"You're okay now, right?"

"Thanks to you."

"If you have a spare, I can change it."

"Lord, no, you've done enough. My husband should be along any minute."

"He's probably stuck in traffic. It's a mess out there. I don't mind."

She glanced at the headlights flickering as they approached. "Where's he coming from?"

"Milton."

"Milton, huh," Danny replied, blowing into his cupped hands. "I have time. I ain't busy or nothing."

"Well," she said, looking out the window as bands of snow whirled around Danny. "I have a spare in the trunk. I feel terrible putting you out; you've been so kind."

"It's not a problem."

"Are you sure? It's awful cold out."

"I've been colder. Why don't you stay in the car? No sense in you freezing."

"Thank you," she said as she removed the keys from the ignition and handed them to Danny.

"Roll your window up," he said.

Danny walked to the rear of the car and opened the trunk. It was cleaner than the operating room at the Carney. The jack was stored next to the spare tire, snow chains, and a box of road flares, looking like they had been gift-wrapped. Danny removed the large screw that held everything in place, lifted the tire out, and placed it on the ground, along with the jack, lug wrench, and tire iron. He walked back to the driver's window, knocked on the windows, and gave her the keys back. "Can you put the emergency brake on?"

"Of course."

He returned to the tire and started chipping away at the ice beneath it, using the new tire iron that would have been at home at a Christmas dinner spread, stopping to rub his freezing hands every few minutes. "Why don't you start the car?" he asked. "It'll keep you warm."

As soon as she started the engine, he stuck the tire iron into the exhaust pipe and put his hands alongside it, rolling them around until they were warm. He removed the iron and continued chipping until he had enough room to place the jack beneath the car. He banged his hand against the fender on the second crank, opening up the skin near his wrist. "Fuck," he muttered. He wiped his hand on his pant leg and placed a handful of snow over the cut. After wrestling with the frozen lug nuts, he tossed the flat tire in the truck and replaced it with the one from the trunk. After closing the trunk, he tapped on the window. "All set."

"Thank you so much," she said, rolling the window down. "Here, let me pay you," she said, reaching for her purse.

"Naw, that's okay. I don't want anything. I was glad to help."

"I insist," she said, fingering a five-dollar bill.

"It's okay. I'm good," Danny said, holding his hands up.

"Are you sure? You didn't have to stop and help as you did."

"I know. You were in a bad spot."

"Heavens, please take it," she said, extending the bill.

"No, thanks. You know, I think you're gonna need the money for a new tire."

"Oh, that won't be a problem," she said, suddenly noticing his worn dungarees and thin canvas sneakers. "Can I give you a ride home?"

A cold breeze blew up from the river below. Danny rubbed his hands and pulled his collar up. "Um, sure. If it's not out of your way."

"For heaven's sake, it's the least I can do."

"Okay," he said, pulling his head deeper into his neckline. "Are you sure?"

"Of course; please, let me do it."

"Okay," Danny said.

After he got in, she noticed his bloodied hand. "What happened?" she asked, reaching for his hand.

"This?" he replied, pulling his hand closer and rubbing it. "It's nothing. I banged it on the fender."

"Here, take a handkerchief," she said, leaning forward and opening the glove compartment.

The handkerchiefs, with lacy edges, were neatly stacked and ironed, reminding him of the stuff in the trunk. "Are you sure?"

"Yeah, no problem."

He took one and wrapped it tightly around his hand. "Thank you," he said.

"If you need another one, take it. They're not doing any good just sitting there." The glove compartment was so clean Danny was afraid to grab another. "Are you sure you're okay? That looks painful."

"It's okay. It doesn't hurt or nothing." Danny squeezed the handkerchief tighter and stretched his legs so his feet were closer to the heater. She couldn't help but notice and slid the heater lever higher.

"Which way?" she asked.

"Straight ahead; Four Corners."

She put the car in gear, flicked her direction, and took off. "I must say, you're pretty good with cars," she said.

"Thanks. I like working on them," he said in a voice filled with pride.

"Where did you learn to do mechanic work?"

"I don't know. Ever since I was a little kid, I liked taking things apart—radios, TVs, toys, all kinds of things. There's a gas station in my neighborhood, and I go in there sometimes to watch. The owner is really nice. He sometimes lets me work on stuff, putting things together and mostly taking things apart."

"Do you own a car?"

"Naw. I can't afford one," Danny replied with a hint of embarrassment.

"I see."

"A couple of my friends got cars. I help them with tune-ups and oil changes, stuff like that."

"They're fortunate. You're quite a resourceful young man," she said. "Do you have a job?"

"Naw, I'm still in school. You can turn here," he said, pointing.

"Do you know Port Gas, next to the skating rink at the bottom of the hill?"

"Sure."

"My husband and I own it."

"Are you kidding? You must be rich."

She laughed and shook her head. "Heavens, no, we're not rich. We work very hard, both of us. He runs the business, and I do the books."

"You don't look like a bookie, not like any I know."

"Heavens, no. I do the bookkeeping," she said. "It's accounting. I manage the money. I write the checks and pay the bills and the employees. I also handle the deliveries and order supplies; gas, oil, wiper blades, and the things we sell at the station."

"Oh, I get it. I never heard of that. That must be great, owning a gas station and everything."

"Well, it is, for the most part. It's a lot of work, but it's worth it."

"I ain't never met anyone who owned their own business before."

"Before we married, I worked as a cashier at Filene's. That's where we met. We both worked weekends and a few nights a week when we went to school. And look at us now. Heavens! We're still working weekends. That didn't work out so well," she said, laughing. "And nights!"

"Take a right, up ahead," Danny said, "at the lights. How long have you owned it?"

"Nine years. We own two stations."

"You own them all by yourselves?"

"Well, they're franchises."

"French fries?" he asked, scrunching his forehead.

She laughed. "No, no, honey, it's called a franchise. We have the right to use their business name along with others. They do all the advertising for us. If you ever see a sign or a commercial for the station, that's our advertising. The *franchisor*, they call them, puts all the signs up."

"Sounds like the thing that cooks the French fries," Danny said, chuckling. She joined him in laughing.

"Plus, by being a franchise owner, along with other owners, we get a better deal on our rent and the price we pay for things like the gasoline we buy and then sell. The more we buy, the cheaper we get it. It's the same with McDonald's. Those are franchises, like the one on Gallivan Boulevard. They're the ones who sell the French fries," she laughed. "That's a franchise owned by two brothers, Tom and Vincent Kelly. They live in Braintree."

"I never heard that word before. I never thought about stuff like that, people owning a business and everything. I didn't know regular people could own a business."

"Well, they can. Like any business, you have to put a lot of money into the deal. The Kelly brothers do pretty much the same thing we do. The more burgers they sell, the more money they make, and because they sell so many, they can buy them a lot cheaper. It's the same with us. The more gas we sell, the more money we make. We buy it cheaper, and when we sell it, we make a profit. That's how a franchise works. It's really how a lot of businesses work."

"Darn it," Danny said suddenly, interrupting her. "We should have turned back there. I'm sorry. I was distracted."

"Oh, don't worry about it. I'm not in a rush," she said as she turned and retraced her route. "You know, we have an opening at our station down at the Port. Would you be interested?"

"Interested? Are you kidding?" Danny sat up in his seat and twisted toward her. "Are you serious?"

"If you look inside the glove box, there's a little box in the corner. You'll find some business cards." Danny popped the small door open and removed the box. "There, take one. It's got my husband's name and number on it. Give him a call tomorrow afternoon. I'll let him know you'll be calling. He's usually available after three."

Danny smiled so hard he thought his jaw would snap. "Thanks, ma'am," he sputtered. "There," he said, pointing, "you can drop me off at the Texaco station."

"Stanley's?"

"Do you know him? He's the guy I was talking about, the one who lets me work on things."

"What a small world. I know Stanley. We both do. He's a really nice man, and he runs an excellent business. Tell him I said hello the next time you see him."

"I will. I see him every day."

She pulled into the gas station. "I can't thank you enough for your help," she said.

"You're welcome." He grabbed the door handle and clicked it. "It just dawned on me—I forgot to ask you your name."

"Please don't apologize; it's my fault. I forgot to tell you. My name's Margaret. Margaret Erickson. My husband's name is Richard."

"Just like on the card."

"Yes, and yours?"

"Daniel; Daniel McSweeney. Everyone calls me Danny."

"Well, Danny, I'll tell my husband you'll call."

"Thank you, ma'am. That'd be great."

Danny swung the door open, got out, and crossed the street, running as fast as he could, nearly falling on the snow and ice that had taken over the neighborhood, up the stairs to his apartment.

# 19

Danny hoped someone was home when he flew through the front door. It was not every day he was offered a job by a rich person who owned two gas stations. He ran to the kitchen, yelling, "Ma! Ma! Chrissy!" No one answered. He worked his way back toward the front of the apartment, sticking his head in every room. "Frankie! Hey! Anyone home?" The wind rattling the windows was the only response he got. He turned the radiator on in the front parlor, listening to the pipes hiss at him. He tugged his socks off, placed them over the heater, and slid his sneakers beneath the metal casing. The color gradually returned to his blue-and-white toes as he rubbed and bent them. He flipped the TV on, shuffled to the bathroom, grabbed a bath towel, sat on the couch, wrapped the towel around his feet, and placed them on the rattling radiator, sighing in relief.

Another story about the Vietnam War was on. The broadcaster—a tall, middle-aged man wearing a dark suit, every hair in place—was spitting out the names of places Danny had never heard of and couldn't pronounce: Khe Sanh, Xuan Loc, Ben Suc, Cholon, all sounding like choices from a Chinese menu. When his toes matched the color of his fingers, he got up and walked across the cold wooden floors into the kitchen, where he lit the stove and placed four hot dogs in a frying pan. He poured a glass of milk, sipping it as he rolled the dogs around with a fork. When they were done, he placed them between a couple of slices of bread, buried them beneath a blanket of ketchup, and headed back to the parlor. When the weather came on, the scratchy voices on the television gave way to the sound of feet shuffling through the front door. His sister came in first, followed by his mother and Frankie; no one was talking.

"Is everything all right?" Danny asked, getting up and following them. Bridie and Chrissy went straight into Chrissy's room and shut the door behind them. "What's going on?" Danny asked Frankie.

"Chrissy got beat up by her boyfriend!"

"Beat up? What do you mean beat up?"

"Her boyfriend; he beat her up! Chrissy called Ma, and she was crying and everything, and IhadtogetMrs.BabcockshedrovemadowntowntogetChrissy. Mawasreallyupset. Iain'tneveseenhersomad!"

"Slow down, will ya? I can't understand anything you're saying."

"Okay, okay!" Frankie replied, panting as if he'd just run around the block. "LikeIsaidChrissycalled."

"Slow down!"

"Okay, okay. It was around four o'clock or something. Chrissy was on the phone, and she was crying. Ma said she had to go downtown to get her. She told me Chrissy was calling from a phone booth. Ma said her boyfriend punched and kicked her and . . . and," he sputtered like a steam engine, "then knocked her down . . . that's what she said." Frankie swallowed another lungful of air and continued. "Chrissy said they were fighting, her and her boyfriend; that's what Ma said; she did."

"Fighting?" Danny's voice grew louder.

"Yeah, you shoulda heard Ma. And I saw Chrissy; she's got a black eye and a fat lip, like jigaboo lips, and her blouse was ripped, and, oh yeah, her legs were bleeding; I saw them!"

"Did she say anything else?" Danny asked.

"Who?"

"Ma."

"Naw, Ma didn't say nothing, not to me. She kept asking Chrissy a bunch of questions, but she didn't say nothing; she kept crying. Ma wanted to call the cops, but Chrissy didn't want her to. So, she and Ma were arguing, and Chrissy started crying again, and Ma started crying. And Mrs. Babcock, she didn't say nothing; she just drove. I think she was crying. They were all crying."

"Did you talk to her?"

"Who? Chrissy?"

"No, the Virgin Mary! Who the fuck do you think I'm asking about?"

"Jeez, I don't know, don't get mad at me. I didn't do nothing. She didn't say nothing to me." Frankie peered around Danny. "Can you hear anything?"

"Did Ma say anything else?" Danny replied.

"Naw. I remember. Chrissy said he threw her out of his car and left her downtown at Park Street."

"That motherfucker!" Danny spat, turning and heading into the parlor with Frankie shadowing him every inch of the way. Danny peeled his socks off the radiator and bent them back and forth several times to loosen them up. He put his sneakers on, grabbed his coat, and headed to the front door.

"Where're you going?" Frankie asked, wide-eyed.

"Out."

"Out where?"

"Out."

"Can I come?"

"No! And if Ma asks, tell her I went down the Corner."

"When are you coming back?"

"I dunno."

Frankie bent his head down and went back into his bedroom. Danny could hear his sister crying and his mother talking. He paused briefly before bounding down the stairs two at a time, down to the sidewalk. He ran all the way to the schoolyard. Several of the kids were huddled at the front gates. Charley impulsively took a few steps toward Danny. "What's wrong?"

"My sister got beat up," Danny said.

"By who?"

"Her boyfriend."

"What's his name? Where's he from?"

"He ain't from around here. The motherfucker's from Newton."

"Newton?"

"Yeah, he's a fucking Jew."

"Are you shitting me?"

"No, I'm serious," Danny said.

"Is it the kid with the 'Vette?" Billy asked.

"Yeah," Danny replied. "The red one. How did you know?"

"I seen it around. Fuck, who hasn't?"

"Do you know where he lives?" Charley asked.

"Newton. That's all I know."

"That's where they all live. Jew Town," Charley said.

Danny nodded in agreement.

"So, what're you gonna do?" Charley asked.

"I'm gonna find him and fuck him up!"

"Want some help?" Charley asked.

"Yeah, sure," Danny responded, looking around. "Can we get a car?"

"Yeah, no problem," Mooch replied.

"Thanks, man. If you can get a station wagon, that'd be great. We can all fit in."

"I'm gonna need ten or fifteen minutes. Is that okay?" Mooch asked.

"Sure, of course."

"So, what do you know about Newton?" Mooch asked.

"Not much. It's out past Route 128, past Dedham. I ain't never been there before."

"What do you know about this cocksucking Hebe?"

"Not much. Just his name. Robert Hensel. No, wait. It's Henschel. His father owns a Chevy dealership on Comm Ave."

"Do you mean Henschel Chevrolet?"

"Yeah. How'd you know that?"

"You're kidding me. It's the biggest Chevy dealership in Boston."

"No shit, I didn't know that."

"You're kidding. That guy's a fucking millionaire!"

"We'll be back," Mooch said to the other kids.

He and Danny continued chatting, trying to figure out how rich Henschel was, as they walked down to Fields Corner and stopped at Bradlees' parking lot, where they sat on a low metal traffic barrier and watched the cars come and go. One cigarette later, Mooch stood up like a jack-in-the-box. "Come on," he said, swinging his legs over the railing. "There," pointing, "See that lady over there—the fat one with the lard-ass kids that just got out of the station wagon?"

"The blue one?" Danny replied as he watched the trio waddle across the lot.

"Yeah, that's it. Walk down that first lane," Mooch said, pointing, "over there, next to the Ford pickup. See it?"

"The blue one?"

"Yeah. That's the one. When you reach the end, go down the other lane," he continued, pointing again. "Between the green Chevy and the red Mustang. Back toward the street."

"Yup, I see 'em."

"If you see any cops, whistle loudly and wave, okay?"

"Sure."

"As soon as I start the car, head over to Hi-Fi. I'll pick you up there."

"Got it!"

Mooch took off. Danny watched the two-legged blimp and her kids balloon across the parking lot through Bradlees' swinging double doors, a smaller version of the Macy Day Parade. As soon as they entered, Mooch jimmied the car so fast, it looked like he had the keys. He got in, popped the ignition, and took off, driving around the block and stopping in front of the neon-lit pizza house. Danny got in and kicked the ketchup-stained McDonald's bags; empty potato chip bags; and torn, emptied Oreo cookie packages aside.

Mooch turned the radio on, rolled it to WMEX, and took off. As soon as he pulled up to the schoolyard, Misfit, Mikey, and Charley opened the rear doors and climbed in. Billy passed the beers to Charley and got them.

"So, where does this cock-sucking Hebe live?" Mooch asked in the same breath, "Billy, give me a beer, will ya?"

"Newton. We can get there by Columbia Road. But, if you stop when ya see a phone booth, I can figure it out better," Danny said.

"No problem."

A few minutes later, Mooch spotted pulled over at a corner gas station. Danny got out, grabbed the chained directory, and flipped through the pages, swinging from the end of a short silver chain. When he reached the aitches, he tore the pages out and stuffed them in his pocket. "Let's go," Danny said, returning to the car.

"Which way?" Mooch asked, shifting into gear.

Danny pointed. "There. Take a left on Dudley Street." He ran his finger down the first page, *Ha, He, Hel, Hem, Hen—Henschel.* There were three of them: a Gloria, the dealership, and one at 324 Walnut Street. "Anyone know where Walnut Street is?"

The kids responded in sequence: "Fuck if I know." "Beats me." "Shit, I dunno." "I dunno."

"Mooch, can you find a gas station?" Danny asked.

"Sure."

"So, how long has your sister been dating this fucking Jewball?" Mikey asked.

"I don't know. A while, I guess. She doesn't check in with me or nothing."

"Don't take this wrong or nothing, but what's she doing dating a Jew? Ain't that against the law or something?" Mikey looked around at the other kids. "Father Driscoll said that if a Catholic and a Jew had kids, they'd be retarded. He said Jew blood was all fucked up; it ain't pure or nothing."

"Yeah, I heard that," Mooch said.

"Me too," echoed Charley. "Father McLellan told me the same thing. He said all kikes were dirty and messed up. He said they carry diseases. Nothing for nothing, Danny, but I hope your sister ain't been fuckin' him or nothing."

"No offense taken," Danny said, jerking his arm and pointing. "There's a Gulf station. Can we stop there?"

"Yup," Mooch replied, signaling and turning.

Danny rolled his window down and spoke as soon as they pulled up. "Hey. Do you know where Walnut Street is?" he asked the attendant, a tall, gangly man wearing greasy overalls, an oil-stained baseball cap, and a pair of thick glasses.

"Sure," he replied, describing the best route he knew, waving his arm around, fortifying the directions he was giving.

"Thanks, man," Danny said.

Mooch drove, never exceeding the speed limit, rolling through quiet, tree-lined streets in front of well-lit homes with broad, veranda-like porches. Soon, the roads grew wider, the trees taller, and the houses bigger. "It's gotta be coming up on the right," Danny said.

Mooch slowed down. "Can anyone see the numbers?" he asked.

"I can," Charley said, calling out the house numbers. He stopped when they reached Henschel's house, a majestic structure that looked like a small hotel flawlessly trimmed with louvered shutters and surrounded by thick, white railings. The 'Vette was parked at the end of the driveway, basking in the yellow glow of a pole-mounted light.

"There it is," Danny yelled, "That's his fuckin' car, right there," jabbing his finger against the car window. "Motherfucker!"

"Be cool," Mooch said. "Be cool." He pulled over in the next block, beneath a broad, branched tree, beyond the streetlights' pool of light. "So, what's the plan?" he asked, turning to Danny.

"I want to scope the place out first." He looked at the other kids. "Does anyone want to come?"

"I do," Mikey replied. "I gotta drain a vein."

"Me too," Misfit said, followed by Charley and Billy: "Yeah, I gotta go too."

After everyone finished, they strolled down the road as if they'd been there their whole life. "There's the 'Vette!" Danny yelped, pointing.

Mikey grabbed Danny's arm. "C'mon, man, you gotta be cool," he said. "You can't do shit like that. Someone'll see us and call the cops or something." They continued around the block, returned to the station wagon, and got in with the rest of the kids.

"So, whatd'ya think?" Mooch asked.

"Gimme a minute," Danny replied. "I gotta think."

Mooch turned the radio down and slid his seat back. "I don't mean to push you or nothing, but we can't stay here forever. The cops are gonna come by sooner or later. If they find out we're from Dorchester, we're fucked."

"Yeah, I know. I'm sorry," Danny replied. "I know."

Mikey glanced at the house. "We can't do nothing now—there's too many people in there."

"I've been thinking; he's gotta be going out. Look at where he's parked. It's like he's ready to go." Danny glanced around at the other kids. "If he were staying in for the night, he'd have parked in the garage. There's no way he'd leave his car outside like that. He's going out; I'm sure of it. You kids don't mind waiting a little longer, do you?"

"I'm okay," Mooch said, adjusting the rearview mirror. The other kids nodded. "But I think we oughta move in case the cops come by."

"Anyone know what time it is?" Danny asked.

"Quarter to nine," Charley replied, passing Danny another beer.

"Hey! Look!" Billy said, waving his hand around. "He's leaving!"

The Corvette's tail lights got brighter as the car backed into the street, turned, and pointed toward them. "Get down!" Mooch yelled, flapping his arms. Mooch waited until the car passed before starting the engine and pulling a tight U-ey, following Henschel down to Route 30. As they neared the 'Vette, Danny banged his hand on the dashboard and yelled, "Look at that motherfucker! He's with another girl."

"What did you expect?" Charley said. "He's a Jew. It's probably his sister. He's probably banging her."

Henschel took a right toward Route 95. Mooch followed, maintaining his distance. They continued into Lexington, where Henschel drove to the center of town and parked. Mooch drove past him, made another U-ey further down the street, and parked in the shadows, where they could see the 'Vette. Henschel got out, walked to the other side, and opened the door for a tall, leggy blonde. "She ain't no fucking Jew," Charley said. "That's for sure."

"She's gotta be a Protestant. They'll fuck anything," Misfit said. "Even Jews."

Danny whacked the dashboard again. "That motherfucker!"

Henschel and the blonde entered a fancy-looking restaurant that took up the first floor of an old brick building.

"So, what do you want to do?" Mikey asked.

"Fuck him and his car up," Danny replied.

"Sounds good!" Mooch said as he reached under his seat, pulled his slim jim out, and slapped it in his hand. "But not before we take it for a joy ride."

Danny slapped the dashboard again. "Fucking right!"

"I want the Jewball," Mikey said.

"That's good. I can't let him see me," Danny said, nodding. "So, here's the plan. Mooch, you circle around the block and boost the 'Vette. I'll meet you down the street. Mikey and Charley, you guys, wait outside the restaurant for Henschel to come out. Make a scene, you know, anything to get him going. Call his girlfriend a slut or something. No, call him a fag. Yeah, that's it. Call him a fag and start a fight with him."

Mikey cracked his knuckles. "Sounds good to me." He spat out the window as if he had coughed up a slice of pizza.

"Let's fuck this Jew prick up!" Charley said.

"Okay. Let's do it," Mooch said. "Let's meet at Houghton's Pond when we're done."

Mikey cracked his knuckles again. "Billy, gimme another beer," he said.

Mooch and Danny got out. Mooch crossed the street and headed in the other direction while Danny took off the opposite way. Wooden fences gave way to stone walls and tall, stately trees that arched over the Norman Rockwell-themed Road. Mikey, Charley, Misfit, and Billy grabbed a handful of beers and walked to the top of a low hill covered with pine and maple trees and sat deep in the shadows, far enough from the road that they couldn't be seen but close enough that they could see everything going on.

Ten minutes later, Danny felt the low rumble of the Corvette coming up behind him. Mooch pulled over, and Danny climbed in. Mooch turned the car around and parked under the shadows of some leafy trees that lined the sidewalk.

From the hill, Misfit and Billy watched through the restaurant window. After dessert was served, the waiter handed the check to Henschel. After paying it, he and his date, dressed in a fluffy white rabbit coat and knee-high boots, stepped outside. She glanced at her reflection in the window, as she had done on the way in. Henschel stood alongside her, admiring himself, dressed in a black-and-orange letterman's jacket with a basketball on the left side of his chest. An orange-colored number twenty-three was sewn in the middle of the ball. As soon as they stepped on the sidewalk, Charley walked straight into Henschel, knocking his shoulder so hard he stumbled into his girlfriend and knocked her on the ground.

"You fucking asshole!" Henschel said, gathering himself up and helping his girlfriend get to her feet. As soon as she was upright, Henschel barrel-chested toward Charley. "What's your fucking problem?" Henschel bellowed, pulling his jacket open. He pushed Charley's shoulders with both hands straight out. "You got a problem?" Henschel bellowed.

"I do, you fuckin' fag!" Mikey shouted behind him.

Henschel turned, and Mikey hit him with a quick shot to the stomach. Henschel keeled over and sucked a chest full of air, trying to stay on his feet. Mikey came around with another left, swinging upward. Henschel tried to block Mikey's punch but failed and fell to his knees. Mikey stood over him. Henschel's girlfriend screamed, flapping her arms like a baby bird trying to fly.

Henschel started to get up, but Mikey kicked him in his knee, sending the pride of Newton to the ground screaming. Mikey kicked him in the gut as soon as he hit the sidewalk. Henschel rolled over into the fetal position, hugging his knees to his chest, moaning.

Henschel's girlfriend screamed. "Stop it! You're hurting him!"

Mikey grabbed Henschel by his collar, yanked it until his jacket came off, and tossed it aside. Charley grabbed it and kicked Henschel in the ribs, leaving a darkened footprint on Henschel's monogrammed shirt.

"Keep the fuck out of Dorchester!" Charley yelled. "If you come back, it'll be a lot worse." Henschel looked up, wide-eyed, and nodded rapidly.

Mikey pulled Henschel onto his knees and punched him in the face, sending a spray of blood across the sidewalk. "I'm done with this piece of shit," Mikey said, spitting at him and dropping him. Charley flipped Henschel's jacket over his shoulders and strolled back and forth like a barnyard rooster, flapping the sleeves in the air. Henschel's girlfriend remained glued against the wall, whimpering like a newborn baby.

Victorious in battle, the kids returned to the station wagon and joined Misfit and Billy. Charley got in, stuck the screwdriver in the ignition, and started the car while Mikey leaned over the back seat, grabbed a couple of beers, and opened one for Charley and himself.

"Pissah! You showed that motherfucking Jew," laughed Billy, holding up his beer, toasting.

"Yeah, good one. Let's get the fuck out of here before the cops show up," said Misfit.

They drove slowly past the restaurant, where a small crowd huddled around Henschel and his girlfriend. He was crying louder than she was. "Fucking cry-baby," Mikey said. "Next time I see that motherfucker, I'll give him something to cry about."

---

Further down the street, Mooch started the 'Vette, banged a U-ey, and headed toward Route 128, grinding through the gears. When he reached the on-ramp, he double-clutched, and the car jumped like a jackrabbit, while the tires screeched like a couple of eight-year-old girls at Disneyland. A billowy cloud of thick white smoke wafted from beneath the wheels. The tachometer windmilled as Mooch barreled down the highway, redlining at 7,100 rpm. Mooch pumped the clutch and popped the car into fourth gear, and the tires squealed again, sending another cloud of smoke in the air. *The Rolling Stones* screamed from the radio.

"I love the fuckin' Stones," Mooch said as he hit 112 miles an hour. Danny squeezed his door handle as they entered Route 95. Mooch turned the radio up louder.

# 20

Mooch turned onto Route 495 and headed north toward Franklin, a small, rural town known chiefly for its Christmas displays, bedroom-bound drunks, and an Amtrak station, marking the end of the commuter line from Boston. Mooch rattled on like he was at the Indy 500. "This car's a fucking beast. It's got three two-barrel Holley carburetors. They suck like a coupla Hingham whores! The rear end's geared for some serious torque."

Danny listened, too embarrassed to admit he didn't understand all the car talk. When they hit an open stretch of road, Mooch punched it. "There! Did you hear it?" Mooch asked.

"Hear it?" Danny replied. "I fuckin' felt it!" The speedometer kept climbing: 107, 108–110. Danny's stomach tightened as everything outside turned into a blur.

"The clutch is really light," Mooch yelled over the engine's din. "It's got a real close-ratio transmission, four hundred and sixty pounds per foot of torque."

Danny nodded, pretending he knew what Mooch was talking about.

"Let's see what kind of balls this has," Mooch said, double-clutching and dropping the car into third gear. The rear end jumped, and the transmission shrieked as they hurdled down the road, spinning the tachometer at 7,200 rpm. Mooch slammed the car into fourth gear, and the tach spun like an outboard engine. Danny's fingers throbbed, and his hands sweated as they hit 132 miles an hour. They neared the Bellingham turn-off at 142. Danny felt like he had to take a shit; his knuckles throbbed. Mooch downshifted and let up on the gas. The car slowed down as quickly as it had accelerated.

"So, what d'ya think?" Mooch asked, rolling his window down and tossing his empty beer can.

"Fuck! How fast were we going?" Danny asked.

"Close to a buck-fifty, maybe more. If we had enough road, we coulda hit one-eighty, maybe one-ninety. Shit, maybe it coulda been two hundred. You can see why a car like this will get you laid," Mooch said. As soon as he heard himself, he quickly added, "Fuck, I'm sorry. You know what I mean."

"Yeah, no problem," Danny said. All he could think about was his sister leaning over the front seat, giving Henschel a blowjob while he drove down Dot Ave. Mooch continued toward town. "You wanna drive?" he asked.

"Yeah! That'd be cool."

Mooch pulled off at the next ramp. "I gotta drain a vein," he said, jumping out and running into the woods. Danny joined him, both turning their backs to the wind. "It's like flying a fucking rocket!" Mooch yelped, jumping around, almost pissing on Danny.

"No shit! I ain't never been in anything that fast before," Danny said.

"And you won't ever be in anything faster unless you're getting laid by Fathead's mother."

Danny laughed so hard he nearly pissed on Mooch's feet. "Save that shit for Fitzy's mother. Don't waste it on me," Mooch said as he took a few steps back, waiting for Danny to stop laughing.

When they were done, they headed back to the car. Danny ran to the driver's side and slid into the seat while Mooch got in the other side. "Okay," Mooch said, lighting a filtered Marlboro. "You gotta be careful with the clutch. It's kinda like fucking. If you don't do it right, you'll blow your load too soon. And, when you let it out, you gotta let it out slowly, you know, just like fucking. You want it to last."

Danny laughed again, "You gotta stop that shit. You're killing me."

"I'm serious, man," Mooch said. "This is one of the most powerful cars on earth. If you dump the clutch too quickly, it'll stall. You gotta time it just right. When you let the clutch up, you gotta hit the gas at the same time. You gotta listen to the engine."

"What about all the dials and everything?"

"Don't worry about them. They don't mean nothing. You gotta listen and drive by your ears. Fuck the dials. They don't mean shit."

"Really?" Danny retorted, rubbing his sweaty hands on the sides of his pants. He grabbed the wheel, pumped the clutch a few times, and revved the engine while listening to the cylinders pound away.

"You ready?" Mooch asked.

"Yup." Danny shifted into first gear and watched the RPMs rise from 2,200 to 2,300 to 2,400.

"Go on," Mooch said, popping smoke rings out his mouth.

Danny squeezed the wheel tighter and pressed the gas pedal. He let the clutch out, and the car lurched forward and bounced a couple of times before stalling.

"Don't worry, man, you'll get the hang of it," Mooch said. "Like I said, you gotta listen to the engine. It's like fucking—find your rhythm, and don't blow your load too early."

Danny nodded, popped the car into neutral, and turned the engine over again, letting it settle into a smooth idle. He pressed the clutch and shifted into gear. When the engine sounded right, he slowly let the clutch out, and the car moved forward, sputtering a few times. It lurched, and within a few seconds, they coasted at thirty miles an hour. Danny pressed the gas pedal, and the engine started whining. "You gotta shift now," Mooch said, tapping the dashboard. "Now! NOW!" Danny hit the gas, and the car lurched forward; the engine whined. "Shift! You gotta shift!"

Danny let the clutch out and pressed the gas pedal. The car jerked several times in short, stuttering motions before smoothing out and accelerating. Mooch opened the glove compartment and rummaged through a small stack of papers before tossing them out the window. He removed a pair of sunglasses, put them on, checked himself in the mirror, smiled, and stuck them in his pocket. Danny shifted into third gear and listened to the engine hum. At the fourth gear, the car accelerated smoothly. After repeatedly glancing in the rearview mirror, Danny said, "I'm done," wiping his hands on his pants. "Why don't you drive?"

"Sure," Mooch replied. "Put it in neutral and pull over." Danny released the gas and tapped the brakes several times until they stopped. "I gotta take a piss," Mooch said as he swung the door open and hopped out. Danny put the brake on, got out, and lit a cigarette. After a long and noisy piss, Mooch returned to the car, and Danny followed. Mooch pumped the clutch and let it out, spraying dirt and leaves everywhere. They hit the ramp doing ninety miles an hour. Mooch banked into a curve, and the rear end slid around like a freshly-hooked flounder. Mooch downshifted as he came out of the turn. The motor howled again, and the differential box stuttered and shook the car. Danny gripped the door handle to keep from sliding onto Mooch's lap. They flew down the road as if everything around them was frozen. To Danny's white-knuckled relief, Mooch slowed down when they reached the Granite Street off-ramp. When they got to Codman Square, a cop car from the other direction put its lights on and banged a U-ey in the middle of the street.

"Hold on," Mooch yelled, slowing down.

"What the fuck are you doing?" Danny gasped, watching the cops in close pursuit.

"Don't worry, I'm just fuckin' with 'em," Mooch said, coolly puffing on his cigarette as he turned onto Talbot Ave.

"Are you fucking crazy?"

"Depends on who you ask," Mooch said.

When they reached Blue Hill Avenue, the cops pulled alongside Mooch. Mooch smiled and gave them the finger. "Hold on," Mooch said, grinning as he slammed the brakes. To Danny's amazement, the 'Vette stayed in perfect alignment and came to a sudden, screeching stop, leaving a pair of seven-inch wide burned tire strips behind them. The cops hit their brakes half a second later, fishtailing and bouncing off several parked cars, sending broken mirrors and various car parts all over the street.

"How the fuck did you do that?" Danny asked.

"Pure fucking skill," Mooch replied, glancing at Danny and then at the police. "Amateurs," he said, flicking his cigarette out the window. He waited until he locked eyes with the cop driving the car, then jammed it in reverse and left another streak of acrid-smelling rubber on top of the asphalt as they shot back toward Codman Square. When they passed under the New York and New England railroad bridge, Mooch yanked the parking brake and spun the wheel to the right. The car spun around in a small, tight circle and stopped, pointing in the other direction. Mooch shifted into first gear, punched the pedal, and shot through the intersection. He took a right at Washington Street, and they flew toward Gallivan Boulevard at eighty miles an hour. Mooch and took another right to merge into the traffic flow, slowing down to forty miles an hour. He turned onto Blue Hill Ave. and took a left into the Franklin Park Zoo, screeching to a stop beneath a small grove of low-hanging trees.

"Jesus Christ! You're out of your fucking mind!" Danny yowled.

"Shit. That was too easy," Mooch said, glancing at Danny's hands, still glued to the door handle. "Relax; they'll never look for us here. Hey, want a smoke?" he asked.

"Sure," Danny replied, loosening his grip on the door handle, grateful that he didn't need a crowbar to do it.

"So, what's up with this Jew fuck?" Mooch asked. "What did he do to your sister?"

Danny took a drag on his cigarette and stared out the window.

"I know it ain't none of my business or nothing," Mooch said, "but I want you to know I'm here for you; we all are."

"To tell you the truth, I'm not sure. I mean, I didn't talk to her or nothing. When she came home, she was crying. She was with my ma, and they were really quiet. I didn't hear what they said. I saw that her coat was ripped, and her legs were bleeding. My little brother, Frankie, heard them talking and said he beat her up, threw her out of his car, and left her downtown."

"If it means anything, Mikey did a good job fucking him up."

"Yeah, I know. That was good. That fucking Jew deserved it."

"Can you imagine the look on that cocksucker's face when he found out his car was stolen? He musta had a canipshit."

"Fuck him," Danny said.

"Hey! Let's see what's in the trunk," Mooch said, banging his hand on the steering wheel. Mooch swung the door open, and they both got out. Mooch pulled a screwdriver from his back pocket, jammed it in the lock, and twisted it. The trunk flipped open, and the interior light shone on a chrome-trimmed tire. "Hey, there's a toolbox," Mooch said. He flipped it open. It was full of shiny Craftsman wrenches, ratchets, screwdrivers, and stainless-steel sockets, clean enough for open-heart surgery. "Can you use these?"

"Are you serious?"

"Fuck yeah, I got plenty of tools."

"Really?"

"Yeah." Mooch poked around a little more. "Hey, you wanna drive?" A moment later, he laughed at Danny's long, blank stare. "I'm just fuckin' with ya, man. Let's go. We gotta meet the kids at Houghton's."

"Can we drop this stuff off at my house?"

"No problem."

Mooch started the engine, keeping the lights off until he pulled up to the park entrance. He shot across the street and stopped at a red light, where four black kids walked straight toward the car. Danny looked at the lights, then back to the kids, and then to Mooch. "We gotta get outta here! Those fuckers ain't delivering pizza."

"Fuck them and the boat they came in on," Mooch replied, crushing his cigarette out on the leather seat and creating a small cloud of nasty-smelling smoke.

The first kid reached for Danny's door, two went behind the car, and the fourth came up to Mooch's side carrying a brick. "C'mon, let's get the fuck outta here," Danny said.

The kid with the brick lifted it up. "Get outta the fucking car, honky."

Mooch stuck his middle finger in his nose and pressed it against his window. "Fuck you." The kid stepped backward, ready to throw the brick. Mooch dropped the car into gear and let the clutch out so fast, that Danny's head bounced off the seat. The kids scrambled in every direction while the car fishtailed and left a plume of smoke so dense the kids couldn't see each other. "Fucking spear-chuckers!"

They drove until they were near Danny's apartment, Mooch making sure not to get too close. After he pulled over, Danny got out, popped the trunk open, grabbed the toolbox, and disappeared behind the side of his three-decker, returning two minutes later. Mooch took off and pulled up in front of the schoolyard. "Hey! Anyone got a beer?" Danny yelled to the crowd of kids.

"Danny. Is that you, you fucker?" Bugsy responded.

"Well, it ain't the fuckin' Pope," Danny hollered back.

"Is that the Jew's car?" Grunta asked, running over.

"Yup," Mooch replied.

"Hold on a sec," Bugsy said, running down the alley and returning with a six-pack. He pulled a couple of beers out and handed them to Danny and Mooch. "So, how'd it go? Did you get the cocksucker?"

"Oh yeah. Mikey did!" Mooch replied. "He jacked that piece of shit up. Dropped him like a bad habit."

"No shit," Bugsy replied.

"We're meeting the rest of the kids at Houghton's Pond," Mooch said.

"Wanna come?" Danny asked. "You'll have to squeeze in."

Bugsy looked around, "Yeah, okay."

Danny slid his seat back as far as he could. "Get in."

Bugsy crawled into the passenger seat and folded himself up like a pretzel. "Let's get outta here," Mooch said, revving the engine and shifting into reverse while letting the car roll downhill. The tachometer spun like a windmill in a tornado past the red line. He let the clutch up, and the car started bouncing up and down like a basketball, sending a thick cloud of nose-burning smoke high in the air. He jammed the car into first gear. The engine heaved and groaned, and the tires howled in protest. As soon as the wheels caught the pavement, the 'Vette took off like it had been shot from a cannon, leaving behind a blinding cloud of smoke.

"Holy fuck!" Danny yelled, looking back.

"That was fucking great!" Bugsy yelled.

They shot through the red-lit intersection at the bottom of the hill, doing 106 miles an hour. House lights went on up and down the street. Mooch slowed down two blocks later when he ran out of a straight road. When he did, the engine's sound changed, and the tachometer bounced around like it had hiccups.

"That doesn't sound good," Danny said, staring at the gauges. "Is everything okay?"

"Probably not, but who gives a fuck?" Mooch replied as he pressed the accelerator. The car made more grinding noises. Bugsy leaned forward and turned his head to listen better. "That sounds fucked up."

"It is," Mooch said, laughing.

"Can we do it again?" Bugsy replied through a shit-eating grin.

"I don't think so. We gotta meet the other kids at Houghton's, and this piece of shit might not make it."

"Are you kidding me?" Danny asked.

"No, I think I blew out the rear end," Mooch said.

"No shit!" Danny said.

"Yeah, no shit. We gotta keep moving. If it stalls, it might not start," Mooch said as he put the car in gear and coaxed it down the street, double-shifting and double-clutching his way through Milton to the Blue Hills. When he reached Houghton's, he circled past the parking lot to make sure there were no cops around. After making a second turn, he nursed the car to the far end of the lot and backed in. When he turned it off, it heaved and shuddered before belching and shutting down. He turned the radio up and lit a smoke.

"Who's that? I never heard this band before," Danny said. "The music's different."

"It's FM," Mooch said, sounding like Mr. Dowling, the history teacher. "It's a different kind of music. It's not like that AM shit. FM's different."

"Different? What do you mean?"

"I dunno. Different. It's hard to explain. They play a lot of psychedelic stuff."

"Psycha-what?" Bugsy asked, scrunching his face as if he'd swallowed something sour.

"Psychedelic. It's hippie stuff; it's what the long hairs play," Mooch replied.

"I ain't never heard a guitar played like that before. This psycha—whatever you call it—is wild," Danny said. "What did ya say the name of the band was?"

"The Grateful Dead," Mooch replied.

"The Grapeful what?" Danny asked, looking over to Bugsy. "That a fucking cereal."

"Did you say the Gracious Dead?" Bugsy asked. "That's a weird fucking name."

Mooch tilted his head back and smiled. "It's the Grateful Dead. They're great. The lead guy's a guitar player named Garcia."

"Garcia? Is he a spic?" Bugsy asked.

"I don't know. But, I gotta tell you, the fucker can play the shit out of a guitar," Mooch said.

"Where's he from?" Danny asked.

"I dunno, somewhere out in California. San Francisco, I think," Mooch replied.

"That place is full of fags," Bugsy said.

"Sausage smokers," Danny said.

"Fudge packers," Mooch added.

"Hey!" Danny yelped. "There they are!"

The wagon quietly pulled up alongside them. Charley got out first, followed by several empty beer cans that bounced around at his feet. "So, did you guys have a good time?" Danny asked.

Charley, wearing Henschel's jacket, swaggered toward the 'Vette, holding his crotch with both hands. "Yeah, I'm taking his girlfriend to the prom," he said, rubbing his hand on his sleeve. "She gives great head, just like his mother."

"Does she swallow?" Bugsy said.

"She's a Jew, ain't she?" Charley said.

"Fitzy's ma ain't a Jew, and she swallows," Danny said.

"We ain't talking about niggers," Bugsy said.

"So anyways, was he surprised?" Danny asked.

"Are you shitting me? He never knew what hit him," Charley said. "And Mikey here, he fucked him up really good!"

"That piece of shit was a fucking lightweight. He fought like my little sister and cried like her," Mikey said. "His girlfriend had more balls than him."

"Seriously, Mikey," Danny said. "I owe you."

"No problem. It was my pleasure. He won't be back in Dorchester again."

"Let's strip this thing," Bugsy said, walking to the car.

Mooch tossed his screwdriver over to Billy. Billy slid it underneath the hood emblem, popped it off, and stuffed it in his back pocket. The other kids opened the doors and rummaged, looking for anything not bolted down. Mikey pulled the tire iron out of the trunk and popped the hubcaps off, tossing them in the back of the station wagon. "Those are mine," he said. The kids continued, taking anything they could tear off or take out—carpets, mirrors, the lighter, door handles, and everything that shined. Two smokes later, Danny spoke up. "You kids done? The Staties are gonna show up sooner or later, so we better get the fuck out of here before they do."

"Yeah, you're right," Mooch said. "Are you guys all done?"

The kids looked around at each other, shrugging.

"Okay. You kids gotta move back a little." The kids looked at each other and then stepped back a few steps. Mooch got in and started the engine, turning it over a few times before it came to life, and when it did, it spewed a cloud of smoke and sounded like a fork in a garbage disposal. He had to keep revving the motor so it wouldn't die as it kept choking out. When it ran as smoothly as possible, Mooch slipped the car into gear and nursed it across the parking lot, leaving a long, dark trail of dark fluids on the asphalt paving. He revved the engine, threw the car in reverse, and popped the clutch when he was halfway across the lot. The car howled and screeched as it took off backward, sounding like a large skipping turntable. He put the car in gear and pressed the gas pedal to the floor. The engine made a stuttering sound, and metal parts snapped, sending a cloud of smoke from beneath the vehicle. Mooch throttled his way onto a small dirt bank, and when he reached the top, he put the emergency brake on, got out, grabbed a large rock, and put it on the gas pedal. He got back in, shifted into first gear, released the brake, and jumped out. The car spun down the hill into the pond and made a loud sizzling sound as it sank into the water beneath a cloud of billowing steam and oily-smelling smoke.

"It looks like that Jew's gonna be walking for a while," Mikey said, tossing his empty can in the water.

Danny walked over to the water's edge, pulled his fly down, and pissed in the pond. "Fuck him." A sheen of oil rose to the surface, leaving an iridescent halo around the car.

# 21

When Danny spoke to Mr. Erickson on the phone, he told him to be at work at six thirty so he could show him the ropes. Danny went to bed early to be ready, but it didn't help. He dragged himself out of bed and sleepwalked into the parlor after a pit stop in the bathroom. He scraped some frost from the window and watched a slow line of cars wind up the hill, spinning and sliding on the black-iced road. After a few minutes of watching, trying to figure out who would make it, he slippered into the kitchen and stuck some Pop-Tarts in the toaster. He ate the first while tugging his pants on and the second while pulling a long-sleeved undershirt over his head. He laced his new boots, of which his mother had said, "They're steel-toed," like she was announcing her firstborn baby. "Your father wore a pair just like them."

Danny grabbed his pea cap and gloves and went outside, surprised at how dark and cold it was, grimacing when the wind sliced through his skin. A slow-moving bus, filled with miserable people, bundled for the winter, howled as it fought its way up the street, spinning and sliding as it made its way up the hill. He followed it, walking in the middle of the icy tire tracks worn by the early morning traffic. The rest of the way wasn't any different. When he neared the gas station, he saw a tall, clean-shaven man shoveling the driveway. Danny approached the man, removed his gloves, and extended his hand. "Hi, I'm Danny."

"Danny! I'm pleased to meet you," the man said, removing his gloves and shaking Danny's hand. "I'm Mr. Erickson." His grip was firmer than Danny had expected.

"Good to meet you."

"They haven't plowed yet, have they?"

"No, not yet."

"A day like this, it'll be a while."

"No kidding."

"I've heard some wonderful things about you. You impressed my wife, and that's not an easy task. She said she offered you some money, but you wouldn't take it."

"Yeah, I just wanted to help her. She was stuck," Danny said, slipping his gloves back on.

"If you don't mind me asking, why didn't you take the money?"

"It didn't seem right to me. She needed help, and I was there. I didn't do it for the money. I was glad to help."

"Most people would have taken the money, some before they did anything. And a lot wouldn't have done anything; they wouldn't have even stopped."

Danny fiddled with his gloves. "I don't know. It was the right thing to do."

"It was, son. It was indeed."

Danny smiled and nodded.

"Are you ready to get started?"

"You bet. What can I do?"

"There's another shovel inside the bay," Mr. Erickson said. "I've got some customers coming in later this morning. Unfortunately, I wasn't able to get here any earlier."

"That's why I was running late. I had to run half the way here. It's pretty fucked up out there," Danny replied.

Mr. Erickson suddenly retreated into a stern face. "I'd prefer you not use that kind of language around here. It's coarse and offensive. I don't appreciate it, and my customers won't. As long as you work here, you must speak and act like a gentleman. You're not on a street corner or in a pool room. You're at work, at your job."

Danny bowed his head in embarrassment. "Yes, sir. I . . . I'm sorry. It won't happen again."

"Everything you say and do reflects on me, my wife, and our business. There's no room for vulgarity around here—not here, not anywhere."

"I'm sorry. It won't happen again, I promise."

"Good," he replied, nodding. "We have a lot of work to do. Can you start over there, at the front door? I need the front shoveled and the area in front of the garage bays cleared."

"No problem," Danny said enthusiastically.

Danny walked over to the single-story station, a green-and-white block building, grabbed the shovel, and stuck it in the snow, not getting very far as a thick layer of ice lay beneath the surface. Danny stabbed at it; his shovel bounced and rattled in his hands.

"There's a better shovel in the garage," Mr. Erickson yelled from the other side of the driveway. He walked over to Danny. "I forgot to mention. There's a coffee pot and some donuts if you're interested."

"Thanks. I don't drink coffee, but I'll grab a donut when I'm hungry if that's okay."

"How about some hot chocolate?"

"Yeah, that'd be great."

"Okay. Let me show you where everything is."

Danny resumed shoveling after two cups of cocoa and a couple of jelly donuts, while Mr. Erickson cleaned the pumps off. When he was done, he called Danny over. "Can you give me a hand, son?"

"Sure. What do you need?"

"See that wheelbarrow over there? Can you fill it with some rock salt and spread it over there?" he requested, waving his hand around. "And over there," he added, tilting his head in the other direction. "You can use the big shovel to spread it out."

"No problem," Danny said.

"When you're done, we can go over running the pumps and setting up the oil rack."

"Sounds good."

Danny chipped away over the next hour and spread the salt, eventually clearing the walkway. "How's it look?" he asked, stepping into the office. Mr. Erickson got up from his paperwork and stepped outside.

"Splendid, son, splendid. You did a great job. Why don't you sit down so we can discuss some of the other things I need you to work on."

"Can I grab another cocoa?"

"Of course."

Danny made another drink, sat down, leaned back in the office chair, and studied the room. A stack of papers was on the desk, some pens and pencils, and a couple of notepads. The shelves and desk were covered with books, boxes, and files that did not appear well organized. Mr. Erickson cupped his hands around his coffee. He spoke, starting with the basics: gas—regular and premium, motor oil, transmission fluid, windshield fluid, fuses, wiper blades, shutoffs, emergency valves, and deliveries. "Take some notes if you want," he said, sliding one of the pads across the desk to him. "See that drawer over there, the bottom one? That's yours. You can put your things in there." Danny started writing some things when an old Ford pulled up. The driver, an older woman, peered over the steering wheel while wiping her front window with a little white doily. "You want to give this one a try?" Mr. Erickson asked.

"Umm, yeah," Danny responded, sounding less than confident.

"Are you sure?"

"Yeah, I'm good."

"If you need anything, I'll be in the stock room."

"Okay," Danny replied, pulling his gloves on. He stepped outside and walked up to the car. "Good morning. Can I help you?"

"My, yes, thank you. My defroster's not working, and the windows are fogged. I can hear something spinning around. There's air coming out, I can feel it, but it's not hot."

"I can take a look at that if you'd like."

"That'd be wonderful."

"Do you need any gas?" Danny asked.

"Yes, please."

"Why don't we take care of that first and get you inside where it's warm?"

"Thank you, that would be nice."

"Fill it up?"

"Yes, please."

When he was done with the gas, Danny pointed at the garage and said, "You can drive right in." Danny guided her and held his hands up. "That's good," he said. "You can shut it off and wait inside. It's warmer in there. It shouldn't take too long."

"Thank you," she said as she exited the car.

"Would you like a cup of coffee?"

"Oh no, thank you. I'll be fine."

"There are some magazines if you're interested."

"Thank you."

Danny went back into the garage, opened her front door, lay on the plastic-covered bench seat, and stretched out so he could reach the fuse panel. He spotted a blown fuse, pulled it out, and slid back out of the car, only to be greeted by a scraggly-looking guy with an acne-pocked face leaning on the door frame. "Whatcha working on?"

"The defroster. I think I found the problem," Danny said, holding up the fuse and rolling it around in his fingers.

"Did you look under the hood?"

"Naw, I think this is it," Danny said. "You work here?"

"Yeah. You must be the new kid."

"Yeah, Danny. Danny McSweeney," he said, extending his hand.

"Larry McMahon," the guy offered with a slight nod. "Are you related to Tommy McSweeney from Saint Mark's parish?"

"No." Danny glanced into the office. "I don't know him."

"It's a common name."

"I'm not being rude or nothing, but I gotta get back to work," Danny said.

Larry nodded and left. Danny walked over to the workbench and looked through a box of fuses bolted to the wall. After finding the right size, he crawled back under the dashboard, popped the fuse in place, and turned the defroster on. He placed his hand over the dashboard and felt the warmth blast from the heater. He returned to the office, "Your car's ready, ma'am."

"That was quick. What was it?" she asked, getting up.

"A fuse."

"Wonderful, wonderful. How much will that be, young man?" she asked.

"I'm not sure. I need to ask the owner. This is my first day."

Danny popped his head inside the storeroom. "Mr. Erickson. I fixed this lady's car."

"What was it?"

"A fuse; a twenty amp. She asked me how much it cost, and I told her I didn't know."

"Tell her a dollar twenty-five," Mr. Erickson replied, "including labor."

Danny returned to the office, wrote the charge on a small slip of paper, and handed it to her.

"What do I owe you for the gas?" she asked.

"That'll be another two dollars and forty-five cents."

She counted out the money and handed him another thirty-five cents. "That's for you," she said.

"Me? You don't need to give me nothing extra."

"Yes, I know. It's a tip."

"Well, okay," he said, putting the money in his pocket. "Thank you."

"You're quite welcome. Is Mr. Erickson here?" she asked.

"Yes, would you like me to get him?"

"If you don't mind."

Danny popped his head into the storeroom. "Do you have a minute? This lady asked to see you."

Mr. Erickson wiped his hands with his pocket rag and entered the office. "How are you today, Mary?"

"I'm fine, thank you."

"I see you met Danny."

"I did. He's a fine young man."

"How can I help you?"

"Well, I'd like to tune the engine up this week. It's running a little rough."

"No problem," Mr. Erickson said. He walked over to a large calendar on the wall. "How does Tuesday morning sound? Say, nine o'clock?"

"That'll be wonderful," she replied.

"Tuesday, it is. We'll see you then."

She turned to Danny and Larry, who had entered the office. "Thank you all."

Danny stepped outside and guided her as she backed out of the garage. After she left, he grabbed the shovel and started shoveling. "You have a natural way with people," Mr. Erickson said as he stepped outside. "That's a rare trait."

"Thanks."

"And did you see what just happened? She gave you a tip, and she'll be back for a tune-up. The pumps pay the bills, but the repair work is where we make our profit."

"Profit?" Danny asked, baffled.

Mr. Erickson chuckled. "When a business makes money, it's called income, and after paying all our bills, the leftover is called a profit. It's how we make money; it's what we keep. When we pay for things, that's called an expense. For example, when I pay you, that's a business expense. Some of the income goes to you. And then, there's the loss, and that's what it sounds like. It's when you lose money. It doesn't make sense to be in business if you're losing money, right? That's why they call it *profit and loss*."

"I never heard that before. There's a lot to this business stuff, isn't there?"

"There sure is, son, there sure is. Running a gas station takes a lot of money, like any other business. It's sort of like running a household. You work to pay your bills, buy food, and pay the rent or, if you're lucky, the mortgage." Danny nodded, thinking about the countless times he'd seen his mother, late at night, placing bills and coins into little marked envelopes, writing down the names of the things that had to be paid: the rent, groceries, heating oil, gas, and electric bills.

"While we have a minute, let me show you where we keep the supplies," Mr. Erickson said.

They stepped into the storeroom, lined with shelves filled with boxes of all shapes and sizes stacked to the ceiling. Tires, belts, wires, cords, and tools hung from the rafters above. Labels with numbers and part descriptions were attached to each of the pieces. "Here, on the right, we store the motor oil. And over there," Mr. Erickson said, with a wave of his hand, pointing to the containers neatly stacked on the metal racks lined up against the wall, "is the transmission fluid, and next to that is the antifreeze. We have what we call an *incentive* for selling oil and any other car fluids. You can earn an extra fifteen cents for every can of oil or windshield washing fluid you sell. It's called a *commission*, which is extra money for you. It's part of the company's business plan. They figure if they give you some of the sale prices, you and every other employee will be motivated to sell more oil and other products. It's an incentive."

"What do you call it?" Danny asked.

"A commission. It's sort of like a reward for going the extra mile. You get to keep some money for selling the oil, windshield washing fluid, transmission fluid, and anything else we offer. It can be pretty profitable. As an example, let's say you sell twenty cans of oil. That's an extra three dollars a day at fifteen cents a can. Now, if you worked full-time, five days a week, you'd make an extra fifteen dollars a week. It can add up pretty fast. In a month, you can earn an extra sixty dollars. That's a lot of money."

"Sure is," Danny said, distracted by visions of long black Cadillacs and yachts floating off the shore of Miami.

"Do you know how to do an oil change?"

"Yup, sure do."

"Good. As you know, you have to be careful with the filters. You can't mis-thread them. That's the only trick." He pointed at the far wall. "The oil filters are over there, and the gaskets are over here."

"Got it," Danny said, looking around, and nodding.

"And I have a full collection of Chilton manuals."

"No kidding. Stanley does too. I learned a lot of things from them."

"They're a great resource. Here, let me show you how to operate the lifts."

"Mr. Erickson, can I ask you a question?"

"Of course."

"How long's Larry been working here?"

"A little over four months. Why do you ask?"

"I was curious, that's all."

"Do you know him?"

"Not really. I seen him around the neighborhood."

"Between you and me, I'm not really happy with him."

"Why's that? I mean, if you don't mind telling me?"

"He doesn't come in on time, and he's not a hard worker like you." He placed his hand on Danny's shoulder. "I've been watching him."

Danny nodded.

"And I've been watching you, of course."

"I appreciate it."

"Well, let's keep this between us."

"Of course. Sure."

After learning how to run the lifts, Danny continued shoveling and spreading rock salt. Mr. Erickson started making some calls. Twenty minutes later, he stepped outside and yelled, "Danny, can you take over the pumps?"

"Sure," he yelled back. Over the next half hour, Danny watched Larry pace around the office, waving his arms and yelling, while Mr. Erickson sat behind his desk at the other end of the conversation. Eventually, Larry stormed out, grabbed a shovel, and headed over to the far end of the driveway, where he started shoveling. Mr. Erickson came out a few minutes later and called Danny over.

"Danny, I'd like you to work with Larry. He can show you where everything is and what he does."

"Sure." He glanced over to Larry, shoveling and banging his shovel around. "Is he okay, I mean, you know, working with him?"

"Of course. He'll be fine."

"Okay."

"I have to head over to the Quincy station. One of my guys called in sick. I'll be back around noon."

"Sounds good. If you need anything else, let me know."

"Will do."

Danny walked over to Larry. "Mr. Erickson asked me to help you. He said you could show me around and stuff."

"Is that right?" Larry said, leaning on his shovel. "Did he say anything else?"

"No. That was it."

Larry lit a cigarette and took a long drag. "He didn't say nothing else?"

"No. He told me he wanted me to work with you and help you stack the shelves. He said you were going to show me all the stuff you do. Said you'd teach me."

"Did you say anything to him?"

"What? What do you mean? Like what?"

Larry stared at Danny, then said, "Fuck it. Never mind."

"Okay. So, what can I do?" Danny asked.

"You can help shovel this fucking snow."

"He wanted me to work on the other stuff, stacking the shelves and getting things in order."

"I don't give a shit what you do. Fill the oil racks over there," Larry said, pointing at the island of pumps. "Make sure all the racks are clean and stocked."

"No problem," Danny said. He went inside, grabbed an old box for the oil, returned to the racks, and started removing the oil cans, using his pocket rag to wipe the grease and oil off the shelves, stopping when he noticed some cans were punched on both ends. The pump bell rang. Danny looked around for Larry; he was on the phone, with his feet on Mr. Erickson's desk, drinking a cup of coffee. Danny waved at Larry to get his attention, in vain. He kept waving and pointing at the car, but Larry didn't acknowledge him, nor did he look up. Danny finally gave up and walked over to the pumps, where an older gentleman patiently waited. "Sorry for the delay. I was busy inside."

"It's not a problem. I'm not in any rush. Can you fill 'er up?"

"Sure," Danny replied. "Regular or premium?"

"Regular."

Over the next hour, a steady stream of cars pulled in, needing gas, oil, and occasionally wiper blades. Meanwhile, Larry stayed on the phone, while Danny ran from pump to pump, trying to get Larry's attention. Half an hour later, Mr. Erickson pulled up. As soon as Larry saw him, he hung up the phone and ran outside to help the next customer, wiping his brow as if he had been working.

"I can see you fellows have been really busy," Mr. Erickson said.

"Yeah, we sure have," Larry said, glancing over to Danny, silently pumping gas into an old Buick.

"How about I grab a couple of spuckies for you fellows? How about some chips and a couple of tonics?"

"Yeah, that'd be great," Larry said.

"Danny?"

"Yes, thank you."

"I'll be back shortly," Mr. Ericskon said.

"Sounds good," Larry said.

As soon as Mr. Erickson left, Danny returned to work; Larry got back on the phone, staying there until Mr. Erickson returned. As soon as he did, Larry ran out and busied himself, wiping his brow for added effect. Mr. Erickson dropped the lunches off and took off again. Danny continued working as customers kept coming in. Larry made no effort to get up. He spread his lunch across the office desk, started eating, and got back on the phone. Once things slowed, Danny grabbed his lunch, went into the storeroom, closed the door, and started eating. The pump bell went off. Danny kept his head down, reading a Chilton manual on 1963 Chevy Impalas.

Larry knocked on the storeroom door. "Are you gonna get that?" he said.

Danny reached back over his head and locked the door. The pump bell rang again. Larry kicked the door and cussed. The bell rang again. Danny closed his eyes and leaned against the wall, staying there a while. Half an hour later, he got up, washed his hands, and went back out. To his surprise, the oil racks were filled and neatly stacked. Danny picked a couple of the cans up and turned them over. "So, what's up with all the holes in the cans?"

"I gypped 'em," Larry replied.

"What do you mean?"

"The customers. I gypped 'em."

"I don't understand."

"You gotta keep this between you and me, okay?"

"Yeah, sure. Of course."

"There's a couple of ways. The easiest is to fake the stick."

"Fake the stick? What the fuck does that mean?"

"What you do is you pull the dipstick out of the engine. You wrap a rag around the top like you're being neat. Then, when you put the stick back in, you hold your other hand just above the top, just like this," Larry said, pinching his fingers together. "When you stick it in, you hold it about half an inch above the top of the tube; you never stick it all the way in. It works best if the driver's watching you. When you pull the stick out, you'll always be at least a quart down, you know, because you never stick it in all the way. You walk over to the window and show it to them, so they can see for themselves. Then you say, 'Looks like you're a quart low.' They never question you, not after they see the stick."

"I get it," Danny said, nodding.

"It's a great fucking scam. See down here," Larry said, pointing, "the cans in the bottom drawer. They look okay, right?"

Danny picked one up. He could tell it was empty as soon as he touched it.

"Those are the ones I use."

Danny turned the can around in his hand. "What about Mr. Erickson? He's gotta notice."

"He's an old fucking man. He don't notice shit. If he did, he'd have said something before. He ain't never said nothing. If he knew, he'd have said something."

"I guess. You know he ain't that stupid."

"Whatever. I keep the good cans on the top, so everything looks good. When Erickson compares the receipts with the can count, everything checks out. It's free fucking money! And besides, all the old ladies that come in here are easy marks, dumb bitches."

"Aren't you worried about getting caught?"

"By Mr. Erickson? Naw, that's not gonna happen."

Danny put the can back in the rack, rotating it so the label was in front. "I'm gonna go back to work."

# 22

Larry left at five thirty and Danny a little after eight. When he got home, he devoured a sandwich his mother had made for him with a tall glass of milk. After running a wet hand cloth under his armpits, he put his shirt back on and went back out. As soon as he stepped outside, an Impala full of kids he didn't recognize slowed down and stared at him. Danny lit a cigarette and stared back. The car continued slowly scoping the neighborhood. Danny crossed the street and walked along the front of a four-story brick apartment building across the street from his home. The car came back and slowed again. Danny stepped back into the shadows, where they couldn't see him. The car continued slowly down Westville Street.

Danny stumbled alongside the building, stopping when he found a two-by-four frozen to the ground. He kicked it a few times until he dislodged it. He picked it up and walked back to the corner of the building. The car drove by again. When it disappeared down the street, he leaned the piece of wood against the wall and waited, before stepping out and walking down Westville Street, to the schoolyard, where the snow was deep and largely untrodden. The kids were hanging in the brick-walled alcove. The boys were on the left, drinking, smoking, and talking, and the girls were on the right, doing the same but with more talking. Danny was greeted by a serenade of *heys, hi's*, and *what's ups*, carried aloft by small clouds of smoke-infused steam.

"Man, it's fuckin' cold out," he said.

"Well, put it back in," Bugsy said. "Want a beer?"

"Yeah, thanks."

Bugsy pulled a Gansett out of a mound of snow and tossed it to Danny. "Can you grab me one?" Fitzy asked.

"What am I, your fuckin' waiter?" Bugsy replied in a don't-ask-me-again tone.

Danny took a swig and pulled his smokes out. He snapped the pack and popped a couple out, extending them toward Bugsy and Mooch. Fitzy made a move, and Danny stuffed his cigarettes back in his pocket. "Hey, guys," he said. "A Chevy full of kids drove by when I was on the way down. I didn't recognize none of 'em. They slowed down, eyed me, and then went down Westville to check things out. They came back a couple of times."

"What color was the car?" Charley asked.

"Maroon."

"Could be the fags from Uppies," Charley said.

"They wouldn't have the balls to come around here," Mooch said.

"I wish the motherfuckers would," Charley said, looking at Billy.

"Well, they ain't here now. Anyone wanna make a run?" Bugsy asked.

Danny put his hand into his pocket and ran his fingers through the coins filling its bottom half. "I'll go," he said.

"Anyone else?" Bugsy asked, looking around.

"I can't. I gotta head home," Mooch said. "My grandma's visiting, and we gotta go to church in the morning."

"Gimme a minute," Danny said, jogging over to Patty.

"Hi. How are you?" he asked, stopping as close to her as possible without touching her.

"Fine," she said, with a smile that made him think of tall cold drinks, white sand, and blue water. "That was a scary story about that car and those kids. Weren't you afraid?"

"Not really. They would never have caught me if they came after me."

"So, how's everything going?" she asked.

"Good. Really good."

"How's your sister?"

"Okay," he replied, wondering if she knew what was happening and, if so, how.

"I heard you got a job," she bubbled like a root beer float. "Working at the gas station down near the Port."

Danny's throat filled with sand. "Yeah, it's pretty cool. I got lucky."

She took his hand and gently squeezed it. "I'm really happy for you. I think it was more than luck."

"I don't know."

"It is."

"I gotta tell you, it's a great job. Best of all, the owner's a nice guy. He's teaching me about business and stuff. I get a commission for every can of oil I sell; fifteen cents a can. I even got a tip for fixing this lady's defroster."

Her cheeks turned pink with pleasure. "Sounds like a great job!"

"Hey! You coming?" Bugsy yelled from the other side of the schoolyard.

"Um. I gotta go," Danny replied, stuffing his hands in his pockets, turning, and walking away.

"Danny," she called, semi-skipping over to him. "Would you like to come to my house for suppah next Sunday? We're having a pot roast. I asked my folks, and they said it'd be all right."

"Really?"

"I told my parents about you, and they said they'd like to meet you."

"Have you ever had a boy over for suppah before?" Danny asked.

"Not since I was in kindergarten. And it was lunch. My old neighbor, Tony LaCivita, and I had fluffernutters. Wait, it could have been PBJs." She laughed when she heard herself.

"What time?"

"Four o'clock."

"How should I dress?"

"Just like you are. It doesn't have to be anything fancy. My father might be dressed up 'cuz it's a Sunday, but you'll be fine. Promise."

"Danny! What the fuck're you doing?" Bugsy yelled from the top of the stairs.

"I, um, gotta go," Danny said, running off.

"I'll see you on Sunday," Patty said, waving. "Make sure you're on time. My father likes everyone to be on time."

"Okay," he replied, waving back at her.

"Hey, I heard you got a job at the Port Gas Station?" Fitzy said when Danny caught up with him and the other kids heading down to the packie.

"Yeah, I started today." He turned to the other kids. "Hey. Do any of you guys know a kid named Larry McMahon?"

"McMahon? A little taller than me? Ugly pizza-face? Lots of acne?" Fitzy replied. "A pockmarked motherfucker?"

"Yeah, that's him."

"I know him. He's a piece of shit. How do you know him?"

"I work with him."

"No shit! What's he do?"

"Pumps gas mostly. Other than that, not much. He's a lazy fuck."

"That don't surprise me. He's a fuckin' thief too," Fitzy said, spitting out a chunky loogie. "He'd steal the fillings out of his grandma's mouth."

"What parish is he from?"

"Saint Matthew's."

Danny suddenly stopped and yelled. "There it is! That's the Chevy I was talking about, the one that was following me!"

"C'mon," Mooch said, running across the street toward the loading platform behind Supreme's. The other kids followed; the car slowed down.

"Anyone recognize anybody?" Bugsy asked.

"Naw, not me," Fitzy said.

"I ain't never seen 'em before," Mooch said.

"Me neither," said Billy.

"If they had any balls, they'd have stopped," Bugsy said.

Mooch grabbed a couple of pallets, leaned them against the loading dock, and kicked them, breaking them into smaller pieces before joining the other kids leaning against the building. Danny stepped onto the sidewalk and looked up and down the street. It was quiet; he walked back to the kids. "So, how much money have we got?" Danny asked, pulling out a pocketful of change. The other kids did the same.

"We got enough for a case and a half," Danny said after collecting everyone's money. "Let's find a buyer."

# 23

After watching Larry fiddle around, not doing much of anything, Mr. Erickson walked over to him. "Can you give me a hand and change the oil in the Chevy?" he said, nodding toward a brown-colored car in the end bay.

"No problem," Larry said. "What about Danny?"

"What about him?"

"Why doesn't he do it?"

"He's busy."

"Doing what?"

"Does it matter?"

Larry looked over at Danny. "Not really."

"Okay. Let's get to it."

While Larry worked on the Chevy, Danny pumped gas, sold a lot of oil, and managed to schedule four tune-ups. The afternoon pace broke when Tommy Sweeney drove in after lunch. "Danny! How's it going?"

"Great, man!" Danny said, wiping his hands with a long red cloth. "Gimme a minute."

He walked over to Mr. Erickson. "Can I take a break for a few minutes?"

"Of course; you've been working very hard," he replied, saying it loud enough for Larry to hear, not that it had any effect.

"What're you up to?" Danny asked Tommy.

"Nothing much. I need some gas."

"How much?"

Tommy counted his change. "A buck thirty-six."

Danny stuck the nozzle in the gas tank. "Hey, can you do me a favor?" Tommy said.

"Sure, what do ya need?"

"I gotta change my oil, and it's wicked cold out. Can I bring my car around later? I have nowhere to do it, and I don't want to lie down in that fucking slush."

"Let me ask my boss. I think he'll be okay with it." After pumping the gas and being paid, Danny went inside and handed the money to Mr. Erickson. "Mr. Erickson, can I ask a favor?"

Looking up from his paperwork, "Sure, what is it?"

"That guy outside's an old friend. He's gotta change his oil, and he asked me if he could do it in one of the bays. He can do it after hours if it's okay. I'd be with him the whole time. He's a good kid. He's got his own job and everything. There's a lot of slush in the gutters, and he'd get wet and cold if he did it out there."

Mr. Erickson got up and looked out through the plate glass window. Tommy saw him and waved. Mr. Erickson waved back and turned to Danny. "Okay, but I don't want a bunch of kids hanging around."

"Thanks! I 'preciate it."

"Don't have him come before six, okay? And remember, just him, no other kids."

"Got it. No problem."

"He said it's okay," Danny said as he jogged back over to Tommy. "We close at six, so come by any time after that," Danny said. "And he doesn't want anyone else coming with you, okay?"

"Yeah, no problem. Thanks, man. I owe you."

"I'll see you later. Bring a couple of beers."

"Sure."

Mr. Erickson left at two thirty. "I doubt I'll be back," he said. "I have a lot to do. You guys should be okay."

As soon as he was gone, Larry came over to Danny. "Hey, can you do me a favor?"

"What kind of favor?"

"I need you to punch me out when you leave. I gotta be someplace."

"You gotta be kidding! Why didn't you tell Mr. Erickson before he left?"

"It's none of his fucking business. C'mon, man, don't be a pussy."

"I'm not a fuckin' pussy. I'm doing most of your fuckin' work as it is. What if Mr. Erickson comes back? What the fuck am I supposed to tell him?"

"Tell him I left. Tell him I had to go home. I don't give a fuck. Tell him whatever you want; make something up."

"Man, you're putting me in a bad spot."

"I wouldn't ask you if it wasn't important."

Danny said nothing in response; he returned to work, and, to his relief, the rest of the day went by quickly. He closed up at six, locked everything up, emptied the cash register, and put the day's receipts in the bottom of Mr. Erickson's desk. He counted the money twice, wrote it down on a piece of paper, and removed an oil-stained canvas bag from the bottom drawer of the desk. He placed the money and the note in the bag and carried it to the storage room. He pulled a can of Quaker State Oil—where the bottom had been removed, from the oil shelf—stuffed the money inside, and pushed the container to the back of the rack.

After washing his hands, Danny returned to the office and turned the radio on to WMEX—he'd had enough of Sinatra, Martin, and Crosby to last a lifetime. After loosening his shoelaces, he put his feet on the desk, leaned back, and closed his eyes. Ten minutes later, Tommy pulled in with Whitey and Paulie, holding cans of Gansett. "Here," Tommy said, tossing one to Danny as soon as he entered the office.

"Thanks," Danny said.

"So, what's going on?" Tommy asked, rubbing his hands together, warming them.

"Nothing much; been busy," Danny said. "How about you kids? What'd you do today?"

"Drove around mostly. We went to Kresge's for a coupla chili dogs. Whitey's got a hard-on for some pig from Eastie, Mary . . . Mary Anne Bonnatelli," Tommy said, spreading his fingers apart and wiggling his tongue between them.

"Yeah, Mary bone-her-and-tell-me," Paulie laughed.

"You guys are fucking assholes. She ain't a fucking whore," Whitey said, defensively.

"I don't know about that. She's from East Boston, and she's gotta swallow, right?" Paulie said.

"Yeah, on the first date," Tommy added, "just like her mother."

"Fuck you," Whitey snorted back.

"C'mon, man, we're only fucking with you," Tommy said. "Don't be so fucking serious."

Danny lifted his beer, toasting fashion. "Let's get your car up on the lift."

"Sounds great!" Tommy said. "I really appreciate it."

"No problem," Danny said. He entered the garage and opened the large, loud overhead door to the first bay. Tommy went outside and pulled the car in while Paulie and Whitey went into the office, turned up the radio, and opened another beer. After Tommy got out, Danny closed the overhead door and pulled the lever for the hydraulic motors that lifted the car. Danny stopped it when it was high enough for Tommy to walk under. "You got an oil wrench?" Tommy asked, studying the oil pan.

"Sure." Danny grabbed the wrench from the clips on the wall and handed it to Tommy. "What the fuck," Danny muttered, turning when he heard something fall. He returned to the office; Whitey had knocked a box full of metal screws over. "C'mon, guys," Danny said. "This is where I work. You ain't even s'posed to be here. If my boss comes in, you're gonna get me fired."

"I didn't do nothing," Paulie said, defending himself. Whitey kneeled down and started putting all the screws in the box.

"Put the box back where you found it, okay?" Danny said. "I gotta check in on Tommy." He spoke louder to get his point across. "Don't touch nothing else, okay? Stay here in the office; it's warm; listen to some music." Danny stepped back into the garage. "How's it going?"

"Good. I finally loosened the motherfucker."

"Let's roll the drain wagon over so we don't get any oil on the floor," Danny said. After everything was in place, Danny spoke again. "Let me know if you need anything else." He turned, picked some tools off the workbench, and started cleaning them.

"I thought you were done working," Tommy said, glancing over.

"I am."

"Then what're you doing?"

"Cleaning."

"Why?"

"The tools are dirty, and they need to be cleaned. I don't mind doing it."

"Why? Ain't you off the clock?"

"Well, yeah, but my boss is a good guy; he let me use the bay so you could change your oil, right?"

"Yeah."

"Well?"

"Well, I think you're kinda stupid."

Whitey stepped into the bay. "You guys want a beer?"

"Sure," Danny said.

"Me too," Tommy said.

"I gotta tell you, man. You're nucking futs. I wouldn't do nothing like that if I wasn't getting paid," Tommy said to Danny.

Danny shrugged. "I don't mind."

Danny pulled the hydraulic lever again. The metal footplates on the lift clattered when the car came to rest, filling the room with the pulsing shudder of air as the compressor rumbled to rest. Tommy removed several oil cans from his trunk, opened the hood, poured them into the oil opening, and then screwed it shut. He waited a couple of minutes before checking the dipstick.

"Looks good," he said.

"Great," Danny responded, placing the clean tools on the wall clips.

"Where do I pour the oil out?" Tommy said.

"I'll take care of it. Why don't you clean up and move your car out?"

"Sure."

Danny lifted the tray, carried it outside, and emptied it into a rusted fifty-five-gallon drum alongside the building. "Where's Whitey and Paulie?" Danny asked when he stepped back into the office.

"I dunno," Tommy responded.

"Whitey! Paulie!" Danny yelled.

"In here," Paulie yelled from the rear of the storeroom.

Danny stormed through the rear door of the office and yelled, "GODDAMN IT! DON'T YOU GUYS LISTEN? YOU GUYS ARE GONNA GET ME FIRED!"

Whitey emerged from behind a tall metal rack filled with tires and a stack of oil-stained boxes. "Relax, man," he said. "We're just looking around. There's a lot of cool shit here."

"Fuck. This ain't Sam and Becky's. If my boss shows up, I'm screwed!"

"Okay, okay. I'm sorry, man," Whitey said. "You don't have to blow a fuse."

"It's my job, Whitey, and it's a good one!"

"Okay, I get it."

"Do you know what all this stuff is for?" Paulie asked, rolling one of the engine parts in his hand.

"ARE YOU FUCKING DEAF? PUT THAT DOWN," Danny screamed, "and get out of here!" He swung the door open and waited for the two kids to leave. As soon as they did, he slammed the door behind them and stormed back into the bay. "Are you done?" he yelled at Tommy.

"Yeah. Just finished up."

"Okay," Danny grumbled. He swung the door open, went outside, lit a smoke, and paced back and forth as he watched the kids through the plate glass window. Two smokes later, he flicked his snipe and walked back into the office. "I'm sorry, guys," he said. "You kids want to see how the hydraulic lift works?"

"Yeah," Whitey said.

"Sure," Paulie mumbled.

Tommy nodded a *yes*.

Danny pulled the lever down as soon as everyone was in the garage. The walls shook as the lift descended. "That's the compressor over there," he said, pointing to a large, grease-covered piece of machinery with black hoses and colored wires sticking out of it. "It's really powerful. This is the safety latch. You gotta always lock it in place. It's the most important part of operating the lift. And that's the pit," Danny said, pointing with his beer hand. "If something leaks or if you spill anything, it goes down there."

"How'd you learn all this shit?" Paulie asked.

"Like I said, my boss is really cool. He's been teaching me all kinds of shit."

"So, do you know how to use the rest of this equipment?" Whitey asked, looking around. "I ain't never seen shit like this before."

"Most of it," Danny replied. "I got a lot of opportunities here. I've learned more from my boss than I have from the teachers in school."

"Man, you're one lucky motherfucker," Tommy replied.

"Yeah, no shit," Paulie said.

"I know, believe me, I know. My boss is really smart; the best part is that he trusts me. That's why I got so pissed when you guys were fucking around in the back."

"Yeah, sorry about that," Paulie said. "I wasn't trying to be an asshole or nothing. I was just curious."

Danny nodded. "Man, you've got the best job of anyone I know," Paulie said.

"You do," Whitey added. "You're a lucky son of a bitch."

Danny got up and grabbed another beer. "Anyone want one?" he asked. Everyone responded with an approving nod or a *yes*.

"We're gonna have to go after this one," Danny said. "It's been a long day. Tommy, can you give me a ride home?"

"Naw, I got someplace to go."

"What?"

"I'm just fucking with you, man. I gotta take these mooks home. I was gonna ask you anyway. I was afraid these two homos would make a move on me."

"Fuck you," Whitey said.

"Yeah. Fuck you. You're the homo," Tommy said.

"Blow me!"

# 24

The weekend melted like a stick of butter in August. Danny stayed home, bored, watching *Bowling for Dollars, Dialing for Dollars,* and other insipid shows while his mother cooked—meatloaf, soup, and sloppy joes, filling the refrigerator with a week's worth of food. Frankie lay around, burping and farting. Chrissy spent most of her time in her bedroom. If anyone asked, Bridie would say, "She's not feeling well—she needs some rest; leave her alone." Every time Chrissy's name came up, all Danny thought about was Henschel's Corvette sinking below the murky waters of Houghton's Pond; he remembered the rancid smell of the burning engine and the oil that floated on the surface of the pond.

Danny finally came to life when he popped his head into the kitchen. "I'm gonna shower," he said, "is that okay?"

"A shower?" Bridie replied. "It's three-fifteen on a Sunday. How in the world did you get dirty? You haven't done anything."

"I ain't dirty, Ma," he replied. "I'm going to Patty's house for suppah. They're having roast beef."

"Where does she live?"

"On Melville Ave, near Washington Street."

"Does she have any brothers or sisters?"

"Yeah." She nodded. "Hey, Ma, I don't want to be rude or nothing, but I gotta get ready. I don't want to be late."

"Are you supposed to bring anything?"

"No, her ma made everything."

"What are you wearing?" she asked, stirring a simmering pot.

"I dunno. I'll find something."

Danny went into the bathroom and looked in the mirror. He leaned forward, popped a couple of pimples, and fingered a few stubborn blackheads. After showering, he spread a small glob of Vaseline in his hair and combed it back, tapping everything into place. His mother had laid out a freshly ironed blue shirt and a pair of *good* pants across his bed. He dressed and strolled into the kitchen. As soon as his mother saw him, she lifted her hands. "My, you look smart," she said.

"Thanks, and thanks for ironing my clothes."

"I was glad to do it."

"I gotta get going."

"Hold on a sec," Bridie replied. She stepped out of the room and returned with three one-dollar bills. "Here, honey, it's not right to go empty-handed. You should bring dessert with you."

"I got money, Ma."

"I know. But it's something I want to do."

"Are you sure?"

She pressed the money into the palm of his hand. "I'm sure."

"Thanks, Ma," he responded, stuffing the money into his pocket.

"Have a good time." She gave him a quick peck on his cheek.

"I will," he said, turning to go.

"Oh, honey, there's one more thing."

"I really gotta go, Ma. Can it wait?"

"It'll only take a minute, honey. Come with me."

Danny harrumphed, but not loud enough for her to notice. He followed her into her bedroom, where she removed a bottle of cologne from the top of her dresser. "Here, honey, let me put some of this on you. It was your father's favorite."

He closed his eyes as she placed a couple of dabs behind his ears. When she was done, he opened his eyes. Tears trickled down her cheeks, filling the thin lines that had widened over the last year. She tried to speak but couldn't. He held her a moment longer, letting her go when she moved from him and sat down on her bed, clutching the perfume tightly against her chest.

"Go on," she said, wiping her eyes. "You don't want to be late."

"I love you, Ma," he said.

"I love you, honey."

A frigid blast of air filled his lungs as soon as he stepped outside. He stuffed his hands in his pocket and hopped around the patches of ice that had formed on the sidewalk, stopping when he reached Shur's Corner Store. There, he peered through the plate glass windows, scanning the upper racks for the latest comics and the lower shelves for the dirty magazines. After a few more minutes of ogling, he lit a cigarette and walked past Mother's Rest to the corner store at Aspinwall Street. He went in and strolled through the narrow aisles, stopping at the dessert section, where he picked up four packs of Hostess Cupcakes. He paid for them, and the clerk placed the plump mounds of sugar-coated sweets in a small brown bag and rolled the top over to close it. Danny stepped outside, darted across the street, and turned at Melville Avenue, where, unlike in his neighborhood, the sidewalks were shoveled, and the snow was neatly stacked like pillows on sale at Filene's Basement. He followed the addresses painted on artful plaques, stopping when he reached Patty's house. After combing his hair, he walked up the front steps and looked at his reflection in the thick leaded window that filled the front door. After smoothing his hair again, he pressed the doorbell and heard Patty yell, "I'll get it!"

The door swung open, taking Danny's breath away with it. Patty smiled at him, looking gorgeous in a blue wool dress, long white stockings, and black patent leather shoes. Her hair was tied in a bun tethered with thin red ribbons that flowed over the collar of her dress. She looked like a Christmas ornament. "You're right on time," she giggled as she let him in.

"Mom, this is Danny," she said, beaming as they bounced into the kitchen. Patty's mom looked just like her. Her hair was done up in a low beehive, and her cheeks were dusted with a light layer of rouge. She wore a festive red dress under a red-and-white checkered apron.

"Hi, Danny. It's a pleasure to meet you," she said, extending her hand after patting both hands on a kitchen towel. "I've heard a lot about you."

"You have?" he replied, blushing.

"Oh, it was all good."

"That's a relief," he joked. "I'm pleased to meet you, ma'am. I got these for dessert," he said proudly, holding up the rumpled bag. "It's cupcakes—Hostess Cupcakes!" he said just as a crystalline dome covering the largest chocolate cake he'd ever seen caught his eye at the other end of the counter.

"Oh!" she replied. "That was sweet of you. Honey, can you put those over there on the counter?" she asked Patty. "These are wonderful. The boys will love them. You know, they're Mr. McNulty's favorites." Danny smiled and looked at the package of cupcakes, dwarfed by the massive chocolate cake that dominated the kitchen counter.

"I hope you're hungry," Patty's mother said.

"I sure am," Danny replied, glancing at Patty.

"I'm going to introduce him to Daddy and the rest of the family," Patty said as she playfully pulled him into the parlor.

"Daddy," she said as they entered the double glass doors. Her father looked up from his magazine. The first thing Danny noticed was his hair—neat and closely cropped, trimmed at the edges—and his shirt, an expensive one with white buttons on the collar, held in place with a bright red tie.

"It's a pleasure to meet you," Mr. McNulty said, standing up and greeting him, something that had never happened before; no one had ever stood up to greet him when they met.

"Same, sir," Danny said, extending his hand.

"These are my brothers, Petey and Tommy," Patty said, nodding to her blond, blue-eyed, freckled siblings. "They're Irish twins."

"I kinda figured."

"And these are my sisters, Peggy and Jeannie." The girls put down the Sunday comics and came over, studying Danny from every angle. They looked to be around nine and eleven. Both were neatly dressed in matching blouses and checkered dresses, a mix of blue and white. Their hair was done up in a bundle of curls that looked like they had an interview with the heirs of Shirley Temple.

"Hi, glad to meet you guys," Danny said.

"Where do you live?" Peggy asked.

"Don't be so nosy," Patty gently scolded her.

"That's okay," Danny said. "I live near Four Corners. Do you know where that is?"

"I do!" Jeannie answered, bouncing up and down. "It's near the zoo, right?"

"No, it's not that far away. It's kinda in the middle," Danny replied, laughing.

"Okay, you two, quit pestering Danny," Patty said. The girls frowned in reply.

"Everyone ready for suppah?" Patty's mother called out from the kitchen. The boys answered by scrambling to their feet and running into the dining room, bouncing off Danny's legs as they flew by.

Mr. McNulty smiled and extended his arm to his side, inviting Danny. "Please," he said, guiding him into the dining room. "Have a seat."

"Why don't you sit down here?" Patty said, patting the back of a tall, upright chair at the end of the table. The girls followed, giggling like a gaggle of geese.

"Thanks," Danny said. He sat down and placed his hands on his lap while everyone else took their seats. Patty's father sat at the far end of the table, closest to the parlor. The younger children sat down, a chorus of hungry children, leaving the other end of the table, nearest the kitchen, open for Patty's mother. Patty sat alongside Danny, picked up her meticulously ironed napkin, replete with doily edging, and spread it across her lap. Danny picked his up and laid it across his lap as she did.

"Can I help with anything, Mom?" Patty inquired.

"Would you mind filling the milk pitcher?"

"Sure," Patty said, getting up and walking to the refrigerator to remove a tall bottle of cold milk. "Excuse me," she said, reaching in front of her brothers to set the perspiring pitcher on the table. Danny readjusted his napkin and realized he was still wearing his windbreaker. He carefully slipped it off and draped it over the back of his chair.

"You can call me Mike," Mr. McNulty said, noticing the threadbare jacket.

"Thanks. My real name's Daniel, but you can call me Danny. All my friends do."

"Well, then, Danny it is."

"Everyone ready for some salad?" Mrs. McNulty called out. A serenade of yeses filled the air like a band of butterflies.

"I don't want any onions," Petey said, scrunching his face until it looked like a baked potato that had been in the oven too long. "They make me sick."

"Can I have extra tomatoes?" Tommy asked.

"Onions are good for you," Mrs. McNulty replied.

"I don't like them," Petey whined.

"You will someday," Mrs. McNulty said.

"No, I won't," Petey replied, in protest, scrunching his face again.

Danny's stomach rumbled when Mrs. McNulty placed a large, colored bowl filled with fresh lettuce, chopped tomatoes, and thin slices of onion in the middle of the table. The bowl matched the smaller ones, neatly laid out around the table, making him think about the battered cabinet in his kitchen, filled with chipped bowls, dishes of varying sizes and colors, plastic Flintstone cups, and an assortment of Welch's Jelly glasses.

Everyone passed their bowls to Patty, and she filled each with an appropriate share of fixings, removing onions from one plate and adding tomatoes to another, adjusting as she went along. Danny handed his bowl to Patty. She arranged the serving, placing the tomato slices along the edge and scattering sliced onions on the lettuce. "How much do you want, Mom?" she asked her mother, busy filling another bowl with mashed potatoes.

"Half a bowl, please."

After filling her mother's bowl, Patty placed it between her mother's silverware alongside several bottles of fancy-looking salad dressings with names Danny didn't recognize. He stuck his fork in a plump tomato slice and took a bite, making the girls giggle. As soon as he looked around, he realized he was the only one eating. Embarrassed, he put his fork down and placed his hands on his lap. Mr. McNulty folded his hands and bowed his head. "Bless us, Oh Lord, and these thy gifts, which we are about to receive, from thy bounty, through Christ, Our Lord. Amen."

"Amen," said Mrs. McNulty, choired by the rest of the family.

"Amen," Danny said, trying to remember the last time his family had sat down and prayed over a meal. The dressings were passed around and poured, and the silver forks, all matching, came out. Steaming rolls covered with melting slabs of butter followed. While the bowls were passed and filled, Mr. McNulty carved the roast beef into thin slices while Mrs. McNulty added thick slabs of butter to the mashed potatoes. The younger kids started eating, too busy to yammer or quarrel with each other.

"So, how's school?" Mr. McNulty asked Patty.

"Fine, Daddy. I have two more reports to do in English and one more in my history class," Patty replied, somehow making school sound fun. "And how about you two?" he asked the girls.

"Good! Great!" they said in unison, giggling, glancing again at Danny. They continued talking, in circles it seemed, crisscrossing their conversations about favorite classes, favorite teachers, best friends, yucky boys, and school vacations. When the girls finally petered out, Mrs. McNulty tried to coax a conversation out of the boys, an impossibility; they were eating.

"And how about you, Danny?" Mr. McNulty asked. "Where do you go to school?"

"Dot High. Umm, I mean Dorchester High."

"Excuse me." Mr. McNulty said, turning to the boys. "Use your fork and chew your food. "I'm sorry," he said, apologizing to Danny. "Do you have any special interests?"

"Naw, not really. I'm taking all the regular classes so I can graduate. I'm not studying anything special."

"I see. Are there any classes you like?"

"I don't know, math, maybe. I like my math teacher, Mr. Valenti. He's smart and a really good teacher. And I like my English teacher, Mr. Rockwell."

"What about your other classes?"

"To tell you the truth, I don't like history too much. My teacher Mr. Mellon's a real jerk. I don't know anyone who likes him. Who cares about the pilgrims and all those Indian wars and the Constitution of Independence?"

"You mean the Declaration of Independence?" Mr. McNulty politely corrected him.

"Yeah, that's what I meant. The Declaration of Independence," Danny said, glancing over to Patty.

"You know, son," Mr. McNulty said, speaking in a tone that always made his family pause and listen. "All of the laws of our society and the rules that govern everything we do are based upon the Constitution of the United States. Our history is important, and it's certainly worth studying."

Patty spoke up, much to Danny's relief, tossing him a lifesaver. "He knows about all that stuff, Daddy. Danny's one of the smartest boys I know."

Mrs. McNulty artfully piped in before Mr. McNulty asked another question. "Do you play any sports?" she asked, stopping suddenly to speak to her sons. "Use your forks," she said to the boys. "And chew your food. This isn't a race."

"A little baseball and some football. Pick-up games, mostly. I play some street hockey. I'm a big Red Sox fan," Danny replied, lifting his voice a notch.

"Who's your favorite player?" Mr. McNulty asked in an enthusiastic voice that took ten years off his age.

"Tony Conigliaro, hands down. Man, I hope he makes it back. And Yaz is fu—" He stopped and swallowed his words as fast as he could. "Um, I mean," stuttering, "Yaz is incredible. Can you imagine if Tony C. was in the lineup in the series? We'd have beaten the Cardinals to a pulp."

"So, how do you think they'll do next year?" Mr. McNulty asked, switching the conversation to his wife for a moment. "Honey, would you mind making a cup of tea? Would you like one?" he asked Danny, who was amazed at the volley the conversations went through, changing every couple of minutes to keep the kids focused.

"No, thank you. I'm okay. If Boomer can stay healthy, we should be all right at the corners. I think Reggie Smith's gonna do a good job at center. Joe Lahoud's okay in right; he ain't no Tony C., of course. I don't know about Lonborg." Danny took a deep breath and a matching sip of milk. "It's gonna be a tough season with all our injuries."

"And what about the Cardinals? How do you think they'll do next year?" The kids were quiet; they'd never heard their father talk about baseball like this before, not with so much enthusiasm.

"I hate to say it, but I think they're gonna do it again. I mean, how do you stop Bob Gibson? And what about Lou Brock? He hits everything that comes near the plate. And you know, the American League is full of hitters, while the National League's all about pitching. Plus, you got McCarver behind the plate. God, they're a great team; tough to beat." Patty's little sisters were quiet, goggle-eyed, listening to Danny and their father talk about baseball.

"Would you like some more?" Patty said, gently interrupting the conversation.

"Sure," Danny said, looking around. "I mean, if there's enough."

"There's plenty," Patty's mother said, getting up and gathering some dishes. "Honey, do you want seconds?" she asked Mr. McNulty.

"I'm stuffed. Maybe later."

Patty followed her mother into the kitchen, returning with Danny's plate, covered with several slices of meat, a small mountain of mashed potatoes covered in thick brown gravy, and a fat-buttered roll.

"So, Danny, what parish are you from?" Mr. McNulty asked.

"Saint Peter's."

"What's your father do?"

Danny fidgeted with his fork. "I . . . I don't know." He spoke in a quiet voice. "My father left us when I was little; me and my ma and my big sister Chrissy and my little brother, Frankie."

"I'm sorry," Mr. McNulty responded, glancing over at his wife. She smiled, saying a million things without speaking a word.

Danny shrugged. "It's no big deal."

"I'm ready for dessert!" Petey shouted, holding his plate up.

"Me too!" Tommy screeched. "Me too!"

"Settle down, boys, settle down," Mrs. McNulty said. "How about you girls?" she asked while already knowing the answer. "Mike?"

"Yes, a small piece, please, and a little more water for my tea, if you don't mind."

Danny, eating alone, hurried his way through his plate. When he was done, Patty picked it up, and a minute later, her mother came out of the kitchen with a large dish loaded with the Hostess Cupcakes, all neatly arranged, like they were filming a television commercial.

"Cupcakes!" the boys yelled, bouncing up and down like a pair of beach balls. Their mother placed the goodies in the middle of the table. The boys nearly knocked over their glasses, overreaching for the sweets. Mr. McNulty sighed in response to his wife's look. She returned to the kitchen with another dish covered with several slices of chocolate cake. Patty placed one on her father's dessert dish along with one of the cupcakes. She put a thick piece of cake on Danny's plate.

The boys continued chattering, reminding Danny of the Disney chipmunks. Patty's mother gave all the little kids half a cupcake. When they were done, they smiled chocolatey grins. She stopped them as soon as they started to get up. "All of you, straight to the bathroom, brush your teeth, and wash your hands."

"Aw, Ma, do I have to?" Petey asked, speaking for all of them.

"Listen to your mother," Patty's father said, ending the conversation.

Patty gathered the dishes and went into the kitchen. "Excuse me," Danny said, getting up and following her. "Where's your dish towel?"

"Oh, don't worry. I'll take care of it. Why don't you relax?"

"I'd rather help you. Besides, if I can help you, we can sit down sooner, and I get to spend more time with you."

Patty blushed to the point of embarrassment. "Okay. Over there, in the top drawer."

He grabbed the cottony towel, came back, and stood alongside her. "You're so lucky," he said.

"What do you mean?" she replied, turning the water on and running her hands beneath the faucet, adjusting it until it was the right temperature.

"I mean, you have the most incredible family. Your dad is so cool and smart. And your mom, she's beautiful and really friendly, and man, can she cook. That's the best suppah I ever had."

"Really?"

"Yeah, I'm serious."

"And I like your little brothers and sisters. I can't believe they get along so well."

"They don't always. They're on their best behavior because we have company."

"You mean me?

"Who did you think I was talking about?"

"Gee, I don't know." Danny shook his head as if in disbelief. "Your folks make me feel special."

"You are special."

"Me? No, I'm not."

"You're so silly. My father really likes you." She smiled, filled the sink with soapy water, and began washing the dishes.

"You think so?"

"Did you see how he lit up when you started talking about the Red Sox? I didn't know you knew so much about baseball."

"Me? I love baseball. I gotta tell you, your dad knows a bunch too."

"It was nice hearing him talk about all that stuff. He sounded like a kid."

"Wait until your brothers get older."

"They're already growing up too fast."

"Did you see the way they listened to him?" Danny asked.

"Yeah, it's sweet, isn't it?"

"It sure is."

Patty hummed while she passed the dishes to Danny. He watched her while he dried them and placed them in the dish rack. "What's your family like?" she asked, handing him the salad bowl.

"I got a little brother, Frankie. He goes to the Marshall. And I got a big sister, Chrissy. She wants to be a nurse."

"What about your mom?"

"She's nice; she's my mom."

"Does she work?"

"Yeah, downtown."

"What about your father? What do you remember about him?"

"Not much. He wasn't around a lot. When he was, he and my mom fought a lot. There was lots of screaming."

"I'm sorry."

"Thanks, but there's nothing to be sorry about. It is what it is."

Patty glanced at the clock hovering above the sink. "Let's finish up so we can watch some TV."

"Sounds great! What do you guys like to watch?"

"*Lassie* and *Voyage to the Bottom of the Sea*. The girls like *Lassie*, and the boys like to watch *Voyage to the Bottom of the Sea*. What do you like to watch?"

"Me? *Voyage to the Bottom of the Sea*. What do your folks like to watch?"

"They don't really care. They're okay if my brothers and sisters don't fight. My dad mostly likes to read, and Mom likes to knit."

"What do you like?" Danny asked.

She lifted her shoulders. "I don't care, except around the holidays, when they have all the special shows on, like *The Wizard of Oz* or *Peter Pan*."

"And *It's a Wonderful Life*."

The television crackled from the other room. "Let's finish up," she said. "It sounds like they're watching *Voyage to the Bottom of the Sea*."

"Sounds good."

# 25

Danny got up early to try a few jujitsu kicks he'd learned about in a book he'd bought from an ad in a Superman comic. It was an official book from New York, taught by Master Wang, a martial arts expert. Wang had written a special section about fighting two assailants at the same time. Danny went over those parts every time he picked up the book, practicing those moves repeatedly. When he was done, he put on an extra pair of pants and bundled up with two shirts and the woolen scarf his grandmother had given him. Mummified, he walked up to Four Corners and waited for the bus, crunching his toes to keep them warm. He turned his back to the wind, pulled out a cigarette, and fought to light it. He turned at the sound of a car horn; a green Buick, sounding like a jukebox on wheels, pulled up to the curb. Robby McElliott rolled the window down. "Hey! Danny! Need a ride?"

"Robby?"

"Yeah!"

"Get in," Robby said, pushing the door open and lowering the radio's volume. Danny flicked his snipe into the street, slid into the front seat, and extended his feet to the heater.

"Man, it's cold out," Danny said, closing the door, rubbing his hands together, and extending them in front of the heater vent.

"No shit," Robby said. "So, what've you been up to?"

"I got a job," Danny said.

"No shit? Where?"

"The Port Gas station, down on Neponset."

"I know the place. How'd you get that job?"

"It's a long story. I helped the owner's wife when she broke down. She had a flat."

"So, what do you do?"

"Mostly pump gas, change tires, oil, and things like that. I'm learning how to do tune-ups, change the spark plugs, and drain radiators."

"I didn't know you knew how to do all that stuff."

"I've been learning. Stanley, who owns the Texaco at Four Corners, lets me hang around and shows me stuff. Sometimes he lets me work on things."

"You don't own a car or nothing, do you?"

"No, I've just been around them a lot."

"That's good shit, man."

"Yeah, I figure I'm kinda lucky. Plus, my boss is really cool. He has the biggest collection of Chilton books I've ever seen."

"That's great; I hate my fucking job."

"Where do you work? I forget."

"I stock shelves at Bradlees. It's boring as fuck."

"I thought you were a mechanic?"

"Sort of, I guess. I keep this thing running," Robby said, tapping the dashboard. "Last summer, I rebuilt the engine. I removed the whole block, rebuilt the cylinders, re-sleeved them, and put in new gaskets."

"That's pretty complicated shit. My boss has been talking about getting someone to work on the weekend, tune-ups, and stuff like that. You interested?"

"Are you shitting me?"

"No, I'm serious. I can't promise nothing, but I'll ask."

"Man, that'd be fucking incredible!"

Robby pulled up to the school parking lot, filled with cars and soot-covered snowbanks. After driving around, he found a spot next to one of the corner snowbanks. "Are you working today?" Robby asked, turning to Danny.

"Yeah," Danny replied.

"How 'bout I drive you to work? If your boss is in, maybe I can meet him and ask about the job? What do you think?"

"That's a great idea. How 'bout I meet you here after school?"

"Sounds like a plan."

It was a long day. Danny struggled to stay awake through his last class, English. As soon as the bell rang, he sprinted down the corridor and outside, inhaling a breath of painfully cold air that felt like he was swallowing a pack of razor blades. Robby saw him and waved him over.

"You want a smoke?" Danny asked.

"Yeah. Thanks. So, how are your classes going?" Robby asked, turning the engine over and throttling the car to life.

"Not bad. You?"

"Same."

"Have you thought about what you're gonna do when you graduate?"

"No, not really. I ain't going to college, I know that. If I don't have a good job, I'm gonna join the army."

"I was thinking about doing the same; it depends on the draft board."

"The draft board? Do you have some medical issues?"

"Yeah, I got a big dick."

"You're a fucking asshole."

"Takes one to know one."

"Fuck you."

They bantered all the way to the gas station, continuing until Robby tapped Danny's leg. "What's going on?" A squad car was parked in front.

"Slow down," Danny said, gripping the dashboard and leaning forward. Mr. Erickson was in his office talking to a tall, dark-haired cop scribbling on a leather-bound notepad.

"What the fuck's going on?" Robby asked. "Do you know that cop?"

"No, I ain't seen him before." Danny slammed the dashboard. "Pull over?"

"Sure."

Danny got out, flicked his cigarette onto the sidewalk, and walked to the office. When he stepped inside, Mr. Erickson and the stone-faced cop stopped talking and stared at him.

"This him?" the cop asked.

"Yes," Mr. Erickson replied stiffly, staring at Danny.

"Is everything all right?" Danny wheezed through a dry throat.

"No! I was robbed this weekend," Mr. Erickson said, standing up from his seat.

"What? When? How did it happen?" Danny asked, nervously sticking his hands in his pockets. "Is . . . is there anything I can do?" he rasped.

"What time were you here until on Saturday night?" Mr. Erickson asked, seating himself on the edge of the desk.

"I don't know. Nine, nine thirty, maybe." Danny glanced over to the policeman. "Why?"

Mr. Erickson picked up the trash bucket full of empty beer cans and placed it on his desk. "Who was here with you?" he asked.

"A couple of friends," Danny replied, shoving his hands deeper into his pockets.

"Who?"

"Some friends."

"I'm gonna need their names and addresses."

"Why? They didn't do nothing."

"I need the names, and I need them now."

"Okay." Danny looked over at the cop, scribbling away in his notebook. He tore a page out and handed it and a pencil to Danny. Danny sat down and wrote everyone's information down as best he could remember, glancing up every few minutes to look at the cop and Mr. Erickson, who said nothing to Danny or each other. He handed it to Mr. Erickson, who scanned it and then gave it to the police officer.

"They're all from Saint Peter's or Saint Ambrose," Danny told the officer.

"I have all I need. I'll be in touch," the officer said to Mr. Erickson.

"Thanks again," Mr. Erickson replied.

The officer left. Danny wiped his hands on his pants and cleared his throat. "I don't know anything about the robbery. I really don't."

"I think you ought to go home," Mr. Erickson said, returning to his seat where he shuffled papers on his desk.

"But . . . but Mr. Erickson. I didn't rob you, and my friends didn't."

Mr. Erickson got up, walked over to the plate glass window, and stared out the window. "The kids were just looking around, but they didn't take anything. They're good kids. They wouldn't steal anything, I swear," Danny said apprehensively, taking a few steps closer.

Mr. Erickson turned. "Son, you were the only one who knew where I kept the money. How do you explain that?"

"I don't know. I . . . I can't." Danny wiped his hands again. "I wouldn't steal from you. I wouldn't. I'm not a thief, and my friends, they aren't either."

"I'd like to believe you, Danny, but the facts are the facts. You and your friends were the last ones here. Right?" Danny said nothing and suddenly felt sick; he wanted to vomit. "I'm very disappointed in you. My wife and I thought you were different. She's going to be very disappointed, too, with good reason."

Danny started breathing hard. "It wasn't me. I swear on my mother's grave. It wasn't. I would never steal from you." His voice cracked like a broken vase. "Never."

Mr. Erickson picked up the trash barrel and shook it, rattling the cans around. "What's all this? Did you watch those kids the whole time?" He waited for Danny to say something, but he remained silent, fighting the urge to puke. "Did you?" He repeated, "DID YOU?"

"No, I didn't watch them the whole time; I couldn't; I was busy. I'll talk to them. If one of them stole the money, I'll get it back. I promise on my mother's grave, I will."

"Do what you want. I've filed a complaint with the police, and they've opened an investigation. The truth will come out. It always does." Danny started to speak, but Mr. Erickson cut him off. "We're done. Get your stuff and leave."

"But," Danny started, stopping when Mr. Erickson waved him off.

"What was that all about?" Robby asked when Danny got back in the car.

"Someone robbed the place over the weekend. Mr. Erickson, my boss, blames me."

"Aw, man, I'm sorry," Robby said.

"I got shit-canned."

"Aw, man. That's not good."

"No kidding." Danny stared out the window, looking for something that wasn't there. "C'mon. Let's get outta here! Can you drop me off at Four Corners?"

"Yeah, sure, of course."

"I'm sorry things didn't work out," Danny said when Robby pulled over.

"That's okay. It wasn't your fault."

"Yeah, I know. Still . . ."

"If I can help or anything, let me know."

"I will, thanks," Danny sullenly replied.

Danny exited the car, crossed the street, and entered Harmon's. The soda jerk—a studious-looking kid with hollowed cheeks, blackheads, a whiffle cut, and small-rimmed glasses—looked up from his math book. "What can I get you?" he asked.

"Do you have any hot chocolate?"

"Small or large?"

"Large."

"Marshmallows?"

"Yup."

Danny grabbed his drink, shuffled to the corner stool, sat down, and looked out the window thick with condensation. A smoke-spewing bus unloaded a small crowd of worn, tired men and ragged, weary women. Most of the men headed across the street to Scanlon's for dinner—hard-boiled eggs, pig's feet, a baked potato, and for those with bigger pockets, a stale roast beef sandwich soaked in mustard.

The women, wearing scarves or pocket bonnets, trudged down the street to freezing apartments two flights up, where they would turn the heat on, hoping the place would warm up by the time their husbands got home. There, they would drag a frozen piece of meat out of the refrigerator and pour a cup of instant potatoes into a chipped ceramic bowl, ready for whenever their husband came home.

Danny's drink warmed his belly, making him think about the burglary. *Could the kids have done it?* He'd kept his eyes on them as best he could. They would have had to move a lot of things around and make a lot of noise. *How would they know where the money was?*

Another bus pulled up and dumped another load of people out. Danny watched them drag themselves along the sidewalk. By the time he finished his drink, four more buses had unloaded their passengers. He glanced at the clock, carried the empty cup and saucer to the counter, thanked the kid, stepped outside, lit a cigarette, and walked toward Mother's Rest. The place was loud. A rowdy bunch of kids, screaming like banshees, were running around with sleds, toboggans, and large cardboard sheets. Danny sat down at the far end of the park, where two little black kids were towing an old rusty sled through the still-fresh, white snow. Small clouds of steam sputtered above their heads as they chatted.

One of the bigger kids jumped onto his cardboard sheet and aimed straight for the black kids. They looked up just before they were hit and tossed high into the air, screaming as they bounced down the hill. The kid on the cardboard coasted to a stop and rolled over, laughing. His friends hooted along with him. "Stupid fuckin' niggers," one of the kids yelled, laughing like he was at the circus.

The little girl, crying and bleeding from her head, slipped while getting up. The kids pelted her with a stream of snowballs, making her scream louder. Danny got up and ran down the hill toward her. The rain of snowballs stopped when Danny neared the kids. When the girl saw him coming, she put her hands over her head to protect herself. The little boy fell several times, trying to get to her. As soon as he reached Danny, he raised his arms to fight.

"Hey, hey, be cool," Danny said, waving his arms like he was fanning a fire. "I'm not gonna hurt you." The boy stared at him and then over to his sister before slowly lowering his arms. "You can trust me," Danny said. The boy wiped his nose, leaving a wet streak on his sleeve. "Come on, let's get your sled," Danny said. "You don't want anyone to steal it, do ya?" The little girl ran her hand over the splotch of blood that had started to freeze her hair. "No," she said.

"Okay then."

Danny grabbed the clothesline tied to the rusted tow rail. The little girl came around behind him to peer at the kids from behind his legs. He passed the cord to her; she sniffled and wiped her face.

"Let's go," the boy said, grabbing the rope from her.

They trudged up the hill, nervously looking at the kids above. "It's okay," Danny said. "I won't let them hurt you." He escorted the kids across the street. After they were out of sight, Danny crossed over, sat on one of the benches, and lit a smoke. The kids laughed and glared back at him. He shook his head, finished his cigarette, hiked down the hill, and hopped over a low chain-link fence onto the sidewalk. A snowball whistled over his head. He looked back, too tired to figure out who'd thrown it.

Danny passed rows of three-deckers where television screens flickered behind thinly frosted windows. Occasionally, he could see the silhouette of someone walking by the windows. After passing Stan's gas station, he crossed the street and hopped up the frost-covered steps leading to his apartment building. As soon as he opened the door, he smelled his mother's beef stew. He double-stepped the stairs, swung the apartment door open, and headed straight to the kitchen, where his mother was ladling dinner for Frankie, who was sitting in front of a bowl covered with four spongy pieces of Wonder Bread smothered in oozing slabs of butter.

"Hey, Frankie, what's up?" Danny said, grabbing one of his pieces of bread.

"Ma! Danny took my bread!"

"There's plenty for both of you," Bridie said, not bothering to look up from the stove.

"Are you staying out of trouble?" Danny asked his brother.

Frankie encircled his hands around his dish and continued eating as if it was his last meal. "I was sledding at the Rest," he mumbled through a mouthful of food. "Me and a coupla friends."

"I just seen a bunch of kids up there."

"It was a lot of fun," Frankie said, swallowing half a piece of bread.

Bridie spooned a ladleful of stew onto Danny's plate. He scooped it up with a slice of bread and stuffed it in his mouth. "What's up with you?" Danny mumbled through a full mouth, speaking to Chrissy, who was sitting at the end of the table, staring out the window.

"Robert's picking me up at seven thirty. We're going shopping at the Lexington Mall," she said, drawing the word *Lexington* out as if it were accompanied by a symphony.

"I gotta go to the bathroom," Danny said, squeezing out a small fart, nearly giving himself a hernia.

"Asshole," Chrissy muttered.

"Did you get out of work early?" Bridie asked when Danny returned.

"Yeah."

"Now that the holidays are over, work has slowed down. I wanted to get home early so I could do some cooking," Bridie said.

"That'd be great," Danny said. He turned to Chrissy. "So, how's Robby doing?"

"It's *Robert*. His name's *Robert*, not Robby. *Robert*."

Danny shrugged. "Okay, so how's he doing?"

"Fine," she said, slicing her answer off.

"I haven't seen him around in a while. Do Jews do anything special for New Year's Day?" Danny asked.

"No," she said, speaking in a tone reserved for funerals.

"Huh," Danny said, resuming his meal.

"Actually, he had an accident," Chrissy said.

"An accident? What happened?"

"One of his tires blew out."

"Mother of Jesus! Was he hurt?" Bridie asked, turning from the stove.

"He's okay. He was lucky. He went off the road and ended up in Houghton's Pond."

"Mother Mary."

"He broke his nose and banged his legs up, but otherwise, he's okay," Chrissy said.

"Mother of Jesus. Why didn't you say something?"

"I just did."

Bridie shook her head and harumphed.

"That's terrible. How's his car?" Danny asked.

"It's totaled," Chrissy said.

"He musta been going really fast to end up in the pond," Danny said.

"*He was*," she said coldly.

"Ma, can I have some more stew?" Frankie said, interrupting the conversation.

"Here, give me your bowl."

Danny passed his bowl to her. "Can I have some more?"

"Of course. Chrissy?"

She got up. "I'm gonna lie down," she said.

"G'night," Bridie said.

"G' night," Chrissy said.

# 26

As soon as Danny got to school, he asked for Whitey, Tommy, and Paulie. The more he searched, the madder he got. He ran into Bugsy in the cafeteria, where he was eyeing half a dozen chatty cheerleaders. "What's up?" Bugsy asked when he spotted Danny coming toward him. "Is everything okay?"

"No! I'm fucking pissed!"

"About what?"

"My work got robbed. I think a couple of the kids did it."

"What kids? Who?"

"Paulie, or Whitey. I don't know; it coulda been Tommy."

"Tommy? Tommy Sweeney? No fucking way, not Tommy." Bugsy nodded toward the right. "Look at the ass on that blonde."

Danny glanced at the girls. "I let Tommy come by my work on Saturday night to change his oil. Paulie and Whitey were with him. I told them to stay in the office and not to fuck around with anything. Every time I looked around, they were in the backroom, going through shit. That's where we keep the money. We put it inside an old oil can. Those fuckers must have found the can."

"That doesn't sound like something they'd do. Besides, how would they know the money was in a can? You didn't say nothing to them, right?"

"Of course not. It don't make sense."

"How can you be sure it was them? I mean, ain't there some other people that work there?"

"Not over the weekend. We were the only ones there?"

"You know those kids; they wouldn't do nothing like that. They might be stupid, but they ain't that stupid."

"Fuck! That's it!" Danny yelled. "FUCK!" He screamed so loud, that the cheerleaders stopped talking. "THAT MOTHERFUCKER SET ME UP!"

The girls gathered their things and walked over to another table.

"That cocksucker knew where the money was!"

"Who? What the fuck are you talking about?"

"Larry McMahon! He's the only one besides me and Mr. Erickson who knew where the money was."

"McMahon? From Codman Square?"

"Yeah."

"That kid's a piece of shit. I wouldn't trust that motherfucker as far as I could throw him."

"Fuck, everything's starting to make sense now. What're you doing tonight?"

"I was gonna fuck one of them cheerleaders," Bugsy said, "but you messed that up."

"No, seriously."

"Nothing," he said, shrugging. "What's up?"

"I gotta find that asshole. I'm gonna see if I can find Robby, see if he can drive us."

"Robby from Bowdoin?"

"Yeah."

"What's he got to do with this shit?"

"I ran into him, and he gave me a ride to school. We talked about my work, and he told me he was looking for a job. So, I brought him down to meet my boss, and when we got there, all hell broke loose. I'm gonna see if he can give us a ride."

"I get it."

"You know any of the kids from his Corner?"

"Naw, no one I can think of," Danny said.

"You can't go down there and accuse him of this kind of shit. Not on his Corner."

"Fuck him."

"You think you can take him?"

"I don't know. It doesn't matter. I can't let him get away with this shit."

"I'll talk to my brother Matty. If you and that douchebag gotta duke it out, I'll make sure it's a fair fight. He knows kids from that Corner."

"That's cool," Danny said. "I'm gonna kick his skinny fuckin' ass."

"Hey, you don't need to convince me."

"How 'bout I meet you at the Marshall tonight?"

"Sure. What time?"

"Eight."

"Sounds good."

After Bugsy left, Danny continued looking for Robby, poking his head in different rooms, ending up in the corner bathroom, where he lit a cigarette and stared out the window, waiting until the period ended. When the bell rang, Danny walked up to Robby's car, pulled his hands out of his pockets, and rubbed them together. "Hey, what's up?"

"Nothing much."

"I was wondering if you could do me a favor."

"Name it."

"Can you give me a ride later tonight?"

"Sure, where to?"

"Rocco's."

"Um, yeah, I guess. Can I, uh, ask what for?"

"I'm looking for this kid—Larry McMahon."

"McMahon?"

"Do you know him?"

"Naw, but the name sounds familiar."

"I think he's the prick who robbed my boss," Danny replied.

"Are you shitting me?"

"No, I'm sure it's him. I've been asking around. That kid's a thief. Bugsy's gonna join us. Is that cool?"

"Umm, yeah, sure. How old's this kid?"

"I dunno. Nineteen, twenty, maybe?" Danny pulled his smokes out and extended the pack to Robby, who took one. "So how 'bout I meet you at the Marshall?"

"Sure. What time?"

"Quarter to eight?"

"No problem."

"I'll see you then."

"Hey. You want a ride?"

"Naw, I'm gonna see if I can find that asshole."

Robby nodded. Danny walked to the schoolyard entrance on Peacevale Road, willing to put up with the shitty weather and frozen feet for the chance he'd run into someone who knew where to find Larry. After passing Rocco's and seeing no one, he made the long trek to the Lucy Stone playground, where he lit a smoke and watched a game of street hockey, staying long enough to see a few goals scored, each of which was punctuated by some kid wearing a cuffed wool beanie and waving his hockey stick in the air, yelling, "GOAL!"

"Nice shot," Danny yelled just as loudly. He flicked his snipe and walked toward the school beneath the glow of incandescent lights that carved out a butter-colored path for him. At the top of Claybourne Street, he looked at the Prudential, stacked like a tall loaf of bread, remembering when it was built, slice by slice, until it was the tallest building in Boston. His mother used to take them to the upper deck when it was warm. It was a great place to see and hear the sounds of the city—traffic, sirens, police cars, ambulances, fire engines, screams, and sometimes gunfire.

The budding evening unfolded before him when he reached the end of the street, which was filled with the same characters as the night before, the night before, and the night before that. And of course, Cerier's bar was warming up. The regulars were milling about, inside and out; beacons marked by the orange glow of cigarettes, smoke wafting through the air, carried aloft by the sound of clinking glasses and voices—conversations about the Sox, the Pats, the Bruins, the Celtics, work, bosses, wives, ex-wives, girlfriends, former girlfriends, getting laid, and plans for the next weekend. Over the next few hours, the conversations would turn into arguments, compliments into cusses, and hand-shaking into fistfights. After the street lights went on and the air cooled, the musical clinking of tall drinks and bottles of beer would give way to the sound of shattered glass.

Across the street, at Abe's poolroom, Danny could hear pool balls clacking into each other. Inside, Rats in white T-shirts and black leather jackets prowled around, wielding wooden pool sticks buffed with blue chalk at the end. Cigarette smoke poured out the front door as if the Vatican had just nominated another pope. A bus went by, filled with people fighting to be friendly. Men read their newspapers, surgically folded into four-inch strips, carefully keeping their elbows tucked in. The women read romantic pocketbooks, dog-eared, and passed from one to another until they fell apart, only to be replaced with new ones. Everyone was eager to get home to watch TV behind steam-covered windows fueled with the residue from a boiled corned beef and cabbage dinner.

Danny took the ice-covered stairs two at a time until he was inside, passing Mrs. Feeney on the first floor and the Cochrans on the second, arguing loudly, as they often did. The old man, Charley "Chuckles," was an ex-con from Charlestown.

He lived with his foul-mouthed wife, Mary Elizabeth, and their three sons, Ricky, Butch, and Patrick, the last of whom they called Paddy; it was an apartment full of shitbags. Chuckles's wife always introduced herself as *Mary Elizabeth*, never Mary, as if she was royalty or something. Chuckles had done time at Walpole for a botched bank job. After he'd gotten out for good behavior, the judge had told him he would put him away a lot longer if he didn't move out of Charlestown and stay away from his bank-robbing friends. Chuckles had agreed, swearing to keep out of trouble. Despite objections from his kids, he'd moved his family to Dorchester. Nothing had changed. His friends came over on the weekends to play cards and plan more heists. Danny bumped into them now and then, usually on Sunday mornings, on his way out, when his mother thought he was going to church. They were usually packing, making it hard to tell if they were cops or townie thugs—not that there was much difference.

The three boys were sometimes there, sometimes not. They were all dropouts and petty thieves. They shared their time between Juvenile Hall, Deer Island, and an uncle or aunt in New Hampshire. On more occasions than he could remember, Danny had heard Mary Elizabeth talking to his mother, telling Bridie her sons were *good boys*. She'd always spoken with a cigarette bouncing around her mouth, like a mackerel hooked on the end of a fishing rod. Her voice had been raspy as if her larynx was being dragged across a cheese grater. "You don't need to worry about nothing. They wouldn't hurt nobody," she'd said, coughing up half her lung in the middle of the conversation.

When Danny hit the second floor, he smelled his mother's goulash—spiced meat and vegetables—and followed the smell through the front door straight into the kitchen. "Hi, Ma," he chirped.

"Hi, honey," she said, rubbing her hands on her gravy-stained apron. "Are you hungry?"

"Are you kidding? I could eat a horse!"

"Why don't you wash up and sit down? I'll fix you a bowl and some bread."

Danny stuck his nose in the pot.

"Go on," she said, tapping him on the rear end. He kissed her cheek, hurried into the bathroom, ran his hands under the faucet, skipped the soap, returned to the kitchen, and sat down, spoon in hand, watching his mother fill his bowl with the thick, steaming meal. She slid a dish of doughy Wonder Bread in front of him alongside a small chipped tea saucer with a stick of butter on it. "Would you like a glass of milk?"

"Uh-huh," he slurred, talking around a mouthful of goulash and a piece of bread buttered so thick, he could have used it as a pillow. Bridie filled his glass, prepared her bowl, and sat down.

"This is nice," she said. "We don't get to do this too often, the two of us, do we?"

Danny swallowed his food and ratcheted up a quick "Yeah." Then, after another mouthful, he spoke. "You know, Ma, this is the best goulash you ever made." He buried another piece of bread beneath a fat slab of butter, swallowing it in three bites, barely chewing it. "Did you put something different in it?"

"Yes. I'm surprised you noticed," she said, laughing. "Instead of yellow onions, I used red ones. What do you think?"

"It's great. I didn't know they had different onions, colors, and everything. I kinda thought they were all the same."

"You'd be surprised how many different onions they have these days. There are white ones and sweet ones and little ones called shallots."

"Shallots? Sounds kinda Jewish or something."

"I suppose," Bridie said as she buttered another piece of bread and put it on his plate. "So, how's school going?"

"Good. Real good."

"I wanted to ask you"—She suddenly stopped so fast she scared him into putting his spoon down—"Mary, Mother of Jesus! I forgot to tell you. Your boss Mr. Erickson called. Twice. He said it was important."

"He did?"

"Yes. The last time was about an hour ago. He said he needed to talk to you. He gave me his home number and asked that you call him as soon as you got home. I'm sorry, honey, I forgot."

Danny left his spoon in his bowl and stood up.

"Is everything okay? I'm sorry, honey. Is everything all right?"

"Yeah, yeah. Everything's fine. Do you have the number?"

"Oh yes, I wrote it down." She dabbed her mouth with her apron, grabbed a small piece of paper from the countertop, and handed it to him.

"I gotta make this call."

"Go on. I understand."

Danny grabbed the phone off the wall, pulled the cord behind him, entered the bathroom, closed the door, and dialed. "Erickson Residence."

"Mrs. Erickson?"

"Yes, may I ask who's calling?"

"Danny, Daniel McSweeney." He spoke so fast she didn't understand him.

"Who?"

"Danny. I work, er, I worked for your husband. Danny McSweeney. At the gas station."

"Daniel! Oh yes! How wonderful to hear from you. We were expecting your call."

"You were?"

"Why yes, dear. How are you doing?"

"Fine, thank you. Fine."

"And how is your family doing?"

"They're fine, ma'am. They're fine. Everyone's doing well, thank you."

"That's nice."

"My ma told me that Mr. Erickson called. She said it was something important. Is he okay?"

"Oh yes, yes, honey. He's fine. He wants to talk to you. He has some good news."

"Good news? Really?"

"Oh yes. It's about the robbery at the gas station and Larry, the other boy that worked for us."

"*Worked* for you?"

"Oh yes. Mr. Erickson fired him after he was arrested."

"Arrested?"

"Oh, yes, dear. He's the one who stole all that money."

"Arrested! When? How? What happened?" With each word, his voice lifted an octave.

"Mr. Erickson can explain it all to you."

"Is he there?"

"No, I'm sorry. Unfortunately, he's out at the moment."

"Do you know when he'll be back?"

"He should be back in a half hour. I'll have him call you."

"Gee, that'd be great, ma'am. That'd be wonderful."

"Heavens, Danny, I know you didn't steal from us. When Mr. Erickson told me what happened, I scolded him good and hard. I told him you'd never do anything like that, not in a million years. He should have listened to me. I gave him my two cents worth. I told him so. I did."

Danny felt tears well up. He tried to keep them in so they wouldn't take over his voice. He started to speak but stopped, coughing over his words.

"Are you all right?" she asked.

"Yeah, yeah . . . I'm fine. It's just, I dunno, a surprise."

"My gosh, I think it's wonderful news."

"Yes, ma'am, yes, it is. I can't thank you enough for letting me know."

"Honey, I'd like to ask a favor of you."

"Anything, ma'am, anything."

"Don't be too hard on him. Mr. Erickson feels just horrible. Things were fine until he hired you, and then things started to go wrong, and he wrongly associated you with the burglary and other problems. The receipts weren't quite matching up, and some money was missing. It turns out you were, oh, what do they call it? A fall guy. Yes, that's it. That's what Mr. Erickson called it. You were the fall guy for that other boy."

"Yeah, I figured that out. I was a patsy."

"A what?"

"A patsy; it's the same thing."

"I see. Danny, it was nice talking with you, but I have to go. I'm making suppah. Mr. Erickson will be home soon."

"I understand."

"Don't worry about a thing. Mr. Erickson would like you to come back to work."

"Okay. Thanks!"

"Bye-bye."

"Bye-bye. Good night."

Danny pressed his back against the door and stretched his neck. He gathered the phone cord up and walked into the kitchen, smiling. "Would you like me to reheat your dinner?" Bridie asked.

Danny sat down and chuckled to himself.

"It must have been a good call. You seem to be in a good mood."

"I am, I am. I don't know if I told you, but I had some problems at work."

Danny explained everything while they ate—how Mr. Erickson had blamed him, how he had been fired, and how he had planned to go to Rocco's and all that would have followed. When he was done, Bridie stood up.

"I'm glad everything worked out. He's such a nice man."

"He is. He's the best."

"Let's celebrate. I got some ice cream and chocolate cake. Would you like some?"

"Yeah, sure, Ma. Thanks."

"Do your friends know what happened?"

"Well, um ..." They were interrupted by the front door opening. The clomping of feet meant Frankie was home.

"Come and sit down honey," Bridie said, placing a bowl on the kitchen table. He hollered from the hallway, "I gotta go to the bathroom, Ma."

"Wash your hands, honey."

"Okay, Ma."

Bridie ladled a large serving into a chipped blue bowl. Frankie sat down, and Danny watched him devour his supper. "How are you doing?" she asked Frankie.

"Mm, fine," escaped from a mouth too full of food to say much more.

"Slow down, honey. There's plenty more!"

Frankie wiped his nose and replied with a quick nod.

"I gotta go out, Ma. I gotta meet someone," Danny said, getting up.

"Will you be late?"

"Naw, I shouldn't be."

"Okay."

"If Mr. Erickson calls, can you ask him what's a good time to call him?"

"Sure, honey."

"If he ain't gonna be up, can you ask him if I can go by after school tomorrow?"

"Sure."

Danny grabbed his jacket and headed out. It was warmer than he'd expected. He left his coat unzipped, enjoying the cool air. He shuffled through the slush that had replaced the snow and, after crossing the street, ran into Mooch on Westville

Street, carrying a bag of beer. "What's up?" Mooch asked, handing Danny one of the cans.

"Nothing," Danny replied. A few steps later, he asked, "Seen anyone tonight?"

"Naw. Who are you looking for?"

"Robby McElliott. Remember him?"

"McElliott? I ain't seen him in a long time. Is everything okay?"

"Yeah. I'm s'posed to meet him tonight. He's gonna give me a ride."

"Huh? I didn't know you were hanging out with him."

"I'm not. We got something going on."

"That's cool," Mooch said.

They turned at the end of an asphalt driveway hugging the face of the brick school where the pavement opened into a playground painted with squares, circles, and hopscotch patterns. The older kids were slumped against the doors at the top of the granite steps, while the younger ones held the walls up on both sides of the alley.

"Hey, Danny," Fitzy called out loudly. "I heard you were playing with a coupla spooks at the Rest last week. Is that true?"

"Whatever I did ain't none of your fucking business," Danny said, walking up to the circle of kids.

"So, what are you, a nigger lover?"

"Me?" Danny replied. "If it's the ones you're talking about, I seen 'em before. They were running out of your house. Your mother was in her nighty, chasing them and yelling, 'Come back! I need some more chocolate sauce.'"

Fitzy put his beer down and lunged at Danny. He grabbed Fitzy by the collar and rolled backward, jamming his foot into his stomach and flipping him headfirst into the side of the building. Just as fast as he had flipped him, Danny sprang to his feet and stood over Fitzy, who was thrashing around, trying to get up. When he did, he leaned against the wall and waved Danny off. "Enough," he mumbled, wiping a stream of blood from his mouth.

"You give up?" Danny asked, stepping forward with clenched fists.

Fitzy nodded, *yes*.

"Okay then." Danny nodded and walked away.

"How did you do that?" one of the younger kids asked. A rabble of voices followed:

"He didn't even hit him."

"Did you see that?"

"Danny kicked Fathead's ass."

The girls clambered behind the younger kids, chatting and pointing. Mooch, Bugsy, Misfit, Mikey, and the other kids laughed at Fathead. Misfit held a can of Schlitz in the air and called out to Danny, "Hey killer, you want a beer?"

Danny turned to make sure Fitzy was staying put. His concerns faded when Fitzy walked away, followed by the younger kids asking questions.

"Where'd you learn that one?" Mooch asked. "It's pretty fucking cool."

"Yeah!" Mikey added. "That was great. Fucking Fathead deserved it. He's such an asshole."

"I got tired of all his shit. The motherfucker never stops. I had to do it," Danny said.

"So, where'd you learn that stuff? I can't believe how far you threw him," Mooch said.

"I've been practicing it for a while. I bought a book I saw in a comic," Danny said. "It cost me a buck and a quarter. They call it jujitsu." Danny enunciated it: *Joo jitz zoo.*

"Jew, what?" Mikey replied. "What the fuck do the Jews have to do with it?"

"Nothing. It ain't a Jew thing. It's Japanese, sorta like karate. It's the kind of stuff Napoleon Solo and Illya Kuryakin do on *The Man from Uncle*. You use the other guy's weight against him."

"Oh yeah, I seen 'em do that stuff on TV."

"So, when Fitzy came at me, instead of running into him as he expected, I used his weight against him. I let him come to me. That's how I flipped him over."

Everyone oohed and aahed. The explanation got the younger kids babbling and the girls chatting again. "Anyone know what time it is?" Danny asked.

"Quarter past eight," Mikey replied.

"Shit, I gotta go." Danny downed his beer and ran out to the street, where Robby was waiting. "Shit, I'm sorry. I got tied up," Danny said.

"No problem. I was a few minutes late myself. Everything okay?"

"Well, yes and no. I mean, I don't need to run that errand anymore."

"Really? That's great."

"Yeah, no kidding. You won't believe it. The cops busted Larry with the stolen money."

"Are you kidding me? That's great!"

"Yeah, it is. Let's get some beers so we can celebrate. Then, you and me can see Mr. Erickson about the job. Now that Larry's gone, there's gotta be an opening."

"Sounds good to me!"

# 27

The usual forty-five-minute walk to work took a little over half an hour, which meant he made great time, especially considering the weather. As Danny neared the gas station, he could see Mr. Erickson sitting at his desk with a box of Dunkin' Donuts—a meeting was in the works. A cruiser pulled up, and a tall, dark-haired cop clad in tall black boots emerged. Danny stopped next to a street light to see what was going on. Mr. Erickson got up, coffee in hand, and opened the door to let the cop inside. They each grabbed a donut and started talking, sometimes accenting the conversation with a wave of arms and a fluttering of hands. Danny's stomach lurched. He couldn't figure out what was happening. If the cops wanted to arrest him, they could have picked him up at home. He leaned alongside a tall maple tree and watched.

Two donuts later, the cop returned to his car, waved at Mr. Erickson, and left. Danny flicked his snipe, thrust his hands into his coat pockets, headed across the street, and strode into the office. A grease-stained bag of donuts sat in the middle of the desk alongside a small stack of napkins. Danny entered the garage, where Mr. Erickson was working on an old Chevy station wagon. He turned as soon as Danny came in. "Good morning, son. I'm so glad to see you."

Danny stuck his hands in his pockets. "Morning to you."

"Danny," Mr. Erickson said, wiping his hands with a mechanic's rag and taking a few steps forward. "I made a big mistake. I owe you an apology."

"An apology? For what?"

"For what? I should never have doubted you. I feel horrible," he said, shaking his head. "I hope you can forgive me. I feel like a dammed fool. I was just so damned upset—I wasn't thinking right. I should have known better." He waited for Danny to say something, a futile effort. "You remember that officer that came by that day?" Mr. Erickson said.

"Yeah," Danny replied coolly.

"His name's Lonardelli. Tony Lonardelli. He's the one who arrested Larry. He's a good cop; I've known him for a long time." Danny unzipped his jacket and loosened his collar, more relaxed now. "Sit down, son. Have a donut and some hot chocolate."

Danny followed Mr. Erickson into the office, sat down, and grabbed a donut. "So, what happened?" he asked.

"Well, after you left, I was stewing pretty good. A little while later, the phone rang. It was Larry calling in sick. He went on about having a cold and not feeling good. It didn't sound right. The next thing he tells me, he might be out all week. I told him to call me when he felt better. So, the more I thought about it, I'd seen Larry come to work sick before, with a cold and sniffles. It didn't make sense. So, I called the station and spoke to Officer Lonardelli, who offered to check Larry out. He called me a few hours later to tell me he was booking Larry at the station. Can you believe it?"

"Are you serious?"

"Lonardelli went down to his house. He spotted the oil can in the back seat of his car. So, he goes upstairs to Larry's apartment to talk to him. His mother doesn't know anything, so she lets him in and calls Larry out into the kitchen. But he doesn't come out, so his mother asks Lonardelli to follow her into Larry's room. She opens the door, and Larry's stuffing the money under his mattress. Can you believe that?"

"Really? That's pretty stupid."

"No kidding. Lonardelli lifts the mattress, and there's the money. Larry starts yelling at him about search warrants, and Larry's mother starts yelling at Larry.

I guess it was pretty funny because she was trying to hit Larry. Lonardelli had to protect him from his own mother."

"That musta been a riot."

"I'm sure it was. So Lonardelli tells his mother he's gotta take him down to the station and asks if she has a paper sack. She gives him one, and he puts all the money in the bag and heads out. That's it."

"I can't believe it. Did you get all your money back?"

"I got most of it. He'd spent about a hundred bucks. Judging from Lonardelli's take, he must have tied a good one on."

Danny took another bite of his donut. "I kinda figured it was him. Me and some friends were getting ready to look for him."

"I have to tell you, son, I'm glad to have the money back, but I'm even happier you're back. I feel like a real bum. I shouldn't have gone off, half-cocked like that, blaming you."

"It's okay. It's no big deal. I can't blame you for feeling that way. Heck, I'd have thought the same thing."

"I appreciate that, but I was wrong. I hope you can forgive me."

"No problem. Don't worry about it."

"Great! Are you ready to work?"

"You bet."

"Good. I have three tune-ups today and a couple of oil changes."

# 28

It was dark when Danny got home. He was tired and hungry and wanted to eat and watch *Hawaii Five-O*. Climbing the stairs to his apartment, he heard voices from the television, louder than usual. He slid onto the sofa beside his mother and remained quiet; Bridie was staring at the television, and Frankie sat alongside her. "You've come a long way, baby," wafted from the tinny little speaker inside the brown cabinet. President Johnson appeared, holding a handful of cards, in front of a podium covered with an array of microphones.

> *America is shocked and saddened by the brutal slaying tonight of Dr. Martin Luther King. I ask every citizen to reject the blind violence that has struck Dr. King, who lived by nonviolence. I pray that his family can find comfort in the memory of all he tried to do for the land he loved so well. I have just conveyed the sympathy of Mrs. Johnson and myself to his widow, Mrs. King. I know that every American of goodwill joins me in mourning the death of this outstanding leader and in praying for peace and understanding throughout this land.*
>
> *We can achieve nothing by lawlessness and divisiveness among the American people. It is only by joining together, and only by working together, that we can continue to move toward equality and fulfillment for all of our people. I hope that all Americans tonight will search their hearts as they ponder this most tragic incident.*

> *I have canceled my plans for the evening. I am postponing my trip to Hawaii until tomorrow. Thank you.*

Bridie sighed and clutched her apron, rolling and unrolling it. Then, as quickly as the president had appeared, Raymond Burr replaced him, rolling across a room in a high-backed wheelchair, *Ironside*. "Frankie, please turn that down," Bridie said. Burr remained on the screen, moving around silently. "Danny, did you see anyone . . . or anything on the way home?" Bridie asked.

"No," he said, shaking his head. "Why? What's up?"

Bridie walked to the front window, pulled the curtain aside, and peered outside. "They're rioting in Roxbury."

"Who?" Danny asked.

"The Negroes."

"The Negroes? Who cares?" Danny said with a shrug. "They did that before. They burned Grove Hall down last year, remember?" Bridie said nothing. She continued looking out the window. "Let them do it again. They can burn the whole place down if they want," Danny said.

Bridie turned and spoke in a funeral ceremony tone. "This time, it's different. This preacher man, Martin Luther King, was their leader." She turned back to the window at the sound of a police car flying up the street, its blue lights painting everything it passed. "The last time, they stayed in their own neighborhoods, with their own people. They say the riots are getting worse; they're not just burning places in Roxbury."

"Does that mean we get to stay home?" Frankie asked, bouncing up and down.

"Well, *you'll* be staying home," she replied.

"What about you?" Danny asked.

"I'll be all right," Bridie said. "They're not going to bother me. Besides, I can't afford to stay home. We still have bills to pay. Money doesn't grow on trees, you know."

"I can't stay home. I promised Mr. Erickson I'd help close this week."

"Honey, I don't think it's safe for you to work at a gas station, especially at night. Who knows what these people are going to do?"

"I doubt they're gonna come over here looking for trouble. They'd never go down to Neponset, not in a million years."

"Can I stay up late and watch TV?" Frankie asked, interrupting the conversation.

"Frankie, sometimes . . ." Bridie said, petering out.

"What?"

"Nothing."

Danny got up and stretched his arms over his head. "Is there anything to eat, Ma? I'm starved."

"No, but I can make you a tuna fish sandwich."

"That'd be great!"

"Can I have one too?" Frankie asked.

"Sure," Bridie said.

Danny headed down the hall, pausing to listen at his sister's closed door, figuring she was inside. He was tempted to knock but decided otherwise. He went into the bathroom and studied his face in the mirror. He ran his finger over several pimples, popped a few, watched his hands, walked into the kitchen, and sat at the kitchen table where Bridie had laid his sandwich out next to a Fred Flintstone glass filled with Zarex.

"Thanks, Ma," Danny said, taking a large bite of his sandwich, followed by half a glass of Zarex. After two more bites, he stopped eating, sensing something else. "Is everything okay, Ma?"

"Yes," lifting her apron to dab her eyes.

"What's up?"

She waited a moment before responding. "Nothing. I'm okay."

"C'mon, Ma, something's bothering you. What is it?"

She hesitated for a moment before responding. "This Martin Luther King man getting killed is not good," she said as she started sobbing. Danny got up, wrapped her in his arms, and held her closely. "Let me get you a cup of tea," he said after she calmed down.

After preparing her cup and handing it to her, he studied the corners of her eyes, noticing small, thin lines trailing across her face. Once silky and wavy, her hair was now coarse and streaked with strands of gray that met the lines on her face. Her skin, no longer pink and soft, looked harder and darker.

"I'm sorry, honey," she said.

"For what? There's nothing to be sorry for."

"Yeah, I know, it's just . . . a lot is happening."

"Like what?" She pursed her lips and tried to reshape them into a smile but failed. "C'mon, Ma, what is it?"

"They say the Negroes are attacking white people, not just in Roxbury; everywhere," she said.

"You don't need to worry about nothing, Ma. Nothing's gonna happen to us. They're not gonna come over here."

"Honey, have you ever thought about having a family?"

"I ain't never thought about it or nothing. Why?"

"Your sister's pregnant."

"What?" *That motherfucker!* was all he could think. He clenched his fists, and his arms froze.

"Danny, are you okay?"

"I'm . . . I'm sorry, Ma. I . . . um . . . when's she due?"

Bridie reached over and held his hand. "Sometime in late August. Mother of Christ, what was she thinking?"

Danny slammed the table, sending Bridie's cup and saucer on the floor and spreading shards of china everywhere. Bridie's eyes opened wide. She grabbed

Danny's arm. "She's my daughter, and she's your sister. Your sister," she said; words that fought their way through her tears.

"I know, Ma, I know. It's just this fucking Henschel. It's not that he's a Jew or nothing. It's just . . . it's just he's such an asshole. That fucker's so full of himself!"

"I know, honey. I know. We have to wait to see what's going to happen. If she has the baby, you'll be an uncle. Can you imagine that? An uncle."

"Yeah, I know, I know, but . . ."

"But what? I've tried to talk to her; it's not easy. She won't tell me anything. I've tried. Lord knows I've tried."

"I believe you, Ma, I do. What do we know about him? What about the time he hurt her? What about that? He's a fucking Jewball."

"At least he's not a Protestant," Bridie replied.

"I guess." Danny walked over to the window while Bridie returned to the stove to make another cup of tea. Danny grabbed a broom, picked the broken pieces up, tossed them in the trash can, grabbed a broom, and silently swept the rest up.

"I'm sorry, Ma."

"Don't worry about it," she said tremblingly. "I need your help, honey. We can't let her go through this alone. We're her family. We're all she's got."

"I know, Ma, but he's a fucking Jew. This is wrong!"

"I know, honey, I know. But, unfortunately, there's not much we can do about it now. What's done is done, and nothing's gonna change that."

"I know, Ma, I know. But . . ."

"And I know what happened in Newton," Bridie said, interrupting him. "The thing with her boyfriend and his car."

Danny lost his breath, unsure of what to say. He banged the table again. "You know, Ma, he deserved it. Chrissy might be a pain in the ass, but he had no right to do what he did to her. He had no right to beat her up. He got what he deserved."

"I know, honey, I know."

"Does Chrissy know?"

"About the car and her boyfriend getting beat up? I'm not sure what she knows."

"How did you find out?"

"Your brother told me. He heard it from some friends. He said everyone knows."

"Everyone?"

"I told him not to say anything to Chrissy."

"That's good."

"And I spoke to Robert; I went out and saw him at his work."

"Are you kidding me?"

"No, I did."

"I don't believe it."

"It's true."

"Really?"

"I wouldn't lie to you, would I?"

"No, I guess not. What happened?"

"Well, your sister wouldn't talk to me. I needed to know what had happened. I'm still her mother, and I have a right to know, right? So, a few days later, I took off from work early, got on the Green Line, and went to his work."

"Ma, you kill me."

"So, I show up at his work. Jesus, Mary, and Joseph, you should have seen the look on his face. As soon as he saw me, he ran right over. I could see he was really nervous and didn't know what to say."

"So, what did you do?"

"I asked to meet his father. 'My father?' he says, 'My father? Why?' I told him we had business. He told me he wasn't in. I told him I could wait for him, and I had all day. So, I started walking around, looking at the cars, and he followed me everywhere, a Nervous Nellie he was. I asked him if I could sit in one of the cars, one of the big ones, with all the chrome and everything. He says, 'Can we talk in private?' I said, 'Sure,' and off we went. He takes me outside to a trailer, like the ones you see on construction jobs."

"Yeah, I know the ones."

"So, we go in, and he asks me if I'd like a glass of water, and I said, 'Yes, thank you.' So, he gets me a glass of water, and I take my time drinking it like I have all the time in the world. I ask him about his father, and he doesn't want to talk about him. He wants to know what I'm doing there. So, I figure I *do* have all the time in the world. I mean, I took the day off and went all the way out here, right?"

Danny, still stunned, leaned forward.

"So, I took my time drinking the water, and he's sitting there, waiting, you know, for me to say something, so I asked him for another glass. After I finished, I asked him why he hadn't been by. He said he'd been busy at work, so I asked doing what. He hemmed and hawed for a few minutes, not saying anything. So, I asked him about the fight they'd had downtown. That made him really fidgety; Lord, you should have seen him."

"He asked me what Chrissy said, but I didn't say anything, so I sat back and drank my water. He says again he's been really busy at work. So, he goes on again about how busy he's been. When he's done, I ask him again, 'So why haven't you called?' He didn't say anything, and he got more fidgety. I let him fidget for a few minutes. Finally, I asked him what happened that night and why'd he hit her."

"What'd he say?"

"He said they had been arguing, and it had got out of hand."

"Out of hand! What the fuck?"

"Language, honey."

"I'm sorry."

"So, I finally got up and said, seeing as his father wasn't here, I'd come back."

"What'd he do?"

"Nothing."

"What'd you do?"

"I left."

"Just like that?"

"Yup."

"Sounds like some kind of day. Huh?"

"It sure was." She turned to the window and stared at several pigeons cooing on the roof next door.

"Is everything okay?" Danny asked.

"I think Chrissy must have done something wrong to upset him; that's why she won't tell me. You know Danny, men don't usually hit their girlfriends like that. When they do, it's because they've had a bad day or something. When things go wrong, like they sometimes do, a wife or girlfriend needs to be quiet and listen. That's what a wife's supposed to do, what a girlfriend should do. She has to listen to what her husband says, and sometimes he might get angry and have to hit her. He doesn't mean it, but those things happen sometimes. A woman's s'posed to listen in times like that." Bridie reached over and held his hand. He wanted to say something but wasn't sure what to say. She hugged him and left for the bathroom just as Chrissy walked in.

"How was the show?" he asked.

"Fine. Is Ma okay?"

"Yeah, as far as I know."

"What were you two talking about?"

"Nothing much. School and stuff like that."

"What kind of stuff?"

"Stuff."

"Like what?"

"Stuff." She put her hands on her hips and waited until he spoke. "Martin King and all the bullshit going on in Roxbury. She was worried."

"Uh-huh."

"I told her they'd never come over here."

"Anything else?"

He ran the water over his dish and pretended he didn't hear her.

She spoke again, "Was there anything else?"

He turned and spoke. "No. I told her I had to go to work and wasn't going anywhere near Roxbury. I told her not to worry about nothing." Bridie shuffled into the kitchen. "Can I get you anything?" she asked Chrissy.

"Thanks, Ma. I'm okay. I just wanted a glass of milk."

"Are you sure, honey? I got some ginger snaps," Bridie said. "I told Frankie not to eat them all."

She poured some milk into a small glass and drank it. When she was done, she placed the glass in the sink. "I'm going to bed," she said.

"I'll see you in the morning," Bridie said.

"Good night," she said to Danny and left. As soon as she closed her door, Bridie said to Danny, "Did she say anything?"

"Naw. She asked a bunch of questions, but I didn't tell her nothing."

"That's good."

"Do you think she knows I know she's pregnant?"

"I don't think so. She wanted to tell you, but she's not ready yet."

"That don't make no sense. She's gonna start showing soon, ain't she?"

"Yes, she will."

"What about Henschel? Does he know?"

"I don't know. She hasn't said anything."

"Are you gonna tell her I know?"

"I'll have to sooner or later. Let me talk to her and see what she wants to do. I . . ." she paused to correct herself. "We need to be there for her. No matter what happens, we need to be there for her. We're her family."

"But, Ma . . ."

"But nothing! She's your sister, and she needs us. She might not say that, but she does. Trust me, she needs us."

"What about her boyfriend, the Jew?"

Bridie crossed herself. *Father, Son, and the Holy Spirit.* "We'll just have to wait. She needs to figure it out. She's under enough pressure as it is, and she's going to have a baby."

"I know, Ma, I know. She can't marry him or nothing, right? That's not legal; she's Catholic."

"Hail Mary, full of grace," she said, crossing herself. "It's complicated."

"I'm gonna lie down."

"Okay, but will you do me a favor?"

"Sure, Ma. What is it?"

"I'd like you to think about tomorrow. I'd feel much better if you stayed home and watched your brother and sister. You can't be too careful these days."

"Jeez, Ma, I can't do that. They can take care of themselves. And besides, I promised Mr. Erickson I'd come in. I got a job—I ain't a kid anymore. Chrissy can watch Frankie. She doesn't leave the house anyway, right? They'll be okay, Ma. They'll be fine."

"I don't know, honey. It'd make me feel a lot better if you were around."

"How about I come home a little early, before work? I can skip a couple of classes. There's not gonna be many kids at school anyway, not with all that crap going on. I'll come by after lunch and make sure everything's okay."

"Okay, I guess. It's just . . ."

"What?"

"Nothing."

"Are you sure?"

"Yes."

"Okay."

---

Danny got up early, hauled himself into the parlor, and turned the television on. There had been more riots and fires along Columbia Road and at Dudley Station. The MBTA had stopped running buses through the area, and they had shut the Orange Line down. The riots in other places were much worse. When the next commercial came on, he went into the kitchen, stuck a couple of Pop-Tarts in the toaster, and poured a glass of milk. Halfway through his second serving, his mother came down the hall in her tea-stained slippers. She popped her pink-curlered head into the kitchen. "Good morning," she mumbled before going into the bathroom. He turned the burner under the tea kettle on, removed a cup and saucer from the strainer, and dropped a teabag in the cup.

Bridie came back in. "How'd you sleep, honey?"

"Not too bad. I had a couple of dreams."

"Anything special?"

"Naw, I don't even remember them." The kettle whistled. "I made you some tea."

"Thank you." She sat down at the kitchen table and sighed. "Is anyone else up?"

"No." Danny placed the cup in front of her. She spooned some sugar into it and stirred it around.

"Was there anything on the news?"

"Yeah, but nothing much. Most of the news was about other places; Detroit, Washington, and, umm, Chicago."

Bridie stirred her tea some more and gazed out the window. She eventually turned as if she had found whatever she was looking for. "Can I make you something?" she asked. "Pancakes? Oatmeal?"

"Naw, I'm fine. I had some Pop-Tarts."

"You should take a couple more for later if you're hungry. They're good for you."

Danny made himself a cup of tea. They chatted some more about Chrissy, wondering what she would do. After finishing his drink, he got dressed, and while doing so, he bumped into his dresser, waking Frankie up.

"Hey, douchebag," Danny said. "Ma wants me to stay home to watch you, but I can't; I got things to do."

Frankie pulled his cover over his head, and as soon as he did, Danny threw a sneaker at him.

"Hey, that hurt," Frankie said, rolling onto his stomach.

"No, it didn't."

"Yes, it did."

Danny tossed another sneaker at Frankie's head. "How about that one?"

"Stop it, or I'm gonna tell Ma."

"You're such a fucking pussy."

Frankie pulled the sheets down and stared at Danny.

"Listen. I'm gonna go to school for a while. And then I'm gonna come home to check on you. After that, I'm going to work. You can't fuck around, you got it? Chrissy's gonna be home, so don't give her a hard time or nothing, you got it?"

"Yeah. So, why're you going to school? Ain't you worried or nothing?"

"Naw. Them fucking spooks ain't gonna fuck with us. They ain't got the balls. Thay ain't that fucking stupid."

"You don't have to worry. I can take care of myself. I'm not a baby."

"Then quit acting like one."

Frankie pulled his sheets aside and stretched his legs first, then his arms, back over his head, and then sat up. "Is Chrissy all right?"

"Yeah, as far as I know. Why?"

"I dunno. I've seen her puke a few times."

"When?

"I don't know. Early in the morning, usually."

"Did you say anything to Ma?"

"Naw."

"Okay. Don't say nothing. I'll find out what's going on."

"Okay." There was a long pause. "Danny?"

"Yeah."

"Is she gonna be alright?"

"Who?"

"Chrissy."

"Yeah, she's fine."

Frankie nodded.

"Hey, I gotta go. Remember, don't piss your sister off. Ma's pretty wound up about this Martin King bullshit; the last thing she needs is you bugging her."

"Okay."

"I'll see you later."

Danny walked down the hallway and popped his head into the kitchen. "I'm going, Ma."

Bridie looked up from the table. She was crying. Her makeup ran down her cheeks, leaving black streaks across her face. Danny quickly stepped forward and kneeled in front of her. "C'mon, Ma. Everything's gonna be okay. There's nothing to worry about. They'll stay in their own neighborhood."

"I know, honey, I know. It's not that. It's just that . . . I was thinking about Chrissy. She's gonna need us."

"I know, Ma, I know. She don't need to worry about nothing, and you don't need to worry. Everything's gonna be okay. We're here to help her. I'll be here to help her. I promise."

# 29

Danny watched the Number 23 bus, packed to the gills, chugging up the street, spewing smoke, and causing dogs to bark. Finally, the bus turned left on Washington Street and stopped in front of the A&P supermarket. Danny started to cross the street but stopped when a cop car barreled through the intersection with its lights spinning. The bus remained by the sidewalk, idling and coughing, as more people fought to get on. *Fuck that noise*, Danny thought. *I'm walking*. It wasn't until he passed Sam and Becky's *Five and Ten* that the bus pulled out and continued down the street, weighted down with more weary souls than when it had stopped.

When he reached Mother's Rest, he lit a smoke. Another cop car went by, faster than the first one, headed in the same direction. He continued walking and spotted someone walking up the concrete steps at the edge of the park. He picked up a piece of broken concrete and rolled it in his hand, ready to throw. As he got closer, he recognized Billy's gait. "Hey, asshole!" Danny yelled before tossing the chunk of concrete in Billy's direction.

"You missed!" Billy said. He bent over, picked the concrete up, and threw it toward Danny.

"What's up?" Danny asked.

"Nothing much," Billy said. "Hey, you got any smokes?"

Danny extended his pack. "How ya feeling?"

Billy shrugged. "Ah, you know." Danny looked at the purple scar above Billy's eye, a remnant from the trash can beating. It ran across his forehead and disappeared into the edge of his hairline.

"So, what's up with these fuckin' spear chuckers?" Billy asked. "Are the stupid bastards gonna burn down their own homes?"

"Fuck if I know."

"They ought to send them all back to Africa."

"I don't give a fuck what they do as long as they stay away from us."

"Yeah, no shit," Danny said, spitting a loogie on the sidewalk. "You got any plans after graduation?"

"Yeah, I'm gonna join the army."

"The army?"

"Yeah. Like my father. He was a grunt. He killed a bunch of Japs. I'm gonna kill a buncha them slant-eyes too."

"Why not the navy or the marines?"

"I hate fuckin' boats. I get seasick. The marines are a buncha faggots. Naw, I'm gonna join the army."

"John Wayne, motherfucker!"

"What about you?" Billy asked. "What're you gonna do when you graduate?"

"I don't know. I got a job I like. If I go, I think I'll go in the marines."

"Gung ho motherfucker!" They paused as another cop car went by.

"It must be a fuckin' mess in Roxbury."

"I heard a lot of shit going down in Grove Hall."

"That's where they're shooting the firemen."

"Did you know my Uncle Ricky's a fireman?"

"No."

"My ma talked to him last night. They had some calls in Roxbury, and those fucking jungle bunnies started throwing rocks at them. Can you believe that?"

"If you ask me, the firemen should let the whole place burn down; they should stay home."

"No shit." Billy paused to light a cigarette. "So, what're you doing today?"

"I gotta watch my little brother. My ma wouldn't let him go to school today. She's worried he might get jumped or something."

"Jumped? Doesn't he go to the Marshall?"

"Yeah."

"He ain't gonna get jumped down there."

"Fuck, I know that. That's what I told her. It didn't matter. I wasn't going to argue with her or nothing."

They continued walking to the end of the schoolyard. Several cop cars were parked at the end of Peacevale Road. They stuffed their heads into their shoulders and their hands in their pockets and crossed over to the other side of the street. When they did, one of the cops hollered at them. "Hey, you!"

The cop, a tall Italian built like a wide receiver, walked toward them. Danny and Billy started to walk faster. "Hey!" If they hadn't heard him the first time, they did now. "Billy! How're you feeling?" They stopped and turned. The cop stuck his hand out. "It's Billy, right?" the cop said.

"Um, yeah," Billy replied, fidgeting. "Do I know you?"

"Well, not really, I guess."

Billy scrunched his forehead, confused.

"I'm the cop who responded when those kids jumped you last winter."

"Sorry. I don't remember too much from that day."

"That's okay, I remember you. You're one tough bastard."

"Umm, I guess."

"You don't remember much, do you?"

"Naw, not really. I'm sorry." Billy shrugged.

"So, what're you guys doing out today?"

"We're going to school," Billy replied.

"You should stay there when you get there. It's not a good day to be roaming around. He turned then to Danny. "You work for Richard Erickson, don't you?" the cop asked.

"Um, yeah," Danny responded.

"Rich speaks highly of you. He says you're a good kid and a hard worker." He extended a thick, dark hand to Danny. "I'm Tony Lonardelli. Rich called me after the station was robbed."

"Oh yeah, I remember you."

"Well, your buddy's out of action for a while."

"He's not my buddy. He's a punk. I hope he rots in jail."

"He's gonna have his hands full in there. He doesn't seem like a tough guy."

"He ain't. I was gonna kick his ass if I caught him."

"Well, you don't have to worry about him for a while. We got him on grand theft."

"That's good."

"Listen, whatever you do, stay away from Franklin Field. We're expecting a lot of trouble over there."

"We don't ever go to Franklin Field," Billy said. "That place is a jungle. It's full of jigaboos."

"Is it true the niggers are shooting at you guys, umm . . . I mean, officers?" Danny said.

"Well, not us. Not yet. They're shooting at the firemen. If they shoot at us, we're gonna shoot back."

"Really?" Danny said.

"Really. And we don't miss."

Danny and Billy nodded their heads in unison. Danny lifted his head in Billy's direction. "It was nice talking to you. We gotta go," Danny said.

"Same here," Lonardelli replied. "Take care of yourselves."

"Thanks. We will."

The boys strolled across the parking lot, hopping around the puddles from the night before's rain. There weren't many cars in the parking lot. It looked like a Saturday morning. The school was as quiet inside as outside, and the classrooms were mostly empty. Billy wandered off while Danny wandered around the hallways, looking to find some of the other kids. He couldn't find anyone, so he headed home after the second period. When he got there, he found his sister sleeping in the parlor, in front of the television, flickering black-and-white images across the screen. He turned the TV off, bent over, and looked at his sister. Her face and neck were fuller, her forearms were thick and chunky, and her swollen stomach was more pronounced. He grabbed a quilted blanket from the corner chair and covered her.

Danny shuffled into the bedroom. Frankie was propped up on his bed, reading a comic book, surrounded by a stack of others, some on his bed and some on the floor.

"Hey! What's up?" Danny asked.

"Nothing," Frankie replied, looking up for a second before returning to his magazine.

"How's Chrissy?"

"Fine," he mumbled without looking up.

"Did you eat?"

"Yeah."

"Need anything?" Danny asked.

"Naw."

"Okay, I'm gonna grab a sandwich, then I gotta go to work." If Frankie had heard him, he wasn't letting on. Spiderman was probably in the battle of his life, which would be more important than anything Danny had to say.

Danny sloshed together a three-piece peanut butter and jelly sandwich and a Flintstone glass full of cherry Zarex, inhaling everything in a few bites and a couple of swallows. After one more look in on Frankie and Chrissy—she was sleeping, and he was reading—he went outside, where he noticed something odd; every car and bus rumbled by as if they were wired to each other and, instead of stopping, they continued through the intersection. When he reached Town Field, a couple of cop cars were parked at the entrance with their front doors open. A pair of shotguns were propped up in the front seat; none of the cops were smiling. There wasn't a lot of traffic on Dot Ave. When Danny arrived at work, Mr. Erickson was unloading a stack of plywood from the bed of his truck. As soon as he saw Danny, he yelled, "Hey, can you give me a hand?"

"Yeah," Danny shouted as he jogged to the back of the pickup.

"Can you grab the other end?"

"Sure. What're you doing?"

"Covering the windows."

"The windows? Why?" Danny asked, lifting his end of the wood and helping get it inside the garage.

"Because of all the rioting in Roxbury. I don't know how long it will go on, so I must be prepared."

"You think there's gonna be trouble?"

Mr. Erickson wiped his arm across his brow. "I don't know. One thing I've learned is never to take any chances. These days, you can't be too sure."

"My ma says the same thing."

"She's a smart lady."

It took them twenty minutes to unload everything. When they were done, they walked to the side of the building where Mr. Erickson had placed a stack of two-by-fours and a carpenter's toolbox full of nails, screws, hammers, saws, and a long wooden drill. "Danny, can you work late today?"

"Sure, no problem."

"Thanks. I have to check the other station to make sure everything's okay."

"Do you need any help?"

"No, but can you do me a favor?"

"What?"

"Can you listen to WBZ?"

"Sure."

"If it sounds like trouble, I need you to lock the place up, padlock the pumps, and go home. If you see anything that doesn't look right or have any trouble, call the police."

"No problem. Hey, that reminds me. I met this cop this morning—Lonna . . . Lorna something or other."

"Lonardelli?"

"Yeah, Lonardelli, that's it. A big Italian guy."

"He's a good man, a good cop. I served in the war with his father, Tony. We were in the same unit in the Normandy Invasion. He earned a batch of medals for shooting down some Messerschmitts in the Battle of Carentan."

"A Mezzer what?" Danny asked, afraid to ask where Carentan was.

"A *Messerschmitt*. They're warplanes. The Jerrys used prisoners of war—our men—to build them."

"That's messed up."

"It is. I have to tell you, Lonardelli comes from good blood."

"Yeah, he was pretty cool. He told me he was the cop that showed up after Larry robbed you," Danny said.

"That's him. I told him all about you, how you gave my wife a hand when she broke down. He's the one that pushed the robbery investigation, and he's the one that tracked that bum down."

"He's the same cop that helped my friend Billy when he got beat up last winter at Dot High. He remembered him and the fight and everything. I couldn't believe it."

Mr. Erickson nodded his head. "Sounds about right. Say, can you grab that ladder and bring it out front?"

"Sure."

"And bring some of those two-by-fours, lean them against the wall. I'm gonna screw them over the windows."

"No problem."

"We'll need to nail a bunch of those spikes in the two-by-fours, then nail them into the top of the plywood. After that, we'll drill some holes in those and hang them on the others."

"Can't they still get in if they want to? I mean, it's only plywood."

"That's true. That won't stop anyone from getting in. If they want to get in, they'll get in. Mostly I want to protect the windows in case they throw anything at them. There's only so much you can do. If they want to burn the building down, they'll do that. It's the vandalism I'm worried about. If they come by, the plywood will discourage them."

"Makes sense to me."

Over the next few hours, they sawed and screwed and hammered and nailed everything together. Then, when they were done, they stood back and admired their work. "Nothing'll get through now," Danny said.

"Let's hope so. You did a great job."

"It wasn't hard once I figured out what you were doing."

"If nothing happens, that's okay too. The plywood'll come off pretty easy."

"That's pretty cool, the way you figured that out."

"So, how 'bout a tonic?"

"Sounds great!"

They washed up and sat down in the office. Mr. Erickson grabbed some drinks and turned the radio onto WBZ. Gangs of roving Negroes had stormed the Jeremiah Burke High School and vandalized the classrooms. Some teachers had been dragged out of their cars and beaten up. More gangs were wandering around Roxbury, torching and looting local businesses. Whites foolish enough to walk or drive on Blue Hill Avenue were attacked and dragged into the street or out of their cars, where they were robbed and beaten. Mr. Erickson shook his head, stretched his arms, and stood up. "C'mon, we'd better get back to work."

Every other car that pulled up was tuned to WBZ. The regulars stopped by, most wanting their tanks filled, their radiators topped off, or the pressure in their tires checked. All in all, things were quiet, and everyone was patient. Danny couldn't figure out why his mother had been so anxious. Mr. Erickson left at five thirty. Danny continued working until seven thirty. He closed at eight, thinking about a couple of slices at Hi-Fi. As he neared the restaurant, the sounds of cars and buses screeching and people hollering and laughing filled his ears. He inhaled the scents of the avenue: Chinese food, stale beer, car exhaust, urine, and cheap perfume. A small crowd shuffled in front of the taxi stand, where the drivers were bickering with customers, arguing about how much it would cost to haul them to the North End, Neponset, or Quincy.

The smell of exhaust gave way to the scent of tomatoes, pepperoni, onions, and cheese when Danny opened the door to Hi-Fi. Tony C. was spinning large slabs of dough into pies while guzzling a tall glass of tonic and tugging away on a Camel, now and then tapping a few ashes into a glass ashtray and sometimes in the sauce. "Hi, Danny, what'll it be?" Tony asked, tilting his head slightly to keep his carpet in place, the words spilling out like a spoonful of fresh tomato sauce.

"A coupla slices of cheese and a coupla pepperoni."

"Anything to drink?" Another flick of his cigarette.

"Coke," Danny said as he pulled some money out of his pocket and counted.

"Drink's on me," Tony said.

"Really?"

Tony nodded.

"Thanks, man."

Tony lifted his eyebrows and nodded toward the door as two girls dressed in Catholic school uniforms with knee-high white socks came in. Tony grabbed another piece of dough and shaped it into a long chubby cylinder. "Psst," he muttered, catching Danny's attention, holding the roll of dough in front of his crotch, shaking it up and down. Danny laughed so hard that everyone looked over. Tony rolled his eyes and whistled like a choir boy as he flattened the dough.

"You're a crazy fuck," Danny whispered.

"Who, me?"

"Yeah, you. Whod'ya think I'm talking to?"

Danny waited until the girls sat down before grabbing a table close to them, doing his best to appear uninterested. A few minutes later, Tony whistled at Danny; his slices were ready. He got up, covered his pizza with cheese and red peppers, and carried them back to his table, taking a bite before sitting down. Tony called out in as sweet a voice as he could muster. "Girls, your pie is ready." Danny bent his head, pretending to study his pizza, and when he looked up, one of the girls, a redhead, was staring at him. Danny looked at her momentarily and then over to Tony, who shrugged. When he looked back at the girls, they had started eating and resumed talking. Danny tore off a corner of his paper napkin, rolled it into a ball, tossed it on the girls' table, and watched it bounce across the pizza. They stopped eating and looked at him. "Hey, do you girls know Patty McNulty?" he asked.

"Yes," they giggled. "We both do," the redhead replied, looking at her friend.

"Yeah, I kinda figured that out. The uniforms were a dead giveaway."

"Of course," they replied in unison.

"Patty is one of my best friends," said the brunette, smiling from inside plump cheeks and beneath a head of curly hair held in place with a simple white ribbon. Her skirt was precisely ironed, and her shoes shined like glass. "I'm Emily. We've met before." Danny kept chewing to buy time; she looked familiar. "It was in the Marshall schoolyard. I was with Patty. Remember?"

Danny nodded. "Oh, yeah, yeah. Sure," he said, lying. "Did you girls go to school today?"

"Yes. Why wouldn't we?" the redhead replied.

"You know, the riots in Roxbury. The Martin King thing; the colored guy that was killed."

"Oh, *that?*" the redhead said. "We go to Catholic school. They don't allow riots at Catholic schools; it's against the rules."

Emily piped in. "Someone asked about the riots, and Sister Madeline McCarthy told us it has nothing to do with us and not to worry; Mother Mary would look over us."

"What's your name?" Danny asked, turning his attention back to the redhead.

"Joann. But my friends call me Jojo."

JoJo was different; her skirt was not as sharp as Emily's; it wasn't ironed, and her blouse was wrinkled. Her shoes were scuffed, her socks were mismatched, and her blouse was not tucked in.

"Anyone need another drink?" Danny asked, getting up to refill his.

"No, thanks," Emily said. JoJo smiled and shook her head. *No.*

"You think the redhead swallows?" Tony asked, filling Danny's cup.

Danny grabbed a handful of napkins from the counter and placed them over his mouth to stifle his laughter. "You're a sick fuck. You know that?"

"Yeah. So, what else is new?"

Danny shook his head. "You need help."

Tony grabbed another roll of dough, lowered it to his waist, and waved it in Danny's direction. "You gonna help me?" Danny smiled, shook his head, and walked away.

"So, are you two going steady?" Emily asked when Danny returned.

"Steady?"

"Oh, I thought you two were going steady, you know, 'cuz Patty talks about you all the time."

"She does? About what?"

"All kinds of things."

"Like what?"

"For one thing, she says you're different and not like the other boys."

"Yeah, she says that all the time," JoJo said. "She says you're smart, and she said you're a really good kisser."

"Well, compared to the mutts I hang out with, being smart ain't nothing special."

"She also said you beat up some kid using karate, like Napoleon Solo."

"Is that true?" JoJo asked. "Are you a black belt or something?"

"No, I wish I was. It's called jujitsu."

"Where'd you learn it?"

"I bought a book I saw in a comic book; I taught myself." The girls stared at him, mouths agape. "The kid deserved it. He's a real jerk and a bully. You know the kind of kid I'm talking about?"

"I do," Emily said. We have a kid like that in our neighborhood. His name's Pestico, Johnny Pestico. He used to pick on my little brother until my cousin beat the crap out of him one day and broke his nose."

"He probably likes little boys; guys like that are usually fags," Danny said.

"Really? Are you serious?" JoJo gasped.

"Yeah. I've seen it before."

"No!" Emily exclaimed.

"It's true," Danny said. "You can't trust them fags."

The girls huddled together, whispering to each other. Danny finished his last piece of pizza, got up, tossed everything in the trash, and returned to the girls' table. "It's been nice talking to you girls. I gotta go, I gotta get home, I gotta get up early for work."

"Where do you work?" JoJo asked.

"The Port Gas station, near the skating rink at Neponset."

"I know that place. I'll come down to see you if I ever need a fill-up," JoJo said.

Emily gasped as if it were her last breath.

Danny sputtered through a dry mouth. "Umm, it was nice meeting both of you." They smiled back at him.

As he headed out the door, Danny heard Emily say, "I can't believe you said that. You embarrassed him."

"Did not."

"Did too."

"Did not."

"Did too."

"Well, maybe a little."

# 30

"We gotta find a place for Ditch Day," Bugsy said, turning his head and blowing a mouthful of smoke to the side.

"It's gotta be down the Cape," Danny said.

"Yep. Let's hope it doesn't rain. Remember the last time we went to the Cape?"

"Yeah."

"Fuck, yeah. It rained the whole day," Bugsy said.

"If it does, we can go to Turner's," Mooch said. "There's a coupla places we can go to if it does rain. You know they have covered benches. We'd have to get there early to save one."

"I know the place," Bugsy said.

Suddenly, Mooch yelped, "I got it!"

"Got what?" Bugsy replied. "The clap?"

Danny laughed so hard he spit his cigarette out.

"Doesn't Charley's family have a cottage at White Horse?" Mooch said.

"Yeah, I think so," Danny replied.

"We gotta see if we can talk him into using it," Mooch said.

"Fuck me! That's a great idea," Bugsy said. "Where is he?"

"He'll be down, I'm sure," Danny said.

Sure enough, Charley showed up a little after eight; they started in on him as soon as he did. "We won't fuck the place up," Bugsy said. "I promise."

"No fucking way. What do you think I am, a fucking idiot or something?" Charley said.

"No one said that," Bugsy said. "You're one of the smartest fucks around."

The kids pressed him further, making sure he had a full beer in his hand and a bottle nearby. "Fuck no!" Charley said, shaking his head like it was on a blender.

"Aw, c'mon, man. We won't make a mess," Danny said.

"No fucking way!" He drew the words out so long; you could have driven over them. "NOT IN A MILLION FUCKING YEARS!"

"I know these girls from East Boston," Bugsy said, passing a bottle of OT to Charley. "Take a swig. They work at Kresge's and love giving head. You're not gonna pass up on a blowjob, are you? You ain't a fag or nothing, are you?"

"Fuck you, of course not."

"They like to swallow," Danny said.

"Really?" Charley said, slurring his words.

"Oh, yeah," Bugsy said.

A half-hour later, Charley gave in and agreed to everything the kids had planned; the booze, the beer, and the bimbos from East Boston. Ditch Day planning was over.

---

Charley's family retreat had started as a small, shingle-clad cottage built by his grandfather, Daffy, a former fireman and a bull of a man in temperament, stature, and drinking skills. According to family lore, he ate as many nails as he hammered; he was a tough bastard. The drafty little building was tucked away at the end of an unpaved, sandy roadway, overlooking a small beach surrounded by shifting dunes and crooked little fences, weather-worn and embedded in the landscape. Over the years, the place had grown from one large room with a wobbly old stove to a three-bedroom cottage with two bathrooms, several closets, a full kitchen, and two showers, one inside and one outside.

Charley picked up Danny, Bugsy, and Billy and made a pit stop for donuts before driving down to Rocco's, where a large crowd was hanging around drinking, smoking, and getting louder with each passing minute. "So, what time are we leaving?" Bugsy asked Charley.

"I don't know. Around nine," Charley replied, looking around, muttering to himself, *fuck, too many kids. Fuck, fuck.*

"So, are those pigs from Eastie coming?" Danny asked, glancing over to Bugsy. "You promised Charley he was gonna get laid, right?"

"And me too," Billy yapped, "me too, right?"

"Yeah, with five-finger Mary," Bugsy laughed.

"What?"

"You'll get laid, don't worry."

"I better."

"Hey, I gotta grab some smokes. Anyone need anything?" Bugsy asked.

"I do. I'll join ya," Danny said.

They strolled into Rocco's, shuffling their feet across the well-worn oaken floor that squeaked with each step. "Can I have a pack of Winstons?" Bugsy asked the clerk, a plump woman in her forties, smoking and chewing gum at the same time.

"Box or pack?"

"Box."

Bugsy tossed a crumbled dollar bill on the countertop. The clerk grabbed a pack of smokes from the shelf behind her and began counting his change with her nicotine-stained fingers.

"Twenty-seven, twenty-eight, twenty-nine," she droned. "Thirty . . ." Danny came up behind Bugsy. "Twenty-two, twenty-two, twenty-nine, twenty-one, thirteen, twenty."

The clerk stopped, peered over her glasses, and started counting again from the beginning. Ashes from her cigarette dropped onto the countertop. Danny walked toward the door, counting louder, "Thirty-six, thirty-one, twenty-two, twenty-one, twenty-nine, thirty-seven, nineteen."

"Can I help you?" she asked, restacking the coins. "I don't have all day."

"Get out of here, you retard. We gotta get going," Bugsy said. As soon as Danny stepped outside, the clerk muttered, "Your friend's an asshole. You know that, doncha?"

"He ain't my friend. He's a fag. I ain't never seen him before."

She rolled her eyes around and started counting again. When she finished, she slid his change across the countertop. "Thanks," Bugsy said, grabbing a pack of matches advertising discount rates for *Paragon Park, the World's Largest Roller Coaster.* When he got outside, Charley stood beside the open trunk at the back of the car. "Anyone want a beer?" he asked.

"Is the pope Catholic?" Danny answered.

Charley fished some Gansetts out, opened them, and passed them around. He stuffed a couple of cans in his pockets and closed the trunk. After everyone got in, Charley handed the beers to Billy, who was sitting next to him, fiddling with the radio dial. The vehicle shuddered before giving an exhausted wheeze when Charley turned the engine over. "Hey, Billy. We're all gonna get laid. Twice maybe," Charley said.

"Really?"

"Yeah, and they're gonna blow us, too," Charley said. "They're from Eastie. They like to swallow almost as much as the girls from Hingham."

"I read in Playboy that the cum's good for their complexion," Bugsy said. "It keeps 'em from getting acne and shit. That's why the girls from Hingham look so good."

"Is that true?" Billy asked, taking a sip of his beer.

"It has to be. I read it in Playboy," Bugsy replied.

"Anyone got any Frenchies?" Billy asked.

"I got plenty," Charley replied, tapping the glove compartment. "I don't know if I got any in your size, though. They're large and extra-large."

"Fuck you."

"Anyone know what time it is?" Danny asked.

"Hell, if I know. I ain't got a watch or nothing," Charley said.

"Me neither," Bugsy said.

"It don't matter. They'll wait," Charley said. "The girls from Eastie like Irish dick. They're not greasy like their father's dicks."

"Hey, did you get the rum?" Danny asked.

"Does a porcupine piss on a flat rock?" Charley rejoined. "Does a bear shit in the woods? Does Fathead's mother swallow?" Everyone laughed so hard that the windows steamed up.

"I got half a gallon of Bacardi," Charley replied. "Billy, you know what I'm gonna do? I'm gonna pour the rum on my dick, so it'll be sweet and sticky. I'll bet they'll love that! It'll remind them of their brothers."

"Are you really gonna do that?"

"Fuck, yeah!" Bugsy said.

"So, where are we meeting them?" Danny asked.

"At the far end of the station, at the bottom of the bus ramp. Where the trolleys leave," Bugsy said.

"Got it," Charley said, running a red light as he neared the station.

"There they are!" Billy said, pointing, banging his hand against the window.

"I hope that's not the hand you jerk off with," Danny said.

"That's them, ain't it?" Billy said, leaning forward again and bouncing in his seat.

"Yeah," Charley said. "Don't squirt your shorts."

"I've been laid before. I've gotten a blowjob too," Billy said oversensitively.

"Yeah, but your sister doesn't count," Bugsy replied.

"And your mother doesn't count either," Danny added.

"You guys are assholes; you know that, right?"

"We're only fucking with you. You know that, right?" Danny said.

"Yeah, I know, but . . ."

"Look! There they are," Bugsy said.

Charley pulled up to the curb, shifted the car into neutral, gently braked to a stop, and rolled his window down. "Mary Anne?"

"Yeah," she bubbled, poking her head through the window, filling the car with the scent of cheap perfume and stale cigarettes.

"What's up?" Bugsy asked.

Billy was about to say something but lost his breath when she leaned closer, bringing her bouncy breasts to eye level.

"Can you fit us all in?"

"Yeah, of course. We got plenty of room. If we don't, we'll stick Billy in the trunk," Bugsy said.

"One of you might have to sit in the back or on someone's lap," Danny said.

She slid back out the window and looked at Billy and Charley, smirking when she noticed the bulge in Billy's crotch. Billy fumbled around, trying to find the best place to put his hands, making things worse. "How 'bout I get in front with you two," she said.

"Yeah, sure," Billy stuttered.

"This is Joanne," Mary Anne said, "and this is Betty."

"Hi," Charley said. A reprise of greetings from the other kids followed.

The girls walked around to the other side of the car. Billy swung the front passenger door open and got out while Bugsy opened the back door. Joanne and Betty got in the back, and Mary Anne slid into the front seat by grabbing Charley's thigh and pulling herself across the seat. She was wearing a pair of hip-huggers so tight, Danny couldn't figure out how she got them on, never mind off. He looked closer; there were no underwear lines.

Joanne wore a pair of purple-colored slacks that looked like they had been painted on. Her blouse hugged her tightly, exposing her belly and, above it, a light-colored bra barely hiding a couple of chocolate quarters tightly tucked behind it. Her hair looked like a second-floor room addition, stacked atop her head. Her eyebrows had been heavily plucked and painted back on, reminding Danny of a doll he'd seen at Bradlees.

Betty was an endless bundle of boobs, hips, and giggles. Whenever she laughed, her tits bounced up and down like circus seals, and her blouse flipped open every time she moved, leaving little to the imagination, something no one complained about.

"You girls want a beer?" Charley asked. Before they could answer, Bugsy opened a few cans and passed them around.

Charley took off and turned the wipers on as soon as they hit the expressway. "So, how was the ride over?" Danny asked.

"It was okay," Betty said, popping her gum. She stuck her finger in her mouth and twirled it around, nearly putting Billy into cardiac arrest.

"Wasn't as long as I thought it would be," Mary Anne said. "I never come this way."

"Charley, can you pull over?" Billy said. "I gotta see a man about a horse."

"Can you hold it? Hojo's is coming up."

"I'll try. I really gotta go, man."

"Would you like me to hold it?" Mary Anne said, giggling and rubbing Billy's leg, nearly sending him into his grave. A few minutes later, Charley pulled into the Howard Johnson parking lot and drove to the far end, next to the woods. "Be right back," Billy said as he, Bugsy, and Danny ran into the woods.

"Jesus Christ!" Bugsy said. "Did you see her tits?"

"How could you miss them! They're all fucking stacked," Danny said.

"I'll bet you it's because of all the cum they swallow," Billy said as he pulled his fly down.

"You don't believe that shit, do you?" Danny said. "If that was true, why don't the girls from Hingham have big tits? They swallow, right?"

Bugsy laughed so hard he wobbled and pissed in every direction.

"Hey, point that thing somewhere else," Danny said. They all turned at the same time, distracted by the sound of crunching leaves and breaking branches; Charley was coming toward them.

"Man, these chicks are hot, ain't they?" Danny said as soon as Charley reached them.

"How about them bazookas?" Charley responded.

They remained silent, finishing their work, zipping up, and running back toward the car when the rain came down harder. "What're you gonna do if a bunch of kids show up?" Danny asked Charley. "What the fuck, with all this rain and everything? Everyone's gonna be looking for someplace dry."

"Yeah, I've been thinking about that," Charley said. "I thought everyone was going to Nickerson Pond. I wonder how many kids know about my family's place?"

"All it takes is one," Bugsy said.

"Yeah, one with a big mouth," Charley muttered.

"I didn't say nothing," Bugsy said.

"I didn't say you did."

Charley opened the trunk, and everyone grabbed a handful of beers and got back in the car, now a steam bath on wheels. Charley rolled his window down to let some air in while Billy ran his hand across the windshield, puckering the moisture off so they could see where they were going. Mary Anne turned and tapped Betty on her knee, sending her into giggles and launching her breasts into action. Betty responded by opening her purse and removing an emaciated-looking cigarette. "Anyone got a match?" she asked.

Bugsy looked at the rumpled paper stick as he handed his matches to her. "What the fuck is that?" he asked.

"A joint," Betty said.

"A what?"

"A joint; you smoke it."

She lit it and took a long drag. The scent reminded Danny of a skunk. All the kids watched her, fascinated with everything she did. Instead of blowing the smoke out, she pursed her lips and kept the smoke in, expanding her chest until her tits nearly popped out of her blouse. The car filled with a cloud of light gray smoke after she exhaled. She closed her eyes, took another drag, and held the smoke in before passing the paper stick to Joanne, who smoked it the same odd way, inhaling and holding it in.

"God, that thing stinks," Danny said, fanning his hand in front of his face.

The girls laughed in response.

"So, what are you smoking?" Danny asked.

"Marijuana," Betty replied.

"Marijuana! Are you serious?" Billy cried. "You gotta put that fucking thing out! I'm serious! We could get arrested!"

Mary Anne calmly put her hand on Billy's thigh. "Relax. It's cool," she said. "It's just a little pot. No one's gonna die or nothing."

Joanne passed the half-smoked cigarette to Danny, who just stared at it. "Are you gonna take a hit or not?" she asked.

"A what?" Danny asked.

"A hit. A toke. A drag. I don't know, a puff," Mary Anne said like she was reading the newspaper.

Danny lifted the joint to his nose and rolled it around, inspecting it.

"It's not gonna kill you. All you gotta do is take a drag and hold it in for as long as you can," Mary Anne said, taking the joint from him. "Like this," she continued, drawing the smoke in, puffing her chest out, and inflating her tits again. After she exhaled and didn't die, Danny reached for the smoke and lifted it to his lips. "Don't worry. You're gonna like it," Mary Anne said, patting Danny's knee. He took a long drag, inhaling until the joint glowed and burned close to the end. He kept the smoke in for as long as he could before letting it out, expecting things to change, but they didn't. *What the fuck?* He took another drag and kept it in even longer, but nothing happened.

The other kids, wide-eyed, stared at him. He inhaled again, closed his eyes, and tilted his head back, listening to his heartbeat, something he hadn't noticed before. He let the smoke out and noticed the windshield wipers slapping the water aside, leaving broad, iridescent streaks on the glass. One of the kids asked him something, but he didn't respond. The voices faded like the morning fog. He heard the doors opening and closing and the rain pitter-pattering on the car's roof, content not to move or do anything.

# 31

Danny wasn't sure how long he'd been in the car. It could have been a few minutes, or it could have been a few days. His only clue was the color of the sky, and it had not changed much. He moved his legs around, glad his feet were still attached. He watched the steady stream of showers that looked like strings of diamonds dangling from the belly of the dark gray clouds that rolled gently across the sky. The sounds of cars and muddy wheels sounded like a summer symphony. After tugging on his laces, he made sure his socks were on, his pants buckled, and his fly zipped. He fumbled with the door, and after figuring out how it worked, stumbled out of the car and stepped into a muddy puddle. He got out, turned his back to the rain, tugged his collar up, and tried to figure out which way to go. He studied the uneven roadway, a path marked by ponds and puddles flanking a row of cottages, all looking like they'd been built at the same time by the same crew. He walked up and down the road, studying everything until he spotted one of the cottages surrounded by beer cans, bottles, footprints, and heaps of trash. He leaped over the puddles until he was in front of the noisy beach house. He swung the door open, stepped in, and spotted the kids hanging around a long countertop separating the parlor from the kitchen.

"Hey, how ya feeling?" Bugsy yelled, causing everyone to turn and look at Danny.

"I'm good, man, I'm good," Danny said, rasping through a dry mouth. "Is there anything to eat?" The girls started laughing.

"Let me check," Charley replied. He left the room and went into the kitchen, rummaging around in the cabinets and stopping when he found an old box of Saltine crackers. Charley tossed them over to Danny. He grabbed a handful and stuffed them in his mouth. After another mouthful, he offered the crackers up. The guys passed. The girls each took a couple and chewed them to death. Danny smiled and stuffed another handful in his mouth. The girls started laughing again, getting louder with each bite Danny took.

Bugsy shook his head and sidled up to Betty. "What's so goddamned funny?"

"Him!" she replied, pointing at Danny.

"Is he gonna be okay?"

"Yeah."

"I never seen him eat like that before."

"He's okay. He's got the munchies."

"What are those?" Bugsy asked.

"The munchies; he's hungry. When you smoke pot, you get super hungry. Everything tastes good. They call it the munchies."

"I ain't never heard of that before," Bugsy said.

"It happens when you get high," Betty said.

"What is it like? Getting drunk?" Charley asked.

"Sort of, but better. You get really hungry, mostly for sweet stuff, like cake and cookies. Last week, Mary Anne and I got high and ate a whole pack of Oreos in ten minutes."

"Does it do anything else?" Charley asked.

"Yeah," she replied. "Everything looks and sounds really cool. You hear things you never heard or noticed before."

"Anything else?"

"Lights and bright stuff. You can almost hear them. I don't know how to explain it. It's really cool."

Joanne piped in. "You might have heard a song maybe a hundred times before, maybe a million, and then you hear all kinds of things like you heard it for the first time. If you listen to the Beatles' new album *Sergeant Pepper's Lonely Hearts Club Band* when you're high, you'll hear all kinds of sounds, like a whole orchestra and everything. It's amazing."

"And fucking," Mary Anne said, stopping the conversation cold. "Fucking is like nothing else you've ever done."

"And cum tastes really good," Betty said, giggling. "It's kind of sweet and salty."

The guys stared at each other, speechless.

"Is Danny gonna be okay?" Mooch asked. "I ain't never seen him like this before."

"He'll be fine," Mary Anne said.

Charley looked around the room. "You girls wanna go in the back, where it's quiet?" he said.

"Sure," Mary Anne said.

"Let's go." Charley got up and led everyone to the master bedroom at the back of the house. "I'll get some beers."

Danny walked over to an old rocking chair in the corner of the room, where he sat down and looked out the window at the rain. Suddenly Charley started screaming, "GET THE FUCK OUT. NOW!"

Danny and Mooch ran out of the room. "What's up?" Mooch asked. Danny stood next to him, looking at everyone in the room.

"I gotta start throwing some of these fuckers out," Charley said. He turned back to the kids. "Get out, all of you, get the fuck out!" The kids got up slowly and left, trudging out into the constant rain. After the last one left, Charley closed the door and grabbed a beer. "You got anything else to eat?" Danny asked. Charley ignored him.

"Ricky," he said to one of the kids, a tall, overweight guy who looked like he could have been a lineman for the Patriots. "Don't let nobody in."

"Sure. No problem."

"Thanks," Charley said, handing him a beer.

He went back through the house. Mooch and Danny followed. Charley swung the main bedroom door open. Billy was sitting on his grandmother's hope chest, and Joanne was on her knees, giving him a blowjob. Bugsy was on the bed, spread-eagled. Mary Anne, ass up in the air, was bobbing her head up and down on his dick. Fitzy had Betty bent over the dresser, fucking her from the rear. Her blouse was off, and he was squeezing her pink-tipped breasts, rotating them in his hands. Danny was in the corner of the room, laughing and rocking himself.

"Jesus Christ," Charley said. "Save some for me."

"I'm ready," Betty said, glancing over her shoulder at Fitzy.

Fitzy grabbed her by the hips and pumped harder. She glanced at Charley. "Don't be long," she said. "I wanna get laid." Danny laughed so hard that he nearly fell out of his chair. Fitzy looked at Danny. "We're done," she said, pushing Fitzy off.

"I'll be right back," Charley said, returning five minutes later. "Danny. I need your help. I gotta throw some more of these assholes out," he said.

"What about the other kids?" Danny said, looking over the guys, half-naked and sprawled on the bed and around the room.

"Are you shitting me? What're they gonna do? Run out there with their dicks in their hand?"

Danny slowly stood up and followed Charley back into the kitchen, where Charley started yelling again. "GET THE FUCK OUT OF HERE! NOW!" The kids began shuffling around, mumbling in protest. "WHO THE FUCK INVITED YOU?" Charley screamed, waving his arms. No one moved; they just stared at him. "Fuck this!" he thundered. "Danny, can you get the other kids? I need some help."

Danny scuffled into the master bedroom; the kids were almost dressed. "Hey, guys. There's a bunch of kids out there Charley doesn't know. He's having a hard time throwing them out."

"We'll be right out," Bugsy said, zipping his pants up and tucking his shirt in.

Danny waited while watching the girls get dressed, giggling and tugging their panties on, slipping their bras over their shoulders, adjusting their blouses, putting on fresh lipstick, and brushing their hair. The guys finished dressing and followed Danny into the living room.

"What the fuck's going on?" Bugsy yelled as he walked over to the tallest of the bunch and grabbed him by the collar. "Who the fuck let you in?" he shouted, half dragging the kid out the door, stopping when the kid stepped outside. Bugsy turned and yelled, "Who's next?" The rest of the kids grabbed their beers, left their cigarettes burning in the ashtrays, and went outside. "Don't hang around here. If you do, I'm gonna kick your fucking asses down to the beach."

Bugsy slammed the door and turned. "Is that it?" he said, chuckling.

"You're such a badass," Charley said, laughing.

"That big goofy fuck is a fucking pussy," Bugsy said. "Did you see him?"

"Fuck yeah," Danny said. "I think he pissed his pants."

"Anyone know him?" Charley asked.

"I think I seen him around," Danny said.

"Fuck him. Hey, Mooch, put some music on, will ya?" Charley said.

Mooch fumbled with the radio until he got a strong signal, one without much static. Charley lit a smoke, sat on the couch, put his feet on the coffee table, and sighed. As soon as the conversation started again, there was a knock on the door.

"What the fuck?" Charley yelled. "Danny, can you see who it is? If it's those fucking kids, tell them they gotta leave, or they're gonna get fucked up." Danny got up and opened the door, expecting trouble. It was Becky, Kat, and Patty, their faces wet from the gently falling rain.

"Hi," Becky said, strolling in, shaking the rain from her jacket. She was dressed in a red pantsuit that accented her hips and legs. Her hair was held in place with a white headband that matched her blouse. Kat followed, in a buttoned pink blouse and black slacks that looked like she had slept in them. She was wearing a red windbreaker over a white sweater that looked like it had been glued on. Her hair was done in a tightly bound ponytail. Patty was the last to come in. She was wearing a blue hooded rain parka, a pair of fur-lined boots, and a multi-colored chiffon blouse tucked into a pair of tan slacks that flattered her legs and backside.

The girls flirted across the room, parting the kids like Moses making his way through the Red Sea. Becky stopped at the end table and turned the radio up. The harmonies of Archie Bell and The Drells filled the room, singing *Tighten Up*. Kat and Patty peeled their coats off and started dancing while Becky removed her jacket as if she was on stage at one of the cheesy strip bars in the Combat Zone.

"Can I get you girls something to drink?" Charley asked.

"Can I have a beer?" Kat asked.

"Sure."

"I'll have a tonic if you have one," Patty said.

"Sure."

Becky glanced over to Charley. "Do you have any wine?"

"Naw, just beer and some hard liquor."

Becky looked at the other girls as if they would solve the problem. "I guess a beer'll have to do. Can I have a glass?"

"I'll get them," Danny said, stepping forward before Charley said anything else. He went into the kitchen, grabbed the beers and the tonic, and looked around for a clean glass, to no avail. He grabbed a dirty one from the sink, ran it under the hot water for a minute, pulled his shirt out, and used it to clean the glass. He returned to the front room and handed the drinks and glass out.

"It looks pretty messy out there," Danny said to Patty.

She brushed her hair back and glanced out the window. "Yeah, the roads are really muddy."

Danny joined her, looking out the window, watching the drops hit the ground and explode. "Are you okay?" she asked.

"Yeah, yeah, I'm sorry. I ain't never seen it rain like this before."

"You seem a little—I don't know—funny or something."

"I'm okay. I'm . . ."

"I'm worried about you," she said.

"I'm okay," he said. "I'm tired."

"So, who's here?" she asked, looking around.

"A bunch of the kids. Bugsy, Mooch, Charley, Billy, and Fathead. There's a bunch of other kids from the Corner. They're hanging out back."

"We passed a bunch of kids outside. They didn't look very happy."

"Did you recognize any of them?"

"No."

"They're from school, most of them anyway. They weren't invited. Charley had to toss them."

She nodded and sipped her tonic.

"So, how are your college plans coming along?" Danny asked.

"Well—" she stopped, interrupted by a tidal wave of voices surging down the hallway—it was Mooch, Fitzy, Billy, and the Eastie girls, fluffing life back into their dark, sweaty hair. Mary Anne and the other girls strolled across the room, opened the front door, and lit their cigarettes. Fitzy sidled up next to Mary Anne. "You got a smoke?"

"Sure," she said, tugging on her blouse, removing her cigarettes tucked into her bra, exposing a pound of wet cleavage. She turned her backside to Becky as she passed a cigarette to Fitzy. After placing a cigarette in Fitzy's mouth, Mary Anne wiggled her matches out of her back pocket and lit his smoke. After it lit, she lifted the match to her lips and blew it out, exaggerating the pursing of her lips. Mary Anne slid her matches back into her pocket as Becky strolled across the room toward her.

"Am I in your way?" Mary Anne asked in mock innocence. The room became quiet.

"You're not in my way, skank," Becky hissed.

"Whatjusay?" Mary Anne said.

"You heard me. SKANK."

"What the fuck did you say?"

"I said you're a fucking skank."

Mary Anne looked at Becky's feet. "You know I've seen those shoes before. They were on a fat old hooker who works the Zone. She likes chocolate dicks." She took a drag on her cigarette. "Musta been your mother, huh?"

Kat and Patty gasped while Joanne and Betty laughed.

Becky grabbed the beer from Fitzy's hand and tossed it in Mary Anne's face. Mary Anne grabbed Becky by the hair, pulled her down, and dragged her across the floor while Becky shrieked and swung her arms wildly over her head. Becky fought back, got a hold of Mary Anne's arm, and pulled her down with her, where they wrestled and screamed as they rolled around the wooden floor, covered with sand and a thin layer of dirt. Mary Anne kicked her way until she was straddled across Becky's chest. She tore Becky's blouse open, bouncing her buttons across the living room floor.

"Stop it!" Becky screamed. "HELP!"

Patty grabbed Danny by the arm and screamed, "Stop them!"

Danny looked at her.

"DANNY!"

"What?"

Mary Anne pulled on Becky's bra; two cups of flesh-colored foam popped out and bounced across the floor.

"FALSIES!" Fitzy screamed like the drunken idiot he was. "FALSIES!"

"Stop it!" Patty screamed. "STOP!" she cried, grabbing Danny by the shoulder. Danny put his beer down and walked over to the girls, a thrashing bundle of hair and clothing.

"She's had enough," he said to Mary Anne, grabbing her by the arm. She continued pulling Becky's hair. "C'mon," he said, "Let her go."

"YOU FUCKING CUNT!" Mary Anne yelled, pulling Becky's hair one last time before letting her go. When she did, Becky crossed her arms over her chest, rolled over, and curled up into a ball.

Mary Anne got up, pulled her smokes out, lit one, and stuffed her matches in her back pocket. The room filled with the raucous sound of hoots and hollers.

# 32

Danny gave Becky a beach towel to wrap around herself before she and the girls left. Mooch put the radio back on, and everyone resumed drinking and talking about what had just happened. Fitzy stuffed the pieces of foam under his shirt and paraded around the house, laughing, mostly by himself. After the shitshow ended, Mary Anne coaxed Charley into trying one of the marijuana cigarettes with her in the back of the house. When he returned nearly an hour later, he looked like he'd had a religious experience. "C'mon, Danny," Charley said. "You gotta go for it. She gives great head, and she swallows."

Danny shook his head. "Naw, I'll pass."

Drunk and tired, the rest of the kids spread out, crashing on the furniture and anyplace else they could lie down. Danny remained on the couch and fell asleep. When he got up the following day, the place smelled like a cesspool; the floors were sticky, and there were spilled cans of beer everywhere. Someone had puked in the corner of the living room, leaving a small mound of ripe-smelling vomit. After finding a clean coffee cup, he ran the faucet until the water was cold. He drank three cups of water, hardly taking time to breathe between swallows. He stepped outside, lit a cigarette, and tried to remember what he had said and done, foggy memories that he wanted to purge from his mind.

When he went back in, the kids were still sleeping, snoring, and farting. After finding a plunger, he unclogged the kitchen sink. He went into the bathroom; the toilet was overflowing with shit, toilet paper, urine, and other things he didn't recognize, maybe cigarettes or vomit. He wasn't sure. It took him ten minutes of rummaging around in a shed in the backyard before he found a bucket, a pair of gloves, and a small garden shovel. He fought waves of nausea as he cleaned the toilet, pausing to gag every few minutes, puking a couple of times. When he was done, he poked his head into the bedrooms. Charley was in the back bedroom, lying spread eagle on the bed. Mary Anne was crouched over him, blowing him. When Charley saw him, he waved as if he was in a parade.

Danny went back through the house, cleaning up and sweeping. After he turned the radio on, the rest of the kids started getting up, coming to life by groaning and farting. The girls got up, scurrying about, taking turns taking showers, dressing, and coating themselves in perfume.

"That was fucking great," Charley said when he finally stumbled out, looking over to Danny, who said nothing. "Is everything okay?" he asked.

"I've been cleaning this shit up all morning," Danny said.

"I would've helped if you woke me up," Mooch said.

"You want to help?"

"Sure."

"Why don't you get some coffee and donuts?" Danny said.

"That's a good idea," Charley replied.

The guys reached into their pockets and put money on the kitchen counter.

"Want any company?" Betty asked.

"Sure," Mooch said, smiling so hard he almost broke his teeth.

Charley went outside and, seeing the trash cans were full, took some from a few houses down. Mooch and Betty eventually returned. After everyone ate and drank their coffee, they started cleaning up. After filling the cans, Charley and the kids returned them, now overflowing, to where they had been taken from. "I'll have to come back tomorrow," Charley said.

The drive home was quiet.

The weather got worse, hot and humid, and the cicadas were chirping away. On his way home from work, Danny stopped at the Corner, tired and hungry. The kids were talking about the Sox and their chances for their series with the Yankees, the dreaded rivals from New York. "Here," Bugsy said, handing Danny a beer. He opened it and looked up when he heard voices coming down the street. It was Patty and some of the girls.

Danny stepped away from the guys, catching Patty by surprise. She froze like a statue. The other girls stopped, looked at each other, and walked around the guys to the other side of the store. Patty smiled at him the way he remembered. He took a swig of his beer and stepped onto the sidewalk. "Hi," he said sheepishly.

"Hi," Patty answered softly. "How are you?"

"Fine. How's your family?"

"Good. Everyone's been asking about you," she replied.

"Really?"

"Yes, especially my dad."

"No kidding? How's he doing?"

"Good. He's been busy at work."

"What did you tell them?" Danny asked.

"I told them you were sick." They stared at each other to the point of discomfort. "Danny . . ." she started to speak.

"I . . . I need to let you know what happened."

"I heard."

"Heard what?"

"I heard what happened . . . what was going on that night at Charley's cottage. You were smoking marijuana and getting high. That stuff's bad for you. It leads to harder drugs," she said.

"I . . . I wanted to tell you, but I couldn't. I didn't know what I was doing. I'd never done anything like that before. I hadn't planned it or nothing. You know what I mean?"

"I do, I think."

"I hope so."

"After I learned what happened, I figured out why you acted so weird."

"Was I that bad?"

"Bad? I tried to talk to you, and you acted like I wasn't even there."

"I'm sorry. I was messed up."

"No kidding!"

"It was so weird. I was sort of there and not there. It's hard to describe."

"Well, I hope you never do that again. That stuff can make you a drug addict."

"Yeah, I don't think I'd do it again. I really didn't like it."

"What about those girls? How do you know them?" The tone of her voice changed as if someone else was talking.

"They're *Charley's* friends," he said, doing all he could to disassociate himself from them.

"Where did he meet them?" It was now an inquisition.

"I'm not sure. Downtown, I think."

"They weren't very nice."

"Yeah, I don't know what to say. They aren't from around here."

"And what about Becky?"

"What about her?"

"What about her!"

"Well, she kinda started it."

"No, she didn't."

"I don't know what to say. They were Charley's friends, and it was his place."

"What about Becky and me? Weren't we invited? Was it supposed to be a private party or something with those girls? Was that the plan?" Her voice tightened.

"I don't know. It was supposed to be just the guys. It was Charlie's place, and he invited whoever he wanted to. A lot of kids showed up, and they weren't invited. He threw them all out; man, was he pissed."

"I understand. Still, it wasn't nice, what happened to Becky. That was terrible."

"Yeah, I know. It was pretty messed up. How's she doing?"

"How do you think she's doing?"

Danny bent his head down and kicked a small stone to the side. "Not good, I suppose."

"Can you believe that jerk, Fitzy?" she said.

"I know. He's a real piece of shit. He's got no class and no couth."

"I'm glad you're not like that."

"No way."

"So, do you promise not to smoke that marijuana anymore? It scares me, Danny. I don't want to see you become a drug addict."

"Yeah, of course. I shouldn't have tried it. It kinda just happened."

"So, do you promise not to do it again?"

"Yeah, I promise."

"Good. You know I care for you. You know that, right?"

"Yeah," he blushed, "I do."

"My father asked me if I ran into you, and you were better, that you're welcome to come over for family dinner anytime you want."

"I'd like that."

"And my mom keeps asking about you."

"Really?"

"She does. And she asked me if I missed you."

"What did you tell her?"

She blushed and said, "That I did."

Danny stepped closer. "I missed you too. I'm really sorry about what happened. It wasn't planned or nothing. I would never do anything to hurt you. You know that, right?"

Patty leaned closer and gave him a kiss on the cheek. "Let's forget about the whole thing."

"I will. It won't happen again."

She gave him another kiss. "Why don't you come by for breakfast after church?"

"Sounds good."

---

Danny got up early on Sunday morning and went to work. He liked going in to ensure the shelves were stocked and the place was clean, even though he wasn't getting paid, usually leaving by ten thirty when Mass was getting out of Saint Anne's. He'd pass through a steady stream of parishioners, strolling through quiet, tree-lined streets and houses, where the smell of bacon filled the air. After work, he stopped for some donuts. Patty was waiting for him on her front porch. As soon as she saw him, she hopped down the wooden steps and greeted him. "Good morning," he said.

"Good morning, back at you," Patty replied, reaching for his hand. They rolled their fingers together like a ball of yarn, leaned into each other, and kissed. "Come on in. Everyone's been asking for you."

Patty spun around and headed back up the stairs, reaching her hand behind her for him to grasp, flopping it around like a dish towel until he grabbed it. She tugged him up the porch, and when they were at the entryway, he stopped, tucked his shirt in, and made sure his shoes were tied and his fly zipped. Patty swung the door open and bounded through a long, wallpapered hallway covered with pink and blue flowers over a maroon-and-gold carpet, with large gold *fleurs-de-lis* patterns endlessly repeated. They entered the kitchen, where he was overwhelmed by the smell of ham, toast, eggs, and coffee. He hadn't thought much about eating, but by the time he was in the kitchen, that was all he could think about.

"Good morning," Mrs. McNulty said as she dried her hands on her apron.

"Good morning. How are you?" Danny replied, trying not to look at the thick slabs of sliced ham on the countertop. "I got some donuts," he beamed.

"I can see. You don't have to do that," Mrs. McNulty said, relieving his arms and putting the donuts on the counter. "How was work today?"

"Great! It was a good day. I got a lot done." He slipped another glance at the ham.

"Patty tells me you go in every Sunday morning even though you aren't getting paid."

"Well, yeah, sort of. I don't mind going in. I stock all of the shelves and get everything in order. It makes the week a lot easier when everything's stocked, and the place is clean. Plus, I don't need to worry much when working. I like to be ready."

"You're an awful smart boy." Danny blushed, unable to stop it from happening. He peeked into the living room. "I'm gonna check in with Mr. McNulty."

"I'm sure he'll be glad to see you."

"I'll help you, Mom," Patty said.

Danny strolled into the parlor. Mr. McNulty was in a large brown recliner, reading the Sunday Globe. His feet were propped up on a leather-covered hassock. The boys were sprawled across the floor, pressing blobs of Silly Putty on the cartoon strips and then transferring the images to other parts of the newspaper. Dick Tracy was in the business section, and Li'l Abner was in the help wanted ads. It remained to be seen where Beetle Bailey was going.

"Good morning!" Danny said, not wanting to interrupt him too much.

"Good morning, Danny," Mr. McNulty said, setting the paper aside and getting up. "How are you?"

"Fine, thanks."

"Patty tells me you've been promoted at your work."

Danny blushed. "Yeah."

"She's very proud of you," Mr. McNulty said.

"I'm pretty lucky, I guess."

"Luck has nothing to do with it. You've earned it, son," Mr. McNulty said.

"You're a good boy and a hard worker. I'm glad Patty has a friend like you. Most boys are hanging on the Corner, getting into trouble."

"So, what do you think about this new pitcher, the kid from Philly? Rizzo, or something?" Mr. McNulty asked.

"The right-hander? The kid with the wicked curveball, down in Pawtucket?" Danny replied.

"Yes. Darn it, I can't remember his name!" Mr. McNulty rolled his head back. "Razzo? Rankie?"

"Rankowski!" Danny offered.

"Yes, that's him. He's one heck of a ballplayer."

"No kidding. I can't wait to see him play."

"Me too!"

"Are you boys ready?" Mrs. McNulty called from the kitchen. No time was wasted; the boys jumped up and sprinted into the kitchen.

"Girls," she yelled into the hallway. They came bounding down the stairs almost as fast as the boys.

"Let's grab a plate before everything's gone," Mr. McNulty chuckled.

When they sat down, Patty handed Danny a tall glass of orange juice.

"Thank you."

"You're welcome. Do you want one, Daddy?"

"Yes, honey, thank you."

"The Sox've got a few tough weeks ahead of them," Mr. McNulty said.

"Yeah. They'll get through it okay, I'm sure," Danny said.

"I hope so." Mr. McNulty took a sip of his juice. "And what about the Tigers? They're having a great year."

"Yeah, they are," Danny said, nodding. "I gotta tell you, Minnesota's gonna be tough."

"The whole division's tough. It's not like the National League. I prefer a hitting game."

"Me too!"

"Between you and me, I'm still upset at Lonborg."

"No kidding," Danny responded. "Skiing! Can you believe it?" What was he thinking?"

"Imagine where we'd be if we had him *and* Tony C.?"

"We'd win every game. There's no doubt."

Patty dished out breakfast. When everyone's plate was filled, she sat down. Mrs. McNulty folded her hands, bowed her head, and prayed. "Bless us, O Lord, and these, thy gifts, which we are about to receive from thy bounty, through Christ, our Lord. Amen."

The rest of the family bowed and, hands folded, replied, "Amen."

Danny and Mr. McNulty continued talking, solving all the Red Sox's problems and half of the Celtics'. All the while, Patty kept serving Danny and her father. They finally looked up and realized the table was clean; they were the only ones left.

"Wow, where did the time go?" Mr. McNulty asked.

"Gee, I don't know."

"You'll have to excuse me," Mr. McNulty said. He grabbed the newspaper from the parlor, handed it to Danny, and went upstairs.

Danny loosened his belt and opened the paper to the sports page. He was in the middle of studying the baseball standings when he heard footsteps. He looked up to see Patty wearing a brightly colored blouse and a freshly creased pair of white slacks. Her hair was tied up in a bun, and she wore a pair of small silver earrings.

"Ready to go?" she asked.

"Sure," Danny replied, mindlessly putting the paper down. "You look incredible!"

Patty glanced at her black patent leather shoes and blushed before smiling at Danny. She turned and called behind her upstairs, "I'll be back in a little while, Mom."

Danny got up and walked over to the stairway. "Thank you for breakfast," Danny said.

"You're welcome," Mrs. McNulty replied from above.

"Tell Mr. McNulty I said goodbye."

"I will. You two have a nice day."

"We will," Danny responded while looking at Patty, smiling and beckoning him toward the front door. She swung it open, stepped onto the front porch, and kissed him. He closed his eyes and kissed her on the lips. She took his hand, and they strolled down the stairs and turned toward Washington Street.

"Man, I can't believe how much I ate. That was the best breakfast I ever had," Danny said.

"My mom likes to cook, especially Sunday breakfast," she said.

"I usually have cornflakes or Frosted Flakes for breakfast." She squeezed his hand. "It's nice of your mom and dad to have me over."

"They like you. And my dad loves talking about baseball with you. He doesn't have anyone else to do that with. Did I ever tell you? He thinks you're one of the smartest kids he's ever met, knowing all the players' names and their statistics."

They flicked their fingers in and around each other's hands, remaining silent until they reached the end of the street. "Your family's pretty religious, aren't they?" Danny said.

"Not more than anyone else."

"Yeah, I guess."

"Did you know my father used to be an altar boy?" she asked, stepping in front of him and spinning like a ballerina. "He can say the whole Mass in Latin."

"You're kidding. I've been to Mass sometimes when they say it in Latin. I can never figure out what they're saying."

"Besides learning the Bible and all about the church and the history of Jesus, one of the things I like best is it's the one time of the week we all get together. After Mass, everyone sits around the table, and we eat, talk, and catch up on things."

"You're pretty lucky."

"Doesn't your family go to church?"

"We used to, but not anymore. I can't remember the last time we went."

"Don't you go?"

Danny pondered the question; she didn't rush him. He replied half a block later, gauging his words. "No, not anymore. Don't take me wrong or nothing, but it seems they just want more money whenever I go. It's like some kind of racket or something. You know what I mean?" Danny changed his voice as if standing at the altar, making his best priest-like impression. "Our third collection is for Father Murphy, who's vacationing in Bermuda, and our fourth is for the bishop, who's building his new library. You know, stuff like that."

She looked over at him, remaining silent.

"We ain't rich or nothing. None of us are, but the parish is," Danny said. "They got all kinds of money. I mean, look at the churches." She said nothing. They walked along quietly as if they were going to a funeral. Two blocks later, Danny spoke again. "I don't mean to say anything bad or nothing, but when my Aunt Sue needed help after her husband died, the church didn't do nothing for her. She was religious; she went to church every Sunday, even Saturdays, and always gave them money. Then, when she needed help, the priest told her to pay a dollar and light a candle for her dead husband, and he'd pray for him. That was it! It was as if she hadn't given them enough over the years." Danny shook his head and grew more animated. "The first time she needed something, they told her to pay for a candle, as if that was gonna do something!"

"What parish was that?" Patty asked.

"Saint Anne."

"Oh, Saint Anne," she repeated.

They grew quiet again, continuing to Codman Square, where rows of staccato-stacked structures lined both sides of the street, casting lazy shadows onto the pale gray sidewalks that tied the buildings together. Almost every one of the stores was closed, making it a great time to window shop. They headed toward the church in the middle of the square, invigorated by the pleasant breezes that fluttered the trees and blew curly brown leaves down the street, leaves so crisp, you could hear them. The church bell chimed to announce the hour.

"Danny, you never talk about your father," Patty said. "I don't mean to pry, so I'll understand if you don't want to talk about it."

Danny continued walking to the end of the block, where he stopped, turned, and spoke in a voice that scared her. "He was an asshole! He left my ma and me and my brother and my sister; he left us nothing. He was a jerk, and I'm glad he's gone! He used to beat my ma up when he came home. He drank a lot and hurt her, and there was nothing I could do. I was too little, and there was no one around to help. I could hear her screaming and crying." Danny's chest heaved, and his eyes filled with tears. "I couldn't do nothing. I couldn't!" He closed his eyes, bent his head down, and shook. She put her arms around him and held him as they both cried. It took a few minutes before he composed himself and spoke again. "And then . . . then he had an accident at work and . . . and he was in the hospital for a long time." He paused and wiped his nose, dragging his sleeve across his face, leaving a wet trail of sorrow. "They put him on some pain medicine." Patty held him tighter, draining the sobs out of his chest. "After that, he was never the same. He'd changed. And then, one day, he left and never came back. He was gone, just like that. Gone."

Danny loosened his arms, and she lifted her head from his shoulder to wipe her tears. An older couple across the street looked over. Patty wiped her eyes, smiled at them, and made a small wave. The man tipped his hat, and the woman smiled and nodded before continuing on their way.

Danny stood erect and flexed his shoulders. "I'm okay with it. I am," he said. "A lot of the kids don't have a father. Some don't even have mothers. Look at Mikey, Billy O'Reilly, and Muffinhead. They don't have fathers. And Ricky

Lancione doesn't have a mother. Charley don't either. His mother was killed when he was little."

Patty squeezed his hand and kissed him.

"Me, I don't give a shit. It's my little brother and big sister. I know that's why my sister's so fucked up. It's why she makes so many such stupid mistakes about her boyfriends." Danny took a deep breath. "Yeah, he was a real role model." His chest heaved one last time. He wrapped his arms around Patty and pulled her so close he could feel her heartbeat.

"C'mon. Let's take a walk," Patty said, tossing her hair over her shoulder. They locked fingers and walked across the street into the sun's path as it melted into the horizon. "What a beautiful day," she said.

Danny squeezed her hand. "It sure is."

They started the long descent toward Franklin Park, passing small stores and apartment entryways jammed into closet-sized pockets and flanked by redbrick walls and granite stoops. Danny stopped at the joke shop, one of the most popular places in the square for him and his friends. "I used to buy those all the time," he said, pointing to a small, cigarette-sized box containing little gray balls that exploded when you threw them. "Remember them?"

She shook her head. "Not really. I had a pair of those when I was little," she said, waving her finger at a pair of plastic teeth that you wound up like an alarm clock and that clattered and bounced around when you put them down.

"Those were great! And what about those?" Danny said, pointing again. "Stink bombs! We used to light those in school. Man, those things smelled nasty!"

"We'd never have been able to do that in our school. The sisters would have killed us. My father would have killed me if I did anything like that."

They continued laughing and looking at the array of items: fart cushions, dribbling cups, X-ray glasses, trick cards, and itching powder, enjoying the memories they brought back.

"Would you like a sundae?" he asked.

"Sure, that'd be nice. It sounds good."

"Great! Let's go."

They turned and headed back uphill, passing other couples, kids with a dog, and a few foul-smelling, ragged little men. When they reached Brigham's, they stepped inside and looked around. "Let's get that booth in the corner," Danny said, nodding toward the back of the restaurant. He glanced at the menu posted on the wall behind the countertop. "What's your favorite flavor?"

"Vanilla."

"Vanilla? Mine too."

# 33

As the school year ended, Danny put in more hours at work, staying late and usually working Saturdays, settling into the rhythms of a full-time job, getting up early, going to work, and getting to know the regular customers. Mrs. Reynolds stopped by every Saturday morning to have Danny check the air in her tires and wash her windows. She was always generous with her tips. "You've earned it, young man," she'd say, handing him a small handful of coins. And then there was Old Man Sweeney, who liked his oil changed every month, whether he needed to or not. He'd get out of his car and look over Danny's shoulder, watching everything he did, anxious like an expectant father. He always tipped too, but, unlike Mrs. Reynolds, he handed out bills instead of pocket change.

Danny's favorite customer was Mrs. McPherson, a twenty-one-year-old widow who'd lost her husband in Vietnam. He'd been there less than a month before he stepped on a landmine, ending his short married life. His body parts ended up splattered in a grove of banyan trees alongside a paddy field in the Mekong Delta, leaving little to send home.

Mrs. McPherson owned a black Mustang, and she came by twice a week, rain or shine, to get her tank filled and have her oil checked. Danny enjoyed watching her when she pulled up, got out, removed a chamois cloth from her trunk, and shined the chrome mirrors and bumpers, all the while bent over, unknowingly taking Danny's breath away.

Every Friday afternoon, he'd put half his money in the bank, pretending it didn't exist, just like Mr. Erickson had told him to do. Most of his friends weren't so lucky. They didn't work, so they had nothing to save. They knew Uncle Sam would get them a job. All they had to do was visit the recruiting office in Codman Square, and there they could sign up for the army, the navy, or the marines.

"C'mon in, kid, let me tell you what the army can do for you."

"This is a great chance to serve your country."

"We'll teach you how to kill some slant-eyes."

"Geez, kid, don't you love your country?"

"You ain't a faggot, are you?"

"If you had any balls, you'd join the marines. Don't be a pussy."

---

Bridie was busy working hard, making plans for Danny's graduation. "After all," she told him, "it's not like a birthday. Everyone has a birthday. How much work does it take to get older? Graduating from high school. That's special. Not everyone graduates, you know." She must have said it a hundred times. She was very proud of him. On Friday, coming home, he passed his mother's room and saw her trying on a new dress in the mirror. "How do I look?" she asked, turning from side to side.

"Great, Ma, you look great!"

"I borrowed a suit for you from Mrs. Feeney. It's in your room. Can you try it on?"

"Yeah, sure. I wanna grab something to eat first."

"I made you a tuna fish sandwich. It's in the fridge."

"Thanks."

"I also bought you a nice button-down shirt. Can you try it on?"

"Sure, Ma."

"Can you turn the tea kettle on?"

"Sure," he yelled back.

Bridie returned to her modeling and humming while Danny ate and poured her a cup of tea, bringing it to her when it was ready. He got dressed and went into her bedroom.

"My, you look so handsome. Let me look at you." She turned him around, tugged on the tail of his jacket, and pulled on his pants. "Let me get a tie." She removed several of them from the closet and held them up, one by one, against his neck. "Which one do you like?" she asked.

"The blue one."

"That's my favorite," she said. "Let me help you put it on." She fiddled around with his collar. "You know, I used to always tie your father's."

Danny tilted his head back to make it easier for her. "Can I ask you a question?"

"Of course," she said.

"When's the last time you heard from him?" Danny asked as she looped the tie around his neck.

"I don't know. Over a year ago."

"Is he still in Florida?"

"I'm not sure."

"Do you think he's okay?"

She pulled the tie up, tightening and adjusting it under his collar. "I don't know. It's hard to tell. I don't know, honey. I don't know."

"Did he say anything?" She kept fiddling around with his tie in silence. "Did he ask for me?"

"Here, turn around. Let me check the length. You have to turn it a little here, like this, and pull it up closer to your collar. Like this," Bridie said, tugging the knot. "There, how's that feel?"

"Good," looking at himself in the mirror.

"You look like him," Bridie said.

"Dad?"

"Yes," she replied, nodding.

Danny stared at himself in the mirror. He ran his hand over his chin, feeling the whisker nubs, listening to them. "Do you know if he's married?"

"I don't know, honey."

"Is he working?"

"I don't know, honey. What I do know is he's in a lot of pain. He has been for a long time. Ever since he had his accident."

"Still?"

"Yes. And there might be some other things. It's complicated."

"What about Aunt Sue? Do you ever hear from her?"

"No," Bridie said, shaking her head. Her voice dropped. She sounded sad. "It's been a long time. The last I heard, she moved to New York."

"Do you think he'll ever come back?"

"I doubt it. He doesn't keep in touch with his own family."

"Have you ever thought about seeing him?"

"I used to, but that was a long time ago. Here," she said, reaching for her dresser top, "I bought a snap-on tie for Frankie. Can you make sure he puts it on tomorrow? I also got him a new shirt." She removed it from her closet and handed it to him. "What do you think?"

"It's nice, Ma, real nice."

"We'll have to leave at five thirty. It'll be busy, and I want to get good seats."

"Okay."

Danny went into his room, got undressed, and lay down, thinking about his father, eventually drifting off to sleep.

After getting home and taking a hot bath, Danny spent the rest of the afternoon getting Frankie ready.

"Jesus Christ, it won't kill you to look nice for one night."

Frankie looked back like he was going to the dentist.

"C'mon Frankie, you gotta help me. This is important to Ma." After a few more prods and several threats, they were ready by five. Bridie called a cab to take them to the graduation.

"We'll sit here," Bridie said, walking to the second row of chairs. "C'mon, Frankie. Sit here, next to me. Chrissy, is your chair comfortable?"

"Yes, Ma. It's fine."

"Do you need anything?"

"No, I'm good," Chrissy said, fidgeting, trying to get comfortable.

"I'll be back. I gotta get my stuff," Danny said, getting up and strolling to the back of the hall. Mr. Valenti, Danny's math teacher, handed him his cap and gown, taking them from a rolling rack of coat hangers. "Good luck, Danny. We'll miss you."

"Thanks, Mr. Valenti. I'll miss you," Danny said as he stepped away and sniffed the garments, wondering how many kids had worn them, surprised they smelled better than his dungarees. He stepped to the side, put his gown and cap on, and checked himself in the mirrors that lined the walls. Happy, he turned and waved at Mr. Valenti and walked back to his seat. Many of the families, excited, were taking Polaroids, waiting for them to develop before passing them around for everyone to look at. He heard familiar voices from the back of the hall; Bugsy and a couple of the kids were standing behind the last row of chairs, no one dressed for graduation. Bugsy broke through the crowd and walked over to Danny. "What's going on?" Bugsy asked.

"How come you ain't dressed?" Danny joked.

"What? And wear all that corny shit?"

"Well, yeah. It's a big day. Plus, I earned it."

"It don't matter to me. I don't need no high school diploma where I'm going."

"So, what are you doing here?"

Bugsy looked around the room. "I don't know. Maybe settle a few scores."

"With who?"

"Who knows?" he chuckled.

"Yeah, right," Danny replied. Bugsy pulled a pint of Jack Daniels out of his back pocket and took a swig. He passed it to Danny, who glanced quickly over his shoulder before swallowing.

"Who ya here with?" Bugsy asked.

"My ma, my big sister, and my little brother. They're over there," Danny said, pointing with a nod of his nose.

"So, what ya doing tonight?" Bugsy asked.

"My ma's got some dinner plans at some fancy restaurant." Bugsy took another swig and passed the bottle to Danny; he took a quick shot.

"How about you? What're you doing?"

"We're coming to dinner with you and your family. Your ma invited me."

Danny started to speak, to protest, but Bugsy punched him in the arm before he could spit anything out. "Hey man, I'm just fucking with you."

"You fucker. You almost had me," Danny said.

They bantered back and forth for a few minutes but quieted down when a small group of teachers, led by Mr. Garrison, the phys. ed. teacher, and Mr. O'Brien, the three-hundred-pound English teacher, walked by. Mr. Reynolds, the good-looking math teacher—as the girls said—and Mr. Baron, the goofy science teacher, joined them.

"Hey, Bugs. I gotta get back to my ma. If I get in any trouble, she'll kill me."

Danny glanced over at the teachers and then back at Bugsy. "Later."

"Later."

Danny walked back to the front of the auditorium and strolled in front of the long row of seats, glancing back at Bugsy. Bugsy had always said that if he ever saw "that little prick Garrison" outside of school, he'd kick his ass. It didn't take long. Danny heard some yelling and hollering from the back of the room. Bugsy was screaming at Garrison. A security guard was running toward Bugsy, and as soon as he saw the guard, he swung at Garrison, missing him. "Motherfucker!" Bugsy yelled as he wrestled Garrison to the floor and continued throwing punches at him. Several of the teachers got ahold of Bugsy and pulled him off, but not before he'd torn Garrison's jacket sleeve off. Mr. O'Brien grabbed Bugsy, wrapped him in a bear hug, and lifted him up. The kids hooted and hollered as O'Brien carried him to the back of the room, kicking and screaming. Everyone shut up after several cops ran over, holding their clubs high.

"You fellows need a hand?" asked a whiffle-topped sergeant with arms as thick as Danny's legs.

"Over there," Mr. Baron said, pointing at the crowd of kids yelling. "These gentlemen were just leaving." As soon as the cops approached, the kids turned and left. "That one," Mr. Baron said, pointing at Bugsy. The four cops nodded. A few minutes later, the cops escorted Bugsy out, accompanied by a cacophony of hoots and cheers that filled the room.

# 34

Danny headed down to the Corner the following day after graduation. The Corner was packed and felt like New Year's Eve. Everyone was celebrating. Bugsy was the center of attention, telling everyone how he'd duked it out with Garrison. "That motherfucker's lucky he had all those other teachers around him," Bugsy said as he drank from a tall can of Gansett.

"Garrison said you fight like his sister," Danny said as he walked over.

"Who?" Mooch sputtered.

"Garrison," Danny answered.

"Fuck you, asshole," Bugsy said as he tossed a beer to Danny.

"Thanks," Danny said, snapping the beer open. "So, what happened last night? Did those cops fuck you up?"

"Naw, they tossed me in the can and called my old man." Bugsy took another mouthful of beer. "My brother Matty had to drag him out of Layden's. He was pissed 'cause the game was on. I figured he was gonna kill me."

"No shit," Mikey said. "You caused quite a fucking mess. There were cops all over the place. Fucking Timmy got busted with a half-pint. The cops threw him out on his ass. He didn't get to graduate with the rest of us. My ma asked me if I knew you, and I said, 'hell no, I don't know that kid.'"

"So anyway, my old man shows up, and he's got a few under the belt, and I'm expecting the worst, right?" Everyone nodded in agreement. "Well, I didn't know, but when the cops called my house, my brother Matty took the call. I don't know if any of you kids remember, but Matty had Garrison, and my father remembered that little prick. He was always complaining about Matty and my other brothers. So, after Matty told my old man I was duking it out with Garrison, he told Matty he was happy about it, knowing they can't do shit to me anymore. Anyways, my father comes to the station, acting really pissed. He lays into the cops, screaming and hollering, 'Where's the guy that beat my son up? Where is he?' He gets really loud and everything, and he's going on and on, telling them he's gonna press charges and sue all the fucking cops in the station. 'He's just a kid,' my old man says. So, my brother Matty's trying not to laugh the whole time. He almost pissed his pants—hey Danny, can you grab me another beer?—Matty told me he had to sit on a bench and cross his legs so he didn't piss himself. So, Matty says a big fat sergeant comes up, 'cause my father's making this big commotion and everything, and he's trying to calm him down 'cause he's so excited. So, the next thing you know, they're bringing my old man back to see me, to make sure I was okay. I'm in the drunk tank with some guys from Southie and some fucking idiot from Charlestown. He's all fucked up, and he's trying to sleep it off, and every time he dozes off, one of the kids from Southie pulls on his jacket, and this stupid fuck rolls off the bench and lands on the floor. The townie looks up, and these guys from Southie look at him like they're innocent, and this poor prick can't figure out how he got on the floor. It was a fucking riot. So, my old man comes in, and I figure he's gonna kick my ass, and so I'm getting ready when I see my brother Matty standing behind him, waving at me like it's okay. You know, don't worry or nothing. So, they all come in, and my old man looks at me, and instead of whacking the shit out of me, like I figured he'd do, he starts hollering again: 'Which one of you guys beat him up?' So, Matty's standing outside the cell, and he's got a shit-eating grin. That's when I knew I was okay."

Bugsy took another swig and continued. "So, these cops ask me if I'm okay, and I'm looking at my old man, and he's just standing there, staring at me. When no one's looking, he winks at me, the fucker. So, I start moaning and rubbing my neck like I'm hurting. Then my old man goes off again. He's on a fucking roll. He tells the cops he wants Garrison's name and address 'cause he wants them to arrest him. He has them all snookered, and they don't know what the fuck's going on, so I say, 'Dad, can I go home? I don't feel good. My neck hurts, and my ribs are hurting too.' I start rubbing my stomach like I'm all fucked up and everything. So, the fat fuck sergeant leans over and asks me, 'Are you okay, kid? Can you stand up?' So, I say, 'I'm not sure, Officer,' real polite like, so I start moaning again." Bugsy stopped, unable to talk because he was laughing so hard. The other kids started laughing with him like they had been infected.

"So, you gotta see the look on Matty's face. He can't take it anymore, so he gets up and looks for the bathroom 'cause he's gotta take a piss and all. So, I stand up slowly, and my old man leans over me like he gives a shit, and he starts asking me if I'm okay again, so I go through the same bullshit with him. So, the cops are watching all of this until the sergeant comes over to my old man and asks him, 'Why don't you take your son home? Get him a good night's rest, and if he doesn't feel better tomorrow, you can come by, and we can follow up, fill out some paperwork and all.' My old man gives them a little more shit and says, 'Okay,' and off we go like a bunch of choir boys going to church."

"No shit," Mooch said. "That's fucking crazy!"

"Yeah, they should give my old man an Academy Award for that fucking act."

"So, what happened after that, when you got home?" Danny asked.

"Yeah, what happened?" Mikey asked, leaning forward.

"We get in the car, and we're heading back home, and my old man asks Matty to stop at Rotary Liquor. So, he grabs a six-pack, and we drink a couple of beers, laughing our asses off all the way home. He told me he was proud of what I did, especially considering how that prick Garrison treated Matty and me. So, Matty drops my old man back off at the bar, and before my old man gets out, he says to me, 'Keep out of trouble,' and that was the end of it. So, my brother and I pulled up in front of our house and finished the beers. Matty goes on about Garrison and how he's such an asshole, and he tells me he's proud of me for doing what I did, sticking up for the family and all. Ain't that the shits?"

"Leave it to you, ya fuck!" Danny said.

Everyone started laughing, lifting beers to Bugsy, talking about the fight and what would happen next fall when school resumed. Danny glanced at Billy, quietly nursing his way through a bottle of Banana Brandy. "Hey, Billy. How is that stuff? Is it any good?"

"Yeah, it's sweet, sort of like drinking a tonic. It goes down really easy. You drink enough, it'll fuck you up; it catches up with you."

Billy passed the bottle to Danny, and as soon as Danny drank some, his stomach warmed, followed by a rush that shot up through his chest and into his head.

"This shit ain't bad," Danny said. "It's kinda sweet like you said. And, it's got a good blast to it." He took another swallow and passed the bottle back to Billy.

"It tastes great with milk," Billy said. "When you mix them, they call it a Jungle Jim."

"Man, those could get you in trouble."

"No shit."

"I gotta see a man about a horse," Danny said. "I'll be right back."

He walked past the girls, huddled against the wall, clucking like chickens. Patty stepped out and tugged at the corner of his jacket, catching him by surprise.

"How's it feel to be a graduate?" she asked.

"Great! I can't believe I'm done!" He tried to think of something else to say but was distracted by her lips and the scent of her hair.

"Are you okay?" she asked. "You're not smoking any of that marijuana, are you?"

"No, of course not. I was, um, thinking about something." This time it was her neck. "Um, when's your graduation?"

"Wednesday. Don't you remember?" she replied, a bit indignantly.

Danny wasn't sure how to answer, trying to remember what she had said, feeling stupid. "It's in the afternoon. I'm so excited. My uncles and my aunts are coming. They're driving up from New York."

"Um, yeah, sounds good. Can you excuse me for a minute? I gotta take a leak."

Patty scrunched her eyebrows. "Sure."

"I'll be right back."

When he returned, Patty was surrounded by a small crowd of girls. She bounced up and down and waved as soon as she saw him. The girls quieted down when he approached and quietly parted as he walked to her.

"I'm sorry," he said. "I didn't mean to be so long. I ran into a couple of the kids. So, we got talking and stuff."

She smiled. "No problem."

"You wanna take a walk?"

"Sure," she said, to the din of the other girls, watching and chatting away.

They walked around the corner, where it was quiet, and they were alone. "I've been wanting to ask you about the war in Vietcong," Danny said.

"You mean Vietnam?" she said, subtly correcting him.

"Yeah, of course, Vietnam." He shook his head in embarrassment. "What do you think about the war and all the kids signing up?"

"What do you mean? Like the reasons? Should they go?"

"I don't know. I guess, sort of the whole thing. I'm thinking of joining. A lot of kids are signing up."

She didn't answer him right away. Instead, she grabbed his hand and held it. "Did you know my father was in the war? He got a bunch of medals." She let his hand go and started to walk. He followed her. "He lost his brother, my uncle, before I was born. In the war."

He could sense the pain in her voice, and he could see it on her face. "We don't have to talk about it if you don't want to," he said, nearly in a whisper.

"It's okay," she said, wiping the tears from her eyes.

"Are you sure?"

"Yes . . . yes, I'm sure."

They continued walking. "My dad says he was the smartest one in the family and a great athlete. He went to BC High, and he played baseball, first base. My dad says he could have played for the Red Sox."

"He musta been pretty good if he could have played for the Sox."

"You remember that day you came by when you and my dad sat around the kitchen table talking about the Sox?"

"Sure, of course."

"After you left, my dad went upstairs and pulled out a photo album he keeps under my parents' bed. He sat around the rest of the afternoon, going through the album. He was looking at some pictures of his brother in his baseball uniform. I was in the hallway; he didn't know I was there and saw him. Later that night, when I was going to bed, I asked my mother if he was okay. She told me he does that now and then when he thinks about his brother. It's why he loves baseball so much. And that's why he doesn't like to talk about the war."

Danny pulled her close. She melted into his arms, sobbing. He held her tightly and rocked her back and forth. She rubbed her eyes a couple of times. "Do I look okay?" she asked when she lifted her head.

"Okay? You look beautiful."

She dabbed her eyes one more time. "Are you sure?"

Danny wrapped his arms around her and kissed her more passionately than he'd thought he could muster. She rolled her head and leaned into his neck, and he fell into the delicate scent of her hair. They remained embraced until the sound of voices echoed across the schoolyard.

She tugged his hand. "C'mon, let's go!" she said.

They left the schoolyard and went up the stairs. Each step made the conversation brighter, punctuated with laughter, smiles, and hand-holding.

"So, what are your plans for the summer?" Danny asked.

"Well, I'm starting college in the fall. My mom wants me to take some summer classes to get a head start."

"Do you wanna do that?"

"I'm not sure. My grades are good, but I guess it wouldn't hurt."

"Where are you going?"

"Boston College."

"I heard that's a good school."

"It is; it's one of the best. My father graduated from there. What about you?" she asked.

"As long as I'm working full-time, I'll continue working. If something happens, I'll sign up to go to Vietnam."

"Aren't you working full-time now?"

"No, not yet. I only work thirty to thirty-five hours a week."

"That's almost full-time, isn't it?"

"I guess. Now that I'm out of school, Mr. Erickson said I could work as many hours as I want, forty or fifty hours a week."

"That's all well and good, but you have to think about your future. You're the smartest boy I know. You should really think about college. I'm sure you could get in. You're not like those other kids. You're smart."

Danny took a long drag on his cigarette, picked up a small branch from the ground, and twirled it in his hand. "No one in my family has ever gone to college. We don't have that kind of money or nothing."

"What about a scholarship?"

"Are you kidding me? I could never get one. I'm not that smart."

"Don't say that. It's not true," she said as her voice lifted an octave.

"C'mon. My grades aren't any good."

"They could be if you tried."

"I don't know," he said, looking down and shuffling his feet.

"Instead of hanging around the Corner, like the other kids, you could be studying and learning things."

Danny fiddled with the stick, twirling it in his hand. "I don't know."

"But what if things don't work out with your job? You need a backup plan. Everyone needs a backup plan."

"I s'pose. Like I said, if things don't work out, I'm gonna join the marines. My old man was a marine. That would make my ma proud of me. And, if I'm lucky, I can learn a trade, maybe become a mechanic or a carpenter. I got all kinds of opportunities."

"That sounds nice and all, but what if you get hurt? You could get shot or something."

Danny tossed the stick across the street and watched as it bounced across the top of a trash can, rattling the lid. "I don't know. When you think about it, no place is safe. I mean, anything can happen at any time. I could get run over by a car tomorrow morning. Heck, I could get run over tonight. You never know."

"Don't be silly. When was the last time you heard of anyone getting run over? You hear about kids getting killed in Vietnam all the time. It's on the news every night."

"I know," Danny responded. "I know."

"My father says this war is different and doesn't make sense. I've heard him talking to my mom, and he always says the same thing. 'What are we doing fighting a war so far away? We have no business over there. It's on the other side of the world.' He reads the paper every day, and he watches the news all the time." They stopped when they reached the next intersection. "Do you watch the news? Do you see what's going on over there?"

"Naw, not really. I'm not into the news or nothing." He looked up, nodding toward Four Corners. "Looks busy tonight. Do you want to check it out?"

"No, not really."

"Why not?"

"I'd rather go to Mother's Rest. It's quiet."

"Okay." They turned around and headed back toward the park. A steady parade of cars and an occasional bus rumbled by, filling their noses with the scent of diesel. It reminded him of Fields Corner. When they reached the top of the hill, they sat on a wooden bench. The lights of Boston Harbor flickered in the distance. Voices wafted up from below, orange-tipped cigarettes glowed in the distance, and small clouds of cigarette smoke hung in the air and drifted skyward.

"I can see why they call it Mother's Rest," Patty said as she slid closer to him on the bench. Danny lifted his arm and wrapped it around her shoulders. "I love this view, especially in the winter when everything is covered in snow. It seems like someplace far, far away, not in Dorchester." She nestled her head against his shoulder. "I could stay here forever," she said.

"Me too."

# 35

Summer was in full flow, melting everything in sight, coating it in a sticky sheen of sweat. Danny took the weekend off. "You deserve a day off," Mr. Erickson said. "Have fun."

The kids met up early and went down to the granite blocks lining the coarse shoreline next to the drawbridge at Malibu Beach. The rocks were preferable to the coarse brown sand and sharp-edged seashells that ran along the bay's edge.

Danny and Bugsy picked a pair of gray slabs alongside the concrete abutment, where it was cool and sheltered by the shadows of the bridge above. Everyone else spread out, settling on other flat rocks, with no guarantee that they wouldn't have a stiff neck or a sore back. Other than small talk about baseball and blowjobs, the only sounds were those of cars rolling by and laughter from families on the other side of the channel drifting across the water. Danny stretched his neck, leaned back, and blew a smoke ring toward Savin Hill, a slight rise in the earth pockmarked with three-deckers, wood-shingled homes, and purple puddingstone. An endless stream of cars and trucks crawled along the Southeast Expressway behind the Dorchester Yacht Club, a sun-weathered two-story building bolted to a creosote pier, held in place by a stack of granite blocks that kept the highway from falling into the bay.

Charley was the first to jump in after he did his best Tarzan imitation, yelling and howling as loud as he could. The rest of the kids followed, swimming out to the channel, where the water was cooled by the corrugated currents of the Atlantic Ocean. Danny swam through the first bridge arch toward the gas tanks where the shoreline, riddled with rusting shopping carts, dead horseshoe crabs, driftwood, cans, and broken bottles, led to the other side of the bridge. He swam close to the creosote pilings bordering the channel, making sure not to stray too far into the deep water where the kids dove or jumped from above. Mikey swam alongside him and, without warning, pulled Danny underwater.

Danny resurfaced and saw Mikey's head bobbing and moving away, swimming toward the other arch into the channel. "Asshole!" Danny yelled, diving deep into the cold water and kicking his legs as hard as he could, through the green-tinted water, around the pilings, toward Mikey's legs. A few kicks later, he grabbed them and pulled Mikey down. They both thrashed around until they heard the thunderous blast of a horn. They let go of each other as a big cabin cruiser headed straight toward them, chasing them to the bridge wall.

"Asshole!" Danny yelled at the cruiser.

"What a fucking jerk," Mikey added.

"No shit."

They said nothing more as they followed the wake to the kids, treading water on the beachside passageway. They swam across the channel to the beach, where they got out and trudged through the sand, passing little kids with sand pails, families lying on old bedsheets, and girls covered in baby oil meticulously positioned to complement each other.

After slowing down to ogle the girls, the kids strolled up to the bathhouse, a stark, white-washed building reminiscent of a state prison. A waist-high concrete wall covered with seated kids ran along the front of the building, flanking concrete steps leading to the entryway. They passed through thick oak doors and stopped at the snack bar, tucked in an arched alcove off to the right. Danny reached into his cutoffs and pulled out two wet, crumpled bills and a handful of change. "Can I have a tonic?" he asked a freckle-faced girl, sweating behind the counter and sunburned on her shoulders.

"Coke, Sprite, or, um, Mountain Dew?"

"Mountain Dew."

Misfit ambled quietly to Danny, almost as if he'd been hiding. "Hey man, can you loan me a quarter?"

"Sure," Danny said, handing him some change.

"Thanks, man. I'll pay you back."

"No problem."

"You want anything?" Danny asked Charley, knowing he probably didn't have any money.

"Naw, I'm okay."

"Fuck you. What do you want? It's a loan," he persisted, knowing he'd never collect and never ask him about it.

"I'll, um, have the same."

The girl removed the bottles from the noisy refrigerator, popped the tops off, and passed them over the countertop. They took a long, slow swig and walked outside, while Bugsy and Mikey remained at the sticky, sugar-coated counter, trying to decide what they wanted.

"You got any plans for the summer?" Danny asked Misfit.

"My uncle has some work for me. Loading trucks. It's part-time, mostly in the mornings."

"That's cool. What's he do?"

"He's a roofer over in Southie."

"What's it pay?"

"I don't know yet." They took another swig. "Speaking of roofs, did you know that side of the roof's open," Misfit said, pointing. "You can see into the girls' bathrooms from up there."

Danny glanced up. "How many times have you been up there?"

"Plenty."

"You're a fucking pervert."

"Yeah, I know." They stared at the roof for a minute. "So, what are your plans?"

"I got a job. I'm working at the Port Gas station, down at Neponset."

"Yeah, yeah, I forgot that. Must be a great job?"

"It is."

"Man, you're pretty lucky. You know my old man doesn't even have a full-time job. He works part-time. The poor bastard has a couple jobs, and my mom works part-time."

"You fags ready?" Bugsy asked, interrupting the conversation.

"Blow me," Misfit replied.

"If you're man enough to take it out, I'm man enough to suck it," Bugsy said.

"I bet you would, you fucking faggot."

"Hey, you fags oughta get a room," Charley said.

"C'mon, you fucking idiots, let's play like the good shepherd and get the flock out of here," Danny said.

Misfit led the way, making sure to pass by the lobster-colored girls. "Fuck this," Mikey yelled, leaping in long strides and running into the water. "This sand is too fucking hot." The rest of the kids followed, and a minute later, they were all swimming their way back to where Billy, Mooch, T-Bone, Grunta, and Headso were spread out on the rocks, lying in awkward positions, like a plate of pasta.

"Where have you guys been?" Mooch asked from behind a cigarette dangling from his mouth.

"Mikey's been at the bathhouse, licking toilet seats," Danny said.

"Blow me," Mikey said, suddenly turning his attention to a box full of MD 20-20. "Where'd you get all that shit?"

"Stole it from a delivery truck down at Supreme's," Headso said proudly, pulling out a bottle and handing it to Misfit. After taking a mouthful, Misfit passed the bottle to Danny, and he passed it around to the other kids, who, in turn, took a deep guzzle, finishing it in one round.

"Anything going on at the beach?" T-Bone asked.

"Nothing much," Bugsy said. "There's a bunch of girls all greased up over there."

"Yeah, I saw me some titties," Mikey said.

"Oh yeah," Mooch replied. "Where?"

"On the other side, this way," Mikey said, curling his hand as if coaxing a dog to come over. "Want to check it out?"

"Maybe later."

"How's the water?" asked Grunta.

"Nice and cool, especially under the bridge," Mikey said.

"I didn't see any jellyfish," Danny said. He walked to the water's edge and stuck his feet in. The other kids followed and passed more bottles around. T-Bone finished his and tossed it into the water, where it bobbed for a minute before sinking. Grunta threw his at the concrete buttress, where it exploded, sending shards of glass beneath the murky water.

"I'm gonna do some jumps," Charley said. He took a healthy swig from one of the bottles and shuffled his way up the steep bank adjacent to the bridge buttress, slipping a few times before reaching the sidewalk. Danny and Mikey swam out into the channel to look for boats that might be coming through the bridge. T-Bone joined them with another bottle.

Charley climbed onto the low wall that bordered the sidewalk, blessed himself, waved at the kids, and jumped, landing in the middle of the channel. Misfit, Mooch, and Billy took a few swallows and climbed up the embankment, following Charley's path. After kissing his Saint Christopher medal, Mooch dove, making a seamless entry into the water, attracting hoots and hollers loud enough to get the attention of the bridge operator, a middle-aged man with a belly that hung out so far over his waist, he surely couldn't see his feet. He swung the control room door open and hollered. "Hey! Stop! You kids can't do that." He stepped outside the booth and waved his arms.

Billy, the next to go, ignored him and climbed over the railing. After blessing himself, he jumped and landed awkwardly in the water, making a painful flopping sound when he landed. He popped up screaming. "Fuck! That hurt!"

"You okay?" Charley yelled, treading water next to the pier.

"I broke my fucking balls!"

"Want me to rub them?" Danny yelled.

"Fuck you!"

"Hey! If anyone else jumps, I'm gonna call the cops," the booth attendant hollered, leaning over the railing.

"Fuck you, you fat fuck," Bugsy yelled back.

"I'm not kidding. I will!"

"Fuck you," Misfit said as he walked toward the booth. The red-faced attendant muttered, remaining where he was. Misfit climbed to the top of the wall, pulled his bathing suit down, and mooned the attendant.

"You little shit!" the attendant said, shaking his fist.

"Fuck him," Bugsy yelled, getting out of the water and climbing the bank to the sidewalk.

Misfit gave the attendant the finger and jumped, curling himself into a perfect cannonball. He sent an enormous splash when he landed, spraying the bridge arches. The kids hooted and hollered when he resurfaced.

Mooch walked to within a dozen feet of the attendant. He turned, bent over, and ripped a loud fart. The attendant's face turned red as a summer apple. Mooch climbed to the top of the railing, yelled, and jumped, feet first, torpedoing deep into the cold, murky green water. He shot back up as fast as he had gone in. The operator cursed, waved his hands, and turned. Bugsy walked toward him. The operator took a few tentative steps toward him and raised his hands. "It's against the law to jump off the bridge," he said, waving his arms like a windmill.

Bugsy came within a few feet of him and stopped. The attendant stared back. Bugsy lurched toward the attendant, catching him by surprise. Bugsy grabbed his sunglasses from his pocket and jumped over the wall, putting them on when he resurfaced.

"Give me my glasses back!" the operator screamed, nearly falling over the railing. "You kids are in a lot of trouble!"

"We better get out of here before the cops come," Danny said.

"What, More Dumb Cops?" Bugsy said, referring to the MDC police force. "They're a fucking joke."

"Yeah, I know," Danny said. "But it ain't worth it to fuck with them. I'm too tired to run. I'm headed back."

The rest of the kids followed. After getting dressed, they grabbed the remaining bottles and left.

# 36

After another miserable night wherein it was too hot to sleep and the humidity made Danny sweat so hard, he could feel the pounds disappear, he headed over to Bugsy's. They met outside, Bugsy hauling his brother's duffel bag filled with beer and dry ice wrapped in newspapers. They hoofed it to Four Corners, passing the duffel bag back and forth between themselves. They met up with Charley and Billy behind Shur's drugstore, and after a quick smoke, they walked across the street and flagged a hackie down.

"Where're you kids going?" asked the cabbie, in his mid-forties, buttons bursting at the stomach.

Charley popped his head in the passenger window. "Quincy."

"Okay, get in," he said, tugging on a Camel. His fingers were so stained, you couldn't tell where his fingers ended and the filter started.

"Hey, mister."

The cabbie turned and stuck his head out the front window.

"Can I put my bag in the trunk?" Bugsy asked.

The driver looked Bugsy and the bag over. "You in the navy?"

"I'm going in pretty soon. Gonna be heading out."

"I was a swabbie," the driver said, stepping out of the cab and pulling his pants up. "Korea. I was on the USS *Rochester*. We lost some good men in that war. A lot of local kids."

"My old man talks a lot about the war," Bugsy said.

The driver grunted, pulled out a yellowed hanky, and wiped his forehead as he lumbered to the back of the cab. "In here," he said to Bugsy, opening the trunk.

"You got an address?" the cabbie asked after everyone was in the vehicle.

"Larry Street. It's off of Willard," Danny replied. "You can take the expressway."

Half a block later, Charley leaned forward. "We gotta drop Kevin here," he said, glancing at Bugsy, "at his aunt's house. She wants to see him before he goes in. Is that okay?"

"Yeah, no problem," the driver said. He lit another cigarette and continued heading south.

A few miles later, the cabbie took the off-ramp, drove a mile or more, and turned into a quiet little cul-de-sac. "You can stop over there," Bugsy said, pointing. "Next to that Chevy."

The driver pulled over and put the car in park. Bugsy got out and waited at the back of the cab. After the driver opened the trunk, Bugsy grabbed the bag and placed it on the sidewalk. "Thanks," Bugsy said to the driver. He leaned in the rear window and spoke. "I'll see you kids later."

"Kev, tell your aunt I said hello," Danny said.

"Will do," Bugsy replied, waving back.

"Nice kid," the driver said. "He'll make a good sailor."

"He sure will," Charley said. "So, can you go back to the end of the street and take a right?"

"Yeah, no problem."

They caught up with Bugsy in the woods, drinking a cold beer and leaning against his duffle bag. "Everything cool?" he asked.

"Oh yeah," Danny replied. "No problem."

"So, what happened?" Bugsy asked, getting up and passing beers out.

"After we dropped you off, we pulled down the street and looked for a house where there weren't no parked cars or nothing, you know, somewhere near the quarries," Charley said. "I get out first, and then Billy, and we stand there like we're waiting for Danny to pay the cabbie. As soon as Danny gets out, we start booking it. Danny starts running in the other direction. The cabbie gets out and starts yelling and running, but he's so fat he can't cross the street. Jesus Christ, I thought he was gonna croak. We're running through the backyards, and there ain't no sign of the cabbie. I figured the fat fuck dropped dead."

"Nice job. Hey, I need one of you guys to carry this fucking bag," Bugsy said. "My back's killing me."

"Here, let me take it," Charley said, lifting the sack onto his shoulder, bending over as he drove his shoulder through the brush and low-hanging trees.

---

The air at the quarries was cool, and the water was inviting. The mirror-like pools reflected the massive granite walls as they rose above the water, passing through a cascade of cold, bleak shadows. Danny figured it was close to ninety degrees, while the humidity made it feel like a lot more. They could hear voices and splashing water as they approached the shuttered Quincy quarries. The drilled, dug, and shafted granite hills, filled with cold spring water, were popular with swimmers, jumpers, divers, and the bad guys when they needed some place to dump bodies or cars. In the winter, when it was really cold, the quarries drew skaters and pick-up hockey games. Over the years, the rocky ledges—or *jumps*, as they were called—earned their names, and, depending on what neighborhood you came from, they weren't always called the same thing as local lore and legend dictated: *Suicide, The Roof, The Point, Black Harry, Jimmie's, Blue Hill, Gray Rock, Slate, Roof Top, 42, Cables,* and *Tar Pit. The Pit* was one of the worst, filled with hotboxes, washing machines, couches, and, depending on who you believed, bodies filled with lead or strapped to cement blocks. And then there was *Ice Box*, a hole so deep, that the walls kept the sunlight from ever hitting the water. The most popular spot was *Goldie's*, *Goldfish*, or *Fishbowl*, its names originating from all the pet goldfish dumped there over the years, a splash of color in a dark abyss.

"This fucking thing's heavy. I feel like I'm dragging a body bag," Charley groaned as he plopped the bag on a large, yellow-painted ledge. Danny and Billy grabbed the lopsided sack and carried it down to a lower shelf. Billy reached inside and pulled a beer out. "Anyone want one?"

"Is the pope Catholic?" Charley replied.

"Does a bear shit in the woods?" Bugsy asked.

"Who gives a fuck?" Charley answered.

Billy tossed the cans around. Danny caught his, walked to the grass line, and watched the cars on the expressway, most heading south to the Cape. He wiped the sweat from his forehead and looked over at the town of Quincy, spread out like a scene from a calendar you'd see at a drugstore; tall white church steeples sticking high in the air, nestled in between patches of broad, summer-leaved trees. Cars, kids, and bicycles came in and out of the picture. The islands in Boston Harbor floated along the shoreline. In the distance, the Boston skyline was marked with tall, gray-colored tombstones.

Behind him, the quarries cast dark gray shadows that jutted over the water. The ledges were painted with a name: *Dick*, *Bob*, *Jimmy*, *Ken*, and *Red*, each marked in honor of the kid who'd jumped them, some never coming back to the surface. Others were faded remnants from prior times, other generations, and neighborhoods: *US Marines*, *US Navy*, *Southie Shamrocks*, *Red Raiders*, *Rockets*, and *Chippewas.*

A bristly yellowed rope hung to Danny's right, leading to a broader ledge high above the water. "Let's go up there," Danny said, pointing with his beer hand.

"I gotta piss first," Bugsy said.

"Me too," Charley said. The rest of the kids mumbled in unison, joining them in the dense stand of bushes.

Danny climbed the rope and waited for Bugsy to follow, while Charley and Billy remained below. They dragged the bag over and tied it to the end of the cord. Danny and Bugsy pulled it, hand over hand, and when they had it, they carried it to the back of the ledge, where it would stay cool, nestled in the granite shadows. Danny and Bugsy opened a beer while the other kids climbed up to join them. Danny walked to the edge of the rocks toward *Canyon*, a watery junkyard filled with rusted cars, refrigerators, washing machines, and other discarded appliances floating alongside large chunks of wood bobbing up and down like oversized fishing floats.

*Table Top* lay across the other side, a massive formation with large iron plates, bolts, and anchors drilled into the stone. A two-inch metal post, a remnant from some old mining machinery, was embedded in a wide, flat ledge several feet from the rocky edge. A popular jumping spot, the kids would run along the top of the quarry toward the pole, and, after leaping high in the air, they'd grab it and swing around, throwing themselves out, beyond the knife-like ledge, into the water below.

Danny leaned back against the side of a tall granite face, listening to the sound of breaking water and laughter echoing from the granite canyons, reminding him of the previous September, when he and Charley had spent the day swimming on a hot Indian summer day. After a couple of hours in the water, they were resting on a ledge, watching a bunch of kids jumping from Table Top. A tall kid, blond and freckle-faced, wearing black high-top Keds and plaid shorts, ran across the shelf. He slipped and rolled backward, slamming his head on the granite and bouncing down the cliff's face like a rag doll. Every time his head bounced off a ledge, it made a sickening sound, sending blood and brains in every direction. When he hit the water, he vanished into the brown murk. Charley dove into the water, guided by one of the kid's sneakers bobbing on the water. Danny climbed down the canyon walls until he felt safe enough to jump in. He swam over to the sneaker and treaded water, trying to stay in place. Charley resurfaced and took in a mouthful of air before making another descent, not stopping to speak.

The kid's friends dropped into the water as they got lower. No one was jumping. Some had pissed their pants, and some were crying. It was a mess. Charley made several more attempts, diving over and over again. Finally, after resurfacing again, Charley cried, "He's gone. I can't get him. I can't. I tried!" He gasped for air, fighting to catch his breath.

"It's okay, it's okay," Danny said. "Why don't you take a break?"

Several of the kids' friends finally swam over. A few were huddled alongside a flat ledge, staring silently at the water. Danny looked at them, all useless. "I'll be back," Danny said to Charley. "I'm gonna get some help."

He got out, jammed his feet into his sneakers, and ran down the hill to a phone booth, where his fingers flopped around like worms as he fumbled to dial 911, dry-mouthed and struggling to speak. As soon as he finished, he hung up, ran back up the hill, and paced back and forth, waiting for the cops to arrive. His heart pounded when he heard the sirens wailing in the distance. Danny stuttered like a chainsaw when two cars pulled up, and the cops got out as he tried to tell them what had happened. When they reached the quarry's edge, he pointed to Charley and the other kids now treading water. The cops walked to the water's edge and peered into the water.

"How long has he been down?" one of the cops asked, removing his hat and tugging on his belt.

"T-t-ten minutes. M-m-maybe fifteen minutes," Danny stuttered.

The other cop walked back to the police car, while the one with Danny waved the kids over. "Everyone, get out. There's nothing we can do now. I want you kids to line up over here," he said. After everyone was out of the water, he started asking them questions, their answers filling his leather-bound notebook.

Fifteen minutes later, a van pulled up, and two scuba divers got out, dragging a rubber raft filled with diving gear up the hill, to the water's edge. An ambulance and a fire truck pulled over. The firemen brought a rope and tied it to the raft. The divers climbed into it and pushed off while Charley yelled instructions, guiding them to the last place he'd seen the kid.

"That's it, that's the spot," Charley shouted, waving his hand. "That way, a little more!"

The divers put their masks and equipment on and rolled backward into the water. Ten minutes later, they resurfaced in a stream of bubbles. They grabbed the rope and went back down while the firemen tethered the other end. The divers resurfaced a couple of minutes later, guiding the body to the surface. Several kids screamed as soon as the boy's head came out of the water. The divers lifted the bloodied body onto the raft and covered it with a thick woolen blanket. They tied the rope off on the raft, and the firemen pulled them to shore.

---

"Charley, how's the water?" Bugsy yelled at Charley, floating on his back, doing a one-handed backstroke while drinking a beer.

"Great!"

Bugsy drained his beer and tossed the empty can toward the bag. He walked to the front of the ledge and looked down. When it was clear, he backed up a few steps, ran across the ridge, leaped, and rolled into a cannonball, sending water high into the air and reaching several ledges.

Danny followed, finishing his beer, and jumped in next to Bugsy. He descended as deep as he could, swam down into the darkened void, and turned toward the water's edge, continuing until he could no longer hold his breath. When he surfaced, he was hidden by the shadows at the other edge of the quarry alongside an overhanging ledge. He could hear Billy hollering, "Where the fuck is he?"

"Fuck if I know!" Bugsy replied, looking around.

Danny tucked himself under the ledge while the kids jumped in and swam around, looking for him and calling his name. One by one, they dove in. Once they were all in, he kicked himself off the wall, propelling himself underwater toward them. When he spotted the first pair of legs, he grabbed them and yanked on them. He could hear screams from beneath the water as the legs thrashed about. He let go, swam a little farther, and grabbed another pair. Nearly out of breath, he pulled one more pair, and after swimming a few more yards, he shot up. As soon as Bugsy saw him, he started yelling, ending whatever he said with, "You're an asshole!"

"Takes one to know one," Danny responded, laughing and pulling his hair back. "Anyone want another beer?" he asked as he swam back to the ledge.

There were a few more yells of "You're an asshole."

When Danny reached the top of the ledge, he grabbed some beers and tossed them to the other kids. Charley followed him, opened his beer, and yelled, "Anyone want to bat some frogs?" He picked a thick branch up from the ground. "C'mon, Billy," he said, waving the branch at Billy. Billy got out, picked up a branch, and joined Charley. They walked along the cobbled dirt path at the quarry's edge, swinging their sticks like golf clubs.

"C'mon Danny, we need a pitcher."

"No, thanks. You know you guys are sick fucks."

"C'mon, grab a couple of beers. You can be the umpire."

Danny grabbed a few beers and followed them. He sat down and watched Charley and Billy spend the next fifteen minutes hunting frogs in shallow water, whacking them on the head, knocking them out, or killing them, continuing until they had a few dozen stacked up, wiggling and bleeding.

"Okay, here's the plate," Danny said, scraping the dirt into a square and placing a couple of sticks around the box. Over the next half hour, Billy and Charley pitched frogs at each other, hitting them with their sticks. Danny stayed far behind the plate, yelling, "Strike, strike, ball, strike, ball, balk, on and on," as frog guts flew at whoever was pitching. When the frogs were gone, the game ended, and they all jumped into the water.

---

By mid-afternoon, the gray-hued ledges were covered with kids from all over the city: Dorchester, Milton, Southie, Roxbury, and Quincy, the hometown kids, hanging in small groups, jumping or diving. "Bugsy!" someone yelled. The kids turned and looked up to see Bugsy's cousin Okie from Shawmut, a kid with more balls than were in the Red Sox bullpen. He dove into the water and swam over to Bugsy and his crowd.

"What are you kids up to?" asked Okie.

"Hanging out," said Bugsy.

"Want a beer?" Danny asked.

"Sure."

"Billy, give me a couple of beers." Billy obliged and tossed a couple to Danny. By late afternoon, the place was packed, and some of the girls had shown up. They stayed close to the walls and paddled around in bikini tops and cutoffs, giggling and flirting without flirting. By late afternoon, the sun turned from yellow to orange, softening the color of the water and the surrounding walls, and the serious diving began. Following a lot of challenges—and failures—three kids were left. One was from Southie, a tall blond kid built like Johnny Weissmuller, and the other two were from Dorchester: Charley and Okie.

The kid from Southie started things off by throwing a large rock in the water, breaking the surface and watching it sink below the green-hued water as the waves spread out, lapping the edge of the excavations. After he'd paced back and forth, measuring his steps, everyone quieted down. He tossed another rock in the water, leaped into the air, and spread his arms out to his sides like a bird in flight. He pitched into a roll halfway down and broke into a perfect dive, entering the water so cleanly, he barely made a ripple. A chorus of oohs and aahs filled the shadowed air. When he surfaced, the guys clapped, and the girls yelped like they were getting laid. He lifted himself out of the water and swung up onto the ledge. One of his friends handed him a beer.

Next was Charley, who had begun pacing back and forth, gauging his steps and quietly measuring the grooves in the granite ledge beneath his feet. He heaved a large rock and watched it land in the water, studying the ripples. He blessed himself, backed up, and leaped, swinging his hands out in front of him. There was nothing fancy about the dive until he was halfway down, when he rolled into the first of two complete spins, breaking at the last minute and landing in the same place the kid from Southie had landed. As soon as Charley surfaced, everyone clapped and cheered. He swam to the kids and glanced over to the kid from Southie, who smiled and lifted his beer.

Okie was the last to go. He stood at the edge of the shelf, studying his shadow as it cast a long, dark image over the water. After tossing a large, flat rock into the water, he watched the waves spread until the water returned to a calm, glass-like surface. Other than the distant drone of traffic on the expressway, the cavernous hole was quiet. Instead of pacing and measuring, he inched his way to the edge and turned backward, stopping when his heels hung over the ledge.

"What the fuck is he doing?" Billy said.

"I don't know," Bugsy said, standing up.

Okie started pulsing like a tall Slinky. He suddenly leaped backward and turned over in two revolutions. Just before hitting the water, he extended his arms over his head, made a slight arc, and turned again, entering the water feet first, so close to the base of the quarry wall that it looked like he had hit it. He descended, disappearing for what seemed like an eternity before coming back up. When he did, the quarry filled with the sounds of cheers, hoots, hollers, and screams. The kid from Southie shook his head in defeat, draped a towel over his shoulders, and opened another can of beer.

"Okie!" Bugsy yelled. As soon as he saw him, Bugsy tossed him a beer. The kids spent the rest of the afternoon, into the early evening, going over the dive and how big Okie's balls were.

"Weren't you scared of hitting the wall?" Danny asked.

"Naw, I had it timed," Okie said.

"Where'd you learn to dive like that?" one of the girls asked.

"In my head, it's all in my head. You gotta plan it out and make it work."

# 37

Danny slept beside an open window, hoping for relief from the heat, restlessly listening to the sounds of cars, dogs, sirens, and screeching tires. Tom "McGlocker" McLaughlin, a DJ with WMEX, complained, "It was so hot, you could fry an egg on the sidewalk." Danny had tried it once, and all that had happened was his mother had hollered at him for making a mess in front of their home. When the morning light filled his room, he kicked his sweat-soaked sheets to the floor, got up, and took a long cool shower. He glanced at Frankie's aquarium. His goldfish were belly up, glued to an oily glaze that had formed atop the water. He thought about going downtown and hanging around Filene's or Jordan Marsh, where it was air-conditioned, but decided against it; it'd be too crowded, and the subway ride would be horrible. He chose to stay close to home as he had a date with Patty. They were getting together with Bugsy and his new girlfriend, Karen Hines, a short brunette with enormous tits. She was a Protestant from Burt Street, near Ashmont Station. The guys had planned to sneak the girls into Sporty's; Bugsy's cousin Johnny was working the door. He'd promised to let them in and keep a booth open for them near the band as long as they were there before nine.

Danny moved from the parlor to the kitchen to the bathroom, where he took a shower every couple of hours, retracing his steps throughout the day. He ate in the late afternoon and put on a blue cotton shirt his mother had given him for his birthday and a pair of freshly pressed chinos, and headed out, walking and listening to the drone of cars as he made his way down Washington Street toward Mother's Rest. The sounds gave way to the echo of voices from across the street. Several black kids were coming down Algonquin Street, heading toward him. Danny pulled his smokes out, lit one, and took a few steps forward, stopping at the curb and staring at the kids. They, in turn, stopped and stared back. Whatever chatter had fueled their stroll dissipated.

Danny looked up and down the street as if waiting for someone. He finished his cigarette, stuck his hand in his back pocket as if he had something, and walked toward the Rest, stopping in front of Levine's funeral home to light another cigarette. When he resumed his walk, the voices continued, shucking and jiving, sounds that faded when Danny walked away. Danny looked out over the park, rooftops, trees, and out toward the ocean, admiring the view. He loosened his collar and watched the sun's waning rays paint the top of the trees red, yellow, and orange. The shadows from the buildings across the street lengthened as the sun dropped behind them, and the street lights flickered as they turned on.

Danny turned and spotted Bugsy, dressed like he was on his way to a wedding or maybe a funeral. The last time Danny had seen him that dressed up had been at a closed casket funeral at Mullens' funeral home for Bugsy's "bless-his-soul" Uncle Kevin. One night, after drinking too much with one of his cousins in South Boston, Uncle Kevin had gotten off at the Fields Corner station and fallen onto the tracks. No one had seen him fall; the rats had got to him first. It took two days before they'd found all his limbs and other pieces scattered across the creosoted railroad ties. Danny and some of the other kids had attended his funeral, an old-fashioned celebration at Uncle Kevin's home in Southie, a two-day affair.

Danny walked behind the splintered wooden benches. He stopped at the rusted railing bolted to the cement stairway leading to the bottom of the park and watched Bugsy climb the steps.

"You're a fucking stud," Danny said as Bugsy neared.

When Bugsy reached the top of the stairs, he grabbed his collar and tugged on it. "Damn right! Elvis fucking Presley."

"Naw. You're a fag," Danny replied, laughing. "You look like a fudge packer from Framingham."

Bugsy grabbed his crotch. "Blow me. All the fudge packers are from Milton."

"Naw, Fathead will do it. So hey, how's everything going with you and Karen?"

"Good. I met her mother last week."

"What's she like? Does she swallow?"

"Fuck you. She's nice. She asked a lot of questions, but she's okay. Speaking of swallowing, is Patty coming?"

"Yeah. She told her parents we were going to the movies. Her old man would kill her if he knew she was going to Sporty's."

"Does she know Karen's a Protestant?"

"I never mentioned it—didn't see why."

"I'm sure she'll be cool."

"She will."

"We got a little time. Let's find a buyer."

"Sounds good."

They headed to Codman Square. "Let's wait and see who's around," Bugsy said. He stuck his hands in his pockets, walked to the front of English's, leaned against the large plate-glass window, and lit a smoke. Halfway through his cigarette, a scruffy-looking bayzo walked toward them, mumbling like a priest holding a private Mass. "Hey, man, can you make a buy for us?" Bugsy asked, offering his cigarettes, shaking a couple out of his pack.

The old man looked at Bugsy and blinked like he'd just gotten out of bed. "Hey, man, can you make a buy for me and my friend? It's his birthday, and we're gonna celebrate," Bugsy asked, nodding in Danny's direction. Bugsy reached into his pocket and took out several bills. "Can I buy you a jug?"

"Shhhure. Whaddya want?" the old man replied, followed by a stomach-turning burp that smelled like dog shit.

"Me and my buddy need a pint of OT for each of us. And you," Bugsy paused to make sure the old man was listening, "you can get one for yourself."

"You can get a pack of smokes if you want," Danny added.

The old man's smile grew larger. The few teeth remaining in his mouth looked like they were going to fall out of his head. "C'mon," Bugsy said, passing a cigarette over. Danny lit it for him. Bugsy went over the buy one more time. "You got it?"

"Yeah. Shhhure."

After the buy, Bugsy and Danny walked to the next block, stopped at Vinnie's Cleaners, and stepped inside the illuminated alcove. They took a long slow swig from their bottles.

"You ever been to Sporty's before?" Danny asked.

"Yeah. I've been there with my old man a few times in the morning before they were open. You?"

"Naw. I been by a few times at night but never went in."

"What about all those spooks? They must be cool, right? Charley Henderson's been in there a few times. He told me the white kids go there because of the music and dancing. They go there because no one wants any trouble."

"Yeah, I heard that. My brothers have been there a bunch of times, mostly Sunday afternoons. They never had any problems with the crows or nothing."

As they neared the Rest, they saw the girls standing beside each other. Patty had her hair done up with yellow barrettes that stood out against a white cotton blouse and a red, knee-high skirt. Karen had her hand on her hip and was smoking. Her dress was much shorter than Patty's, and her nylons darker. She wore a light pink blouse, cut deep at the front, revealing a look-out-for-a-fight cleavage.

As they got closer, they spotted a couple of kids sitting at the end of the park bench, looking at the girls. Bugsy and Danny jammed their bottles deeper into their back pockets and picked up their pace. The girls glanced at the kids on the bench and then toward Danny and Bugsy. The kids turned and saw Bugsy and Danny, and as soon as they did, they got up and headed across the park. "Fucking faggots," Bugsy yelled. "Don't come back!"

"Did those kids bother you?" Danny said.

"Naw," Karen replied with a shake of the head. "They were harmless."

"You sure?"

"Yeah, no problem."

"Man, you look beautiful," Bugsy said to Karen as he walked up.

She blushed. Danny realized he should have said something to Patty. "Is that a new shirt?" he blurted out.

"My blouse?" she replied.

"Um, yeah, your blouse," he fumbled. "It looks really nice on you. And your hair, it looks great." He grabbed her hand and pulled her closer. She rose on her toes and kissed him.

"Hey, get a room," Bugsy said.

"Yeah, one far away from you," Danny replied.

"You girls want a drink?" Bugsy asked as he pulled his bottle out of his back pocket.

"I would," Karen replied.

Danny looked at Patty and lifted his eyebrows; a question. She forced a smile through her clenched teeth and shook her head ever so slightly *no*.

"C'mon, let's sit over there. The view's better," Danny said.

Bugsy and Karen walked across the grass to the steps that cascaded down the hill. "She seems nice," Patty said, respectfully unenthusiastic.

"Yeah, she seems like a lot of fun."

"I guess."

"Bugsy likes her."

"Yeah. I can tell."

Danny pulled his bottle out, unscrewed it, took a long swallow, and held it out to her. "No, thanks."

"Any plans for the weekend?" Danny said.

"No, not really."

"So, how's your family?"

She stuck her legs out and crossed her ankles. "Okay, I guess, 'cept for my little brother Petey—he broke his arm."

"He what? How?"

"He fell off the back porch railing. My mother kept telling him, 'Stay off that railing. You're gonna hurt yourself.' Sure enough, he did. Sometimes, he makes me so mad," she said, flustered. "He's lucky he didn't break his neck."

"Is he gonna be okay?

"I think so. I hope he learned his lesson. He's gonna kill himself someday."

"No kidding."

Danny took another swig from his bottle. "So, have you ever been to a night-club before?"

"No! Never. My father would kill me if he knew I went somewhere like that. I've never been in a bar."

"What about when you go to college? You'll be going to bars and clubs then, right? He can't stop you, then. He's gotta know that you're gonna go out and stuff?"

"I haven't given it a lot of thought. I'm sure he'll see me as his little girl no matter how old I am."

"You know, that's not so bad. It's kinda sweet."

She wrapped her fingers around his. "Did I tell you you look gorgeous?" Danny said.

She blushed like a summer rose and gave him a peck on the cheek. "Where's Bugsy and his girlfriend?" she asked.

Danny looked toward the sound of voices from the other end of the park. "That way," he said, pointing. Hand in hand, they walked toward Bugsy and Karen, leaning against the railing that ran alongside the walkway, making out. Bugsy had his hand under her shirt, feeling her up. He stopped when Danny and Patty walked up. Patty stopped and turned away.

"Hi. Do you know what time it is?" Bugsy asked, bringing his hand out and placing it by his side.

Patty turned back and glanced at her watch. "Almost eight thirty."

"Shit, we gotta go!" Bugsy said. Karen readjusted her blouse, and Bugsy pulled his jug out, "Bottoms up!"

Danny pulled his bottle out and lifted it to Bugsy's, clinking them together. They drained them dry. "Let's play like the good shepherd and get the flock out of here."

Bugsy tossed his bottle over the fence, while Danny stuck his in his pocket. Patty locked her arm in Danny's, while Karen and Bugsy giggled and bounced off each other like a pair of birthday balloons, and together they took off. They stopped at the corner of Bowdoin and Harvard and watched a steady crowd flow into the bar just down the street. A mix of white, Negro, and Spanish women were clad in brightly colored dresses, creating cavernous cleavages you could fill with fruit. Their hair was so puffed up that it must have taken half a can of hairspray to hold them in place. Most wore high heels and short skirts, revealing almost everything they owned. Half of the guys had a cigarette stuffed behind their ears, sitting below afros, some as big as basketballs, while others wore bright-colored sports jackets, competing with the fluorescent lights that lit the sidewalk up with an array of colorful lights. The music was so loud, that the beer signs hanging in front of the windows vibrated.

Karen looked at herself in the drugstore window, fussing with her hair, checking her lipstick, and wiping the edges with a small handkerchief. Patty glanced at the window. Danny peered over her shoulder, joining her in looking at their reflections.

"Everybody ready?" Bugsy said.

Danny and the girls murmured positively.

They crossed the street and got in line. When no one else was in front of them, Bugsy pulled the door open and stood aside, tilting his head for everyone else to follow. Johnny spotted them and waved them in. Karen indiscreetly stepped in front of Bugsy and wiggle-walked to the bar like she owned the place or was ready to perform.

"Hey," Bugsy yelled. "Wait for me." She glanced over her shoulder as if annoyed. He walked toward her, waving her back several times until she rejoined him.

Johnny leaned over to Bugsy. "Is this broad okay?" he asked.

"Ya, she's cool," Bugsy said, wiping his nose. "She's cool."

"Bugsy, you gotta listen to me. Ya gotta keep an eye on her. I don't need any trouble. This ain't the kind of place for this shit." Bugsy nodded and fumbled with his smokes. In the meantime, Karen worked her way back to the bar. By the time her elbows landed on the edge of the bar, two guys had elbowed their way alongside her.

"See, what'd I tell you?" Johnny said. They both looked at her. "What the fuck, Bugsy? Look at her fucking tits. They're hanging out there like they're there for the grabbing. Melons on a tree. She's a walking fuck-fest."

Bugsy shook his head. "I'll keep an eye on her. Promise."

"I don't need no fucking trouble, you got it? And remember, I did you a favor. So don't fuck it up. She's a fucking floozy; keep her in line."

"I will. Promise, I will."

"Okay, I got a booth for you over there," Johnny said, pointing.

"C'mon," Bugsy said to the others. "Let's grab a booth." He called over to Karen. She turned and knocked her drink over. When she realized what she had done, she reached for a bar towel, leaning forward. The bartender, getting a good view of her tits, was in no rush to help her. He continued washing the glasses, stopping when Johnny came over and grabbed Karen's glass.

"I got it," Johnny said.

Everyone watched Karen readjust her blouse; no one was in a hurry to rush her.

Johnny walked back to Bugsy. "Bring her over to your booth, and keep an eye on her. One of these assholes is gonna make a move." Johnny looked over at Danny and Patty, sitting quietly in the booth. "Are they okay?" Johnny asked.

"Them. Yeah. That kid's gonna be a fucking priest. And her," Bugsy said, pointing, "She's Mary Magdalena. She lives in a fucking monastery."

"I think I recognize him. Isn't that Danny? Shit, what's his last name?"

"McSweeney, Danny McSweeney. Yeah, he's a good kid."

"Yeah, that's him. What about his girlfriend?"

"She's okay."

"What parish is she from?"

"Saint Mark's."

Karen got up. Johnny grabbed her by the arm and sat her back down.

"You're hurting me," she yelped.

"Honey, you gotta sit down."

Karen looked through him like he didn't exist.

"Bugsy."

Bugsy came alongside them.

"Put her in the fucking booth!" Johnny shouted, drawing the attention of everyone within a dozen feet of him.

Bugsy grabbed Karen by the arm and kissed her cheek, calming her down. Then, he guided her back to their booth, which was wrapped in red Naugahyde and held together with duct tape, illuminated by a nicotine-stained light bulb. Bugsy coaxed Karen into the middle of the booth alongside Patty. "You guys want anything to drink?" he asked as he started to get up.

"Why don't I grab them?" Danny said. "You two can wait here."

"Okay," Bugsy said, shrugging.

Danny slid out of the other side of the booth. "Can you get me a glass of water?" Patty asked, looking around nervously. "With a straw, please."

"Bugsy?"

"I'll have a beer." He looked at Karen, who was holding her head in her hands. "Can you get her a glass of water?"

"Sure. I'll be back," Danny said as he shouldered through the crowd.

A tall black man with a basketball-sized afro was in the corner of the room, fiddling around with a bass guitar, rattling the windows every time his hands danced across the frets. The pianist, much thinner and darker than the bass player, with long slick hair and a well-manicured mustache, flicked his fingers over the keyboard. The drummer, huddled in the corner wearing a multi-colored dashiki draped over his body, was sweeping his drum heads with his brushes. A wooden-handled 'do-pick stuck out of the side of his afro.

"Danny, right?" Johnny asked, surprising Danny, who turned to see who it was.

"Yeah."

"Where do you live? I seen you around the neighborhood."

"Around the corner, on Bowdoin Street."

"Yeah, I know who you are. You and Bugsy are pretty tight, ain't ya?"

"Yeah."

"Listen, you guys gotta help me, okay? That chick Bugsy's with is a fucking floozy; she's trouble. This ain't the place to fuck around. Them fucking spades will fuck her up if they get a chance."

"Yeah, I figured that out."

"They'll fuck you guys up if you're in the way."

"I know. I ain't stupid."

"I didn't say you were."

"I know. I didn't mean nothing."

"I know." Johnny looked around the room. "She's a fucking Protestant, ain't she?"

"Yeah. How'd you know?"

"Give me a fucking break. It's fucking obvious."

"Really?"

"Yeah, really."

Danny shook his head, trying to figure out what he had missed.

"The last thing I need is Bugsy getting into a beef with some asshole that wants to grab that chick's ass. Fuck, she's serving her tits up like a bowl of fruit."

"I know."

"And then you got all these jigaboos running around. They'd do anything to get some white ass." A saxophone player came out of the bathroom and joined the rest of the musicians still warming up.

"You know I did you kids a favor, right?"

"Yeah, sure I do. And I appreciate it, I do. We both do. Bugsy does—I know it. Between you and me, I don't think he expected his girlfriend to get so fucked up."

Johnny took a big breath and then let out a gallon of air. "If I knew he was gonna bring a lush, I'd have thought twice about letting you kids in."

Danny looked back, having nothing to offer in reply.

"Why don't you sit down? I'll send a waitress over. Her name's Mary. Remember to tip her. She works hard, and she's got a kid."

Danny nodded.

"If you or the girls need 'em, the bathrooms are over there, in the corner. Ladies on the left, men on the right."

"Thanks."

"No problem."

Danny returned to their booth, which was surrounded by a cloud of smoke and a couple of black guys trying to look down Karen's blouse. He slid into the booth and put his hand on Patty's knee. "How are you doing?"

"Okay," she said unenthusiastically and unhappily.

"Our waitress will be coming over in a minute," Danny said.

"Okay," she nodded, glancing around the room and sliding closer to Danny. Patty glanced at Bugsy and Karen, who were oblivious to everything around them. Karen's blouse had slipped again, and she didn't seem to care. Everyone within a dozen feet was waiting for her nipples to rise above her blouse like the sun rising on an early summer morning.

"Bugsy," Danny whispered, tapping Bugsy on his shoulder behind Patty's back, tilting his head toward Karen. Bugsy glanced at her and pulled her top back up, much to the dismay of the guys in the next booth and those standing alongside them.

Mary shimmied over to their booth, carrying her tray by her side. Her hips were wide and hung lower than they had twenty years ago. Danny figured she was in her early forties while noticing she dressed like someone half her age. Her droopy breasts were propped up under a starched white cotton blouse, visible behind a black velvet vest. Her eyes flickered below a pair of false eyelashes, and her skirt revealed more of her loins than was legal in Maine, New Hampshire, Vermont, and maybe Connecticut.

"What can I get you, honey?" she asked Patty, talking through a mouthful of chewing gum.

"Um . . . a Coke, please."

"Put a little rum in it, will ya?" Danny asked.

Patty looked over at Danny, stone-faced. "C'mon," he said.

"Okay, but just a little."

"I'll have a highball," Danny said.

"Hey, I want a drink!" Karen spluttered.

"Whattaya want, honey?" she asked.

"What wazz I drinking?"

"Scotch and water," Bugsy said. "She'll have a scotch and water."

"And you?"

"I'll have a Bud; in a glass."

"Sure."

"And a shot of VO. Can you make it a double?"

"Wanna start a tab?"

"Sure," Bugsy replied as if it was something he did every day.

"Is that all?" Mary asked.

"Yes," Bugsy replied.

"I'll be right back," Mary said.

"She seems nice," Patty said politely.

"Yeah, I guess," Danny said.

The band started playing. Danny tried to talk, but it was too loud, so he started yelling. He looked at Patty, pointed to his ears, and shook his head. They decided to listen to the music, even though neither cared for it. Bugsy and Karen didn't seem interested in it either; Bugsy had his hand up Karen's skirt. Every time she laughed or giggled, Patty turned red with embarrassment.

Two songs later, Mary showed up with a tray full of drinks. She put them down, along with half a dozen cocktail napkins, and left without saying anything. Bugsy sipped his beer, while Karen plowed through her drink, finishing it in a few swallows. Danny and Patty drank theirs slowly; it was still too loud to talk to each other. The band eventually broke into a slow ballad. Several couples got up to dance, wrapping their arms around each other and shuffling across the floor. Patty squeezed Danny's arm. "Can we go now?" she asked.

"I'd like to get one more. We can go after that." He glanced at her drink. She'd hardly drunk anything. "You can finish yours."

"I don't know. I'd really like to go; it's getting late."

Three guys, one as bald as a bowling ball and the other two with afros that touched each other had moved into the next booth. They were staring at Karen, something Bugsy hadn't noticed but Danny and Patty had.

Karen surprised Patty when she waved her hand in front of her. "I gotta take a pee. Wanna go?"

Patty frowned and looked at Danny. "Do you mind? Someone's gotta keep an eye on her."

"I don't know," Patty replied in a whisper.

"C'mon, I'll go with you. I gotta use the men's room." He tossed a crumpled napkin at Bugsy. "I gotta take a leak. You gotta go?"

"Naw, I'm good."

"I'm gonna walk the girls to the ladies' room."

"I'm gonna grab a drink. You want one?"

"Sure," Danny said. "Another highball."

"I'll get one for you," Bugsy said to Karen.

Danny slid out first. The girls followed and then led the way. Halfway across the room, two greasers wearing PFCs and leather jackets came out of nowhere and stepped in front of him. Danny started to walk around the first guy, and as soon as he did, the second one came around and drove his shoulder into Danny, nearly knocking him down. The girls continued walking, oblivious to everything.

"You got a problem, asshole?" the sweaty Elvis look-alike asked, while his friend continued following the girls.

"Me?" Danny replied, standing his ground, noticing the deep scar on the Rat's left cheek, running just below his ear, looking like it had been stitched together with barbed wire. His nose was bent as if it had been twisted with vise grips. Danny spread his feet and clenched his fists, ready to dance. Then, out of nowhere, a fist flew so fast he had to duck. The hand grabbed the leather-clad shitbag by the collar and tossed him to the floor. A second guy came around from the other side and grabbed the first greaser, and threw him to the ground so hard his head bounced off the floor. The girls turned and screamed as the crowd spread like Moses parting the Red Sea.

The greasers and the two guys scuffled across the floor. Someone opened the front door. The guys dragged the greasers out, ass over elbows, onto the sidewalk.

They came back in, and Danny recognized them; it was the Lyons brothers, JL and Potato Head. As soon as Danny saw them, he looked for the girls, relieved that they were okay. He worked his way through the crowd and grabbed Patty by the hand. After walking her back to the booth, he said, "Sit down. I'll be right back."

"Danny, please," she grabbed his arm. "Don't be long. I don't like this place. I want to leave." Her eyes began to water, and she started shaking.

"I'll be back in a minute. I promise. I gotta find Bugsy and make sure he's okay."

As soon as Danny spotted the Lyons brothers, he jogged over to them. "Fuck, I'm glad you guys were here," he said. "I thought I was gonna get fucked up back there."

"What? By those two faggots?" JL said, sipping on a tall glass of beer. "Are you a queer or something?"

"Of course not," Danny said, taking half a step backward. "What the fuck? There were two of them."

"I know. I'm just fucking with you," JL said. "I know them—they're a couple of lightweights."

"How do you know them?"

"They're from Saint Leo's parish. One of my cousins went to school with them."

"Oh yeah?"

"Yeah. They're shitbags."

"The tall one with the scar, he's Ricky Valencia, and the other one, he's George Peroni."

"Yeah, they're a couple of fags," Potato Head said. "They used to hang out with the Parksmen until they chased them off the Corner."

"Yeah, they don't like fags either," JL said.

"I ain't never seen them before," Danny said.

"That's because you ain't a cocksucker," JL said.

"You guys are too much," Danny said. "Hey, can I get you a drink?"

"Sure. A couple of Buds'd be nice," JL replied.

After buying the beers and handing them out, Danny said goodbye. "I gotta check on Bugsy. You guys seen him?"

"Naw," JL said.

"Stay away from fags," Potato Head said.

"Don't worry, I will," Danny said, laughing.

Danny stood on his toes, bouncing up and down, going through the crowd, until he spotted Bugsy at the other end of the bar. "Hey man, you gotta keep an eye on your girl," he said when he reached him. "Did you see what just happened?"

"The fight?"

"Yeah."

"What about it?"

"Your fucking girl was almost in the middle of it."

Bugsy took a sip of his drink and looked around. "I thought she was with Patty."

"She was. It could have been a real mess if it wasn't for the Lyons brothers."

"I didn't see them. Where are they?"

"Over there," Danny said, nodding toward the other end of the bar.

"Where's Karen?"

"Over there, at the end of the bar. Next to those spear-chuckers." They both looked over at the crowd. "Between you and me, you'd better grab her before some more shit goes down."

Bugsy drained his beer and muttered before bumping his way over to the Lyons brothers. Danny followed him. "You know your girl's trouble. She doesn't belong in here," JL said.

"Yeah, I know," Bugsy said, nodding.

"They'll make her shit bleed if they get a chance. You know that, right?" Potato Head said.

"I know."

"Hey, I'm gonna go, guys," Danny said. "I gotta take Patty home.

"Okay," Bugsy said.

"Thanks again," he said to the Lyons brothers, tapping them both on their arms.

Danny walked over to Patty, quietly sitting in the booth, staring straight ahead, hands neatly folded in front of her. "Can we go now?" she said in a tone that left little doubt about her wishes.

"Yes, I'm ready. I'm sorry I took so long. I had to make sure Bugsy was okay."

"What about Karen?"

"I think she's okay."

"I hope so."

"Between you and me, she's Bugsy's problem," Danny said as he stepped aside so she could slide out.

Danny led her across the floor, through the sweaty crowd, past a balloon-bellied cop standing outside. Danny grabbed Patty's hand. They headed toward Codman Square, past a row of four-story apartments neatly stacked side by side. As they walked down the street, they heard voices. Patty squeezed his hand tighter. Danny took a quick look over his shoulder and leaned closer. "Don't turn around," he whispered.

"What?" she replied anxiously, squeezing his hand tighter. "I'm scared, Danny. I want to go home."

Danny gently forced her fingers apart and started walking, gently towing her. He looked over his shoulder again; three black kids were coming toward them. Danny carefully moved away from Patty, unbuckled his belt, slid it out, and wrapped the loose end around his hand. The black kids moved faster and suddenly surrounded them. Patty stopped and froze.

"Hey motherfucker, gimme your money," the tallest of the three said to Danny. He wore a leather jacket over a white T-shirt. His left hand was jammed in his pocket. He held a long, thin knife that flickered from the dull glow of the street lights.

The second kid, the smallest of the three, breathing harder than the others, worked his way around to Danny's side. The last kid, nervous, fidgety, tall, and thin as a rail, was wearing a multi-colored shirt. He kept a close eye on Danny while standing a couple of feet away from Patty, who was shaking and crying. "Yo bitch, give me your fuckin' watch," the kid said. Patty cried through closed eyes.

"BITCH! DID YOU HEAR ME?" he said, spraying spit in her face. Patty's eyes grew wider as he stepped closer, stopped, and rolled his head to the side. "Shit, you nice," he said.

Danny took a half step backward and tightened his grip on his belt. The thin kid took another step closer to Patty. Danny pulled his wallet out; "Here! This is all I got," he shouted, hoping someone other than the kids would hear him.

"Yo, my niggah," the tall kid said, nodding at the thin one. "Get that."

Danny stood motionless as the thin kid snatched the wallet out of his hand. "I WANT THE WATCH, BITCH!" he said as he moved closer to Patty, flashing a mouth full of gold-capped teeth.

"NO!" Danny yelled, putting his arm in front of her. "Leave her alone!"

"MOTHERFUCKER!" the gold-toothed kid yelled. "I didn't ask for your fucking opinion."

The tall kid pimp-walked toward Danny, rolling his shoulders up and down, curling his free hand, and swinging his knife by his side. "Shut your white ass up, or I'm gonna stick you."

"I said NO. LEAVE HER ALONE!"

"Listen, motherfucker!" the knife-wielding kid said, stepping closer. "Stay the fuck outta my business, or I'm gonna cut you!" He turned toward the thin kid. "YO! Motherfucker, grab the watch from the bitch."

"Leave her alone. I gave you my wallet." Danny said, stepping forward. "YOU CAN'T HAVE HER WATCH!"

"I be getting tired of your shit," he said, his knife low by his side. He paused for a second at the sound of a bus rumbling toward them. Danny widened his eyes to get Patty's attention. When he did, he tilted his head in a slight nod as the bus drew closer. Patty's eyes widened again. Danny lifted his head and yelled. "RUN! RUN!"

Patty froze.

"RUN!" Danny yelled again and waved his arms. Patty blinked and came back to life. "RUN," he yelled again as he swung his belt over his head, catching the tall kid with the knife just below his eye, tearing his cheek open. The short kid came at Danny, swinging hard and throwing punches. Danny sidestepped and kicked him in the knee, sending him to the ground howling.

"RUN! RUN TO THE BUS!" Danny screamed. "RUN!"

Patty came out of her stupor and ran in the middle of the street, screaming, "HELP! HELP!" waving her hands. The driver slammed on his brakes and brought the bus to a screeching halt, flinging the passengers out of their seats. Danny swung his belt over his head, backing the kids up and spreading them out. The tall kid came toward him, slicing the air with his knife as blood ran down his cheek. The short kid somehow got behind Danny, got his arm around Danny's neck and tried to pull him down. Danny arched his back, wriggling to stay on his feet. He got his arm loose and swung his belt over his shoulder, hitting the kid on his ear. He screamed and let go of Danny. The thin kid grabbed Danny's arm and pinned it behind his back while the short kid grabbed his other arm. The steely shank of the knife came out of the shadows and vanished as the blade disappeared into Danny's stomach. Danny's eyes fluttered when he saw the knife again, now colored with blood. There were no more reflections. He gasped for air when he saw it strike again under his ribs. He felt the warmth of his blood running down his stomach. He watched the knife go in again, lower and deeper, and then, everything was black.

# 38

"Mrs. McSweeney," a voice called out. "Mrs. McSweeney." Bridie opened her eyes and looked around, trying to get her bearings. "Mrs. McSweeney, Danny's coming around." Bridie turned in her chair toward the voice and felt a stiff ache across her shoulders. She flinched in pain before realizing the voice was Anne's, Danny's nurse's. "Danny's coming to," she said excitedly.

Bridie stood up, struggling with the pain that ran down her back. "Mother Mary, that's wonderful news, Anne." Bridie wiped her mouth with the sleeve of her sweater.

"It is. Would you like to see him?"

"Yes, yes, of course. Yes!" Bridie stood up and grabbed the sides of her dress, fastened at the waist with safety pins, patting at the creases and fumbling to find the seams of her slip so as to adjust it. She smoothed out her collar. She caught a glimpse of her reflection in the window. Her eyes had retreated into her face; she did not recognize herself.

She followed Anne into Danny's room. He was breathing louder than the beeps and buzzes of the medical equipment surrounding him. A young candy striper, with *Jennifer* embroidered on her red-and-white uniform, was taking Danny's blood pressure.

"How's he doing?" Anne asked her.

"Fine," Jennifer replied.

"This is Mrs. McSweeney, Danny's mother. She's a neighbor, a friend of my mom."

"Pleased to meet you," Jennifer said, glancing up.

Bridie looked around. A tray with unwrapped bandages and other medical things sat on the tabletop. Several odd-looking machines with wires and tubes beeped and flashed.

"I called Doctor MacDonald. It looks like he's ready to wake up," Anne said.

"Mother of Mary. That's wonderful," Bridie said excitedly.

"Can I get you anything?" Anne asked, leaning forward and placing her hand on Bridie's shoulder.

"No, thank you, honey. I'm fine. I am."

Bridie sat down, folded her hands across her lap, and looked at Danny. His hair was messy, his face dirty, and his hands dry and chapped. She studied him for a few minutes before rubbing his hand.

"Anne, do you have any lotion?"

"We do. Give me a minute."

Anne returned and handed a small tube to Bridie. She opened it, rubbed some lotion on her hands, and then over Danny's hands. She looked up when Dr. MacDonald came into the room.

"How are you doing?" he asked Bridie in a clinical voice.

"As good as can be. How is he doing?"

"He's improving. He'll need a lot of rest." He placed his hand on her shoulder. "He's a fortunate young man."

"I know," Bridie said, releasing her breath through pursed lips.

Dr. MacDonald picked up Danny's medical charts, a series of papers bound to a clipboard hanging from a metal hook at the foot of the bed. He made a few notations before returning the board.

"How are his vitals?" he asked Anne.

"Fine, Doctor, everything's steady."

"Good. Let's run some smelling salts by him."

Anne picked up a tiny, sealed packet from the tray and carefully unwrapped it. She snapped it in half and waved it under Danny's nose. Danny's head lurched ever so slightly, and his eyelids fluttered. Bridie reached for his hand, but it jerked away. She looked up at Dr. MacDonald.

"That's normal. Don't worry about it. It's a good sign that he's coming to. Can you get a glass of water?" he asked Jennifer.

"Yes, Doctor," she replied, nodding.

Danny's head rolled slowly from side to side, then he coughed, and his eyelids fluttered before opening. "Danny," Bridie said, reaching for his hand again. "It's Ma."

"Mrs. McSweeney." It was Jennifer with a glass of water.

"Thank you," Bridie said. She leaned forward. "Danny, it's Ma. I'm here."

He squeezed her hand. "Thank you, heavenly Father," she said, blessing herself.

"Ma?" Danny said in a feeble voice.

"Yes, I'm here, honey, I'm here!" Danny opened his eyes and parted his lips.

"See if he's thirsty," the doctor said.

Bridie lifted the glass to Danny's mouth; he struggled to take a sip, taking in a small amount before closing his eyes again. When he opened them, Bridie lifted the glass to his mouth, but he shook his head *no*.

Dr. MacDonald walked to the end of the bed and made more notations on the clipboard. "Mrs. McSweeney, we had to remove his spleen."

"His what?"

"His spleen."

"What's a spleen?"

"It's a filter for your blood. It makes sure that everything works okay."

"Doesn't he need it?"

"You can live without one. You know, the human body is amazing. The other organs usually take over and perform the functions of the spleen. If he eats right and takes care of himself, his body will adjust."

"I see, "she said, nodding, wringing her hands.

"We'll get him started on some soup and crackers." He turned to Anne. "I'll check in later this afternoon."

"Thank you," Bridie said, wiping her tears, uninvited guests to the conversation, away. "Honey, can you do me a favor?"

"Sure, what is it?" Anne said.

"Can you call Chrissy and tell her Danny's awake?"

"Of course. Let me grab a piece of paper."

After writing the number down and handing it to Anne, Bridie kissed Danny. "I'll be right back, honey," she said, heading toward the bathroom.

---

Danny opened his eyes; the medicine was wearing off. *PATTY!* He tried to sit up, but a burning feeling in his stomach stopped him; he struggled not to vomit. "MA!" He tried to sit up again, stopping when another sharp pain shot across his belly. "MA, MA! Patty. Is she okay?" he croaked.

Bridie sat up from the hard wooden chair she had slept in, half-asleep and disoriented. As soon as she saw Danny, she calmed down. "Yes, yes, honey, she's fine. Lord Almighty, she's fine."

"Where is she?" he asked, lying back down.

"She's home. She's okay. She wasn't hurt," Bridie said, leaning forward and holding his hands.

"Has she come by?"

Bridie looked out the window and silently shuffled her purse. Danny waited as long as he could.

"Ma!"

"No, honey. She hasn't come by. I'm sorry."

Danny, his head deep in his pillow, stared at the ceiling as if he'd find the answer somewhere in the stained panels above.

"You know, honey, you did a very foolish thing."

Danny bent his head down and hunched his shoulders, contrite.

"God forgive me, Danny, but why would you take her to a place like that? Jesus, Mary, and Joseph, what were you thinking? The place is filled with jigaboos. You shouldn't have gone there, not with her."

Danny closed his eyes and pressed his head deeper into his pillow. Bridie waited for him to respond, but he didn't. Bridie waited and spoke after a while. Her tone was grim.

"She's fine, thankfully, but her father's fit to be tied, and I can't blame him. Mother of Jesus. She comes from a good family. It's been in all the papers and all over the TV. The police, the Negroes, Patty, and the shooting. All of it!"

"The shooting? What shooting?"

"Heaven help us. The shooting." She shook her head. "Of course, how would you know? How much do you remember?"

"The last thing I remember was me and the spooks fighting, and me hollering at Patty to run to the bus . . . and . . . then I remember getting stabbed. After that, I don't remember nothing, really."

"Well, first off, Patty's okay. She wasn't hurt. When the fight started, she ran into the street, and the bus driver stopped. She told him what had happened, and he and a bunch of men ran across the street, and the Negroes ran off. When they got to you, you were lying on the sidewalk, bleeding." She paused and blessed herself. "An ambulance brought you here, and the doctors worked on you half the night to save you. Once word got out about what had happened, a police officer, Lenny, Lonny, Lonna—Lonardelli. That's it. He's a friend of your boss, Mr. Erickson. Well, the next thing you know, him and half the station are out looking for those black bastards. They found them near that old fire station on Harvard Street, near Four Corners."

"I know the station. We used to play over there when we were kids."

"Two of them gave up right away. But the one that stabbed you—Calhoun, Warren Calhoun, I'll never forget his name—he ran away. The police chased him down the street into the Ollie schoolyard. He climbed up one of the fire escapes, and believe it or not, he still had the knife in his hand." She paused to swallow and catch her breath. "This Calhoun tried to stab the cop that chased him up the fire escape, and he shot him right there. Killed him."

"Wow! I didn't know that."

"If you ask me, they should have shot them all, every one of them!" She paused to bless herself. "Mother of Jesus, forgive me. I didn't mean that, not that way."

"Did any of the kids come by?"

"Heavens, yes, a whole bunch of them. They made a lot of noise and caused quite a stir. They were so loud, they got thrown out."

"Really?" Danny replied.

"Oh yes. The nurses were really upset at them."

"Anyone else come by?"

"The police. They came by several times, wanting to talk to you."

"About what?"

"They need you to look at some pictures of the Negro boys."

"What about Mr. Erickson? Does he know what happened?" Danny's voice deflated. "I musta lost my job, missing work and everything."

Bridie put her hands on her lap and smiled. "He and his wife have been by to check on you. She's such a nice lady. And that Officer Lonardelli. He usually comes by in the morning and brings me a coffee and some donuts. What a nice man he is."

"Lonardelli?" Danny propped himself up a little more, fighting the pain in his abdomen.

"Yes."

He looked around, orienting himself. "What hospital am I in?"

"City."

"How long have I been here?"

"Six days."

"Six days? Are you kidding?"

"No."

"And I was out the whole time?"

"Yes. It was touch and go for a couple of days. We thought we were going to lose you. There were so many doctors. I prayed to Saint Christopher every hour I was awake. He protected you."

"How long have you been here?"

"The whole time."

"What about your work?"

"That's not important," she replied, thumbing the seam of her dress. "It's not important."

"Gee, Ma. What about the rent and the bills?"

Bridie's head bobbed as she began to weep. Danny reached for her hand and squeezed it briefly before letting it go. The pain in his stomach was too much. He fell back into his pillow.

"Ma," he said softly, "It'll be okay. The landlord's gotta understand. And I got some money saved." Voices in the other rooms and shuffling feet in the hallway distracted them. Danny rolled his head toward his mother. "Hey, Ma?"

"Yes, honey. What is it?"

"Can you get a nurse? I'm hurting. I need something for the pain."

"Can I look at it?"

Danny pulled his blanket aside, stopping when he felt a small tube stuck into the tip of his penis. "What the fuck? What's that?"

"It's a catheter, honey. It's how you're peeing."

"A what?" Danny yelped.

"A catheter. I'm sure they'll take it out now that you're awake."

"They need to take that thing out of me!" He stared at the thin tube, filled with bloodied urine running alongside the edge of the bed. He grabbed his sheets and carefully tucked them over his groin, revealing a thick mat of bandages wrapped around his stomach. A line of blood ran across his midsection.

"I'll get Anne."

"Anne?"

"Yes. Anne Kenny, our neighbor."

"Has she seen me?" he asked.

"Of course, she's seen you. She's your nurse. She's taking care of you and doing a good job of it. She knows what she's doing."

Danny groaned and pulled his sheets up higher.

"I'll get her." She leaned over and kissed him on his forehead. "I'll be right back."

A few minutes later, she returned with Anne and a freckle-faced redheaded candy striper Danny figured to be about fifteen years old. "This is Betty," Anne said. "She'll be helping me out."

"Hi," Danny said feebly.

"Hi," Betty replied.

Anne placed two fingers on his wrist, glanced at her watch, and counted. Danny brushed his hair aside and waited.

"So, what's going on?" Anne asked.

"I'm in a lot of pain."

"Where's it hurt?"

"My stomach, down here," he said, gingerly tapping his lower set of bandages.

"Can you get me a thermometer?" Anne asked.

"Yes," Betty replied.

"Can you describe the pain?"

"It burns wicked bad. It feels like I've been cut or something."

"Well, that sounds about right. You were cut pretty badly."

Betty handed the thermometer to Anne. "Here, open your mouth." She placed it beneath his tongue and removed it a few minutes later. "You're running a temperature."

"What is it?" Bridie asked.

"A little more than a hundred and one. I'll get you some aspirin."

"Can I help?" Bridie asked.

"Not at the moment."

"Let me take a look," Anne said.

Danny pulled his blanket down over his crotch as Anne leaned forward and gently pressed his stomach.

"Fuck!" he yelped. "That hurt."

"I'm sorry. Let me take a better look."

"Okay."

She peeled his bandage back. "How long have you been bleeding?"

"I don't know. I just woke up."

"It wasn't bleeding earlier," Bridie interjected, peering over Anne's shoulder.

"I'll get you something for the pain," Anne said.

"Thanks. I appreciate it."

"Let me put some new bandages on." She turned to Betty. "Can you get some fresh bandages and tape?"

"Of course."

"By the way, the police want to come by and ask you some questions," Anne said. "Doctor MacDonald wants you up and around for twenty-four hours before he'll let them talk to you."

"I get it. No problem. I'm good."

"Can we get you anything?" Anne said to Bridie.

"A cup of tea would be nice."

"Of course. Betty, would you mind?"

"No, not at all. Cream and sugar?"

"Yes, thank you," Bridie said, folding her hands and placing them on her lap.

"I'll be back," Anne said. "I have another patient to check up on; I won't be long."

Betty returned with the tea, holding it below a saucer she carried in the other hand. She placed it on the bed table and stood up erect.

"Thank you," Bridie said.

"You're welcome."

"Let me know if you need anything else," Betty said.

"Thank you. I will."

Betty smiled, turned, and left.

"So, how's Frankie and Chrissy?" Danny asked.

"Fine," Bridie said, leaning back into her chair. "Chrissy's starting to show."

She slumped inside her shoulders and disappeared. Danny closed his eyes and listened to his mother breathe. Otherwise, it was quiet, remaining that way until Anne's footsteps announced her arrival, drowning out the sound of Bridie's breathing. Anne placed the tray on the small table alongside his bed, holding a glass of water and a metal cup of pills.

"This one's an antibiotic," Anne said, handing him a large red pill. "It should help with the fever. I'll give you one every four hours." Danny popped the pill in his mouth and took a sip of water.

"This is an aspirin." He took it with another sip of water.

"The green one is to help you pee so we can take the catheter out of you."

Danny gulped while taking the pill. "Are *you* gonna do it? Take it out of me?"

"I can if you want."

"I, um, gee . . . I thought the doctor would do it."

"It's a simple procedure. Doctors don't do it."

"Oh . . . I didn't know that."

"These two are for the pain. They're pretty strong. You're gonna feel dizzy like you're drunk or something. They'll probably put you out." He popped them into his mouth.

"Let's change those bandages."

When they were done, she said, "We have to get that catheter out."

He frowned and stared at her uncomfortably.

"Danny, you know this is my job. It's what I'm trained to do."

"Thanks, I know, it's just . . ."

"How about we take the catheter out after the pills kick in. We have a male nurse on the floor. I'll call him."

"Him?"

"Yes, him. His name is Liam, and he's a great nurse. Don't worry. He knows what he's doing."

"Liam? You're kidding me, right?"

"No, not at all. He's excellent. He's been doing this longer than me."

Danny looked down at the tube and followed its path as it wound alongside the metal railing into a small glass container of urine hanging on the side of the bed. "Don't worry about anything. You'll be okay. When you wake up, it'll be gone. You'll never know it was there."

"I hope so."

# 39

When Danny woke up, he felt like he had been run over by a Mack truck. His head felt like it was stuffed with cotton, and his tongue felt like a wad of sandpaper. He spotted a glass of water and drank the whole thing, giving himself a sudden stomachache. He pulled himself up and looked around, trying to figure out how long he'd been out. The first thing he noticed was his mother was gone, and, to his delight, so was the tube stuck inside his penis. His bandages felt better; they were not as tight as the old ones. The bed next to him, empty earlier, was occupied by a kid about his age, hooked up to a string of colored wires and tubes connected to a large pulsating machine.

He heard voices in the hallway, mostly female. He needed to take a leak but didn't want to call for help. His neighbor Anne and the little redhead had already seen his privates. He carefully rolled to his side and spotted a bedpan on a small shelf at his bedside. After retrieving it, he worked the sheets loose, pulling enough material to make a small tent. He slipped the bedpan between his legs and let loose a stream of dark urine. He returned the sloshing pan to the shelf, lay back, and closed his eyes, and it started.

*Walking on the wrong side of the street—at night—with Patty. Jesus Christ! What if something had happened to her? I'd never forgive myself. I am one stupid motherfucker!* His head began to throb. The pain grew more intense. He called out for Anne, but she didn't reply. The droning voices in the hall continued. "Anne!" he called again, this time louder. Still nothing. He opened the top drawer of his dresser and found a Bible. He threw it through the door into the hallway, where it skidded across the floor. A couple of seconds later, a large nurse walked over, picked the Bible up, and marched into the room, tapping the book against her palm.

"Is this yours?" she asked, still tapping the words of the almighty, standing at the foot of his bed. Danny stared at her, wondering if the drugs had confused him. Her pockets were full, and Danny couldn't tell where they ended and where her breasts began. Her legs, thick as ham hocks, hung from beneath her dress like they were in a butcher shop. Her tight socks looked like they had bleached into her skin.

She was big.

"There's a buzzer over there you can use," she rumbled in a voice that could render most men sterile. Danny turned and spotted a small black buzzer connected to a pair of curly black wires bolted onto the side of the bed.

"I'm sorry. I didn't see it."

"Didn't anyone tell you the buzzer was there?"

"I don't know. Could have. I've been on a lot of medication. I don't remember much."

She lumbered over and placed the Bible in the top drawer. "Let me look at you."

She pulled the sheets back and touched him under his ribs and then on the stomach, carefully pressing and feeling around the lower part of his belly. "Does that hurt?"

"Yeah, a little."

She pressed around a few more times before pulling his johnny back. "Does it hurt down there?" she asked, nodding at his penis.

"No!" he replied, quickly pulling his johnny down.

"So, what's the problem?"

"Yeah, I had to go to the bathroom," he said, tilting his head toward the tray.

"I can see that."

"I thought I needed some help, but I was able to go."

"Uh-huh."

"So, can you get me another bedpan?"

"No problem. Anything else?"

"My stomach hurts really bad. Can I have some pain pills?"

She walked to the foot of the bed, lifted his clipboard, and made a few notes. "I'll get some for you."

"Thanks. Do you know what time it is?"

She glanced at her watch. "Nine twenty-five."

"Where's Anne?" he asked.

"Who's Anne?"

"My nurse."

"I'm your nurse," she said.

"I thought Anne was."

"She must work another shift or something."

"Hmm. Do you know where my mother went?"

"No. I haven't seen anyone all night."

Danny nodded. She picked up the bedpan, carried it into the bathroom, returned, placed it on the top of the table, shuffled out the door, and returned ten minutes later with a glass of water and a cup filled with pills. He took the pills, drank the water, and returned the glass.

"Need anything else?"

"Naw, I'm good."

"Okay." She left, wobbling back and forth from leg to leg, like a two-legged table.

He rested and waited for the pills to kick in, eventually drifting off to sleep, dreaming of knives and Negroes, street lights and buses, and Patty. Screaming. Louder. Someone gently shook him, rocking him awake.

"Danny. Danny. Wake up. You're having a nightmare." The hospital lights and his mother's face came into focus. "Danny," she said softly, shaking him again. "Are you awake?"

"Yeah, yeah." He rolled his head from side to side and lifted it. He could hear the cacophony of sounds he had grown accustomed to, not liking any of them: machines, footsteps, moans, buzzers, and voices that echoed in the hallways.

"Where've you been?" he asked, rubbing his eyes. "I was looking for you."

"I'm sorry, honey. I went home to get some rest. I needed it. After you fell asleep, Anne, bless her heart, insisted I go home and get a good night's rest. As soon as I hit the bed, I slept like a log. Mother of Mary, I can't remember the last time I slept that long."

"I'm glad you did."

"Me too. I needed it."

"How's Frankie and Chrissy doing?"

"They're fine."

"Good," he said.

"Praise the Lord."

Danny sat up slowly, shifting himself with his arms. "How long have you been here?"

"I don't know, maybe half an hour, forty-five minutes."

"Huh. I had some weird dreams."

"I could tell. You scared me."

"Did anyone come by?"

"Not that I know." She lifted the metal tray covering a large dish, revealing a cup of apple sauce, mashed potatoes, meatloaf, and a small green salad. "Are you hungry?"

"Yeah, I think I could eat."

"Would you like some help?"

"No, I'm okay. I can do it."

"Okay. Let me help with the table."

After moving everything into place, she propped the bed up. Danny started eating, fighting the temptation to devour everything in as few bites as possible. Anne walked in as he was finishing up. "So, how are you feeling?"

Danny wiped the last of the mashed potatoes from his face. "Pretty good, I guess."

"Glad to see you're eating."

"Me too." He wiped his mouth again. "Hey, Anne, I missed you."

"You did?" she replied, looking at him and Bridie inquisitively.

"Yeah, this battle-ax of a nurse came by last night. She had a really shitty attitude. I didn't like her."

"I'm sorry. Did you get her name?"

"No. I was pretty tired. She was a fucking beast."

"Danny!" Bridie interrupted him. "There's no need for that language."

"I'm sorry, Ma, but she was. You should've seen her."

"Still, there's no need for that language."

"I'm sorry, Ma. She wasn't very nice."

"So, are you ready to talk to the detectives?" Anne asked.

"Yeah, I think so."

"How does this afternoon sound?"

"Good," Danny said, nodding.

"Are you sure?" his mother asked.

"Yeah, I'm sure." Bridie cast a doubtful glance at him.

"What time?" Danny asked Anne.

"How's three sound?"

"Great."

"How's the pain?" Anne asked.

"Not good. My stomach still hurts."

"Want some more medicine?"

"Yeah, but is there anything different? Those last pills gave me some horrible nightmares. I didn't like it."

"That happens sometimes. Let me see what I can do."

"Thanks. I 'preciate it."

"Would you like to get cleaned up?"

"Umm, yeah. That'd be great," Danny said.

"I'll get a basin, towels, shampoo, and toothpaste."

"Thanks. That would be good."

"No problem."

Anne returned with a metal bowl filled with bathing and cleaning supplies. "Do you want any help?" Anne asked.

"No, I'll be fine."

"Okay. I'll get you some hot water." She emptied the bowl onto the small bedside table. Then, she went into his bathroom, filled the bowl with water, and put it on his bed. "I can get a male nurse to help if you need it."

Danny scrunched his face like he'd just eaten a lemon. "Naw, really. I'm okay."

"Okay. If you need anything, call me."

"Will do."

"Do you need any help?" Bridie asked.

"No, Ma, thanks. I 'preciate everything and all. Please don't take me wrong or nothing, but I can take care of myself. Okay?"

"I can help. I'm still your mother," she bristled.

"I know, Ma, I know. I 'preciate you and everything, but I can do it. I need some privacy."

"Are you sure?" Bridie asked, standing up, impatient from the tone of her voice.

"Yeah, Ma. I'm sure. Can you come back in fifteen minutes?"

Bridie hovered around his bed, inspecting his bandages, fluttering his sheets as she looked him over before leaving. "Can you shut the door?" Danny asked.

He pulled his johnny up, soaked the handcloth in the water, and ran the bar of soap across his face until it was covered with lather. He ran it across his neck, dragged it across his cheeks, and rested for a few minutes before washing everything he could, stopping when the pain was too much. He closed his eyes, listening to the machines doing whatever they were doing to the kid in the other bed.

When Bridie returned, the tray was in the middle of his bed. "Let me get that out of the way," she said, lifting the bubbly bowl. She took it into the bathroom and returned with it filled with hot water. "Can I wash your hair?" she said.

He looked up at her and smiled. "Yeah, that'd be nice."

After working the hand cloth with shampoo, she propped him up on a small stack of pillows Anne had brought in and proceeded to wash his hair and massage his head. She gave him tissues to blow his nose, surprised at how much dried blood and mucus came out. Next, she emptied the basin, filled it with cold water, placed it on his lap, and handed him his toothbrush covered with toothpaste. Ten minutes later, his teeth were the cleanest they had ever been. Bridie remained silent the entire time. Finally, she emptied the basin, returned it to his table, and sat down.

"Thanks, Ma! I feel like a million bucks."

"I see you cleaned yourself up," Anne said, walking in just as they finished.

"Yeah, it feels good."

"Let me know if you need anything else. If not, I'll be back in a while."

"Sounds good."

Anne returned a couple hours later, followed by two men wearing dark suits and thin black ties. A tall, uniformed cop followed. Danny recognized him right away.

"Hi, Danny. This is Detective Curriden," Anne said, nodding toward the shorter of the two, "and this is Detective Rocha. You know, Officer Lonardelli."

Lonardelli nodded. "How're you feeling?"

"Not bad, I guess. It could be worse."

"But it isn't. You made sure of that." Lonardelli turned to Bridie. "Your son is very brave. You should be proud of him."

Bridie smiled for the first time in weeks. "I am," she said as she reached over and patted his hand. "I'm very proud of him."

"So, are you up for this? If you're not, we can do it some other time," Lonardelli said.

"Naw, I'm good. I'd rather get it over with."

"Great!" Lonardelli replied. "These detectives have got some questions for you. They're good men, a couple of our best. If you don't remember everything, it's okay; if you want to stop, that's okay too. There's no rush."

"Yeah, of course." Danny looked over at the suits.

"You ought to know: everyone at the station's rooting for you," Lonardelli said.

"Thanks," Danny said, blushing and bowing his head down.

Curriden was the first to speak, but not before looking over to Bridie. "Officer Lonardelli tells me he knows your son."

She nodded *yes*.

"I'm gonna be straight up with him if that's okay?"

Bridie nodded agreeably.

"We've been after that punk for a long time. He's hurt a lot of people, mostly kids and old folks, both white and black. His name is, er, was Warren Calhoun. He deserved what he got. We don't know how much stuff he was into, but we think we can tie him into other crimes. That's one of the reasons we wanted to talk to you. We're hoping you can ID his friends. We want to nail them too. If we can implicate them, we can take them off the streets. You gave us that."

"Really?"

"Yes. There's one more thing you ought to know. When we grabbed the other kids, they only talked about you. One of the kids said you have more balls than a bowling alley."

"What? You're kidding, right?"

"It's true," Lonardelli replied. "You're a bonafide badass. You scared the hell out of them."

Bridie, listening closely, welled up in tears. "I'm proud of you, honey," she said. Danny reached out for her hand and held it for a moment.

"By the way, the Ericksons have been asking about you. I promised them I'd let them know how you're doing. They're very concerned about you," Lonardelli said.

"Really?"

"Of course. They think the world of you."

"That's . . . that's just, I don't know . . . incredible."

"They're good people."

"Yeah, they are."

"So, are you ready?

"Yup."

"The questions shouldn't take too long. First, they need you for a positive ID to close the case. Then, they want you to look at some pictures. After that, it's standard procedure—a case is a case, and the paperwork's all the same."

"Sure, no problem," Danny said. "Hey, how's the other cop—" he stopped and corrected himself, "officer, the one who shot that kid? How's he doing?"

"McDonough? He's fine. They've given him some time off, like always in these situations. After they finish the investigation, they'll let him back to work. It was a clean shooting."

"It must be tough, shooting someone like that and killing him, even though he was a piece of—er, a punk."

"It is. No matter how justified and bad the perp is, it's still tough. The kid should have given himself up. He's got no one to blame but himself."

"Do you have an extra minute?"

"Sure."

Danny turned to his mother. "Hey, Ma. I need a minute to talk to Officer Lonardelli." She shrugged at him. "Alone," Danny responded.

"Oh," Bridie replied, doing her best to sound good with the request. Lonardelli tilted his head at the two detectives and nodded toward the door. Everyone left the room, including Anne. "What's up?" he asked.

"Do you know how my girlfriend Patty's doing?"

"I haven't heard much. Curriden and Rocha interviewed her about the assailants."

"The what?"

"The assailants—the kids that attacked you. The bad guys."

"Oh," Danny replied, nodding.

"Other than that, I haven't heard anything. I know she wasn't hurt."

"That's good; really good. I was wondering, can you do me a favor?"

"Sure. What is it?"

"It's about Patty."

"Okay. How can I help?"

"I messed up. I know that."

"Don't be so hard on yourself. It could've been worse. You saved her, and that's all that counts."

"Yeah, I know, thank God." Danny wiped a tear from his face. "Patty comes from a really nice family. I've been to her house, and I've met her parents. They had me over for suppah a couple of times. They're really nice people." Danny's voice dropped a dozen degrees. "She hasn't come by to see me." He spoke again, sounding like he was in a closet. "I know she would if she could. I know her father's pissed at me." He stopped talking for a moment, sniffling back from crying. "I can't blame him. I know I screwed up."

"I understand."

"I gotta make sure she's okay, and . . . and I need to apologize to her."

Lonardelli placed his hand on Danny's shoulder, and when he did, Danny collapsed into himself and started crying.

"I might be able to help," Lonardelli said.

"I was hoping for that; I figured you could. Her father'll listen to you. I know he will."

"I'll see what I can do. I can drop by and explain what happened. If nothing else, her folks need to know what you did and how you protected their daughter."

"Man, that'd be great."

"You shouldn't be so hard on yourself. It could have happened anywhere. You're the first one who's ever stood up to those kids. More importantly, you protected your girlfriend. You did a good job."

"Thanks."

"All you need to do is get better."

"Yup." He nodded. "I'm working on that."

"Good. I'm rooting for you."

Danny blushed. "I appreciate it. I appreciate everything."

"So, are you ready to talk to the detectives?"

"Yeah, I am."

"Good. I'll call them in."

"Let's do it."

"I'm going to head out. I'll send the detectives back in."

As soon as he left, Bridie and Anne, and the detectives came in. Before Bridie reached the bed, she peppered Danny with questions. "Is everything okay? What did he want? What's so important you had to talk to him in private? Should I be worried?"

Danny shook his head and waved his hand. "Ma, I need a break. We can talk later."

Bridie glanced over to Anne, drew herself upright, pursed her lips, and sat down.

"Hi, I'm Detective Curriden," said the detective that Anne had introduced as such, a thin man with a dark five o'clock shadow and a pair of hollow, sunken eyes anchored to an equally thin, crooked nose. His hair was thinning and his ears were flattened as if they were sewn to the sides of his head. He leaned his head to his right toward the other detective. "This is Detective Rocha, Ricky Rocha."

Rocha was short, stocky, and built like a brick shithouse. His eyes were restless, an unsettling habit that bothered others. He held a leather-clad notebook and a pencil in his stubby fingers. Bridie scooted closer to the bed as if she was the one being interviewed. "We'll need a little time," Rocha said to Anne. "Can you see that we're not disturbed?"

"Sure, no problem," Anne said, smiling throughout.

"Thank you."

Rocha looked at Danny and then over to Bridie. "Ma'am, you'll have to leave."

"But . . ." she protested.

"This is a formal investigation, and we can't have anyone else in the room for the interview."

"But . . . he's my son."

"Yes, I know that, ma'am. You have to understand a police officer shot and killed someone. We're not permitted to have anyone other than the witness present to talk to us."

"I'm sorry, ma'am, but you'll have to leave. You can wait outside," Curriden said.

"But . . ." Her words floated across the room, searching for a place to anchor.

Danny reached over and clasped her hands. "I can take care of this. It's okay."

"I know, honey, but . . ." she looked at Curriden. "Well, I am your mother," she said indignantly. She looked at Anne, expecting some relief, but there was none. Bridie stood up, harrumphing for emphasis. "I'll be out in the hall if you need me," she scowled at the detectives.

"I'll be out at the nurse's station if you need me," Anne said, joining Bridie.

After the door closed, Curriden spoke. "Sorry about that. Rules are rules."

"Don't worry about it," Danny said. "Don't get me wrong or nothing. She's my ma, and she can't help it and everything, but we'd be here all night if she started asking questions. Heck, they'd never end. She'd want to know everything."

"Hey, you're a lucky kid to have her."

"I know," Danny said. "Believe me, I know."

"Let's get started," Curriden said.

# 40

After the detectives finished their questions and scribbled the answers into their notebooks, they left. Danny was surprised when his mother didn't enter. He figured she needed some rest. He thought about the detectives' questions, unable to figure out why they were so hard to answer. *What color was his shirt? How tall was he? What did they say? What time was it? Did you hear any names? What color were their shoes? Where was everyone standing? How much money were you carrying? Did the kid who stabbed him have on black pants or brown pants? Could they have been blue?* Everything had happened so fast.

He sat up and carefully peeled his bandages back, expecting to find more blood, thankful when he didn't. He pressed them back in place, swung his legs over the edge of his bed, got up, hobbled to the bathroom, sat on the toilet, and tried to go but gave up ten minutes later, remembering Anne had told him the medicine would constipate him. He took a couple of deep breaths, stood up, shuffled back to bed, and fell asleep.

He wasn't sure how long he'd been asleep when he heard his name and opened his eyes, fighting the grogginess.

"Hello," Mr. Erickson said.

"Hi," Danny responded, coughing the dryness from his throat, lifting himself up from the bed.

"How are you feeling? I hope we didn't wake you."

"No, you didn't. Heck, that's all I've been doing, sleeping."

"It's good to see you," Mrs. Erickson said.

"Likewise!"

"We were so worried about you," Mrs. Erickson said.

"I guess it was touch and go for a while," Danny replied, measuring his words as if he was counting the vowels and consonants.

"We got you a little something," Mr. Erickson said, handing him a brightly wrapped box and a Get-Well card. He read the card and thanked them.

"Go on and open it," Mr. Erickson said. Danny peeled the ribbon and paper away. The box was filled with comic books and magazines: *Superman*, *Spiderman*, *The Avengers*, *Aquaman*, *Batman*, *MAD* magazine, and the latest edition of *Sports Illustrated,* with Ted Williams on the cover, in an article about *The Science of Hitting.*

Danny studied the magazines and began reading *Superman*, forgetting he had company. "I'm sorry," he said, putting them down. "They're my favorites."

"So, how are they treating you? How's the food?" Mr. Erickson said.

"Horrible. I could use a good meal and a good night's rest. There's a lot going on here."

"I'm sure there is," Mrs. Erickson replied. "Would you like a spuckie?"

"Thanks, I would, but my ma's bringing me lunch." A lie.

"Wonderful. How is she doing?" Mr. Erickson asked.

"She's fine, really good."

"How about the rest of your family?"

"They're all good, thanks."

"I understand Tony's been by?" Mr. Erickson said.

"Tony?"

"I'm sorry. Officer Lonardelli. His first name's Tony."

"It's Anthony," Erickson's wife added with a loving smile.

"Oh yeah. He's been by a few times. I don't remember much, though, except yesterday, when we talked. Anne, my nurse, told me he'd been by. I've been out of it; I don't remember too much."

"I understand. Tony's a good man," Mr. Erickson said, looking at his wife. "He pulled out all the stops to catch the kid that stabbed you. I'm not sure they would have even found him if not for him."

"I didn't know that."

"He did. He sure did," Mr. Erickson said.

"So," Danny asked, "How's business?"

"Fine, thanks. We're down a little, but that's normal this time of year."

"Does your business go up and down like that?"

"Yeah, there are usually patterns. That's normal."

"I'm learning things even though I'm not at work!"

"I have to tell you, a lot of our regular customers have come by, asking for you."

"Really?"

"Really!" Mr. Erickson responded, jokingly imitating Danny. "The story's been all over the news and papers. Mrs. Dunleavy came by asking for you. Do you remember her? She always carries that big purse and wears those broad-brimmed hats."

"Yeah, sure. She's a nice lady. She always asks me to check her tires, oil, and air. She always tips me really well. She lives over near Ashmont, right?"

"Yup, that's her. And Mrs. Doyle? Remember her? She's the older woman from Saint William's, the widow with the green Chevy, who wears those big glasses. She always comes by to let me know she's been praying for you. She lights two candles for you every day. She told me a couple of the women from Saint Anne's have been saying rosaries for you."

Mr. Erickson sat down on the edge of Danny's bed and continued, "You know Danny, you're a real asset to us." He looked over at his wife. "We care about you, both of us."

Mrs. Erickson nodded. "We never had any children, but if we did, we'd want them to be like you," she said.

"I must confess; business has been down since you've been laid up. So, I had to hire a couple of new guys to help out. Your friend Robby came by, and I moved Charley McElroy over from Quincy to help out." Mr. Erickson chuckled. "The both of them don't—heck, *can't*—do as much as you. And they make such a mess. They're not like you. They don't pick up after themselves."

"And they spill a lot of oil," Mrs. Erickson added, shaking her head. "Everywhere. Even in the bathroom. I don't know how they do that."

"I'll keep McElroy on until you return, assuming you want to return," Mr. Erickson said.

"Are you kidding? I still have my job?"

Mr. Erickson laughed. "Of course you do. Why wouldn't you?"

"I don't know . . . I mean . . . I've been out of work for a long time, and I . . . I haven't been able to work or nothing."

"Oh, these things happen," Mr. Erickson replied. "It's like when someone goes on vacation."

"I never thought about it."

"Everyone deserves a vacation."

"I guess. I never had a vacation, except when we been to my grandma's."

"Well, you don't fire someone because he goes on vacation or takes a week or two off, do you?"

"No, I guess not."

"Earning vacation time goes with the job; it's part of the job and part of running a business. Vacations and accidents all happen. You don't fire someone if they have an accident or need an operation, right?"

"No. I never thought about it."

"Well, you don't need to worry about your job. None of this has any effect on your job. What if you had been hurt on the job?"

Danny shook his head. "There's a lot to running a business, isn't there?"

"There sure is," Mr. Erickson said. "But there's nothing for you to worry about. As far as Mrs. Erickson and I are concerned, your job will be there whenever you're ready to return to work."

"I can't believe it. I can't."

"Honey, tell Danny about his paycheck and the insurance," Mrs. Erickson said.

"Oh yes, I almost forgot. Your payroll is covered while you're out. And you don't need to worry about your medical bills. They're covered by your health insurance."

"Huh? What do you mean?"

"You'll get your paycheck, just like you were working all the time, and your insurance covers your medical bills."

"I . . . I don't understand."

"Do you remember all the forms and paperwork we reviewed when I hired you?" Mr. Erickson asked.

"Yeah. I didn't look at it too closely, to tell you the truth. I should have, I know," Danny bent his head and mumbled. "I feel kinda stupid."

"Oh, don't worry about it. It's no big deal. One of those forms was for your health insurance. The other stuff was for your taxes and social security. All the regular stuff."

Danny wiped his eyes. "This is great news. I can't wait to tell my ma. She was so worried."

"I'm sorry. I wish I had seen her so I could have told her," Mr. Erickson said.

"Don't worry. She's gonna be happy. I can't wait to tell her."

"Just get better," Mrs. Erickson said. "We can't wait to have you back. Everyone misses you."

"I will, I promise."

"We're going to get going, and you need to get some rest," Mr. Erickson said.

"Thanks for coming by. And thanks for the comics. I can't wait to read them."

"Let us know if you need anything," Mrs. Erickson said.

"I will," Danny said. "I will. Promise."

Mrs. Erickson patted him on his hand and kissed his forehead. "Get some rest," she said.

"I will."

As soon as they were gone, Danny picked up the *Sports Illustrated* magazine and lifted it to his face to smell it. Whenever he read one, it had been flipped through a hundred times, the ink was smudged, and the pages were sticky. He sniffed it again before putting it down and stacking the comics in his preferred reading order. He opened the Sports Illustrated magazine and started reading, soon falling asleep, awakening when he heard the rustling of a shopping bag. Looking up, he saw his mother.

"Hi, honey," she said, leaning over and kissing him. "How are you feeling?"

"Good; feeling better."

"Did you get some rest?"

She looked over at the stack of comics and the *Sports Illustrated* magazine, still neatly laid out on the table. "Did you have some company?" she asked.

"Oh yeah, Mr. and Mrs. Erickson came by."

"Oh, that's nice. They're such nice people."

"Oh! MA! MA, I got some great news."

"You do?" she asked, perking up. "What is it?"

"Sit down. You gotta sit down." He slapped his hand on his bed and propped himself up, waiting until she pulled her chair alongside him. "Ma, you're not gonna believe this. I got health insurance! My own health insurance! Can you believe it?"

"Health insurance? Are you sure?"

"I am. Mr. Erickson told me it came with my job. My insurance is paying for all my bills. Everything! Can you believe it?"

"Are you sure, honey? You've got a nice job and everything, but health insurance?"

"And I'm getting paid for all the time I've been off. Mr. Erickson said it's like a paid vacation."

"Oh, honey, I'm sure you misunderstood him. Did you take some medicine today? You know, most people don't have that kind of insurance. And paid time off?" She shook her head from side to side.

"I am. I'm sure. They're paying my bills—all of them. Mr. Erickson wouldn't lie to me. I know he wouldn't. He wouldn't say anything like that if it weren't true."

She paused and thought about it for a minute. "No, you're right. Mother, Jesus, Joseph, and Mary, this is wonderful news!"

"It is Ma, it is."

She held her head in her hands and started rocking, back and forth, quietly. After a few minutes, he picked up his Batman comic and reread a few pages to catch up, while Bridie remained silent. After he read a few pages, she stopped moving and spoke. "Honey, I'm gonna go home. I have a lot to do. First, I'm gonna stop at the A&P and buy a cake mix for your boss and his wife. I hope they like chocolate."

"Aw, Ma, you don't need to do that."

"I do, honey. My prayers have been answered," she said blessing herself and murmuring a prayer. She stood up. "Would you like me to bring Frankie with me when I return?"

"Yeah, I guess. Does he want to come by?"

"Don't be silly. Of course, he wants to see you."

Danny grabbed his comic books and reshuffled them, withdrawing a couple and handing them to Bridie. "Can you give him these?"

Bridie leaned over and kissed him on his forehead. "I'm sure he'll like these."

"I know he will."

"I'll see you tomorrow. I want to finish the cake tonight before I go to bed."

"Sounds good." Danny rolled onto his side—it was the first time he'd been able to do that—and started reading until he dozed off, trying to figure out how Aquaman was going to get out of the giant whirlpool he was caught in. He slept without interruption until he heard voices. Danny opened his eyes to see Billy and Bugsy standing at the end of his bed.

"How ya feeling, loser?" Bugsy said.

"You should see the other guy."

"I can't. The cops put that black motherfucker on a slab." Bugsy curled his fingers into the shape of a gun and pointed his hand at Danny. "BANG, you black motherfucker!"

Danny started laughing but stopped when his stomach hurt too much. Bugsy stopped when he saw how much pain Danny was in. Danny composed himself and sat up a few minutes later and reached behind for a pillow. "I can get it," Billy said, helping Danny tuck the pillow behind himself.

"Thanks," Danny said.

"So, you guys hear anything?" Danny asked

"I got a cousin, Peter Campbell. You know him. He's a cop, lives down Neponset."

"Yeah, I remember him. Tall kid with brown hair. Good-looking kid, sort of like, um, what's his name, that guy in Bonnie and Clyde, the actor."

"Warren Beatty."

"Yeah, that's him."

"He says you're one lucky motherfucker. He said it was either that or you're fucking stupid. I told him my money's on stupid!"

"Fuck you, you douchebag." Danny turned to Billy. "What've you been up to? You doing okay?"

"Yeah," Billy muttered, sounding like he had a mouth full of mayonnaise. "I'm still kinda fucked up. I get a lot of headaches; I can't make 'em stop." He came around the other side of the bed and pulled one of the chairs alongside Danny, pivoting his head like it was spinning on greased bearings. He pulled out a pint of VO, a quarter drained, and took a slow, lazy swig. He wiped his mouth and passed the bottle to Danny.

"Naw, not right now."

"Hey, man," Billy said. "Are they giving you those little blue pills, you know, the ones with the little numbers on 'em?"

"I got some blue ones. I ain't never read them, but they're blue." Danny tilted his head, to the left, toward the table. "They're in the top drawer."

Billy opened the drawer and picked them up. "Can I have 'em?"

"Yeah, sure. I can get more."

Billy tossed two of them in his mouth like M&Ms and stuck the rest in his pocket.

"I heard you guys came by," Danny said.

"We tried," Bugsy said, "'cept they threw us out; said we were too rowdy. They let Billy stay, though. Musta thought he was a patient or something."

"Are you serious?"

"Yeah," Bugsy said. "We snuck some beers in, and the fucking nurses didn't like that. So, they threw us out, the fucking cunts."

"What did you expect? You guys are a bunch of idiots. You're lucky you didn't get arrested."

"Yeah, what the fuck," Bugsy said, shrugging.

"I been worried about you," Billy said. "When I was in the hospital, you watched over me, made sure I was okay. I owe ya."

"Shit, you don't owe me nothing. I was interested in them little candy stripers. Me and Bugsy. We didn't give a shit about you."

"You're an azzhole," Billy said.

"Did you know they came in all the time to look at your dick? They wanted to hold your balls and make you cough."

"No, they didn't," Billy blustered. "You're juzz fuckin' with me."

"He's not," Bugsy said. "I was there because I wanted to feed some of them candy stripers my candy cane."

Billy laughed so hard, his eyes rolled up into the top of his head with everything else floating around there: the pills, the VO, and Raquel Welch.

"Seriously, you need anything?" Bugsy asked.

"Naw, I'm good. I was wondering if you've seen Patty."

"I seen her a couple of times, with a bunch of the girls. They didn't stick around or nothing."

"Did you talk to her?"

"Naw. She was with a bunch of them parochial school girls. Bunch of fucking snobs, if you ask me. Like their shit don't stink or nothing."

"So, how'd she look?"

"As far as I could tell, all right."

"Did she ask about me?"

"Fuck, I don't know. She didn't ask me. But, like I said, she didn't come over or nothing."

"What about Karen? Is she okay?"

"She is now. After she found out what had happened to you, she freaked out. We didn't know nothing. After you guys left, we had a couple more. She got fucked up and blew chunks in the booth. It was a fucking mess! We had to take a taxi home. It cost me almost three bucks. I didn't see her until Tuesday—that's when I told her what had happened."

"Do you know if she and Patty keep in touch or anything?"

"I don't think so. She never said nothing to me."

"Well, if you see Patty, can you tell her I was asking for her? Let her know I'm okay? And tell her I'm sorry."

"Sorry? Sorry for what?"

"Are you shitting me?"

"C'mon man. What the fuck were you supposed to do? It wasn't your fault you ran into those spear-chuckers."

"Still, she shouldn't have been there. I should never have taken her there. And, I shoulda done a better job of looking out for her and making sure she didn't get hurt or nothing."

"You did, you dumb fuck! Nothing happened to her. You were fucking John Wayne. Shit! Everybody knows that! If I was there, you and me would've kicked their black asses back to Africa. Either there or to the Franklin Park Zoo. Shit, we'd have stuck them motherfuckers in a cage with the other fucking apes."

"Yeah, I guess." Danny looked over to Billy, busy going through the table drawer. "What the fuck're you doing?"

Billy shrugged and closed the drawer.

"I 'preciate you kids coming by. I gotta get some rest." He tossed his thumb to his left as if he was hitchhiking. "Bugsy, take that fucking dope addict with you." Billy glanced at Danny with one of his growing collections of sad puppy faces.

"I'm just fuckin' with ya," Danny said.

"Yeah, I know," Billy said.

"See you, kids," Danny said.

"Later," Bugsy replied.

"Later," Billy said.

# 41

For the first time he could remember, Danny slept through the entire night in his creaky hospital bed. When he awoke, he read his *Sports Illustrated* for the fourth time, making sure not to crease the pages or smear the ink. He was halfway through when he heard Dr. Armstrong come in, asking in his booming voice, "How are you feeling today?"

"Better. I slept all the way through the night."

"That's good." He removed the clipboard from the end of the bed and walked around. "Let me take a look." After running his stethoscope over Danny's chest, he pressed his stomach, and hearing no complaints, stuck the chest piece of the stethoscope in his pocket and stood upright. "Do you feel well enough to go home?"

"Yeah, I think so."

"From the clinical side, your incisions are healing well. I'm happy with that, as should you. You'll have to come in next week to have the stitches removed. That'll just take a few minutes. You can do that as an outpatient. Other than that, you can go home if you're ready. You'll be better off home than staying here. You're more likely to get an infection here than at home."

"I don't want to sound dumb or nothing, but what's an outpatient?"

"That just means you won't need to check into the hospital. They'll take you in and remove the stitches, and you can go back home. You'll be in and out in no time."

"That sounds good! Can you send a couple of those candy stripers home with me?"

Armstrong raised an eyebrow and ignored Danny's question. "I'll have the paperwork prepared, and we can get you out of here this afternoon."

"Thanks, Doc."

"Do you have any more questions?"

"Um, yeah. How long will I be laid up?"

"It'll be a little while. I don't want you moving around much until the stitches are out. That'll take another five or six days, but it could be longer. It depends on how fast you heal. In the meantime, I'd like you to get a little exercise; nothing heavy—simple things like walking around the house and stretching, bending over. You'll know your limits. I don't want you to go outside yet; there are too many risks. Once your stitches are out, I'll want you walking around and climbing steps and stairs if you're up for it."

"What about work? When can I go back?"

"What do you do?"

"All kinds of stuff. I work at a gas station. I pump gas, change oil, stuff like that. Sometimes I do a little mechanic work."

"I'd say start in with a light detail, something like pumping gas. You can't rush things. It's going to take a few months for your injuries to heal. The last thing we want is to go back in and do another surgery."

Danny nodded. "Sounds good. Thanks."

"Anything else?"

"Naw, I'm good."

"Okay. If you have any bleeding or the pain worsens, get to the hospital right away. Don't wait. I'm going to write you a couple of prescriptions. One's for the pain, and one's an antibiotic to minimize the risk of infections. I can write you one for sleeping if that's a problem."

"Yeah, that's a good idea. It's hard because I can't get comfortable on my side."

"Not a problem."

"Thanks for everything, Doc."

"You're quite welcome. You're a lucky young man."

"I know. Believe me, I do."

"Good luck," Dr. Armstrong said.

Danny knew he was lucky, and more importantly, he was thankful nothing had happened to Patty. He glanced over to the kid in the other bed. Anne had said he was in a coma, but she hadn't told him what had happened, or, if she had, he had forgotten.

"Danny!" a voice caught him by surprise. He looked up to see one of the McKendrys pushing a large hospital cart toward him. Danny couldn't remember his name—there were too many of them, and they all looked alike: blond, blue-eyed, round-faced, freckled, with a chicklet mouth and a gap-toothed smile. It might have been Timmy, Tommy, Ricky, Ronny, or Charley—he wasn't sure. It was the same with the sisters: Millie, Mary, Annie, Janey, and Joannie.

"Hey, I just heard you were here," McKendry said. "How long have you been in?"

"About a week, I think. My head's so fuckin' fuzzy, I really don't know."

"I understand."

"I didn't know you worked here."

"Yeah, I work in the dungeon downstairs. It's where they keep the cleaning supplies and fix things." Danny listened for clues, thinking it was probably Tommy. "My old man used to work here. He got me the job," he added, chuckling. "That's where he met my ma. She used to work in the dungeon. He told me that's where I was conceived, in the fuckin' linen room."

"Are you shitting me?"

"Naw, man, I'm serious."

"I hope they cleaned the fuckin' sheets."

McKendry looked back over his shoulder. "The pay's not bad, and as long as I show up on time and do my job, no one bothers me. I get paid for sick days and holidays. If we're not too busy, I can catch a nap."

"Like your old man, huh?"

"Fuck you."

"I'm just messing with ya."

"I know. Hey, I gotta tell ya, this place gets pretty fucked up on the weekends. A lotta crazy shit goes on."

*Maybe it was Timmy.* McKendry walked over to the door, popped his head out, and looked around. After pulling the door shut, he removed a large box from the bottom of his cart and stuffed it under Danny's bed.

"What's that?" Danny asked, leaning over to look.

"Toothpaste, toothbrushes, and a bunch of soap. I thought you could use 'em."

"Thanks."

"No problem. You got enough toothbrushes to last forever."

"That's cool. I 'preciate it."

"Hey, for what it's worth, a lotta kids thought you were in the Carney. After they went there and didn't find you, they thought you were dead. God, there were a lot of fuckin' rumors out there."

"I didn't know that. But, man, that's kinda fucked up."

"I gotta tell you, you got balls. I don't know a lotta kids who woulda done what you did. Everybody got jacked up after they heard what happened to you. A lotta kids have been takin' it out on the spooks."

"What d'ya mean?"

"It's been a fuckin' circus. A bunch of kids from the neighborhood have been hunting spooks and bashing their heads in. I seen a coupla them fucking jigaboos come in here with their heads split wide open—knocked out cold."

"What?"

"Yeah, with baseball bats mostly. If they don't have bats, they been using all kinds of shit—rocks, bricks, whatever they can find."

"Jesus!"

"Yeah, no shit."

Danny shook his head. "Hey, I just got some good news. I'm going home today. The doc said I'm good, as long as I get some rest."

"Who's your doctor?"

"Armstrong, a tall guy, real business-like. A bit of a tight-ass. You know him?"

"Yeah. I hear he's a smart motherfucker."

"He does know his shit."

McKendry looked around again as if he was being watched. "Well, I gotta get back to work. Whatever you do, don't get jumped by any more spooks."

"Fuck me, I won't."

"I'll drop by if I can get away."

"Give my best to your family."

"Will do," McKendry said. He spun his cart around and headed out, tossing a "See ya" over his shoulder like a wet towel at the beach. An hour later, Bridie and Frankie showed up, just as Batman was in the middle of a fight with the Joker and his henchmen, all dressed like circus clowns. Bridie was carrying an A&P shopping bag. "Are you ready?" Bridie asked. "I brought you some clean clothes.

"Thanks," Danny said, sitting up. "What's going on?" he asked Frankie.

"Nothing much." Frankie looked around the room, stopping when his face grew pale. "How are you feeling?"

"Better. Glad to be going home."

Bridie reached into the bag and pulled out underwear, a sweatshirt, and a new pair of cotton sweatpants. "I got you these," she said. "I thought they'd be comfortable."

He took the clothes into the bathroom and changed. When he returned, he found Frankie fiddling around with the box McKendry had put under his bed.

"What's this?" Frankie asked.

"None of your business," Danny responded. "Put it down."

Bridie glanced at Danny for half a second before turning to Frankie. "Get up," she said. "Leave your brother's stuff alone."

"But, Ma."

"Don't *but* Ma me. Get up, now!"

"Frankie, I can use some help. Can you put my comics in the bag?"

"Do I have to?"

"Frankie, help your brother," Bridie said. It wasn't the voice of a simple request.

"Looks like you're ready to go," Anne said as she entered the room, carrying a clipboard stuffed with papers. "Good morning, Mrs. McSweeney."

"Good morning, honey. How are you?"

"Fine, thank you."

"How's your mom?"

"She's fine, thanks."

"Tell her I said hello."

"Will do." She turned to Frankie. "How are you doing, Frankie?"

"I'm good."

"I have some papers for you to sign," she said to Danny as she handed the clipboard to him. Bridie came around and peered over his shoulder.

"I got it, Ma."

"Are you sure?"

"Let me know when you're ready," Anne said.

Danny took his time reading the papers. He asked Anne a couple of questions, much to Bridie's dismay. When he was done, he signed the papers and handed the clipboard to Anne. She removed one of the papers and gave it to Danny.

"Thank you for everything."

"You're welcome." She turned to Bridie. "He was a good patient."

"Frankie, will you get me my box?"

Frankie pulled the box out, and Danny grabbed it from him. He opened the top drawer, grabbed his pills, and stuck them in the box.

"Do you need any help?" Bridie asked.

"I'm good," Danny replied.

"Are you sure?" Bridie responded.

"I'm sure, Ma."

"I'll be right back," Anne said.

Danny walked over and looked at the kid in the other bed. "What happened to him?" Bridie asked.

"I don't know."

Anne returned, pushing an old metal wheelchair. "What happened to him?" Danny asked.

"He was in a car accident," Anne replied.

"Is he gonna be okay?" Bridie asked, stepping forward to get a closer look.

"I don't know. He's been in a coma for a couple of weeks."

"I ain't seen no one come by to visit him," Danny said. "Doesn't he have any family?"

"We don't know. We don't even know who he is."

"Poor soul," Bridie said.

"They call him John Doe. When the police don't have a name for them, they're called John Doe."

Bridie removed her Saint Christopher medal from inside her blouse, lifting it by a thin silver chain. After kissing it, she bent her head, clasped her hands, and prayed. When she was done, she looked at Anne. "May I?" she said.

"Of course," Anne said.

Bridie placed the chain around his neck and slipped the medal inside his johnny. "Amen," she said.

"Amen," Danny and Anne said.

"Well, are you ready?" Anne asked Danny, placing her hands on the back of the wheelchair.

"Yup."

Danny sat down with his box on his lap and Anne rolled him down the hallway. Bridie and Frankie followed. When they got outside, Bridie flagged a taxi down.

"If you need anything, let me know. Your ma's got my number," Anne said.

"Thanks. I will."

"Remember to listen to your doctor, and keep out of trouble, for God's sake."

"I will."

"Frankie, sit up front," Bridie said when the cab pulled up. Danny got in the back seat and Bridie got in the other side. Danny leaned back and sighed, glad to be going home. When they arrived, Bugsy and Billy were at the top of the porch, leaning against the railing, drinking a couple of beers. Danny's mother led the way, shooing people aside, clearing a path for Danny, who rested every few steps. His neighbors patted him on the back and congratulated him. When he reached the top, he sat down to relax and catch his breath while chatting with his neighbors. Billy and Bugsy drank and listened.

"Honey, do you want to go upstairs?" Bridie said. "You need to get some rest."

"Not yet. I'm not ready."

"Are you sure?"

"Yeah, I'm sure."

"Okay." She turned to Billy and Bugsy. "I have a lot of food upstairs."

"Sounds good, Mrs. McSweeney," Billy mumbled.

"Don't be too long," Bridie said.

"We won't," Danny said. As soon as she left, he asked Bugsy for a smoke.

Bugsy grabbed his crotch. "Tiparillo?"

"Fuck you."

After lighting their smokes, Danny opened his box and removed a crumpled wad of toilet paper. "Here," Danny said, handing it over to Billy.

"What's that?" Billy asked.

"What did you get me?" Bugsy asked.

"Underwear. My dirty underwear," Danny replied.

"Blow me."

Billy popped another beer open and chased it with one of the blue pills. Bugsy finished his beer and stood up. "You ready?"

"Yeah."

"How about you?" he asked, turning to Billy.

"Okay, I guess," he replied, slushing his words out. "I got another fucking headache. They're fuckin' me up."

"I hope those pills help."

"Me too," Billy said. "Doctor said I can't get any more until next week."

"Either of you guys seen Patty?" Danny asked.

"Naw," Bugsy said.

"Me neither," Billy replied, shaking his head.

"I'm sure she'd come by if she could. But, you know, a lot of shit went down that night. Between you and me, I bet her old man isn't really happy with you," Bugsy said.

"Yeah, no shit. I know I fucked up. I just want to make sure she's okay." He flicked his cigarette in a high arc toward the sidewalk and watched it bounce across the ground, sending orange sparks in every direction. "C'mon, let's go. I better get upstairs before my ma freaks out."

The hike up the stairs was more strenuous than Danny had expected. He stopped outside the Cochrans' door on the second floor to catch his breath. "Take your time," Bugsy said. "You got all day." Danny leaned back against the wall and took a deep breath. The smell of corned beef and cabbage filled his nose. "I'm ready," he said.

They climbed the last flight of stairs to find the front door to the apartment wide open. Inside, a large sheet of yellow construction paper was taped to the wall with *Welcome Home* marked in bright red letters. A vase filled with flowers sat on one of his mother's folding aluminum TV tables. A handful of get-well cards were taped on the other wall. Danny flipped through a couple of them, hoping to see Patty's name, but he didn't. Bugsy and Billy continued into the kitchen, and Danny followed. Mrs. Smith, from the corner drugstore, spoke as soon as he entered. "Hi, honey, how are you feeling?"

"Okay, I guess. I'm really tired."

"I'm sure you are. You've been through quite an ordeal."

Danny nodded in response.

"I made a chocolate cake for you. Your mom tells me that's your favorite."

"It is. Thanks, but you didn't need to do that."

"Would you like me to get you a piece?"

"Umm, not right now. I haven't started eating regularly, so I better hold off."

"Okay, honey." She glanced over at the Cochran brothers from the second floor, stuffing a couple of kaiser rolls with thick chunks of cold cuts. Chrissy stood alongside the table, making sure the plates were full, and the condiment cups were clean. "Why don't I cut a piece of cake for you and stick it in the fridge. You can have it later," suggested Mrs. Smith.

"That's a good idea," Danny said, glancing at the brothers.

"Okay. Let me get that cake for you."

"Thanks. I'm gonna check on my friends. They don't know no one."

"I understand. Let me know if you need anything."

He walked over to Bugsy and Billy, who were sipping cans of Coke. "Who are those fucking idiots?" Bugsy asked, tilting his head at the brothers.

"They're the neighbors, the Cochrans."

"They're a couple of fuckin' slobs," Bugsy said.

"Shh, they might hear you."

"Like I give a fuck."

"C'mon, man. They live downstairs. I know they're a pair of assholes, but my ma put this time together, and I don't want to get her upset."

"I was gonna get a sandwich, but I don't want to get into any shit with those fuckin' douchebags. I'm about to whack the tall motherfucker."

"Gimme a minute, will ya? And please, don't do nothing."

"Okay, okay."

Danny walked over to the brothers, who were huddled around the table. "Hey. Thanks for coming. How you kids doing?"

"Good," the older brother, Butch, said, chewing on his Kaiser roll, spitting his words out between chunks of cheese and splats of mayonnaise. "How ya feeling?"

"I'm okay."

"Fuckin' spooks, huh?" said Paddy, the younger brother, wiping a blob of mustard from his mouth.

"Yeah, fuckin' spear-chuckers." Danny leaned over the table and grabbed a couple of plates. "Excuse me," he said. The brothers stared at each other for a minute before backing off. Danny put a roll on each and turned to Bugsy and Billy. "Hey, you kids wanna grab something to eat?"

"Sure," Bugsy said.

Danny gave them each a plate when they came up to the table. "Have some ham before it's gone," he said, speaking loud enough for the brothers to hear. They looked around, too stupid to be embarrassed.

"Our ma made some soup," Paddy said. Danny stared at the bowl of see-through liquid, which was as thin as tea. Bugsy grabbed a piece of bread and dunked it a couple of times, like a donut, watching the bread fall apart. He grabbed two more slices and did the same thing. Then, he picked up a couple of cookies and dropped them in. "Pass the mustard, will ya?"

"Don't be an asshole," Danny whispered. "Here, have some cheese," he said, lifting the plate in front of Bugsy.

"I'll have some," Billy said, reaching out, almost knocking Bugsy's plate out of his hands.

"And some mayo," Danny said, placing a jar with a large knife sticking out of the top in front of Billy. Danny waited until they were done slathering the condiments over their rolls and layering them with more meats and cheese. When they were done, Danny picked up the plate and put it on the other side of the table, in front of his sister. "Thanks for everything," he said to her.

"No problem. How are you feeling?"

"Like shit."

"Why don't you lie down?"

"I will; the walk up the stairs nearly killed me."

"How are you feeling?" Danny asked.

"Tired."

"Go to bed."

"I will."

Danny walked over to Bugsy and Billy, who were huddled in the corner, eating and watching the Cochran brothers.

"I don't like them motherfuckers," Bugsy said. "If they weren't your neighbors, I'd kick the shit out of 'em."

"Don't waste your time. They ain't worth it."

"Pussy," Bugsy said, rolling his eyes.

"Hey, man, I gotta lie down. I'm drained. You guys can hang around and eat, but please don't start any shit. My ma don't need it."

"Don't worry. We're gonna head out," Bugsy said.

"You got some mustard on your face," Danny said to Billy. He grabbed a napkin and ran it across his face, spreading the mustard across his cheek.

"Try again," Danny said. "Hey guys, thanks for coming by. Do me a favor. If you see Patty, tell her I was asking for her."

"Sure," Bugsy said. Billy stuck his mustard-covered thumb in the air.

Danny walked over to his mother, who was busy talking to the Smiths, waiting a minute to avoid interrupting her. When she turned, he spoke. "I'm gonna lie down. I'm pretty tired."

"You should be. It's been a long day."

"Yeah."

"Did you get something to eat?"

"I'm not hungry."

"I'll make you a plate and put it in the fridge for later."

"Sounds good."

He hobbled down the hallway to the parlor, where he found his brother lying on the couch, watching TV. "Hey!"

"What?" Frankie drawled, not bothering to look up.

"Ma needs some help cleaning up, and I need to lie down." Danny shifted his weight from one leg to the other, leaning against the door frame to lessen the pain. "Get your ass up and help her."

Frankie made no indication he had heard his brother.

"Now!" Danny said.

Frankie turned and looked at Danny.

"I swear if you don't," Danny said, suddenly stopping to grab his stomach and speaking through gritted teeth, "If you don't get your ass up right now, you'll wish you were dead."

"Okay, okay," Frankie grumbled. "I'm tired too."

"Tired? What the fuck are you talking about? What about Ma? Don't you think she's tired? Jesus Christ! Tired! You gotta be shitting me. TIRED? Get the fuck outta here!"

Frankie rolled himself over, slipped his sneakers on, and got up. He shuffled past Danny, moaning like he was carrying a cross to his own crucifixion. Danny followed him out, went into his bedroom, and lay down. He'd started to doze off when he awoke to his sister's voice.

"Are you feeling okay?" she asked. The unexpected warmth in her voice caught him off guard.

"Yeah, I'm okay," he said.

"Well, you don't look so good."

She sat down on the end of his bed, moving a few times until she was comfortable. He noticed her belly had gotten bigger, and her cheeks had filled out. Her arms were thicker, and her chest had grown. "How are you doing?" he asked.

"Not too bad. I'm not getting sick anymore."

"That's good. Are you eating okay?"

"Oh yeah," she chuckled as she patted her belly. "Maybe a little too much."

"That's good, that's good." They both paused to smile at each other, something they hadn't done in a long time. "So, look at you, you're gonna be a mother."

She rubbed her belly in a broad, wide circle. "Not soon enough."

"Are you sleeping okay?"

"Pretty much, yeah. You?"

"Could be better."

"Can I get you anything?" she asked.

"Do you know if Ma got my pills?"

"I don't know. I saw her talking to the Smiths. Maybe they're gonna fill the prescription."

"Oh, that'd be good."

"Did you see those Cochran boys? They're a piece of work," she said. "Those slobs ate most of the cold cuts. Then, they wiped out the slices of ham, stuffing their fat faces."

"I saw. Why didn't Ma say anything?"

"I think it's because Mrs. Cochran took care of Frankie while you were in the hospital. She made a couple of meatloaves and tuna sandwiches for Frankie and me."

"Really? I didn't know that."

"Between you and me, I think their ma was embarrassed. How could she not be? I saw her talk to them a couple of times. I don't know what she said, but they kept eating like it was their last meal or something."

"Has their old man been around?"

"I don't know. I haven't seen him around in a while. He must be back in the joint. We'd have heard him drinking and smacking her around if he was here."

"It's too bad her kids don't have the balls to stop him. How long can they stand around and watch him beat her like that?" Danny fluffed his pillow and tucked it behind his head. "Anyways, what's up with you? What are your plans?"

"About what?"

"I don't know. Are you going to keep the baby?"

"Of course I am," she said brusquely, turning stone-faced.

"I'm sorry, I didn't know. I mean . . . we haven't talked in a while, and Ma doesn't tell me nothing."

Her voice softened. "Ma said I could stay here after I have the baby. But I told her, when it's old enough, I'm gonna get a job and my own apartment."

"What about your boyfriend?"

"Robert?"

"Yeah, Robert."

"He's still around, of course. We talked about getting married, but it's not the time." Chrissy straightened herself up and fiddled with her blouse. He waited quietly, giving her a moment.

"Hey, can you do me a favor?" he asked.

"Sure."

"Can you help me with Frankie?"

"What's up?"

"I need you to talk to him. He's pissing me off. I don't need his shit right now."

"You have to give him a break. It hasn't been easy on him, either. He's been pretty good while you were in the hospital—you'd be surprised. He's even helped me a couple of times."

"Yeah, Ma said that. I guess this whole thing has been hard on everyone."

"It has," she said.

"So, is it a boy or a girl?"

"I don't know."

"Do you want to know?"

"I don't know. A boy would be nice. As long as the baby's healthy, I'd be fine."

"Well, if it's a boy, name him after his uncle, Danny. And, if it's a girl, Danielle works."

"Good night, Danny," she said with a smirk. She wobbled as she left. "Get some rest."

# 42

Danny finally fell into a restless sleep as Johnny Carson's voice floated across the evening air from his neighbor's parlor, cascading through the weather-beaten windows. He tossed and turned until he had to go to the bathroom, thankful he could go by himself without calling anyone for help. When the sky grew light, Danny pulled his bedsheets back and ran his hands over his stomach, fumbling with his bandage and the surgical tape, now balled up and sticking to his side. He eased the window open, careful not to strain himself, and was disappointed when the cool breeze he expected did not greet him. He stuck his head out and inhaled the tart summer air. Although not cool, it was a welcome contrast to the smell of filthy socks and sweaty sheets that filled his room, and it was preferable to the antiseptic smell of his hospital room.

After swallowing another lungful of morning air, he grabbed his clothes and went into the bathroom. After he'd had a quick shower and gotten dressed, he could hear voices in the kitchen. They were female, friendly, animated, and in conversation. He listened closely, unsure of how many there were. It could have been four or maybe five.

After making sure his fly was zipped, his hands were washed, and the toilet flushed, he strolled into the kitchen and froze when he saw Patty's mother sitting at the kitchen table, sipping tea with Bridie and Chrissy. Patty and one of her sisters were sitting with their backs toward him. Danny's heart beat so loudly, he thought everyone could hear it. He took a couple of steps forward and stopped.

Patty placed her cup on her saucer, stood up, and turned. She started to speak, but her quivering jaw stopped her. Patty's mother instinctively stood up and embraced her daughter, and, as soon as she did, Patty started crying, a heavy mound of heaving shoulders. Bridie quietly beckoned Chrissy to follow her into the other room. Patty's mother and sister followed, leaving Danny and Patty alone with nothing more than the sound of their breathing. Danny stepped toward Patty, and as soon as he did, Patty threw her arms around him, holding him close as if she was drowning. He started to speak but stopped after she placed her hand over his mouth. "Shh, shh," she whispered. He put his arms around her, and they held each other as tears rolled down her cheek. They remained that way, listening to the pigeons cooing outside and the wooden floorboards creaking.

"Let's sit on the back porch where it's quiet," Danny said, placing his hands around her waist. He led her to the back door, where they sat on a pair of sun-bleached chairs. "Patty, I . . . I want you to know I'm sorry. I'm really sorry. I screwed up. I can't believe how stupid I was!" He shook his head and looked down as if whatever he was searching for would be there. "I . . . I . . ." he stopped.

"It's okay," she said, running her hand over his head and neck. "It's okay. You can't beat yourself up over it. It happened, but it's over. It could have been worse."

"I know. Believe me, I know."

"And besides, no one made me go there. I could have said no, but I didn't. I went with you—it was my choice."

"I know, but I should have been more careful. I put you in danger. I . . . I . . . I shouldn't have gotten so drunk." His voice grew sharper as he sliced himself up into smaller pieces. "We should've taken a taxi so we didn't have to be out there, walking. It was stupid."

She brushed his hair some more. He closed his eyes and rolled his head back. "I'm so stupid. You could've been hurt or worse."

"But I wasn't, and it was because of you."

"I hope you can forgive me," he said, stumbling over the words as if his mouth was full of broken glass. "I'll never do anything like that again! I promise. Never." He wiped his eyes.

"It's okay," she said, hugging him again.

"Can I get you a glass of water?" he asked.

"How about a cup of tea?"

"Sure, sure, of course."

"Can I get it for you? You're supposed to be resting, aren't you?"

"Well, yeah, sure. That'd be good."

"Good. I'll be right back."

"Does your father know you're here? I mean, I was sure he would have . . ." He stopped, leaving his words lingering in the air.

"Would have what?" she asked.

"Would have *killed* me. If I were him, I'd want to kill the kid who did what I did, putting his daughter at risk like that!"

"When he and my mom heard what happened, they were pretty upset. At first, I couldn't talk to him. He was furious. I mean, really mad. I've never seen him that mad before. My mother tried to calm him down, but she couldn't. Later that night, two police officers brought me home after making sure I was okay. They kept asking me if I wanted to go to the hospital, but I told them I wasn't hurt. So, we went to the kitchen, and the policemen started telling my parents what had happened. They were really nice. My dad kept asking them, over and over again, 'Did they touch her? Did they touch her?' That's all he wanted to know. I tried to talk, to let him know they didn't." Her voice cracked. "They didn't, Danny, they didn't, but I couldn't talk. My throat was so dry. I felt like I was suffocating. And my mother, she must have said a hundred Hail Marys. She kept her rosary beads with her all the time. All she did was pray."

She grabbed Danny by his hands and held them tightly. "And whenever I looked at my mother, I started crying; I couldn't help it. And then," she paused to wipe her eyes, "they asked about you. The last thing I remembered was those kids and the knife, and . . . and you fighting with them and me running toward the bus and some men getting off and helping. I remembered sirens and the police. Anyway, my father was getting louder. Finally, one of the policemen tried to calm him down, and they went outside. The other policeman stayed with me, listening while my mom asked me if I was all right. I just nodded really fast so she knew I was okay. And then the policemen had a million questions: 'How many were there? Did you hear any names? What were they wearing?' Stuff like that, and all I could think about was you. I remember you falling to the sidewalk and blood everywhere." She stopped talking to wipe away another flood of tears.

"That's all I remembered. I was so scared. I didn't know what had happened to you. I kept asking the police, and they kept telling me they didn't know anything." Her voice quivered as she spoke. "I thought you were dead, and that's why they wouldn't tell me anything. The next thing, there were more policemen, and then some of the neighbors came over, and some came in. There were people in my house my father didn't even know, and he started to freak out. My mom was trying to calm him down, but she couldn't. She didn't know what to do, so she cried and walked around in circles. And then, the police got a call on the radio. They told us they'd caught the kids that jumped us, and . . . and they'd shot one." She stopped to catch her breath. "And he had died. The policeman had killed him, and they all seemed happy about it. They kept telling us everything was gonna be okay, but no one said anything about you. They just talked about the kid they'd killed." She put her face in her hands and fell into him, shaking like the last leaf of winter. "I thought *you* were dead," she sobbed. Her body heaved and rose every time she wailed.

Danny held her for as long as it took to calm her down. Finally, when she did, Danny leaned close and spoke softly. "What about your father? Is he okay now? Does he know you're here?"

She needed a moment before answering him. "Yes, he does. After the police left, my father went for a walk, and my mom sent the kids to bed, and we sat up and talked. She called the hospital to see how you were doing, but they wouldn't tell her anything. We tried to get your number but didn't have your address. We fell asleep on the couch, waiting for my father to return. When he did, it was late, and my mother asked him where he'd been, but he wouldn't answer. I was petrified. I'd never seen him like that before." She bit her lower lip.

"My father went to bed, and my mother started crying and wouldn't stop. It was horrible, just horrible. We finally went to bed and got up in the afternoon, then we all went down to the police station. They wanted me to pick the Negroes out from a bunch of pictures, but I couldn't. I tried, but they all looked alike." She paused for a moment to compose herself. "Do you remember what they looked like?" she asked him.

"No. They asked me the same questions a bunch of times."

"The only thing I could remember was the smell—especially of the one that grabbed me. I can remember what he smelled like. His breath was horrible. I get nauseous every time I think about it. He was so close to me. I was scared, Danny. Really scared. And then another policeman came. Lenard. Leonardo. No, wait. It was an Italian name. Lonardelli—that's it. He didn't say anything until my father started asking questions."

"What kind of questions?"

"He asked about the bar, how we'd got in, and whether they'd served us drinks. Lonardelli told him we'd snuck in. He didn't say anything about the drinks. And then, my father started asking about you."

"Do you remember what kind of questions they were?"

"I don't know. They sounded like the kind of questions the police would ask. What kind of kid were you? Where did you live? Who did you hang out with? Had you been in trouble before? Did you have a record? They had as many questions about the kids who jumped us, but I couldn't answer them. So Lonardelli told my father he knew you and your boss, Mr. Erickson. He said you were a good kid and had never been in trouble. He said your boss had told him you were hard-working and honest and that he'd never met anyone like you. Mr. Erickson had said if he had a son, he'd want him to be just like you."

"He really said that?"

"Yeah, that's what he said. And he told my father it wasn't your fault we got jumped. He said we were in the wrong place at the wrong time. Lonardelli said that the police had been looking for those kids for a long time, so if anyone was to blame, it was them, the cops, for not arresting them before. My father wasn't sure what to say after that."

"The whole thing's hard to believe."

"How does he know your boss?"

"Their fathers are old friends. I think they grew up together. I can't believe he'd do that and say that. I mean, he hardly knows me."

"Well, that's what he said."

"Did they say anything else?"

"Yeah. My father asked about the colored kids and the one they shot. He wanted to know where they came from and if they had a family. The detectives told him what they knew. One of the kids is from Alabama or someplace like that, maybe Georgia, somewhere from the south."

"Anything else?"

"Not really. They said the investigation was still open, and they'd follow up."

"What happened after that? I'm still kinda confused. What did your father say about you, your mother, and your sister coming to see me today?"

"They had a long talk. My mother told him how much I wanted to see you. And," she paused and grasped his hands, "She told him I loved you."

Danny stared at her, open-mouthed, like a fish feeding. "What did you say?"

"That . . . that I loved you."

Danny looked over the rooftops for a moment. "Did you tell her that? Did you tell her you loved me?"

"I did," she replied, blushing. "I did," she repeated as another round of tears formed in the corner of her eyes.

"I . . . I don't know what to say."

"You can say you love me."

"I can. I mean, I do . . . of course, I do."

She wrapped her arms around his neck. "I do love you. I've loved you from the very first time I met you."

He held her closer, breathing her in. "I love you," he whispered.

"I love you."

# 43

Danny was anxious for his doctor to remove what was left of his stitches. The constant itching and scratching were driving him crazy. He'd pulled most of them out, leaving little wiry stubs sticking out of his skin. He viewed the vanishing threads as proof that he was getting better. "As soon as I get my stitches out, I'm gonna go back to work and hang out with the kids, and me and Patty are gonna go to the movies, and we're gonna have an ice cream at Brigham's."

"Just a few more days," Bridie said. "A few more days."

"I gotta do something, Ma. I'm going nuts. Can I have some of the kids over for a poker game? There won't be any alcohol or nothing."

"Honey, you have to get your rest. You know what the doctor said."

"I know, Ma. I wouldn't be doing nothing but sitting in a chair. I wouldn't do nothing that would hurt me. C'mon, Ma, I'm getting better. Look at me." He lifted his arms in the air like Charles Atlas.

"Okay. But it can't be a late night," she said. "And I don't want anyone wandering around, going into your sister's room, or anything like that. They can use the bathroom and the parlor, but every other room is off-limits."

"Okay."

"And no girls. None."

"Yeah, okay."

"When do you want to do it?"

"How about Thursday?"

"This Thursday? Don't you think that's kind of soon?"

"Ma?"

"Okay, that'll be fine."

"I'm gonna make a couple of calls if that's okay."

"Sure. I have some sewing to do." She got up and left the room. Danny grabbed the phone and towed it into the bathroom, unwinding the curlicued cord behind him.

"Hi, Patty, it's me."

"Hi! How are you feeling?"

"Pretty good. I'm having a good day. I slept through the night."

"That's wonderful."

"I got some good news. My ma said I could have some of the kids over to play cards on Thursday."

"That's wonderful! Can I help? I can serve drinks and snacks."

"I'd love to have your help, and I'd love to have you here, but my ma said I can't have any girls over."

"Not even me?" she asked in a pained voice.

"Yeah, not even you. Please don't take it wrong or anything. It ain't personal. My ma ain't too happy about the whole thing—I had to beg her. She made me promise no liquor and no girls. She ain't worried about you and me—it's the other kids. If you were here, they'd want to bring some girls over. She doesn't want that. She doesn't trust the other kids, and between you and me, I can't blame her." He listened to Patty breathing on the other end. "Are you still there?" he asked.

"Yes, I'm sorry. I was doing something. I . . . I understand."

"I'm looking forward to it. I ain't seen the kids in a long time."

Patty's voice picked up. "Well, how about I grab some snacks? I can get some chips, pretzels, and M&Ms, and come over early and put everything out in bowls."

"Yeah, that'd be great. My ma would be okay with that, I'm sure."

"How about I come over in the afternoon. Say three o'clock?"

"Sounds good. I'll be here."

"See you then."

He hung up the phone and walked down the hall to his mother's sewing room.

"Got a minute?"

She lifted her head and brushed her hair aside. "Is everything okay?"

"Yeah. I'm sorry; I didn't mean to disturb you."

"What's up, honey?"

"Can you do me a favor?"

"Sure."

"Can you make sure Frankie's not around when we play cards? I was hoping you could take him to a movie or something? I don't want him hanging around and bothering us."

"I don't think he'll be a bother," she said, grappling with her hair again, sliding her fingers through a bale of knots.

"I know, Ma, but I don't need him bothering the kids, asking a lot of stupid questions."

"He's not that bad."

"He is. Plus, there might be some swearing or something. You know the way guys talk."

"I do."

"Hey, I talked to Patty, and she's gonna drop some snacks off in the afternoon if that's okay."

"That'd be fine. There's a new Disney movie coming out this week. We can make it a special night, just Frankie and me."

"That'd be great, Ma."

---

Patty came by half an hour early. Her arms were loaded with two grocery bags filled with potato chips, pretzels, cookies, candy, and a couple packs of cigarettes. She filled the bowls Danny's mother had placed in the kitchen and the parlor. Danny put the kettle on the stove and made some tea when she was done.

"So, who's coming?" Patty asked, spooning some sugar into her cup.

"You know, the kids. Bugsy, Billy, Charley, Mooch, Mikey."

"What about Fitzy?" she asked. "Is he coming?"

"Fathead? Are you kidding? I didn't invite him. That kid's such a jerk. I hate his guts."

"I don't like him. No one does. All the girls think he's a horrible person."

"He is."

They finished their tea, taking inventory of the snacks. "Is there anything else I can do?" she asked, placing her cup and saucer in the sink.

"Naw, I'm good. Thanks for all the help."

She dried her hands and looked around. "Call me if you need anything."

"I will. Hey, I just remembered; I forgot to pay you."

"That's okay," she said. "My mom gave me some money."

"No, I gotta. I work, and I have the money."

"Are you sure? I don't mind."

Danny reached into his pocket, pulled out a handful of coins and bills, and handed them to her.

"Thanks."

"Tell your mom I said thank you, and tell your family I said hello. Let them know I was asking about them, okay?"

"I will," she said. She walked over and kissed him on the cheek. "I love you."

"I love you too."

---

Bugsy announced his early arrival by banging on the door, driving Danny out of the tub. He wrapped a towel around his waist, headed down the hall, and swung the door open, where he was greeted by Bugsy with a cigarette hanging out the side of his mouth, his arms loaded down with beers. Karen was behind him, holding a bunch of roses. Danny looked over her shoulder—two other girls stood behind her. Their perfume filled the hallway. "Hi, Danny," Karen said, slipping alongside Bugsy. She gave him an awkward hug. "I got these for you."

"Gee, thanks," Danny said, grabbing his towel to keep it from falling.

"These are my friends, Janet and Pam."

"Um, hi," Danny said.

"We're early, ain't we?" Bugsy said.

"Yeah. It's no big deal," Danny said, trying not to sound angry. "Follow me." He pulled his towel tighter and walked down the hallway into the kitchen. "You can put the beer in the sink. The ice is in the freezer. There's an ice pick in the top drawer. I'll be back. I gotta get dressed."

"Can I see your scar?" Karen asked, catching him by surprise. Danny glanced over to Bugsy, who took a swig of his beer and shrugged. "I told my friends what happened," Karen said giddily.

"I guess," Danny said, pulling his towel tighter, tucking the end in as deep as possible.

"C'mon," Karen said, waving at her friends. The other girls crowded around her. Karen bent down and looked at his bare stomach, the scars, red and jagged, visible just above the edge of the towel. "You're lucky to be alive," she said. The other girls oohed in harmony. "Can I touch it?" Karen asked, twitching her fingers.

"My scar?"

"Yeah, silly. What did you think I was talking about?"

"I, um . . . never mind. Sure."

He closed his eyes and thought of a roomful of fat nuns dressed in black habits with dark mustaches. Karen ran her finger along the edge of his towel, stopping to rest her hand on his stomach. She leaned forward, revealing her cleavage. Danny closed his eyes again and pictured a roomful of gray-haired nurses with wide asses, bad breath, and hairy arms as thick as their legs.

"I, um, gotta get dressed. A lot of kids are coming over."

Karen looked up at him. Her eyes hovered above the line of his towel. She brought her finger to her lips, kissed them, and pressed them against the scar. "I'll be back," he said, stepping back and grabbing his towel. He went straight to his bedroom, stepped inside, and waited for the swelling to subside, thinking about what had just happened, thinking about another roomful of fat nuns.

*What the fuck? Did Bugsy see what happened? Did he give a shit? Jesus Christ.*

He rummaged through his meager collection of collared shirts, deciding on a blue-and-white striped polo shirt his grandmother had bought him and a pair of hardly-worn and neatly ironed chinos. He put his shirt on, tucked it into his pants, and tightened his belt. After one more glance in the mirror, he cupped his hands over his mouth and checked his breath. He went into the bathroom and made sure there was plenty of toilet paper, hand soap, and clean towels on the rack. He opened the medicine cabinet, removed his mother's pills, and stashed them in a box of Kotex under the sink. He stepped into the hall and heard a knock on the door; *shave and a haircut, two bits,* followed by a booming voice. "Anyone home?"

Danny opened the front door, and Charley walked in, lugging a case of beer. Billy was behind him, carrying a large bottle wrapped inside a brown paper sack, holding it like a football. Mikey followed, carrying a smaller bag.

"Hey, keep it down, will ya?" Danny sputtered.

"I'm sorry, man," Charley slurred, his voice hobbled from whatever he had been drinking. "I knocked a couple of times," he said, bouncing the case off his chest. "No one answered."

"You gotta give me a minute," Danny said. "Follow me." As soon as they entered the kitchen, Mooch yelled from atop the washing machine. "I knew them fuckin' spooks couldn't kill you."

"Who let you in?" Danny asked jokingly.

"Your sister."

"Fuck you."

"Seriously, man, I'm glad you're okay. How ya feeling?"

"I'm okay, getting better."

"Did you see his scars?" Karen asked.

"Go on, show 'em," Bugsy said, smirking.

Danny blushed and grabbed a beer from the sink. He took a long swig and suddenly felt sick thinking about that night. He stared into the sink, remaining there until the room was silent, something he didn't sense until Bugsy put his arm over his shoulder. "You okay?" Bugsy asked.

"Yeah. I don't know what happened. I got kinda woozy."

Bugsy glanced around at the other kids with a *mind-your-own-business* look. "Wanna grab a smoke?"

"Yeah. Gimme a minute."

Danny went into the bathroom and ran cold water over a small hand towel and, after running it across his face, pressed it against the back of his neck, listening to the kids talking about him. When he felt better, he strolled back into the kitchen. Everyone stopped talking and looked at him. "Sorry, guys. I'm still dealing with a bunch of shit," he said.

"Don't worry about it," Charley said.

"Here," Bugsy said, passing a beer to Danny. Danny took a swig, put the can down, and lifted his shirt, eliciting a chorus of oohs and aahs. The girls moved around to get a better view, while the guys, interested, tried not to look interested. Danny could feel himself getting a hard-on.

"That must have hurt like a motherfucker," Mikey said.

"It did at first, but not anymore. It's healing." Danny pulled his shirt down. "Anyone wanna play some poker?" he asked.

"Yeah, I do," Mooch replied.

"We all do," Mikey said.

"So, you gotta tell us what happened," Mooch said.

"Okay," Danny replied, buckling his belt, "but this is the last time." The room grew quiet. "So, me and Bugsy met Patty and Karen at the Rest. We had a couple of drinks, and then went to Sporty's. Bugsy got us in; the place was packed. We had a couple of drinks. The place was so loud, we couldn't hear each other or nothing." He glanced at Bugsy. "So, me and Patty left around ten, ten fifteen." Danny drained his beer and shifted his weight. "Bugs, can you get me another beer?"

"Do I look like your slave?"

"Yeah, you do, you ugly fuck."

"Fuck you," Bugsy said, handing Danny a beer.

"Anyways, we headed back to her house; I wasn't thinking; I should've crossed the street, but I didn't; I was kinda fucked up. That ain't an excuse or nothing."

"I coulda told you that, you dumb fuck," Bugsy said.

Danny gave Bugsy the finger. "So, we're walking and heard the spooks walking up behind us."

"How many were there?" Charley asked.

"There were three of them," Danny replied, looking around.

"You said there were seven of them the last time you told the story," Bugsy said. Danny flipped him off again.

"So, we were at the bottom of Algonquin Street, and by then, they were so close I could see their faces."

"Patty must have been scared to death!" Karen said.

"She was," Danny replied, taking another long swig. "I was too. I could've outrun them if it was just me, but I knew Patty couldn't."

"Goddamn it," Mooch said.

"Yeah, we were totally fucked," Danny lamented. "I didn't have nothing near me, no rocks or sticks or nothing. The only thing I had was my belt." The room inflated with a round of *uh-huhs, wows,* and *oohs.*

"They circled us, and I moved around like this." He spread his feet and turned, side to side, changing positions, mimicking the moves he was describing. "The first thing I gotta do is to get Patty someplace safe. I gotta get her into the street, where someone would see her. So, I got my belt off and wound it around my hand with the buckle out." He held his belt out, just like he had that night. The girls gasped all at the same time.

"What'd they do?" Mooch asked.

"The tall one, this big black motherfucker with the blade, keeps telling me he's gonna cut me. Then this other nappy-headed piece of shit comes around to Patty, grabbing her watch. He's got his hand in his pocket like he's got a blade or something. I figured he was full of shit. I was trying to buy time, hoping the cops or someone would show up."

"That's gross!" Karen gagged. "I can't imagine one of them touching me. I'd have to shower for a month." The other girls pulled their heads back and frowned in disgust.

"So, I'm trying to stay on my feet while keeping my eye on these fuckers. One of them got so close I could smell his fuckin' breath." Danny said, wincing. "I'm doing my best to keep 'em all distracted. Thankfully, it worked. A bus came down the street, and when it was close, I screamed at Patty to run, but she was scared to shit, so I kept screaming at her to run. Thank God she did." He took a sip of his beer. "And when she did, I swung my belt around my head and nailed the prick with the knife right above his eye." The girls gasped again. "I fucked him up really good. So, then I kicked one of the other motherfuckers in the knee. That piece of shit went down like Fathead's mother." The whole place erupted into laughter; Bugsy had to explain the joke to Karen and her friends. After another long swig, Danny continued. "Patty screamed and, thank God, ran in front of the bus. That's all I gave a shit about. I figured I could get away until one of those black bastards grabbed me from behind. That's when the cocksucker with the knife shanked me."

Danny felt his heart beat, wondering if anyone else could. He took a deep breath and a sip of beer. "Fuck! What happened after that?" Charley blurted out.

"Yeah! What happened?" Billy asked.

"I . . . I don't remember. That sounds pretty fucked up, but the last thing I remember is the taste of metal."

"Metal?" Mikey sputtered.

"That's all I remember. The next thing I remember, I was in the hospital." The air had been sucked out of the room. The guys were open-mouthed, and the girls were crying. Bugsy came to Danny's rescue when he yelled, "Let's play some fucking cards!"

"Sounds good," Danny replied, setting everyone into motion. Five minutes later, two games were getting started, one at the kitchen table and the other at the kitchen counter. Just as they were getting started, someone knocked at the front door. "Fuck," Danny complained. "I'll be back." Two more kids from the Corner came in. Half an hour later, the apartment was packed; kids were standing in the parlor, the hallway, and the back porch, making a lot of noise. Danny grabbed some ashtrays stamped *Kennedy's, Tom English's, The Desert Lounge, The 1310, Doyle's Cafe, Blinstrubs, Dini's*, and *Pier 4* from the pantry. He placed them all over the apartment wherever there was an open table or shelf. "Hey guys, use the ashtrays, okay. Don't make a fuckin' mess, huh."

Every twenty or thirty minutes, he sat out a few hands to check his sister's and mother's bedrooms to ensure no one was in them. He went out to the front porch, a tilted and splintered platform that listed toward the sidewalk. A low decorative railing wrapped around the edges kept anyone from falling onto the sidewalk below. He lit a cigarette and slid down against the cedar-shingled siding, thinking about Patty. She'd want to know why Karen was there with her friends. Why were they there and not her? He knew he had no good answers.

He finished his smoke and flicked the snipe out into the street, watching it spin to a slow death on the pavement below. Then, he returned to the kitchen. "Bugsy, you got a minute?"

"Sure, what's up?" Bugsy replied from behind a hand of cards.

"Over here," he said, tilting his head to the back door.

Bugsy glanced at his cards. Then he said, "Fold," dropped them on the table, and slid his money aside. He followed Danny into the hallway. "Who'd you tell about the game?" Danny asked.

"I dunno. A few of the kids. I told them not to say anything to no one else."

"Yeah, but that didn't work. My ma's s'posed to be home around eleven, and I can't have the place full of kids. It's a fuckin' mess, and I gotta clean it up before she gets home." Bugsy stared at him with a puppy-dog-eyed, I-fucked-up look.

"Well, I'm gonna need your help," Danny said. "This was s'posed to be a little game with a coupla kids. It ain't. I haven't been able to play because I've been running around cleaning up and passing out ashtrays. I'm not s'posed to be moving around. I'm s'posed to be resting."

"Whatd'ya wanna do?"

"I'm gonna put a note on the door. I'll tell everyone not to answer or open it, and I'll turn the hallway light out."

"Okay," Bugsy said, bowing his head. "I'm sorry, I am. These fuckin' kids are gonna do what they're gonna do. They would've found out once they went to the Corner. I can't stop them or nothing."

"And I told you no girls. Why did you have to bring Karen and her friends? I told Patty she couldn't come over. She came by earlier and set up all the snacks. She's gonna be really pissed at me now. I told her it would just be the guys, and I promised my ma there'd be no girls. She's gonna be pissed at me too. You got me in a lot of fuckin' trouble. What the fuck were you thinking?"

"Fuck, I dunno. She asked me, and I told her it would be okay. I didn't think you'd mind. I mean, shit, she was there that night."

"So was Patty!"

Bugsy shrugged.

"It don't matter now. I gotta deal with this shit before it gets outta hand."

"Yeah, no problem."

They went back inside. Bugsy bellowed, "One of you ugly fucks will have to move. We need a coupla seats."

The kids looked around at each other, not sure who was guilty. "Whoever's down the most, get up," Bugsy said.

Danny shook his head in mock disbelief. "I'll be a coupla minutes," he said to Bugsy. "Why don't you grab a seat until I get back?"

"No problem. These guys are a bunch of chumps."

"Blow me," Mooch said.

Danny strode down the hall to his mother's sewing room, pausing to check the other bedroom doors. He popped his head into the parlor. "Don't make a mess," he said to no one in particular. He closed the door behind him and rummaged through the sewing box, stopping when he found a piece of paper and one of her marker pens. He wrote *DO NOT OPEN* in large bold letters followed by *DO NOT ANSWER* underneath. He put some Scotch Tape on the edge of the paper, went into the hallway, and taped the note to the front door. He stepped outside and unscrewed the hallway light bulb. When he got back to the kitchen, the chairs had been rearranged. One was unoccupied, set aside for him. He grabbed a beer, sat down, and watched as the last hand was played out. Mooch scooped the cards up and banged the edges of the deck a few times before passing them to Bugsy. "Five card stud," he said. "A dime to open."

Everyone slid a few coins to the middle of the table until the pot was full. Bugsy tossed the cards around, spinning them in front of the players. "A lady," Bugsy said, tossing the queen of hearts in front of Charley. "Deuce, no help," Bugsy called as the card spun in the air and landed in front of Danny. He followed it up with, "Niner, nickel, kinker, acer, ocho, ocho, niner, deuce," continuing until all the hands had been dealt. Over the next hour, the money moved around the table as the kids bluffed and bullshitted their way through the game.

When they stopped for a piss break, Charley turned to Mikey. "Hey, is everything okay? You're kinda quiet tonight."

Mikey replied with a shrug. Danny looked over to Bugsy and then spoke to Mikey. "What've you been up to lately?"

"Nothing much. Different day, same old shit."

"How's your brother doing?" Bugsy asked.

Mikey shuffled his cards and dropped them on the table. "What's going on?" Danny asked.

"Well," Mikey said, struggling to speak, "My brother, Stevie, he . . . he stepped on a land mine, and the fucking thing blew half his leg off."

The girls gasped, drawing half the air from the room.

"Fuck, I'm sorry," Danny replied. "I didn't know."

"That's fucked up. Your brother's a good shit," Bugsy said. Mikey started crying, and the room grew quiet.

"That . . . that's not everything." Mikey's voice quivered as he spoke. "They couldn't get to him right away. He and some other guys were under fire; it was a real shitshow. The poor bastard lay there for three days." He paused again. "Three fuckin' days and no one could get to him, and then . . . and then he got an infection and nearly died. He might never walk again." Danny grabbed a beer and handed it to Mikey. He took a swig before continuing. "They're trying to save his other leg. They . . . they might have to cut it off."

"Cut it off? What do you mean?" Danny asked.

"It's infected; his leg is. The infection went up his legs, into his groin."

"Where'd it happen?" Charley asked.

"He was with the First Air Cav in the DMZ," Mikey replied. The words were foreign to everyone.

"What's all that shit mean?" Bugsy asked.

"First Air Cav is the First Cavalry Division. You guys musta heard of them. They've been in the news a bunch. His unit was involved in a big battle. It was named after a unicorn or something. No, wait, it was Pegasus, Operation Pegasus. Stevie and some other soldiers rescued a bunch of marines at this place called Khe Sanh. They transferred him from Kwon Tree, or maybe it's Kang Tee. Fuck, I don't know. It could have been Chop Suey—some fucked-up place like that. Anyways, they sent him to an American hospital in Japan."

The room remained quiet for what seemed like an hour; no one wanted to say anything.

"How's your ma doing?" Mooch finally asked. "This must be fuckin' hard on her."

"She's okay. She's strong."

"Doesn't your brother have a girlfriend? From Saint Marks or something?" Mooch asked.

"Yeah, Tess. Theresa McCone. She's a nice kid and comes from a good family."

"Is her brother Mad Dog McCone?" Mooch asked.

"Yeah," Mikey responded.

"I know that kid. He's one crazy motherfucker," Mooch replied.

"Yeah, he is, but I gotta tell you, he's a good kid, a real stand-up guy. I'd trust that kid with my life."

"Me too," Danny said.

"They don't make 'em any better than that," Mikey said.

"Fucking right," Danny replied.

"Tess and Stevie have been going steady since high school. They were supposed to get married after he got back, and Stevie was going to college. Bugs, can you grab me another beer?"

"Sure, man." Mikey drank half his beer in one long swallow. "They talked about having a big family, you know. Stevie told me he was gonna buy a house on the GI Bill."

"The what?" Mooch asked.

"Yeah, what's that?" Bugsy added.

"The GI Bill," Mikey replied, looking around to a room filled with blank stares. "After you get out, the government'll give you a bunch of benefits if you want 'em. But, of course, you gotta have an honorable discharge to be eligible. Stevie said you could go to college, if you wanted to, on the GI Bill."

"I ain't never heard of that before," Mooch said. "Whatd'ya call it?"

"The GI Bill. You know, like GI Joe. It's s'posed to be a good deal. Stevie told me it's why he signed up; he and Tess had a lot of plans." Mikey took a big breath, filling his chest with the cigarette smoke that floated in the kitchen. "Did you kids know my brother once scored four touchdowns against English High? It was in all the papers and everything."

"I remember," Danny said.

"Me too," Mooch said.

"So, you kids got your draft cards?" Mikey asked a question that upset the girls. A few of the kids answered with, "I did." The girls murmured amongst themselves.

"You know, they're gonna start calling us," Mikey said, flicking his finger around the room, pointing: "You and you and you and . . ." he stopped when he saw Karen crying. "I'm sorry. I didn't mean to mess up the night." His words driveled to the floor.

"Hey, man, let's play some more cards. I wanna take all your lunch money," Bugsy said, looking over to Mooch and pointing his finger at Danny. "Yours too," he said, getting everyone to laugh.

Mikey got up, grabbed a beer, sat down, gathered all the cards, and shuffled. "How many of you homos are playing?"

"Just you," Bugsy replied. "You're the only fag here. So, you can play a game of solitaire."

"Blow me," Mikey said.

A couple of hands later, Karen's friend got up quietly and left. Karen started cleaning up, surprising Danny. The game ended half an hour later after Mooch won a big hand.

"We're gonna head out," Timmy McMahon said. Several of the kids joined him. Danny got up and began to take the trash out.

"Let me get that for you," Bugsy said.

"Are you sure?"

"Yeah. Sit the fuck down."

"Okay, thanks."

Twenty minutes later, the place was spotless.

"Thanks, guys," Danny said.

"No problem," Bugsy replied.

Karen gave Danny a peck on his cheek. "Take care of yourself."

"I will."

Danny went into the parlor and turned the TV on. Ten minutes later, Bridie and Frankie came home. "How was your game?" Bridie asked.

"Great, Ma. Great."

"Did ya win?" Frankie asked.

"Naw, I broke even."

"You boys better get to sleep. It's late," Bridie said.

"Yeah. I'll see you in the morning," Danny said.

"Good night, honey," Bridie replied.

"Night."

# 44

Everything went well at the doctor's office, especially considering Danny had already pulled out most of the stitches, leaving few for the nurse, a pretty little blond from Southie. He would have left more in if he had known how cute she was. She scolded him for yanking them out. "Tough guy," she murmured in a way that made him wish he'd been stabbed a couple more times.

"Maybe I should be a doctor or something," Danny suggested.

"I dunno about that," she teased. "I'll be back with your doctor."

"You're going to have scars there," Dr. Armstrong said after his first glance. "I told you not to pick at them."

Danny shrugged. "Yeah, I know."

After more pokes and prods, Dr. Armstrong stuffed his stethoscope into his pocket. "Remember to get some exercise," he said in his doctorly voice. "Lots of walking and some sit-ups to build your stomach muscles back up."

Danny nodded his head in agreement.

"We'll review things in a couple of weeks. If there's any change or you don't feel right, come back, and go to the nearest emergency room if there's any bleeding. And don't forget. You've had a severe injury, and you can't fool around."

"I know," Danny said. He bent his head and glanced at the nurse before looking back at Dr. Armstrong. "Thanks for everything, Doc."

"You're welcome; remember what I said. Take it slow, and don't push yourself."

"I won't, Doc. I appreciate everything you've done."

"I'll see you in a few weeks," Dr. Armstrong said. As soon as he left the room, Danny slipped his T-shirt over his head, slid his arms through the sleeves, and tightened his belt.

"Do you need anything else?" his nurse asked.

"Naw, I'm okay. Thanks for everything."

"Well, I hope I *never* see you again." She stopped when she realized how it sounded. "I mean, I hope you're never in the hospital again," she stammered. "Oh, you know what I mean."

"Yeah, I do," Danny replied with a throaty laugh. "It's not my favorite place, no disrespect or nothing."

"None taken."

"Thanks for the help."

"You're welcome. Remember to stay away from guys with knives."

"What about girls with knives?"

"They're worse."

"I know. Hey, thanks for everything."

Danny strolled down a long corridor and out through the front entrance. As soon as he was outside, he took a long deep breath to purge the medical smell from his nose. He lit a smoke, stepped onto the sidewalk, and headed toward Boston Common. After passing a corner drugstore, he picked up the smell of incense from another shop. Unlike its sober-looking neighbors, the aromatic storefront was plastered with colorful posters and music he'd never heard before, making him think of belly dancers and camels pulsing from the strange-looking place. Danny peeked inside, unsure if he should go in. A purple light dangled in the middle of the hallway, illuminating the posters hanging on the walls and stapled to the ceiling. The pictures glowed like fluorescent lights. He turned when he heard voices behind him; they came from a couple of long-haired hippies wearing oversized rounded sunglasses. He couldn't tell which was the guy and which was the girl. Danny stepped aside to let them pass. He followed them down the hallway, passing through a series of long, beaded strings he spread apart. They made a pleasant click-clacking sound when they swung back together.

Inside the high-ceilinged room, a large metal rack hung from the far wall, like a giant tie rack filled with hundreds of posters. The couple in front of him looked at racks of clothing filled with pants, shirts, purses, bags, and vests, as colorful as the posters on display, looking nothing like the clothes Danny had ever seen at Bradlees or Filene's Basement. They looked like something you'd see at a circus. The clerk—a petite, freckled girl in her early twenties, Danny guessed—looked up at him from behind long strands of hair held in place by a colorful bandana, like one worn by the Indians. Her loose-fitting blouse, trimmed with delicate ruffles, revealed she wasn't wearing a bra. She nodded and lifted her hand, spreading her first two fingers in a V-shape. Danny gestured back, his fingers folding into the sign of the boy scouts, three fingers held aloft.

Thumbing through the poster rack, inching his way along the wall, Danny looked up occasionally at the clerk. Many of the posters were cartoons or pictures of naked girls and guys with dark glasses, long beards, and crazy-looking clothing. A lot of them had images of marijuana cigarettes, while others depicted perverted scenes of Snow White and the Seven Dwarves or Goofy and Donald Duck engaging in homosexual acts. The word *LOVE* was prominent on a lot of the posters. When Danny ran out of wall, he asked the clerk, "Hey. What kind of music is that?"

She lifted her head and smiled. "The Beatles."

"The Beatles?" Danny replied incredulously.

"Yeah," she repeated in the same tone, smiling.

"That doesn't sound like the Beatles."

Still smiling, she said nothing and continued her work, rummaging through a catalog, making notes, and dog-earing pages. He walked up to the counter. "Are you serious?" She tilted her head to her left. "There, on the second shelf. The new album's called *Sergeant Pepper's Lonely Heart Club Band*."

Danny picked up the album. It was the Beatles, dressed like they'd been shopping in Harvard Square, standing behind a large drum, surrounded by a lot of people he recognized: Mae West, Tony Curtis, Marilyn Monroe, W. C. Fields, Einstein, Marlon Brando, Stan Laurel, Edgar Allen Poe, and others. He turned the album over, shook his head, and returned it to the shelf.

"When? I mean, what happened . . ." He paused to re-measure his words. "When did this album come out? It doesn't sound like their regular stuff: *I Love You, Hard Day's Night, Here, There and Everywhere,* you know, *All my Loving,* all their good stuff."

"They got *turned on.*"

"Turned on? What's that mean?"

"You know, they got high. They smoke pot and drop acid. They got *turned on.*"

"Hmm," was all he could muster, afraid he'd come off sounding like a hick from Franklin. He looked at the flyers and magazines on the counter. One caught his attention: *The Boston Phoenix*. It looked like a big comic book. "Can I look at this?"

"Sure," she said.

He grabbed one and sat in an oversized wicker chair; he'd never seen anything like this before. There were stories about the war, politics, the governor, people, music, concerts, and advertisements for all kinds of things. There were sections covering theaters, movies, record albums, stereo equipment, clubs, *be-ins*, whatever they were, and, at the back, personals, impossible to figure out: *SWF seeks SWM, SWM seeks SWM, SWF seeks BBW, GWM seeks TBM,* and *BF seeks BBM.* All Danny could think about was IBM. He put the magazine back and rummaged through a large apothecary jar filled with buttons and patches with colorful sayings like *Make Love Not War, Fuck for Peace, Try it You'll Like it, Groovy,* and *Love is a Four-Letter Word.*

"How much is this stuff here?" he asked, pointing to some nice-smelling sticks.

"The incense?"

"Yeah."

"Two for a nickel, five for a dime."

"I'll take five."

"Any special kind?"

"I dunno," he said. "What's your favorite?"

"Me? I like the sandalwood," she said. "And the vanilla smells wonderful." She lifted it to his nose. "I like to fuck to vanilla incense, especially when I'm high," she said matter-of-factly, as if they were talking about the weather. Danny fumbled around in his pocket for his money while she placed the long thin sticks into a small paper sack. "Here's an extra one for you," she said, pushing another slowly into the bag. "It's vanilla."

He placed a couple of nickels on the counter. "Thanks," he said with a suddenly dry mouth.

"Groovy," she chirped. "Have a beautiful day."

Unable to look her in the eye while he thought about vanilla incense, he mumbled an anemic "Thanks." Then, stuffing the bag into his rear pocket, he left through the click-clack of the beaded curtains and stepped outside onto the sidewalk, where he rubbed his sweaty hands on his pant legs. He was about to cross the street when a stern voice bellowed from behind him. "YOU! STOP RIGHT THERE!"

He turned; a tall cop, with a short-cropped haircut poking out from beneath a broad-rimmed police hat, was standing in front of him, so close, Danny could tell what he'd had for lunch. A shiny gold badge and a nametag were on his broad chest: *Carney*. Carney's billy club was bouncing up and down on his palm, making a thumping sound that Danny felt in the pit of his stomach. "What've you got there?" Carney demanded.

"Huh?" Danny replied. "Whatd'ya mean?"

Carney grabbed him by the shoulder and wedged the other end of the club under Danny's collarbone.

"There, in your back pocket? What's in the bag?"

"That? It's something I bought."

"Don't get smart with me, you little punk." Carney pushed the club, yanking Danny's shoulder. Danny reached for the bag; Carney yelled. "I didn't tell you to move! I *asked* you what you had in your back pocket. I didn't ask you to get it. Are you looking for trouble or are you just stupid?"

Danny stiffened. "I was just . . ."

"Just what?" Carney demanded, spraying what smelled like stale coffee and bacon in his face. He twisted the billy club until Danny bent over. "Answer the question!"

"Incense," Danny replied. "It's just incense."

Carney pulled the club back, but not before twisting it. Danny handed the bag over to Carney. He opened it and lifted it to his nose. "Are you a queer?" he asked.

"What?" Danny replied indignantly. "Of course not! Fuck!"

"Well, what are you doing with this stuff?"

"I dunno. I was just passing by, and I was curious. It smelled nice. I thought my girlfriend would like it." Carney stared at him. "It's a free country, ain't it?" Danny said.

Carney brought his club around and pressed it into Danny's ribs, making Danny roll over in pain. "Don't get smart with me," Carney said.

Danny yelped and grabbed his side as tears rolled down his cheeks.

"Where are you from?" Carney asked.

"Dorchester."

"You're far from home, aren't you? So, what are you doing over here?"

"I was at the hospital."

"The hospital? What for?" Carney asked in a semi-civil voice.

"For a checkup. I had to get some stitches out." Danny lifted his shirt.

Carney leaned forward and studied Danny's scars. "What happened?

"I was stabbed." Danny went through the story, and with each word, Carney backed off, giving Danny room to breathe. "You should stay away from places like that. They're dopers and fags. You look like a smart kid. Hell, you're from Dorchester. They'll get you hooked on drugs and who knows what else." He slipped the club back into his belt clip.

Danny tucked his shirt in. "Can I go now?"

"Don't let me see you around here again. If I do, I'm gonna haul you in. You got it?"

"Yeah."

Carney turned and strolled down the sidewalk, swinging his club around.

"Fucking asshole," Danny muttered as he tightened his belt.

# 45

Danny spent the next week walking up to Four Corners, where he rested, stopping at Shur's Corner Store, watching his neighbors, beat-up cars, and rumbling buses roll by. As he got stronger, he took longer walks to the Rest, eventually making the trek without needing to stop. In a couple of weeks, he made the round trip, albeit slowly, without stopping. After his speed picked up, he made Saint Peter's his eventual goal.

The first time he reached the church, he half-jogged up the stairway, counting the steps like when he was little. He looked over the town square from the broad, granite landing, wondering if it had looked the same on the day his parents got married. He had seen a few pictures, grainy black-and-white images, but he couldn't make out the faces. He leaned back against the low-slung puddingstone wall, capped with smooth pieces of granite. He ran his hands over the edges, admiring the quality, stones that had been carefully placed there by hard-working parishioners. He admired the large archways and the massive doors, bolted into a thick oaken frame, towering behind him. The entryway was surrounded by intricate layers of concrete, carefully wedged between large puddingstone blocks, and thick windows that separated the door from the top. One of the town's oldest landmarks, a grand square tower, rose upward from the corner of the building.

Danny opened the doors and passed through a tall foyer, illuminated by a soft light that passed through the windows above. He stopped at a pair of marble fonts adjacent to the entryway to bless himself, tapping his hands in the raised bowl of holy water. Then, after passing through another set of doors, he entered the nave, lined with rows of dark, high-backed pews flanking the marble-floored aisle that led to the 1,200-person sanctuary, a high-ceilinged room with an elevated altar surrounded with wooden rails. Three tall stained-glass windows of Jesus and two saints, nestled in deep concrete archways, watched over a forty-foot towering marble edifice. The altar was flanked on both sides with colorful rows of votive candles nestled in shiny brass holders that sent bright streams of light across the altar.

After genuflecting, Danny sat in a pew, watching the parade of colors dance and shimmer across the room as they passed through the large stained-glass window. A ray of colored light ran across his face, warming him. Danny had been in the church so many times, he could guess the time of the day by watching the lights flicker. He said a prayer to the Holy Mother, thanking her for Mr. Erickson being so kind and forgiving. He lifted his Saint Christopher medal from beneath his shirt, kissed it, and dabbed his fingers in the holy water, to bless himself on the way out.

The fresh air greeted him as he jogged down the steps and crossed the street, pausing to peer at the goods for sale at the corner drugstore. He passed rows of businesses that looked like large shoe boxes jammed onto thin wooden shelves. Every one of the smoke-filled bars was packed with locals, sitting on stools that no one else would dare sit on, places like the *Horseshoe Tavern*, *Eddie's Tavern*, and *Burke's Tavern*; the bane of every woman within a quarter of a mile.

Danny picked up his pace as he neared his apartment, pleased he could move so fast. As soon as he got home, he called Bugsy. "I'm feeling great. I'm gonna come by the Corner this weekend."

"That's great!" Bugsy said. "Is it okay with your ma?"

"Shit, nothing's okay with her, but she'll be good with it."

---

"I planned a time for Friday night. Everyone's gonna be there," Bugsy said the next day.

"I don't know," Danny said. "I don't want to have to show everyone my scars and go through all that shit again. I just want to hang out, have a few beers, and catch up with everyone."

"I get it. I ain't gonna let no one touch nothing."

"Promise?"

"Yeah, promise."

"If any of the girls start in with that shit, you gotta help me. I'm serious. Nothing personal, but I don't want Karen making a big scene."

"Okay, but ya gotta know, if you don't come down to the Corner, we're gonna bring the party to your place."

"Why're you busting my balls?"

"I'm doing you a favor. Everyone keeps asking for you, and I gotta tell you, some of the kids are pissed they weren't invited to the card game.'

"Don't say nothing about that fucking card game. Patty musta heard. She won't take my calls or nothing. I know she's gotta be pissed."

"I'm sorry. It got out of hand."

"Out of hand? I told her my ma said there couldn't be any girls over, and you bought a whole fucking bunch of 'em. Other than Karen, I didn't know any of 'em. And all they all wanted to do was look at my fucking scars and touch my fucking stomach. I'm sure Patty heard all about it."

Bugsy walked up to the pantry window and looked into the backyard. "You can't do nothing about it now."

"No shit, Sherlock."

Bugsy watched the kids in the yard playing, tossing a ball back and forth. "So, you gonna be there?"

"Yeah, I guess. Do you know if Patty'll be there?"

"I don't know."

"Did you invite her?"

"No. I ain't seen her around. But I told one of her friends, Ellen or Emily or something." Bugsy belched. "How does Friday at seven sound?"

"Great! That'll work. So, if you see Patty, can you let her know?"

"Yeah, no problem. Why don't you ask her?"

"Like I said, she won't return my calls."

"Let me see if I can fix it. I'll tell her it was my fault."

"Like she's gonna care. As soon as the girls came, I shoulda called her."

"I'll take care of it. I'll get Karen to help. See you Friday."

Danny walked him to the door wearing a glum face.

---

Mooch, Mikey, and Charley joined Bugsy in making plans, offering to do the "shopping." They did this by swiping as much food as they could from the service boxes that rolled along the conveyor belt in front of the Supreme Market. Charley got there first, hanging around the cash registers, pretending like he was meeting someone. Whenever he saw somebody buying steaks, ribs, or roast beef, he'd stroll outside and share the box number with Mikey. As soon as the numbered crate rolled out, Mikey grabbed the bag with the meat in it as he conveniently walked by. He'd take it around the corner and stuff it in a large cardboard box, along with the other bags they'd lifted, continuing until they had enough food to feed the Patriots.

They finished shopping a little after eight thirty. It was a good haul: six hams, nine steaks, a couple of roasted chickens, five packs of bologna, seven bags of chips, two bags of salted pretzels, five loaves of bread, and half a dozen jars of mustard, two of them the spicy brown stuff. They'd also grabbed several packs of cookies and three boxes of crackers. It was going to be a good party.

# 46

Danny spent most of the night tossing and turning every time the lightning lit the skies and the thunder rattled the windows. He fumbled around for his watch, an old Timex that glowed in the dark. It was 3:40 a.m.—an unwanted reminder of his lack of sleep. He kicked his sheets off and hung his legs over the edge of the bed, trying to decide whether to stay in bed or get up. The getting up won. He grabbed a handful of comics and tiptoed down the hall, passing by a band of yellow light that spread out from beneath his mother's bedroom door. He turned on the light in the parlor, sat on the couch, tucked his feet beneath his legs, and started reading. Batman was in trouble. The Riddler had locked the caped crusader in a prison cell. He'd been drugged and didn't know how he had gotten there. Danny pulled his legs in closer, growing tenser as he tried to figure out how Batman would get out of this one.

Danny listened to the rat-a-tat sounds rattling the windows whenever the rain came down hard. The skies lit up every now and then, sending bright rays of light into the parlor. When things quieted down, he resumed reading. Finally, after more spurts of rain and lightning, he finished his comic. Thankfully, Robin had saved the day by picking the locks to the cell, freeing his partner. Danny got up, stretched his legs, shuffled to the front window, and looked down the street as he ran his fingers across the wet, wobbly window that rattled every time the wind blew.

"Good morning, honey," his mother said, surprising him.

He turned and stretched his arms over his head. "Good morning," he replied, rubbing his eyes, noticing that hers were bloodshot. He saw a sprig of gray hair above her temples for the first time. The crow's feet, running from the corner of her eyes over skin once round and smooth, had turned hard and creviced.

"You're up early," Bridie remarked. "Still raining?" she asked.

"Yeah, it's really messy out there."

They stared outside as the wind blew through the rickety windows, cutting them with a razor-like chill. Bridie closed the drapes together, leaned over, and gave Danny a peck on his cheek.

"Can I make you anything for breakfast?" she asked.

"Sure. I was gonna have some Pop-Tarts."

"How about I make some oatmeal with some brown sugar and a cup of hot cocoa to warm you up?"

"That sounds great. You sure?"

"Yes. It's early. I've got time."

He pulled the drapes aside and glanced over to the brick apartments, wondering how many people were leaving for work and how many had just come home after working a night shift somewhere. "Can't you stay home today? It's pretty crummy out there."

She smiled, and the crow's feet faded back into the corners of her eyes, timidly, as if they should never have come out. "Not really," she said, pausing to watch another sheet of rain blow down the street. A steady stream of cars and an occasional bus motored up and down the street, plowing through endless sheets of water. He closed the drapes when the kettle whistled and followed the sound into the kitchen. Bridie smiled and poured some hot water into a couple of bowls filled with oatmeal and a cup filled with cocoa. Danny sprinkled some brown sugar on his oatmeal and watched the bowl slowly turn into a thick, gooey paste. Bridie turned the radio onto WBZ. The weatherman was predicting rain and flooding across the city all week,. "So, are you still going out with your friends tonight?" she asked.

"Yeah, I think so."

"It looks pretty cold out."

"I know. But you know the weather. It'll change," Danny said. "Heck, the sun could be out this afternoon. You never know."

"Can you make sure your brother does his homework? He needs some help with his math, and I don't want him watching TV all day."

"No problem."

Bridie continued talking while Danny continued listening, nodding every time she had a point to make. She rattled on until she realized what time it was. "Mother of Mary! I have to go!" she exclaimed.

She put her bowl in the sink and rushed out of the room, while Danny made another bowl of oatmeal and listened to the radio. Ten minutes later, Bridie popped her head into the kitchen and said, "I'll be home by six. Please make sure your sister eats."

"I will."

"G'bye."

Danny finished his breakfast, wiped the table off, put everything in the sink, poured in some dishwashing soap, and filled it with hot water. He turned the radio off, and went into the parlor and turned the TV on. He was in the middle of a show when he heard Frankie and Chrissy stirring around. He went out to the kitchen, refilled the tea kettle, and lit the burner. "Hey, Frankie," he yelled down the hall. "You want some breakfast?"

"Yeah," Frankie muttered in a sleepy voice.

"Cereal or oatmeal?"

"Cereal," Frankie answered with a moan.

Danny shook his head and went to the pantry; the choice was either Cheerios or Shredded Wheat. He placed both on the table along with a large plastic pitcher, stained from every flavor of Kool-Aid they had ever made. The box of powdered milk needed jabbing with a knife to break up the large white chunks, but it still tumbled into the pitcher in clumps. After filling it with water, he stirred it with a large wooden spoon until the spoon didn't stand up by itself. While waiting for the kettle to boil, he watched a pair of pigeons perched on a wooden railing on the neighbor's porch, sheltered from the lashing rain. When the kettle whistled, he put a tea bag in a cup, filled it with hot water, and carried it to his sister's room. He tapped his foot on the bottom of her door. "Psst, Chrissy. Would you like some tea?" he said.

She coughed and cleared her throat. "Wait a second." He could hear her shuffling around. A moment later, she opened the door. "Thank you," she said pleasantly, surprising him.

"Want it in your room?"

"No, I'd rather have it in the kitchen. Would you mind? I need a few minutes to wake up and wash my face."

"No problem," Danny said.

She ran her fingers through her hair. "I'll be out in a couple of minutes."

"I'll be in the kitchen."

"Danny."

"Yeah?"

"Thank you."

"You're welcome."

Danny went back into the kitchen and put the radio back on. He looked up at Frankie as he shuffled in and grabbed a yellow salad bowl. He farted and filled it with cereal.

"Man, don't do that shit in here," Danny said. Frankie headed into the parlor while Danny opened the kitchen window, hoping a breeze would follow. Chrissy walked in, holding her stomach as if carrying a potato sack.

"What time did you get up?" she asked.

"I didn't," Danny said, rubbing his temples. "I've been up all night."

"I'm sorry," she said while spooning some sugar in her tea. "How come you're not sleeping?"

"Fuck, I don't know. I got too much shit on my mind."

"I know what you mean," she said, rubbing her belly.

"I'm sorry. I got no right to complain."

"Can you pass the milk?"

He slid the pitcher over to her. "So, how ya feeling?"

"Okay, I guess. I haven't been sleeping much, either. It's hard to get in a comfortable position."

"Have you heard from Robert?"

Chrissy took a long, slow sip of her tea and stared straight through Danny as if he didn't exist. He decided to leave it alone, so he got up, took a few steps, and stretched his legs. After a few more stretches, he sat back down. "So, did you buy the shirt we talked about?" she asked.

"Not yet. I was thinking of going today," Danny replied.

"Want any more tea?"

"No, thanks."

"I'm gonna have some oatmeal. Want any?"

"Naw. I had two bowls with Ma."

"She didn't have two bowls, did she?"

"No. She had one bowl."

Chrissy glanced out the window. "You don't need to go out, do ya?"

"Not really, but I gotta get ready for my time."

"Is it outside?"

"Yeah, it's at the Marshall."

"Good luck."

"If it's raining, we'll figure something out."

"I'm sure you will."

Frankie strolled back into the kitchen and put his bowl on the table.

"Hey, you gotta clean up after yourself," Danny said. Frankie turned to go back to the parlor. "HEY!" Danny yelled.

"Leave him alone. I'll take care of it," Chrissy said.

"C'mon, Chrissy. He's gotta learn to pick up after himself."

"He's still a kid."

"Yeah, but . . ."

"Really, I don't mind. I'm gonna be a mother. I might as well get used to it."

She bent over and fiddled around with the radio dial, stopping when she heard Herb Albert's "This Guy's in Love."

"I'm gonna shower and go shopping," Danny said.

"Stay dry."

Danny got dressed, headed out, and took the train downtown, to Jordan Marsh. He pulled the ad from the Sunday paper out of his back pocket and handed it to the first salesgirl he saw. "Do you know where I can buy this shirt?" he asked as he ran his finger over the ad.

"Menswear, second floor," she said, waving her finger toward an escalator.

"Thanks," he said.

When he got off, he heard the clicking of heels coming toward him. A plump, well-dressed salesman smiling from behind a pair of horn-rimmed glasses greeted him. His hair was greased into place. He was wearing a starched shirt, a striped red-and-blue tie, and a belt that matched his shoes. The scent of his cologne was overpowering. "I'm Thomas," he said, extending his hand. Danny took the proffered hand and shook it.

"I'm interested in this shirt," Danny said, unrolling the ad.

Thomas looked at it like he'd seen it a hundred times before. "Oh yes, those are very popular." He looked at Danny. "Turn around," he said. "You look like a thirty-six or thirty-eight. Here, follow me." Two aisles over, they stopped at a long metal rack. Thomas lifted a couple of shirts off their hangers and handed the first one to Danny. "Try this one on. If it's too tight, we'll go to a thirty-eight. There's a dressing room over there," he said, nodding his head toward the corner of the room. "Might as well take this with you," he added, handing him the other shirt.

"Thanks," Danny said. He stepped into the dressing booth. After looking at himself in the mirror a few times and going from one shirt to the other, he decided on the thirty-eight. Thomas greeted him, still smiling, when he stepped outside. "That looks good on you. How's it feel?"

"Fine."

"Do you have a pair of pants to go with the shirt?"

Danny backed up a few steps and looked at himself in the mirror, admiring the shirt's quality and taper. "Here's a nice pair of chinos," Thomas said, holding them at Danny's waist. "It's a great mix, don't ya think?"

"Yeah, I saw it in the paper."

"Try them on. I'll find a nice belt for you."

After Danny got dressed, Thomas handed him a brass-buckled belt, a pair of brown penny loafers, and argyle socks. "If you buy the shoes, I'll throw in the socks," he said.

"Really?"

"No problem."

"Okay. You sold me. I'll take everything. By the way, do you sell taps?"

"Sure. Eagles?"

"Yeah, that'd be cool."

Thomas reached beneath the counter and placed the taps alongside the shoes. "Would you like me to put them on for you?"

"Naw, I can do it."

"You know, we do it for free."

"No kidding!"

"Sure, especially for a good customer like you."

"That'd be great. Thanks!"

"It'll just be a minute."

Thomas reached beneath the counter and removed a small hammer and a rounded block of wood. Then, one by one, he placed the heel of the shoes over the block and nailed the metal taps into the heels with small brads.

"Will that be cash or credit?" Thomas asked.

"Cash," Danny said with pride.

# 47

The rain continued falling throughout the rest of the day, in spurts and downpours, accompanied by loud claps of thunder and spectacular bolts of lightning that lit up the room. "The angels are bowling," Danny's mother used to say to him when he was younger and frightened. Whenever the windows rattled, Danny got up and peered out, listening for the strikes and spares.

"Do either of you need to use the bathroom?"

"Naw," Frankie and Chrissy replied.

Danny grabbed a towel and a face cloth from the pantry closet and went into the bathroom and turned the bathtub faucet on. When the temperature was right, he undressed and climbed in. He wrapped a bar of soap in a face cloth and scrubbed his feet, working his way up to his legs, waist, and rear. He arched his back and dunked his head behind him, bobbing it up and down as he washed his hair when suddenly, the door swung open, and Bugsy strolled in carrying a six-pack of beer. Danny, caught by surprise, jerked himself up. "What the fuck? How'd you get in?"

"I let myself in."

Bugsy lobbed a can of beer at Danny, sat on the toilet, and took a long, slow swig of his, while Danny opened and drained his in a quick succession of swallows. "Thanks, I needed that."

"Anything else?" Bugsy said.

"How 'bout a blowjob?"

"Should I get your sister?"

"Naw, call your mother. Is she up?"

"Up your ass, fag."

"Fag? You're the one who came in while I was in the tub." Danny tossed his empty can to Bugsy. "Did you want to look at my dick or something? I'll show it to ya if ya want."

"Blow me." He opened a couple more cans. "So, how ya feeling?"

"Not bad, getting better. Are you sure you don't want to wash my dick?"

"Naw, your sister can do it. I'll call her if you want."

Danny sputtered like a garden hose. "Don't be so loud. She might hear you."

"So, are you ready for tonight?" Bugsy asked.

"Yeah. You think it's gonna rain?"

"Shit, I don't know. Who cares?"

"Whatd'ya mean?" Danny asked.

"We got us an awning."

"Where'd you get it?"

"Stole it from Lambert's."

"Motherfucker."

"Yeah, me and Mooch and Billy. We snatched it, took the ropes and the poles, everything. It's huge. You can fit like a hundred people under it."

"Cool."

"I invited them pigs from Eastie. They heard about what happened to you. It was all over the news and everything. They're gonna bring some friends."

"Does Karen know?"

"I dunno."

"What do you mean she don't know?"

"I didn't talk to her or nothing."

"Aren't you still going out with her?"

"Yeah, but we're not going steady or nothing."

"Whatever you do, keep them pigs away from Patty and me. Patty is coming, right?"

"Who knows? I told her friends to tell her. So, what time are you coming down?"

"I dunno, seven, seven thirty."

"Sounds good. Whatd'ya want to drink?"

"I still gotta take it slow. Some beers maybe."

"I got a couple pints of VO for us."

"I'll see how I feel. What time are you going down?" Danny asked.

"Six, six thirty. I gotta get changed and eat and set the shit up."

"So, seriously, is Karen coming?"

"Of course. She wouldn't miss it."

"How's everything going with you two?"

"Great! I had dinner at her house. Her father's a cook at some fancy-schmancy restaurant downtown, somewhere on Comm. Ave., near the Common. It's so fucking high-class that they won't let you in if you ain't wearing a tie. Can you believe that?"

"I could believe it, down there."

Bugsy finished his beer, gagged a loogie, lifted the toilet seat, and hacked it into the water. "I'm gonna get going."

"Sounds good. Unless you want to dry my dick off, get the fuck outta here."

"I'll leave a beer for you."

"Thanks."

"Don't be late, fag. We'll have everything set up."

"Thanks!"

After Bugsy left, Danny removed the plug. The tub made a sucking sound as the soapy bathwater spun down the drain. He got out and wrapped the towel around his waist, found his sister's comb, dragged it through his hair, and beat his cowlick into submission. Then, he walked into the hallway, shouting, "CHRISSY!"

"Yeah?" she yelled from the front parlor.

"Can you do me a favor? Can you wake me up at quarter to seven?"

"Sure, no problem."

"Thanks."

# 48

"Danny . . . Danny. It's time to get up." He fought back and wouldn't move. He was on a beach, in Florida, surrounded by a bevy of bathing beauties holding tall, cold drinks. "Danny, you asked me to wake you up. It's almost seven." He blinked his eyes and knocked the glasses from the girls' hands. "Danny, it's time to get up." It was Chrissy, standing above him.

"Yeah, I'm getting up. I was . . . I was dreaming." He bent his arms, arched his back, rubbed his eyes, and sat up. "What time is it?"

"Almost seven." She sat down on the side of his bed. "I tried to get you up, but you were out like a log. I thought you were dead."

He rubbed another dose of daylight back into his eyes and glanced at the window. "Is it still raining out?"

"It's been on and off. It's not as heavy as it was this morning. The thunder and lightning stopped a while ago. You gonna wear the new outfit you got?"

"I don't wear *outfits*."

"You know what I mean—your clothes."

"Yeah."

"I'm sure they look nice on you."

Danny shrugged.

"I'm gonna make some ravioli for dinner. Want some?"

"I appreciate your offer, but the kids got some food."

"Where are you gonna eat if it's raining out?"

"Outside."

"In the rain?"

"Well, sort of. The kids got some tents and shit."

"Uh-huh, okay. I'm gonna leave you alone," she said, standing up and strolling out into the hallway.

"Thanks," Danny said. He walked over to the window; clouds were floating around and patches of gray sky, mixed with a pallet of colors, hovered outside. He looked up into the clouds, searching for more rain. After getting dressed, he walked into his mother's room and studied himself in the full-length mirror bolted to her bedroom door, happy that he didn't look too gay, like he was from Milton. When he stepped outside, a blast of damp summer air greeted him. Danny pulled his collar up, stuffed his hands into his pockets, and walked across the street; the rain started again, a brief downpour, not too heavy.

He turned the corner at the schoolyard and stopped in front of a canvas tarp strung between tall poles and the fence flanking the driveway. Danny quietly slipped through the crowd, the girls on the left and the guys on the right. Danny took one last drag of his cigarette, flicked it aside, and walked toward the tarp. As soon as the girls spotted him, they squealed, "Danny! Danny!"

"My God, how are you doing?"

"Are you okay?"

"How do you feel?"

"Does it hurt?" The questions came from every direction.

Mooch, standing next to a trash can full of beer, grabbed a can of Bud and slid it into Danny's hands, whispering, in a high-pitched voice, "Can I see your scar? Can I? Can I? Can I touch it?"

"Fuck you, fag."

Danny scanned the crowd for Patty, pausing when he spotted Karen. Then, after the clucking quieted down, he walked over. "How's it going?" he asked.

"Fine. You?"

"Good, good. I'm hoping the rain stays away. How long have you been here?"

"Forty, forty-five minutes, maybe."

"Have you seen Patty?"

"No."

"Want a smoke?" Danny asked, pulling his cigarettes out.

"Naw, I'm good."

"I'm gonna see if I can find her."

She smiled as he walked over to the first group of girls and asked about Patty, getting the same answer. Finally, one of the younger girls spoke up: "Did the cops catch the other niggers, the ones that jumped you?"

"Yeah. The cops came by several times and asked me to look at some pictures. It was hard, you know, 'cause they all look alike." The girls laughed and giggled.

Another one of the girls spoke up. "Do you have any restrictions or anything?"

"Not really. My doctor said it'd take a few months before I'm better."

"That's good," she said, followed by a few *uh-huhs* from the others.

"How bad is your scar. Does it hurt?"

He took another swig, slowing the conversation down, hoping that would be its end.

"Can I see it?"

*Fuck it*, he said to himself. *One last time.*

He pulled his shirt out, and everyone grew quiet, even the guys. He rolled his shirt up like a bedroll. When he had it up to his chest, the guys started laughing. The girls oohed and ahhed, and a couple leaned closer to get a better look.

"My sister's a nurse," one of the girls said. "She said you didn't take any pain medicine or anything. Is that true?" Danny shrugged and rolled his shirt down.

"Well, did you?"

"I took a couple when it was really bad."

"How far did it go in?" another asked.

"I think about five or six inches. Pretty deep's all I know."

More gasps followed.

"Are you serious?"

Danny shrugged again.

"Does it hurt . . . I mean, *did* it hurt?" they asked in disbelief.

"I kinda toughed it out," Danny said, tucking his shirt in.

He broke the conversation up after a few more questions and comments, apologizing. "I gotta talk to some of the kids," he said, leaving the girls behind to babble.

As he neared the guys, Bugsy tossed him another beer. "You okay?" he asked.

"Yeah, thanks. I'm okay."

"Man, I was worried about you," Charley said. "I heard they had to take out your speen."

"Spleen. It was my spleen."

"Your what?"

"My spleen. It's some kind of filter or something. It's no big deal. The doctor said I can live without it."

"You're one lucky son of a bitch," Billy said.

"I know."

"What're you gonna do now?" asked Charley.

"I'm going back to work."

"At the gas station?"

"Yeah. My boss kept my job for me."

"No shit?"

"Yeah, I'm real lucky. Say, has anyone seen Patty?" Danny asked. The question floated away, unanswered. After scanning the crowd, Danny spoke again. "Where's Mikey?" Unlike the response to his previous question, everyone quieted down; the laughter stopped.

"Is everything okay?" He pushed Bugsy on his shoulder.

"His brother died."

"Fuck!" Danny downed his beer and grabbed another. Gradually everyone started talking again, and the silence was replaced with chatter.

Danny grabbed a couple of beers and walked to the end of the alley, where he leaned against the fence. Bugsy and a few of the kids followed him. "So, when'd he go?" Danny asked.

"Sometime late last night," Charley said. "I heard he went fast. He was home and started running a fever, puking and shit. His ma called the hospital, and they sent an ambulance over, took him to the emergency room, but it was too late."

"How's Mikey doing?" Danny asked.

"He's all fucked up," Charley muttered, wiping his arm across his reddening eyes. "His brother didn't deserve to die like that. And Mikey and his ma don't deserve none of this shit either." Charley wiped his glossy eyes again. "They gotta be all fucked up and stuff, right?" he sniffled. "How long's their old man been gone?" he asked Billy.

"Three, four years, maybe?" Billy said.

"Not to be disrespectful or nothing, but the old man deserved to go," Bugsy said. "He was a prick. Remember how he used to beat Mikey's ma up? Remember that Easter he broke her arm? Mikey told me she couldn't afford to buy a ham for dinner because they were broke. So, the old man, who'd been on a bender for a few days, came home shit-faced, expecting a fucking dinner. Imagine the balls of that fucking prick?" Bugsy shook his head. "The heat had been shut off, and they were behind on their rent, and this piece of shit's expecting a fucking ham dinner. So, he started slapping Mikey's ma around, and he dragged her to the front door and told her she's got to get a fucking ham."

"Where do you buy a ham on Easter Sunday?" Danny asked.

"You don't," Bugsy said.

"So, then the motherfucker pushed her down the stairs, breaking her arm. Almost broke her neck. He locked her out and told her not to come home until she had the ham. Mikey told me all about it."

"They having a funeral?" Danny asked.

"Yeah, I think so. Saint Ambrose, I heard," Charley said.

"I thought they were from Saint Peter's," Danny said.

"The old man was from Saint Ambrose."

"I didn't want to say nothing earlier, but I talked to Mikey this morning," Charley said. "He's gonna sign up. He wants to be a marine. Says he's gonna shoot a bunch of them slant-eyed motherfuckers for what they did to his brother."

"Are you serious?" Danny asked.

"Yeah. Said he's gonna do it as soon as they've buried his brother. Said he couldn't wait. Told me he has to do it for his family."

"What the fuck is he thinking?" Danny asked, looking over to Bugsy. "What do you think?"

Bugsy took a drag of his cigarette, leaned back, and puffed a chain of smoke rings. "I signed up."

"What?" Danny yelped.

"I joined the army."

Everyone stared at Bugsy. He remained indifferent as he blew more rings in the air.

"Did you tell your ma?" Billy asked.

"Not yet."

"Not yet? What're you, fuckin' crazy?"

"Yeah, I guess, a little."

"Where'd you sign up? Codman Square or Uppies?" Danny asked.

"Uppies," Bugsy replied, popping another ring.

"When?"

"A coupla weeks ago. I got a 1-A," Bugsy said.

"What do you wanna go in for? Mikey, I can understand. But you? I don't get it," Danny said.

"Why not? I ain't one of them smart kids or nothing. My ma and old man got their hands full with my brothers and me. And besides, my old man expects me to pay for room and board. Where am I supposed to get money for room and board? I ain't got no job. Shit, I can't rub two nickels together. Room and board? Fuck me."

"Why don't you go back to school?" Danny said. "They got some good night schools, I hear. You can get your GED; it's just as good."

"Naw," Bugsy said, shaking his head. "School ain't for me. It never was and never will be."

"I don't know, man, it's a big fucking decision," Danny said.

"If I stay here, what the fuck am I going to do? Bag groceries at Supreme's? Work at Seymour's? Signing up is a good deal. The recruiter told me I'd be eligible for the GI Bill, and the army'd train me, so when I get out, I can become a mechanic or something. He said I could make some good money."

"A mechanic?" Charley said. "You don't know nothing about mechanics. Fuck, do you even know how to use a wrench? How about a fucking screwdriver? Jesus Christ, the only thing you know how to screw is your girlfriend."

"He's right," Danny said.

"Seriously, it's one of the things we talked about," Bugsy said. "It doesn't have to be mechanics. It can be something else. The recruiter said I'll have to take some attitude tests to figure out what I'm good at. He said the army's where they'd find a place for me because I was in good health. I told him I wasn't scared of fighting or nothing. I told him, 'I'm gonna shoot some of those slant-eyed motherfuckers,' especially now after this shit with Mikey's brother. I got a reason to go."

"Danny! Can I see your scar? Can I? Can I? Please!" It was a high-pitched voice, crying. Danny turned. It was Mooch. Danny grabbed his crotch and shook it. "Here it is," Danny said.

"It's time to get fucked up!" Billy yelled, passing a jug of OT to Bugsy. After taking a swallow, he passed the bottle around.

"Hey, I gotta ask you something," Billy said, tugging Danny's sleeve.

"What is it?"

"In private," Billy said as discreetly as possible. Billy pulled him over to the curb, where they sat down.

"You okay?" Billy asked.

"Yeah, why do you ask?"

"I dunno. You acted kinda funny when Bugsy said he'd signed up for the army."

"Don't it bother you?"

"Not really. I mean, if that's what he wants to do, who the fuck am I to say?"

"You know, lots of kids never come back."

"I know."

"And when they do, they're usually fucked up. Shit, look at Mikey's brother."

Billy took a swig from his bottle and passed it to Danny. "Bugsy's a good kid and a hard-ass and everything, but the odds ain't so good," Billy added.

"It don't matter, not now. He's made his mind up, and we ain't gonna change it."

"Still?"

"What about you? You ever think about going in?"

"Yeah, I used to. I can't now. My doctor said there's no chance, 'cause my head's kind of fucked up," Billy said.

"I'm sorry."

"Yeah, what the fuck. Shit happens."

They continued chatting about Bugsy and the war, dragging the conversation down into things that made no sense. "I gotta take a leak," Billy said, getting up and stumbling down the alleyway.

Danny lay back on the sidewalk and closed his eyes, listening to the kids behind him laughing and talking. He turned as Billy shuffled toward him with another bottle. After taking a swig, he handed it to Danny, and over the next hour, they passed the bottle back and forth. Someone stuck a sandwich in Danny's lap, cold cuts on bread dripping with mustard and ketchup. He kept moving around as the red and yellow sauces fell on his shirt, shoes, and pants. Every time he tried to clean himself up, he made it worse.

Danny drank whatever was stuck in his hands; it didn't make a difference; he drank it all. When he had to take a leak, it took him three tries to get up. Finally, someone grabbed him and walked him to the end of the driveway, where he lurched over and puked everything up. Whoever it was, helped him back to the gutter and sat him down.

"Are you okay?" a voice asked.

He blinked a couple of times, trying to figure out whose it was and where it was coming from. "You okay?" the voice asked again.

He looked up at Kat, standing over him, smiling. "Hey, Kat, is that you?"

"Yes."

"Hi," he said.

"I've been worried about you."

"Eh."

"You've been drinking a lot."

"Where's Billy?" Danny asked, looking around, trying to focus.

"I don't know. I haven't seen him for a while."

"Huh."

"Would you like a ride home? I've got my father's car."

He stared at her for a moment. "You do?"

"Yeah. It's down the street."

Danny watched as a car came down the street. "Where is everybody?"

"The cops came by, and everyone moved into the schoolyard."

"Humph. I didn't see them."

"They didn't bother with you."

Danny's head rolled around like a helium-filled balloon.

"It's getting late. I can take you. I don't mind."

Danny looked at his mustard-and-ketchup-smeared clothes. "What happened?"

"You got sick."

"Fuck."

"C'mon, I'll help you get cleaned up."

She grabbed his hand, lifted him onto his feet, and led him down the street. "It's over there," she said, pointing at a Ford station wagon. She helped him get in the front seat, where he slumped. "You're a mess," she said. Danny's head rolled around as he looked down at his shirt and pants.

"Do you want to get cleaned up before you go home?"

"Yeah, sure. You got someplace we can go?" he asked.

"Yeah. My house."

"Your house?"

"Yeah. No one's home. My parents are gone for the weekend; they're with my aunt and uncle down the Cape."

"Okay," Danny mumbled.

"Great," she said, starting the car. She drove past Town Field, took a few turns off Park Street, and pulled into a long driveway leading to a garage in the back of a two-story home surrounded by a broad wooden deck. "We're here," she said as she got out and walked around to open the door for him. Once inside, she led him upstairs into a bedroom and put the lights on. "Sit over here," she said, patting the bed. "Take your clothes off so I can wash them. I'll get my father's bathrobe."

"Okay," Danny said, fighting the urge to vomit, brought on by the pink-colored wallpaper covered with red and white flowers, the red the same color as her dresser, end tables, rugs, and curtains. He lay down, rolled his head to the side, and stared at the beady little eyes of a brown fluffy teddy bear sitting on her pillow. He turned when Kat appeared in the doorway, holding a bathrobe and a towel. She placed them on the end of the bed. "After you take your clothes off, hand them to me through the door."

He waited till she stepped outside before disrobing and putting the bathrobe on. Then, he opened the door and passed the clothes to her. "You want anything to drink? A glass of water, maybe?"

"Sure. That sounds good," Danny replied. "Where's the bathroom?'

"Down the end of the hall," she said, pointing.

He glanced at a cherry-red alarm clock on her dresser: ten thirty-five. He went to the window and looked outside, trying to figure out where he was. After a few minutes, he gave up, walked into the hallway, leaned over the railing, and yelled, "Kat, you there?" He waited a minute. "Kat! Kat, you there?!" Hearing no response, he returned to her room and lay down on her bed. As soon as he closed his eyes, his head began to spin. He got up, rushed to the window closest to the bed, opened it, and threw up onto the low roof covering the windows below. After filling his lungs with fresh air, he lay down and fell into a hazy dream; he was with someone, and he was aroused and thrusting. He opened his eyes; Kat, naked, was leaning over him. Her nipples were grazing his thighs, her hands were wrapped around his ass, and she had taken him into her mouth. Her head bobbed up and down; he shook and blew his load. She buried her face deep in his crotch until he stopped moaning.

"Did you like that?" she asked as she licked him on his scar. He grabbed her shoulders and slid her along his chest, pressing her breasts against his body. She pulled herself up and squatted over him while he ran his fingers over her nipples. He grabbed her by her hips and pulled her up until she was directly over his mouth.

He worked his tongue inside her as she moaned and rolled her hips back and forth, continuing until he was hard again. He pushed her onto her back and pulled her legs apart. She reached down and guided him into her. He rammed himself deep into her, slowing down when he was going to come. He made one last thrust and then collapsed by her side.

# 49

Danny squinted when he opened his eyes. The sun shone like it was coming through the ceiling. His mouth was dry, and his head throbbed; his dick, raw and chafed, stung. He glanced at the clock; it was after eight. He sat up and spotted his neatly folded and ironed clothes hanging over the back of the chair. He rubbed his eyes, lay back down, and replayed the night, trying to remember what had happened, wondering where Patty was and why she hadn't been at his party. What had he done with Kat? He curled up into a ball and pulled the covers over his head. A few minutes later, Kat called him. He pulled the covers tighter, knowing he couldn't stay there forever. She called again. "I'll be right down," Danny yelled through a sand lined throat.

He dressed and walked over to the window, still trying to figure out where he was. He took one last look around the room, making sure he had everything, and then lumbered into the hallway, where he heard Kat talking to someone; her voice rose up and down through the conversation. He grabbed the railing to steady himself and walked downstairs, following her voice into the kitchen, where she was at the table on the phone. As soon as she saw him, she blurted, "I gotta go" to whoever she was speaking to. She brushed her hair back and stood up. "Did you have fun last night?"

"Yeah. Who were you talking to?"

"A friend," she said, brushing her hair aside again, draping it over her ears.

"Anyone I know?" he asked.

"I don't think so. It was a friend, um, from school. It's no one you know."

Danny nodded, fostering an extended silence.

"I made some pancakes," she said. "With bananas. Want some?"

"I gotta get home."

"I can drive you if you're worried about the time."

Danny listened to his stomach grumble, knowing he needed something to soak up the alcohol.

"Okay," he said. "I could use some OJ if you've got any. I'm really thirsty."

"Me too," she said, licking her lips and smiling at him as she removed a tall bottle of orange juice from the refrigerator and filled a couple of glasses.

"Thanks," he said, downing his in one swallow. Kat refilled the glass as soon as he put it down. He glanced out the window every few minutes, watching people walk by and kids bouncing balls and yelling at each other. When everything was ready, Kat piled the pancakes onto two plates. She added some sliced bananas and carried everything to the dining room table, where he sat.

"Milk?"

"Sure."

She returned with two filled glasses, and they began eating.

"Kat, I gotta ask you a favor."

She tore off a piece of pancake with her fingers. "What is it?"

"You know, Patty and me, we're going steady. And don't take me wrong or nothing, I like you and all, and I had a good time last night, but . . ."

"But?"

"I was hoping you wouldn't say nothing. I mean, me and Patty got a good thing going, and I don't want to screw it up."

"Don't worry. It'll be our little secret," she said, nibbling on some more banana. "It's none of her business, right?" Her reply wasn't what he'd expected. "I like Patty," she said. "She's a nice kid."

Danny drank some more milk.

"Can she do that, what I did? Has she ever sucked your dick like that?"

Danny lost his breath and blushed.

"I . . . I don't know. She's never done anything like that." He blushed like a ripened tomato. "I mean, we fool around a little. That's all."

"Really?"

"Yeah, we've never done nothing like that—never."

They continued eating in silence. "Did you sleep okay?"

"Yeah."

"I slept like a baby," she said as she finished and stood up. "Let me clean up and get ready." She gathered the dishes and carried them into the kitchen. "I'll be right back. You can watch some TV in the living room." She led him down the hall and turned the television on. Ten minutes later, she came down the stairs, wearing a skintight pair of black slacks and a bright red blouse. "Are you ready?"

"Yeah," Danny said, getting up. She shut the TV off and walked to the front door. He jammed his hands into his pocket, followed her to the car, and waited until she unlocked the doors. Then, instead of getting in, he spoke. "I'm gonna walk home," he said.

"What?"

"I am. I gotta clear my head."

"I don't mind driving you, really. It's not a bother."

"I appreciate it, but I should walk. My doctor says I need to strengthen my legs."

"Suit yourself," she said in a sullen voice. "Don't worry. This is our secret. We'll keep this between us, just you and me, okay?"

"Thanks again. The pancakes were good. Which way should I head?"

"That way," she said, pointing to her left.

He stuffed his hands in his pockets and walked in the direction of her pointed finger. Half a block later, he realized he was at Wellesley Park, the only place in Dorchester that didn't look like Dorchester. The houses surrounded an extensive greenbelt, lit by leaded gas lanterns. The porches were large enough to play football on, and the windows were big enough to drive through.

He turned left onto Park Street and walked past the chain-link fence surrounding the tunneled right-of-way for the Red Line. He stopped and sat down on the steps at the Lucy Stone School to smoke. Try as he might, he couldn't get the image of Kat's head bobbing up and down on his dick out of his mind; all he could smell was her. He wanted to go home and scrub himself with a steel wool pad.

He stood up and headed down Claybourne Street, looking out to the Pru glistening in the morning sun. He made his way to the benches at the top of Mother's Rest, where he sat down and watched a bunch of little kids playing football, most yelling: *I'm open! Throw it to me! Here! Pass! Pass! Blitz! Pass! I'm open! I'm open!*

Why hadn't Patty been at his party? The question haunted him. She'd known about it; everyone had. After watching another twenty minutes of football, he decided to head down to Bugsy's, figuring he'd know what had happened last night. He stood; the football bounced up alongside him. He picked it up and waved at a couple of kids at the other end of the park. Farther, farther. Danny pumped his arms several times before throwing the ball high in a perfect spiral. He lurched forward in pain as soon as he let the ball go. A tall blond, the fastest of the kids, leaped high and caught the ball.

"Did you see that?" Danny heard one of the kids yell. "What a throw!"

He sat back down and held his stomach until the pain subsided, feeling like he was going to puke. He watched the kids until the nausea disappeared, taking his time getting to Bugsy's. He rang the doorbell and waited. He rang it a few more times before realizing it must be broken. After knocking several times, he heard the clicking of bolts and locks. The door swung open, and Bugsy's mother greeted him.

"Danny!" she said, smiling from behind a pair of weary blue eyes and cheeks that hung from her face as if they didn't want to be there. Her apron was freshly dusted with baking powder and soiled with coffee stains.

"Good morning, Mrs. Mulrey. Is Bugsy up?"

"I think so. He came down for a glass of orange juice a little while ago and then went back to bed."

Danny nodded.

"How are you feeling?" she asked.

"Better."

"Everyone's been praying for you. Did you get our card?"

"Yes, thank you," he said, even though he couldn't remember.

"Well, I'm glad you're okay," she said, stepping aside to let him in. "It's a shame they didn't shoot all those black bastards."

"I guess," Danny said, nodding.

She gave him a peck on his cheek. "You can go upstairs if you want, but be quiet. Mr. Mulrey's asleep. He worked a double last night."

"Sure, no problem."

Danny tiptoed up the stairs, walked to Bugsy's room at the other end of the hallway, and opened the door. The shades were pulled down, and it was dark. Bugsy was lying on his stomach; his arms hanging over the sides of the bed. Danny closed the door and sat on the edge of Bugsy's bed. "Bugsy," Danny said, shaking the bed. He pressed his fingers into Bugsy's ribs. "Bugsy!" he said again, louder, with no results. He walked over to the corner window and tugged on the shade, clicking it so it disappeared into a roll at the top of the window, expecting Bugsy to wake up. He picked Bugsy's hockey stick up and pressed the curved end into Bugsy's ass. Bugsy reached behind him and swatted it away. "Asshole!" Danny pushed the stick again, and as soon as he did, Bugsy threw his pillow at him, screaming, "You're an asshole!"

"Fuck you."

Bugsy grabbed his smokes and a cigarette-stained ashtray filled with snipes and ashes. "So, what the fuck did you do last night?"

"I got pretty fucked up," Danny said.

"No shit, Sherlock. I looked all over for you. One minute you were there, and the next, you were gone."

Danny expected more, surprised when there was nothing else. "Yeah," he said, "like I said, I got pretty fucked up."

"What were you drinking?"

"Fuck if I know," Danny said, shaking his head. "Billy and I had a coupla bottles. I think it was rum. I'm not sure. Whatever it was, it was sweet."

Bugsy took a drag of his cigarette and blew it out the window. "Where'd you end up last night? You look like shit."

"Oh, this?" he said, tugging on his shirt. "I spilled some mustard and ketchup when I was eating."

Bugsy took a few more drags off his cigarette and flicked it out the window. "So, where'd you stay last night?"

"Did Karen stay out with you?"

"Naw, we got in a fight."

"About what?"

"Fuck if I know. She was pissed at something. So, what do you remember about last night?" Bugsy asked.

"Not much. I remember talking to a coupla kids. And the girls; they had a lot of questions about me getting knifed."

"Did you ever find Patty?"

"Naw, I never saw her. Did you?"

"Me? No." Bugsy stared out the window scratching his balls. "What time is it?"

"I dunno, nine thirty, ten? Hey, can you do me a favor?"

"Sure."

"If anyone asks, I stayed here last night."

"No problem," Bugsy said as he leaned his head out the window. "Let's get some breakfast," he added, grabbing a T-shirt from the floor.

Danny grabbed the hockey stick and mimicked making slap shots. "Is it okay with your ma?"

"Shit, she feeds so many mouths, she'll never notice. And besides, she likes you. She thinks you're a nice kid because you're polite and have good manners."

"Your ma's pretty cool."

"She doesn't know you're a fudge packer."

Danny brought the stick around like he was swinging an ax, stopping a couple of inches from Bugsy's head. "Fuck you."

"Blow me, needle dick," Bugsy said.

Danny pushed Bugsy with the stick, and they started wrestling, banging into the walls.

"Shh, shh. My old man worked a double last night. I don't want to wake him up. He'll be in a real shitty mood."

"Are your brothers up?"

"I dunno. I don't keep track of 'em."

They crept down the hallway, following the scent of bacon into the kitchen. The countertop was covered with plump muffins, still steaming from the oven, alongside a bowl of home-fried potatoes and thinly sliced tomatoes. "Would you like a muffin?" Bugsy's mother asked. Bugsy grabbed one before Danny could answer.

"Honey," she said tartly. "Can you get a plate for Danny?"

"Sure," Bugsy said, stuffing his muffin into his mouth while handing Danny a plate from the cupboard.

"Have a seat over there, Danny," Bugsy's mother said, nudging her nose toward the far end of the table. "Do you like your eggs fried or scrambled?"

"Whatever's easiest."

"Richard likes them scrambled."

"Yup," Bugsy replied.

"I'll have 'em scrambled too, thanks."

"Of course, honey."

Bugsy removed a pitcher of orange juice from the refrigerator and filled their glasses. "Is the old man coming down?" he asked.

"I don't know," his mother said. "He worked pretty late." She glanced at the clock above the sink. "It's still early. He's gonna want to get some rest. We're going to Uncle Ricky's tonight."

"How's he feeling?" Bugsy asked.

"He could be better. His cholesterol and blood pressure are high." She glanced at Danny. "One or two eggs?"

"Um, two, please. Thank you."

"So, Danny, what are your plans?"

"Plans?"

"You know, your plans now that you've graduated from high school. You must have plans?"

"Oh, *those* plans."

"I mean, it's nice having your diploma," she said, staring at Bugsy. "You can't get by without one. Not today, you can't."

"I got a good job at the Port Gas station down Neponset."

"You're pretty lucky."

"I am. I really am. Is Matty still engaged to that girl in Milton?" Danny asked.

"Oh yes, yes," she replied, glowing when she heard the question. "She's such a sweet girl, that Theresa is. And, she comes from a good family; she's a Daniels."

"*The* Daniels family? Like, as in that politician guy?"

"Yes," she replied proudly. "Thomas—Thomas Daniels. He's a congressman. He's her big brother. He reminds me of President Kennedy, bless his soul, so handsome." Sitting behind his mother, Bugsy spun his finger in an exaggerated circle. *Whoop-de-doo.*

"Here, hand me your plate," she said as she started scooping up some eggs. "How many pieces of bacon would you like?"

"Two, please," Danny replied.

"Can I have a few more?" Bugsy asked.

She forked over a couple of strips to Bugsy. "Honey, can you put some more toast on? Your brother Allen's getting up."

Bugsy stuck a piece of bacon in his mouth and replied, "Sure."

"Ally?" Danny muttered.

"His bedroom's down the hall, that way," Bugsy replied, pointing with a head flick. Danny tilted his head to the side and listened: footsteps, a toilet flushing, running water, then more footsteps. A few minutes later, Allen shuffled into the kitchen, half-dressed, half-asleep, and scratching his head. He glanced at Danny and made no effort to acknowledge him, which was okay with Danny as Ally was an asshole. Instead, he grabbed the milk and called over to his mother. "Ma, can you get me a glass?" Spatula in hand, she made her way over to the cabinet, removed a couple of glasses, and placed them on the table.

"Do you like your eggs?" Bugsy's mother asked Danny.

"Yes, ma'am."

"More bacon?"

"Um, sure. Do you have enough?"

"Don't worry. We have plenty."

"So, Danny," she said. "Have you thought about the service?"

"I thought about it. I mean, who hasn't? I've been to the draft board and all."

Bugsy stared at Danny, as did his mother. "*And?*" she asked.

"And they won't take me."

"Why?"

"I'm a 4-F."

"A what?" she asked, stirring some sugar in her tea.

He cleared his throat. "4-F. It's a medical disability."

"Does that mean you're retarded or something?" Allen asked.

"Allen!" Mrs. Mulrey exclaimed. She put her spoon down, with a loud clink on the china dish, and stared at her older son until he looked away.

"Continue, honey," she said to Danny.

"It means I'm not acceptable because of medical reasons."

"Like what? Are you queer or something?"

"Allen!" Mrs. Mulrey said. "One more time and I will wake your father up."

She reached over and patted Danny's hand. "Go on."

"They won't take me because when I got stabbed, they removed my spleen. They call it a defilement."

"Do you mean *deferment*?" she asked.

"Yeah, that's it. Sorry, deferment. They said I couldn't go, no matter how much I wanted to, because of my 4-F deferment."

"You never told me nothing about that," Bugsy said. "When were you going to tell me?"

"I dunno. I was gonna."

"What the fuck?" Bugsy said.

"I'm sorry. There was so much stuff going on, and I . . . I . . . " Danny stopped and looked at Mrs. Mulrey as her eyes welled up. "They took my spleen out, and . . . and I got knifed in my liver and guts. An inch one way or the other, and I'd be dead. The doctor at the draft board told me I could never go in. My ma and sister are the only ones that know. I didn't even tell my little brother."

Bugsy's mother started sobbing so hard her hands shook. They all stared at their plates for the next few minutes, pushing their food around and avoiding eye contact. The only sound they heard was the sizzling of the bacon and the smell getting stronger. "Oh my!" Bugsy's mother said, getting up and returning to her cooking efforts.

"It's cool," Ally said, nodding at Danny; the first time Danny remembered Ally ever saying anything nice to him.

"Any of you boys want anything else?" Mrs. Mulrey said.

"I'm stuffed," Bugsy said, stretching his arms over his head.

"Me too," Danny said, picking his dish and glass up and putting them and his silverware in the sink. He picked up Bugsy and Ally's plates, glasses, and utensils and placed them alongside his. "Do you need any help washing or anything?" Danny asked.

"Thank you, honey, but the others will get up soon, and I'll have more to do." She wiped her hands on her dishcloth and lifted her hand to Danny's cheek. "You're always welcome to come by, even if you're by yourself."

"Thanks," Danny said. "I appreciate it."

She rubbed his cheek again and then wiped the last tears from her face.

"Ready to go?" Bugsy asked.

"Yup."

"Thanks for breakfast, Mrs. Mulrey," Danny said.

"Catch you later," he said to Ally, who nodded back with a smile.

Bugsy grabbed his windbreaker from the wooden handrail at the bottom of the stairs, swung the door open, and jumped from the porch onto the sidewalk, "Let's get fucked up."

Danny gingerly followed. "Want one?" he asked, extending his smokes to Bugsy.

"Sure."

"So, what the fuck happened last night?" Danny stuck one hand in his pocket and continued smoking. "C'mon, man. Mooch said he saw Kat sniffing around you. She's a fucking pig. You know that, right?"

Danny took a drag of his cigarette. "Yeah, I know."

"Don't worry, man. You're probably the only one that slut hadn't fucked already. Better hope you don't get the clap."

"Do you think Patty knows?"

"Fuck, I dunno. I didn't see her last night. Did you?"

"Naw. But then again, I was kinda fucked up," Danny said. He reached down, slipped his hand beneath his underwear, and scratched his groin.

"You shoulda seen Billy. He fell asleep in the alley, at the back stairs. We tried to get him up, but he was out cold. We body-bagged him under the tarp and left him there, sleeping like a baby, cuz it started raining. That fucker's heavy."

"It's probably all those pills he's taking. They can really fuck you up."

They crossed the street and walked through a bunch of little kids playing football. "I'm open, I'm open!" one of the kids yelled as he ran past them. The ball sailed over their heads, bounced off a car windshield, and landed on a couple of trash cans, making a lot of noise.

"I'm sorry I didn't tell you about the defilement earlier," Danny said as they walked across the street. "Everything's been kinda fucked up since I got stabbed; I'm going through a lot of shit."

"Aw, don't worry about it. It's just, I don't know, you caught me by surprise. I was kinda hoping you'd have signed up with me. Wouldn't that be cool? Imagine you and me shooting a bunch of gooks." Bugsy rolled his right hand over, curling his fingers into the shape of a gun. "BAM! BAM! BAM! Die, you slant-eyed motherfuckers! BAM! BAM!"

"I dunno," Danny said. "Fuck I nearly died. I've been thinking about all kinds of shit like that."

"So, what happened with the doctors at the draft board when you went down?"

"Well, at first, I didn't tell them nothing. Then, when the doctor saw my scars, he started asking a bunch of questions 'cause he could tell it was bad. So, I had to tell them everything."

"So, did they look at your prick?"

"Huh?"

"Your prick. Did the doctors look at your prick?"

"What the fuck are you talking about?" Danny asked.

"If they had, they'd have saved a lot of time. They would have seen it was too small, and they would have classified you right there as a—what do you call it—a 4-F defuckment. So, yeah, that's it. They wouldn't have let you in."

"You're a fuckin' idiot, you know that, right?"

"Takes one to know one."

They continued walking up the hill, past a string of run-down three-deckers and a scattering of modest homes separated by long, pitted driveways. Most houses had a bathtub shrine of the Blessed Mother in the front yard.

"So, when do you go?" Danny asked.

"In about three weeks."

"Then what?"

"Then I go through eight weeks of basic training and then eight more down at Fort Dix in New Jersey for the specialty stuff."

"What kind of stuff?"

"You know, training me on what they want me to do or think I can do."

"Like what?"

"I'd like to learn how to use guns. That's what my old man did in the army."

"You know, dickwad, they'll be shooting back; with real bullets."

"Yeah, so what? I ain't scared of no gooks or nothing." He spat the word *gooks* out like a rifle shot. "I'm gonna blow a whole bunch of them slant-eyed motherfuckers away. Watch me."

"I will, John Wayne. I gotta go home and change. How 'bout I meet you back here in an hour?"

"What do you want to drink?"

"I was thinking rum," Danny said, taking some money out of his pants and giving it to Bugsy.

"Sounds good to me."

"See you in an hour."

"See ya."

# 50

"Bugsy's," Danny replied, answering his mother's question. "I stayed over at Bugsy's." Shutting his bedroom door behind him, Danny plopped down on his bed and took his shoes and clothes off, swapping them for pants and a clean T-shirt. He lay down, listening to the sounds in the bathroom. When he was satisfied no one was in there, he tucked his clothes under his arm, placed his shirt in the sink, and submerged it in hot water. After rolling it around for a few minutes, he tried to rub the stains out with a stiff-faced cloth and a bar of soap, but it didn't work as the stuff wasn't coming out. It was the same result with his pants. After squeezing as much water as possible, he tossed everything into the hamper, overflowing with towels and dirty clothes.

He washed his neck and armpits with a soapy face cloth, wringing it out in the sink. After scrubbing his crotch, he looked for something to rub on his sore penis. He spotted a bottle of rubbing alcohol. He poured some on his crotch, grimacing when it burned. Next, he found a jar of scented white cream, something he'd seen his sister and mother use. He dabbed a little on the side of his penis to see if it stung, and when it didn't, he rubbed on some more. He put everything away, dressed, tucked everything in, and headed out, making it halfway down the hallway before his mother called him.

"Are you going out?"

"Yeah, I'm gonna meet Bugsy. We're going bowling at Ten Pin. I don't want to be late. See ya," he replied, rolling everything together in one long sentence.

"Do you have a minute?" she asked.

"Not really."

"It'll only take a few minutes."

"Okay," he said, taking a seat in the kitchen.

"Let me put some tea on."

Danny stretched his legs and leaned back. The pigeons outside cooed like love birds.

"How do you think your sister looks?"

"I dunno. Pretty good. Is everything okay?"

"Has she spoken to you about her plans?"

"What plans?"

"You know, her plans for the baby."

"No, she ain't said nothing."

Bridie placed the cups on the table, dropped a teabag in each, and filled them with hot water.

"She's gonna have the baby soon, and she's gonna need a lot of help."

"Okay," he said, nodding.

"Have you ever met any of Robert's family?"

Danny shook his head. *No.*

"Well, I met his father."

"Huh? Where? How?"

"At his office."

"At his office? What were you doing out there?"

"Talking business."

"Business? What kind of business?"

"Family business. About your sister, his grandchild."

"Why'd you do that?"

"He has some responsibilities here."

Danny sipped his tea and looked at the pigeons for a moment. "Yeah, I guess he does."

"Well, the Henschels have a lot of money, and Chrissy doesn't. We don't either; we can't afford to feed another mouth and take care of a little baby."

"Uh-huh."

"I spoke to his father, Robert's, and he didn't know about your sister, and he certainly didn't know she was pregnant."

"You've gotta be kidding me."

"No, I'm not."

"That's a gutsy move, Ma. How'd it go?"

"Better than I expected."

"No kidding. So, tell me what happened."

"Well, I took some time off work. I called beforehand to make sure he would be there. I said I was interested in a new car. Heaven help me, I fibbed. When Robert's father came out, I told him why I was there. Mother of Mary, you should have seen his face. He wasn't expecting me, that's for sure. He invited me into his office as soon as I started talking and told him what I was there for." She took a sip of her tea and continued. "Danny, you should have seen the place. The chairs were so soft, and he had a lot of nice pictures on the wall. It was all expensive looking."

"Then what?"

"So, anyway, he had his assistant bring in some bagels and coffee, you know, those good ones like you get in Mattapan, at that Jewish deli. Everything was on one of those fancy silver trays, like in those big hotels downtown. So, I told him everything about how Robert and Chrissy met. I even told him about when he beat Chrissy up. My God, I thought he was going to have a heart attack. I told him that Chrissy was a good girl and didn't call the police. I told him I wanted to, me being her mother and all. You should have seen him. His face turned purple, and his veins popped out of his head. So anyways, he told me that his wife could never know because we're not Jewish, said we were goys or something like that. I didn't understand what he meant. So, he said if she knew what was going on, it would kill her."

"I can't believe you did all that."

"When we were done talking, he sat there and looked out the window for a long time. I sat there and waited. I ate another bagel. He left the room for a little while and asked me to wait there, and I did, of course. I had nowhere to go; I had time. So, when he came back, he had a lot of questions about Chrissy and our family. He even asked about your father and if he was around. I told him he wasn't, and he'd left long ago." She looked out the window and stared at the birds, fluffing their wings, nestling against each other, and cooing.

"So, what happened next?"

"He asked me what I wanted to do and what Chrissy wanted. I told him we had a few options. I told him she could have the baby and keep it or have the baby in a home and put it up for adoption."

"What did he say to that?"

"I couldn't believe it. He said the third option was she could get an abortion, and he'd pay for it. He said he had a friend who handles these types of things. Mary, Jesus, and Joseph, I got so angry. 'An abortion,' I said, 'we're Catholics!'"

"What'd he do?"

"He apologized and got me another bagel and a nice cup of tea. I told him there were a couple of other options. He said, 'Like what?' I told him we could call his wife and give her the good news; her son was having a baby with an Irish Catholic girl from Dorchester. I told him we'd invite the whole family to the baptism. Mother of Jesus, you should have seen the look on his face."

"What'd you tell him was the other option?"

"I told him he could help Chrissy raise the baby."

"How would he do that?"

"He told me he needed a little time to think about it and get back to me. I told him I'd wait; I had plenty of time. So, I settled back in the chair and started reading the magazines in his office. He got up and started pacing around and everything, and I just kept reading like I had all day. He finally told me he'd be back, so I asked him for another cup of tea. He was gone for a little while, and when he came back, he told me he liked the last option."

"So, what'd you tell him? You'd got it all figured out, right?"

"Yeah, I had. I thought about it for a long time. I told him, for starters, he'd have to pay for the delivery and Chrissy's hospital stay, of course."

"That's good thinking, Ma!"

"And I told him she's going to need some help raising the baby, and he's going to have to pay for that too."

"Wow, you thought of all this by yourself?"

"Yes," she said proudly, taking another sip of her tea.

"And I told him I don't want his son Robert coming around or calling her. He has to stay away. If he comes around or bothers your sister, I'm going to tell his wife everything, including how he beat her up and left her downtown, pregnant and bleeding."

"Wow! That's frickin' amazing! Was there anything else?"

"Yes," she replied. "I told him he had to give me a check for fifteen hundred dollars."

"Was that all?"

"No, here's the best part. I told him he'd have to send a check every month for one hundred fifty dollars until Chrissy gets a good job."

"Are you kidding, Ma? That's a lot of money."

"I know it is, honey, but you have to remember, he owns that car dealership and lives in a real hoity-toity neighborhood. Mary, Mother of Jesus, he has plenty of money. He's a Jew."

"You amaze me, Ma. I can't believe you did that."

She finished the last of her tea. "What would you do if it was your daughter?"

"I guess I'd do the same thing."

"Of course, you would. Raising a child is expensive. It's just money to these people. They have plenty of it; they're Jews, for God's sake. And you can bet it's not the first time Robert's got a girl in trouble."

Danny stood up and watched the pigeons flitter around next door. "What did Chrissy say about it?"

"At first, she didn't believe me. Not until I showed her the check."

"Well, that's great. It really is. I still can't believe it!"

"Well, it's true," Bridie said, standing up.

"Does Frankie know?"

"No. He doesn't need to know."

"Yeah, I agree." Bridie picked up the cups and saucers and carried them to the sink.

"That's quite a story, Ma."

"It is. In the end, it worked out as good as it could."

"It sure did," Danny replied, looking at the clock. "Well, I gotta get going. I'm late."

---

The streets were filled with faded leaves, mostly brown, along with some red and yellow ones as the trees had thinned out in preparation for the winter. When Danny walked through the foyer at the Y, he passed a dozen giggling girls in gym shorts, preparing for a basketball game. He found Bugsy and a bunch of kids in the bowling alley. Bugsy was on the far end of the bench, leaning against the wall. As soon as he saw Danny, he reached under his seat and handed him a bagged bottle. "Here," he said. "Put some hair on your balls."

"Thanks." Danny opened the bottle and guzzled a mouthful.

"So, what happened to you last night? You were pretty fucked up," Charley asked from the other end of the bench.

"I was drinking with this idiot over here," Danny said, nodding in Billy's direction.

"Me? I didn't put a gun to your head, did I?" Billy said, laughing like Woody the Woodpecker. "Ha, ha, haaaaaa. Ha, ha, ha, haaaaaa."

"So, what do you kids wanna do?" Danny asked.

"Let's get fucked up!" Bugsy yelled.

"Yeah," Charley followed.

"We can't stay here," Mikey said. "They're gonna throw us out when the little kids come in to bowl."

"What time is it?" Danny asked.

"Who gives a shit?" Mooch replied.

"Let's get the fuck out of here," Bugsy said.

They left and regrouped outside, on the sidewalk. "I hear there's a party at Ricky McKenna's place," Mooch said. "It's a going-away party; he's joined the army."

"I'm not sure I know him," Billy said.

"Tall kid, curly brown hair, stands about this tall," Bugsy said, leveling his hand out and holding it just above his head. "He's got a cousin named Kenny, hangs at Lucky Strikes. Kenny Kerrigan—you know him?"

"Kerrigan. Yeah, he's from Saint Anne's, ain't he?"

"Didn't Ricky get in trouble or something?" Danny said.

"Yeah, he got busted for a couple B 'n' Es. He did six or seven months at Juvie," Mooch said.

"Yeah, I remember now," Danny replied.

"The fucking idiot got busted again. Him and this other kid." Mooch paused. "They broke into this house on Adams Street, and the babysitter was upstairs with a little kid. She freaked out and called the cops, and they got busted. Judge Troy gave him a chance because he hadn't done anything violent, so he gave him one of those fucked-up deals like he always does. He told Ricky he could join the army or do time at Deer Island. Troy told him the army would be a good place for him, said they'd teach him discipline."

"No shit," Bugsy added. "So anyway, Ricky's having a going-away party."

"So, what's he gonna do in the army?"

"If he gets trained right, he could learn a good trade," Bugsy said. "Look at my old man. He's done well. He's got a good job. He's raised a whole bunch of us and bought his own house. He got all that from the army."

"So, whatd'ya think?" Mooch asked Danny.

"Let's go," Bugsy said.

---

After making a buy, they headed down Park Street, stopping at the Sands. Bugsy and Danny walked in, their eyes adjusting to the low light. Tall wooden booths with stiff, hard-backed seats ran beneath dust-covered windows, framed in strips of red oak trim. Yellowed ceilings hovered above, darkened from years of cigarette smoke and rimmed with old fly strips. An old jukebox sat in the corner. It had been there so long that someone would yell "C Seven" instead of calling out songs, translating to "Heartbreak Hotel" by Elvis Presley.

Bugsy walked to the end of the bar. "Lefty, can you give me some change for the cigarette machine?" he asked, putting a couple of dollars on the bar top. Lefty Fay was a local legend. He'd grown up in Southie and had earned Silver Gloves three years in a row. His nickname had more to do with his left hook than him being left-handed. He was one of the best bartenders in Fields Corner, if not Dorchester. He listened to his customers' lies and laments, never passing judgment, never making an argument, always listening. He was a greater confidant than Father McNeely at Saint Ambrose Church, maybe even better than the pope himself.

"Thanks," Bugsy said, sliding the change to Danny, who, in turn, fed the coins into the cigarette machine. Danny pulled the levers until he had two packs of Winstons, a box of Marlboros, and a pack of Camels. Danny grabbed several matchbooks from the top of the machine and stuffed them in his back pocket.

"Thanks, Lefty," Bugsy said.

"No problem." He wiped the bar top with a yellowed cloth, swirling it in broad circles. "How's your ma and your brothers?" Lefty asked.

"Good, thanks," Bugsy replied. "They're good."

"And your dad? Putting up with you and your brothers. I'm surprised I don't see him in here more often."

"He's been working a lot."

"Tell him I said hello."

"Will do," Bugsy said. He turned to Danny. "Ready?"

"Yup."

They rejoined the rest of the kids outside and continued down Park Street, weaving in and out of a row of tilted power poles stabbed into the sidewalks and blackened with creosote. After passing a couple of houses and duplex apartments, shuttered by drawn shades and void of life, they brushed up against chain-link fences and metal buildings, resonating with the sounds of machinery and clanging metal. They passed beneath the railroad bridge, an assemblage of rusty I-beams bolted together like an oversized set of Tinker Toys, painted the same bile green like every other bridge in the Commonwealth of Massachusetts. They stopped at George's spa across the street.

"I got some shopping to do," Mooch said.

"Me too," chimed Billy.

They went inside and spread out in every direction. "Can I help you?" the shopkeeper, George, stammered, shuffling out from behind the cash register. "Hey!" he yelled, as the kids went from aisle to aisle, stuffing their pockets with whatever could fit.

"STOP IT! PUT THAT BACK!" George bellowed.

Bugsy came up behind George, startling him. "Can I have a pack of Marlboros?" he calmly asked.

George glanced at him for a second and then looked around at the other kids, waving his arms. "STOP IT! PUT THAT STUFF BACK! STOP IT! NOW!"

"Marlboros?" Bugsy asked in an exaggerated tone of impatience.

"STOP IT! YOU KIDS GOTTA LEAVE! NOW!" George screamed as his face grew redder and his voice shriller. "I'M CALLING THE POLICE!" he howled as he shuffled over to the other side of the store.

"I'll help myself," Bugsy said as he grabbed a handful of cigarette packs and stuffed them in his shirt.

George grabbed the phone off the wall and fumbled with the dial. By the time the line connected, the kids were gone.

# 51

In 1840, William Henry Harrison visited Dorchester during his campaign to become the ninth president of the United States. A month later, he died of pneumonia, becoming the first president to perish in office. Boston's good citizens commemorated his visit by renaming the train depot he'd arrived at and the residential area adjacent to it in his honor. The name was later shortened to Harrison Square. For years, the splendidly sited subdivision, laid out by master land surveyors, was home to many wealthy families that ran the shipbuilding and maritime trading businesses at the nearby Commercial Point.

The remains of Tenean Creek ran alongside the quiet little subdivision. Years before big homes were planted across the hillside, the tributaries leading to Tenean Creek wound through Fields Corner and halfway up Geneva Avenue. Young boys with wooden branch fishing rods tried their luck along the banks of Tenean Creek. Over time, the creeks were filled, and new roads were built, changing the neighborhood forever with modern subdivisions and commercial buildings. The community's heart and soul were torn out when the Southeast Expressway split the community in the 1950s, leaving behind a gasometer, Tar Wharf, and a narrow stretch of sandy beach that bore the name of the once inimitable creek.

The home sites, a mix of architectural designs, were carefully laid on large lots carved from the gentle terrain. The more prominent streets wound their way through the subdivision and were named Park, Everett, Blanche, Green Hill, Elm, and Everdean. The main street, Mill, was later renamed Victory Road, during

World War I, connecting the city of Boston, through Dorchester, to a military plant in Squantum, where they manufactured destroyers at the naval air station in Squantum. South and east of the railroad stood the Dorchester Pottery Works, a renowned business powered by a massive, thirty-foot diameter kiln housed inside a large redbrick building. A sixty-foot-tall brick chimney towered over the plant. Production peaked in the 1920s when a horde of potters made mugs, cups, plates, and bowls for homes across the country.

Through the middle of the nineteenth century, many successful businessmen and artists called Harrison Square home, building large, French-style mansions adorned with modern architectural features. When the Great Depression struck, commerce diminished, homes were lost, and many residences were carved into smaller units.

After the old, moneyed families had lost their homes, Ricky's grandfather, Maurice, a skilled carpenter, bought one of the majestic homes and converted it into a duplex. He rented one side out while remodeling the other. When he was done, he'd flip them around, renting the renovated side for twice the unimproved unit. After the money started flowing, he acquired more homes and turned them into two-, three-, and sometimes four-unit apartments.

When his firstborn, Bill, came home from the war, Bill moved into one of the new apartments, and his father taught him carpentry, plumbing, and electrical skills. The two acquired and remodeled more buildings, keeping some for themselves and selling some to investors. After Bill got married, he and his wife raised three boys and a girl inside one of the apartments. Ricky was the youngest; George, the middle son; and Kevin, the oldest. Mary was a middle sister.

---

The kids turned onto Everett Street, a quiet roadway lined with broad, leafy trees that arched high above the sidewalk and regularly tossed yellowing leaves at anyone who walked by. Passing several more clapboard-sided Victorian houses, set back behind rows of bushes and small, ornamental fences, they reached the McKenna home, a three-story building on the ocean side of the street. A pleasant-looking chestnut tree claimed the south half of the front yard. Its boughs spread out to the curtained dormers that ran along the house's front and sides and extended beyond the gray slate roof, bound by a wide weathered copper gutter. A broad, sweeping porch, covered with wicker furniture, wrapped around the house like a wooden belt. The door was made of white oak, centered with a thick beveled pane of glass bolted to the frame with large brass hinges. Decorative brick chimneys climbed up both sides of the house, reaching high above the ridgelines, blackened by years of soot from below.

The kids heard laughter and voices coming from a large crowd mingling in the driveway and inside a carriage house in the back. Danny didn't recognize anyone. The kids were older. Several of them were wearing army clothes. Others were crowded around a large wooden picnic table, lost in conversation. A cluster of women hovered nearby, chatting away like the guys.

"You know any of these kids?" Mikey asked Danny as he scanned the crowd.

"Naw," Danny replied, tilting his head toward a couple of girls dressed in miniskirts standing near the back porch.

"Nice," Mikey said, wagging his tongue around.

"Danny!" He looked around, trying to figure out where the voice was coming from. "Up here!" He looked up to a second-floor window to see Ricky McKenna waving and hollering. "We're up here," Ricky said. "C'mon up." Danny waved back. "Front door," Ricky yelled, pointing to his right.

"C'mon, guys. Front door."

Mooch grabbed the bags of rum and tonic, and the other kids grabbed the cookies, chips, candy, and other stuff and went in, passing through a high-ceilinged front room into the dining room. "Be down in a minute," Ricky yelled.

Mikey moved aside the flower centerpiece on the dining room table and neatly laid out some paper cups, filled them halfway with Coke, and topped them off with Bacardi. Danny found a couple of Irish-knit doilies on a dresser and piled the snacks onto them. The rest of the kids emptied their pockets, spreading more candy bars and cigarettes on the other doilies.

"I'll see if there's any ice," Danny said. He went into the kitchen, opened the freezer, removed a couple of ice trays, and emptied them into a large pot on the stove. He carried the ice-filled pot into the dining room and dropped a couple of cubes into each cup. Ricky walked into the room, and Danny handed him a drink.

"How're you feeling?" Ricky asked Danny.

"Not bad, all things considered. It could have been worse."

"Yeah, no shit. You're a lucky motherfucker. I heard there were like five of them."

"Naw, there were only three of them."

"What about the girl you were with? Is she okay?"

"She's fine. Thank God she wasn't hurt."

"I'm glad you're okay," Ricky said, walking to the window and pulling the curtains aside. "How're you kids doing?" he asked everyone else and no one in particular.

*Good, Fine. Okay. Cool. Good.*

Mooch strolled alongside Ricky and pointed his cup toward the backyard, "Who're those kids?"

"Some of my brother's friends."

"Where are they from?" Bugsy asked, peering over Mooch's shoulder.

"All over. Dorchester, Southie, Mattapan, Roxbury, and a couple of 'em are from Lower Mills," Ricky said.

"What're they doing here?"

"They're buddies from the army."

"I don't recognize any of them," Bugsy said.

"They're okay. They been through a lot of shit together."

"So, how's Kev doing? I ain't seen him since he came back from Vietnam."

"He's good. He gets nightmares every now and then. There's times he wakes up screaming. I gotta tell you, it scares the shit out of me."

"How 'bout the rest of them?" Bugsy said, nodding toward the backyard.

"That one over there," Ricky said, pointing. "The one with the blue shirt. That's Ronny Kelleher. Do you know him?"

Kelleher stood five feet, ten inches tall and weighed upwards of two hundred pounds. His hair was dark and curly, and his eyebrows were thick and bushy, hovering above a pair of restless eyes. His lips had an odd twist to them, like a snarl.

"I went to school with some Kellehers," Mikey said.

"Me too," Mooch said.

"Doesn't he have a little brother?" Danny asked. "Mark?"

"Had; he would have been twenty," Ricky said. "He got killed . . . over there . . . in Vietnam."

"What?" Charley asked, lowering his drink.

"Yeah, he was killed as soon as he got there," Ricky said.

"What happened?" Mooch asked.

"He and his squad were ambushed," Ricky replied. "The whole bunch of them. They were only eighteen, maybe nineteen years old. I'll bet some of those kids had never been laid."

"That's fucked up," Danny said.

"You guys wouldn't believe what kind of shit goes on over there."

"I mean, they weren't there long, right?" Bugsy said.

"They were out on patrol to get to know the area. Some hot shot shit from Philly took 'em out. He was 'sposed to know his way around. Someone said he was high, fucked up on dope or something, I don't know; it don't matter; they were killed, every one of them," Ricky said.

"I . . . I'm sorry. I didn't know," Mooch said.

"After they killed 'em, those little slant-eyed pricks cut their heads off and stuck 'em on some fucking tree stumps. And then," he paused and took a deep breath, "they cut their dicks and balls off and stuck 'em in their mouths."

"Are you shitting me?" Charley gasped.

"I'm serious. That's what it's like over there." Ricky shook his head and took a long pull on his drink.

"What the fuck?" Mooch cried.

"That's fucked up!" Bugsy said. "What kind of animal would do something like that?"

Ricky slammed his fist on the table, bouncing a couple of drinks, spilling them over. "That's why I'm going!" he said. "I'm gonna kill as many of those slant-eyed motherfuckers as I can!" He banged the table again, and whatever hadn't spilt the first time, did now. He downed his drink, charged out the front door, and slammed the door behind him. Danny went into the kitchen, grabbed a dishtowel, and cleaned up the mess. The rest of the kids topped their drinks off and went in the front room.

# 52

It took Ricky twenty minutes before he quieted down and came back in. He went straight to the kitchen and grabbed a tall glass, filling it with rum and just enough Coke to change the color of his drink. After taking a healthy swig, he went into the dining room and noticed the mess had been cleaned up. "Thanks," he said.

"No problem," Danny said. "I know it ain't none of my business or nothing, but what's Kelleher doing here?"

"And what's his brother doing here?" Bugsy asked. "There's something about that kid that bothers me."

"He wants to talk to me about enlisting. He and some of his friends were there for a while," replied Ricky.

"How many?" Mooch asked.

"I don't know. I ain't spoken to them yet. I wanted to wait until some more of the kids showed up. A few of 'em are thinking about signing up. And these guys"—he flipped his thumb toward the window— "have a bunch of stories, and they've seen a lotta heavy shit. Some of those guys are marines. They're some bad motherfuckers." A small racket outside drew everyone's attention. More kids, both guys and girls, had arrived.

"Let's go," Ricky said, grabbing his drink and sloshing it around as he headed out the front door. The rest of the kids followed.

"Ricky," Bugsy said. "How 'bout I set the bar up out there?"

"Good idea."

"Danny. Can you help me with all this shit?"

"Yeah." Together, they carried everything out to the carriage house, taking three trips to set the bar up and lay the snacks out. When they were done, they strolled into the backyard and joined the rest of the kids, lounging on some Adirondack chairs spread out across the rear of the yard.

"I overheard them talking about the war. They've all been in, I guess," Danny said. He turned to Bugsy. "You might want to talk to them, maybe see what they have to say." Bugsy shrugged him off. "They musta seen a lot of heavy shit." Bugsy shrugged him off again as if annoyed. "It's an idea, that's all," Danny said. "It wouldn't hurt to listen to them. You never know. If I was going in, I'd want to talk to them."

"I don't know; maybe later." Bugsy downed his drink, got up, and walked across the yard.

Danny stood up and took a few steps toward the house. WMEX was blaring from a ten-pound radio. He walked toward the front of the house and, as discretely as possible, thrust his hand down his pants and scratched his crotch so hard, he bled. After wiping his hand on his pants, he went back around, through the front door, and into the bathroom, where he unbuckled his belt and pulled his pants down. He grabbed a facecloth and bar of soap from the sink, and after lathering the cloth, he rubbed himself so hard, he bled some more.

He grabbed some toilet paper from a metal hanger and folded it neatly into a large square. He placed it over his crotch and pulled his underwear up, the paper holding his crude bandage in place. He tucked his shirt in, buckled his belt, and walked back outside, where he spotted an open cellar door. He cocked his head, listening to the voices coming from below. He looked around and stepped down the half-flight of stairs into the basement, where many kids were scattered about. A small light, hanging from an emaciated cord, illuminated a rowdy card game being played in the middle of the room. There were more chairs scattered around the room; it was too dark to see who was sitting in them, but he could tell there were girls from the smell of perfume and the shrillness of the voices.

He spotted an unoccupied chair, sat down, and watched everyone, an easier task now that his eyes had adjusted. A loud clatter ensued from the other side of the room. It was Ricky bouncing off the walls, furniture, and anyone he passed by. Danny did his best to remain invisible, preferring not to engage with Ricky, who was making a fool of himself. Danny waited until Ricky was busy, mumbling to someone else. Finally, Danny got up and left by a steep, wooden stairway that took him out to the back porch where the older guys were arguing at the picnic table, going at it hot and heavy.

"What the fuck do *you* know?" yelled a tall, bespectacled guy with a long, gaunt face pockmarked from acne. "*You* weren't there!"

Danny had seen him earlier, a heavy chain smoker who kept flicking a Zippo lighter, snapping it open and closed, a constant clicking sound. His cut-off fatigues covered a black-inked tattoo on his left shoulder: the letters *USMC* above a rifle, wrapped in strands of barbed wire. A small green label, embroidered *Connors,* was sewn above his pocket. The ashtray was filled with enough ashes to supply the Boston Archdiocese for Lent.

Ronny Kelleher sat to Connors's left, and next to him sat a blond, blue-eyed Irish kid, well-built and muscular up through his neck and halfway through his ears. Danny heard the guys call him Jackie a couple of times. Jackie's hands were distorted and discolored with a shitty-looking tattoo, *L-O-V-E* and *H-A-T-E,* inked across both hands, below his knuckles.

Two more guys sat at the far end of the table. What they lacked in conversation, they made up for in smokes and drinks. The one opposite Connors wore a cut-off fatigue jacket with *Club Saigon* embroidered on the back in large white letters. His hair was long, greasy, unkempt, and hung down to his collar. His shoulder was tattooed with an image of a skull with a knife stuck through one of the eye sockets. A crow was plucking the other eyeball from its hole from atop the skull. The letters *NVA* were inked below the tat. To his right sat another kid, light-skinned and with a crew cut as flat as a putting green. He drank like he was on assignment, polishing every beer off in three or four throaty swallows.

Ricky's brother Kevin sat to the left of Club Saigon. His aviator sunglasses were tucked close against his face. Danny walked over and tapped Kevin on his shoulder. "Hey Kev, what's going on?"

Kevin turned and spoke in a drifting voice. "Danny, right?"

"Yeah," Danny said. Kevin pushed his glasses closer to his face and slid to his right, nudging Club Saigon over until there was enough room for Danny to sit down. Connors was talking as if he'd been drinking coffee all day. "Like I said, I was part of Operation Hastings," Connors muttered as he took a drag of his cigarette and blew the smoke out as fast as he'd drawn it in, pumping like a piston engine. "We were the first to go in at Cam Lo. I remember that fucking day. It was hotter than shit. The place smelled like a bunch of Hingham whores."

The crew cut spoke up. "Yeah, and I had to go in and save your sorry ass. I was part of Task Force Delta and a CAG. Doncha remember? I was there with a bunch of dumb motherfuckers from Southie. A couple of 'em didn't make it, poor bastards. One got his head blown off, and the other stepped on a land mine, blew both his legs off. The fucker bled out right there." The crew cut guzzled half a can of beer and spoke again. "That's how I ended up babysitting Connors over here," he said, smiling, sharing his nicotine-stained teeth with everyone.

Connors chucked the bird and continued. "I was part of an artillery battalion, three-twelve and the two-one, one-three, two-four, and the three-four. We were near the Cam Lo River. That's where things got all fucked up. In some places, the boonies were so thick, you couldn't touch the fucking ground. Remember that shit, Kev? Remember that fucking elephant grass? It was so nasty, it reminded me of the ass-hair from those skanks from East Boston."

Kevin nodded from behind his glasses. "They brought our battalion through there when we were in this nasty firefight in the Song Ngan Valley. You guys gotta remember that shithole. It was north of Cam Lo."

"Yeah, I remember. It was a few clicks south of the DMZ," Connors said, ping-ponging the conversation.

"That fucking place smelled like shit," Club Saigon replied. "The first time we were out for R 'n' R, we went to one of those fucky-sucky places. That's where I got the clap."

"Yeah, the first time," Connors added, chuckling.

"Yeah, the second time was from your mother," Club Saigon said.

"It wasn't my mother. It was your sister."

"Fuck you."

"Remember those Boom Boom girls?"

Club Saigon took a quick swig of beer and spoke in a high-pitched voice. "Sucky, sucky, love you long time."

Jackie laughed so hard that beer spurted out of his nose. Someone else spilled a drink, and it took a minute before anyone could speak as they were laughing so hard. Everyone else in the yard stopped to listen and laugh.

"So anyway, we were inside a dirt hootch, covered with barbed wire," Connors said. "There were so many snakes and bugs crawling all over the place. Just to be safe, we had a couple of Quad Fifties out front, just to keep shit in order in case we needed it."

"S'cuse me. I don't want to sound stupid or nothing, but what's a Quad Fifty?" Danny asked.

The guys all laughed. "It's four big guns, sort of like four of my dicks," came an answer from Connors that set off more laughter. "They're fifty caliber Browning machine guns." Connors brought his hands up and held them upright. "Rat-tat-rat-a-tat-tat," he said, mimicking the shooting. "Those motherfuckers'll fire up to sixteen hundred rounds a minute."

"No shit! How big are the bullets?" Danny asked.

"A little over five inches, maybe five and a half inches," he said, demonstrating by holding his hands apart. "About this long."

"Yeah, about the size of your dick," Club Saigon said, laughing again.

"Five pounds," Connors replied. "Did I say five inches? I meant five pounds."

Danny laughed and turned at the sound of voices behind him. It was Bugsy and several of the kids, listening.

"They came in from the other side, the SLF battalion, while BLT 3/5, the third battalion, came in. All of us were part of Operation Deckhouse II." Connors took a drag on his cigarette. The kids listened, lost in the conversation, a jungle of foreign words and phrases. "I remember it like it was yesterday. Ronny, weren't you down there when we were getting shot up?"

"When? Oh, you mean *that* time?" Ronny said sarcastically. "I think I was up north in another shitstorm, playing hide and seek with Charlie. Yeah, *that* time," he said, leaning back. "That's when I got nicked here," he added, rolling his sleeve up, revealing a hunk of butchered flesh where his biceps used to be.

"So, we started the assault, working our way through Ngan Valley," Connors said. "Jackie, you gotta remember that day."

"Yup, I do," Jackie nodded.

"Anyways, a couple of A-4 Skyhawks from MAG-12 joined some F4-B Phantoms from MAG-11. Man, they were dumping shit all over the place, bombs, bullets, and napalm. And then," he got more excited, "Morrow's crew hit, and we got some backup. They arrived, a bunch of CH-46 Sea Knight helicopters dropping off a basketful of hard-ass marines. They tried, but things got fucked up." He took a deep breath and continued. "A couple of birds crashed."

"I remember one of them flying into a tree," Kevin said. "It was a total clusterfuck."

"There were too many birds in the sky," Connors added. "After that fiasco, Lieutenant Colonel Vale and a few of his companies established a command post in the LZ, and George's Company I set up a defensive perimeter. Company K came around from the south side of the valley, and that's when all hell broke loose when a bunch of NVA snipers opened fire."

Connors lit a smoke and looked around at the other soldiers. They exchanged glances and said a thousand things to each other without ever speaking. Danny could feel his throat dry up. "It took a while before we beat them back, but we did. Goddamn, we did it!"

"OORAH!" Jackie yelled, surprising everyone. The rest of his green-clad comrades joined in for a second time, yelling, "OORAH!"

"I'll never forget it. It was so fucking dark out, we couldn't see our hands in front of our faces," Connors said.

"Yeah, the only thing you could see was the eyes and teeth of a couple of boneheads from Roxbury," Kevin said. "We had four spooks in our battalion. Believe it or not, two of them were from Roxbury. The other two were from Chicago, I think. Someplace out there."

Connors reached into his top pocket, removed a couple of little white pills, popped them in his mouth, and chased them with a thick swallow of beer. "I gotta tell you, those crows were some tough bastards. They were as good as any white guy."

"Yeah," Kevin said, adding, "There were some good ones. They're not all bad or nothing. To tell you the truth, I hadn't ever spent any time with a spook before."

"Your mother did," Connors said.

"Fuck you. Seriously, these guys had balls; they were tough motherfuckers. And they were some funny bastards. You should have seen them, shucking and jiving and dancing. Those motherfuckers all had rhythm like they were born with it."

"Yup, them fuckers could dance, even when there was no music or nothing," Connors said. "It was like that shit was playing in their head or something."

"So anyways, Lieutenant Colonel Bench and his battalion set up our defenses," Kevin said. "God knows we tried; we did, but the whole thing was fucked. We lost eighteen men that day. Eighteen good men." Kevin took a long swig of his beer. "The next day, Charlie launched another mortar attack on us, and we had to radio in for some more air support. It didn't help, though, as we couldn't flush out the rest of the NVA. It was a fucking shitshow."

"Lieutenant Colonel Bench's second battalion moved off the high ground the next morning toward Song Ngan, while Company G made it over to the river, where they killed some more NVA. After that, we started moving inland to establish a defensive perimeter. After we got set up, another bunch of marines went John Wayne, rappelling from a MAG-16 Huey onto Rockpile, and from there, they blasted the shit out of Charlie," Connors said.

Danny's head spun with all the words and trying to keep up with the conversation. His friends looked just as confused, but neither he nor his friends would admit it.

"How do you remember all this crap?" Jackie asked. "I mean, I can't remember what I had for fucking breakfast."

"I remember what I had," said Connors.

"Yeah, what was that?"

"Your mother."

Kevin shook his head, smiled, and continued. "The third battalion got up and were headed out of the valley, and that's when Charlie hit us again. Mortars were going off everywhere, and they were dropping napalm all over the place like pigeon shit. Ronny, can you get me another beer?"

The crowd had grown larger, and the girls had rejoined, leaning as close as they could to hear everything. "Bell's first battalion, first marines joined up with BLT 3/5 over near Song Ngan. That was your division, wasn't it?" Connors asked Kevin, who, in response, lifted his beer.

"We were pretty lucky," Kevin replied. "Most of the NVA units we ran into were pretty small, maybe a dozen or so. So anyway, we joined Lieutenant Colonel Spaulding's second battalion to block them on the other end of the valley, north of Rockpile. I know you guys remember," he said, looking around at the others.

"So anyways," Connors continued, "A couple of days later, a bunch of marines from the third battalion, fifth marines, as I recall, ran into an NV battalion a couple of clicks north of Spaulding. They were trying to set up a skip station on top of Hill 362, but they couldn't, not right away." He paused and closed his eyes for a moment. "Charlie slaughtered our guys."

Ronny passed him a can of beer. "That continued for a couple of hours until they called for a Huey to get us out of there. That was always fucked because most of the time, there wasn't any place for the choppers to land, and when that happened, we had to burn and blow out everything. If Charlie saw us, we'd end up in another fucking battle."

"What did *you* use?" Danny asked.

"Me? I had an M3 Grease Gun."

"How heavy were those things? My cousin Richie said they weigh a ton," Mooch said from behind Danny's shoulders.

"I don't know, nine, ten pounds maybe. They got heavy after a while. Ronny, what do you figure?"

"I don't know, heavy, really heavy," Ronny said. "Not as heavy as my dick, but heavy." The girls blushed, and the kids laughed.

"How big was the clip?" Mooch asked.

"Thirty rounds."

"I had an M-16," Ronny said. "They worked pretty good if they didn't jam. If you wanted to kill any of those fucking slant-eyes, you'd use a Mike twenty-six or toss some fucking hand grenades; blow the fuckers up."

"That sounds crazy," Danny said.

"That ain't the half of it. Hey, Kevin," Ronny yelped, "Remember those fucking snakes and those goddamn blood-sucking leeches?"

"How could I forget them?"

"Remember that kid from Hyde Park? What's his name? Teddy, Freddy? Shit, I forget. He was the poor fucker who had the leech climb up his ass."

The girls responded with a chorus of oohs, grosses, and yucks. A couple of them started gagging, and as soon as Connors began talking again, they quietly walked back to the carriage house.

"This kid, whatever the fuck his name was, was bleeding out his ass and puking blood all over the place," Kevin said.

"Jesus Christ! How'd they get the leech out?" Mooch asked.

"With a pair of pliers," Connors said matter-of-factly.

"Are you shitting me? Pliers?" Danny said.

"Yup, a pair of pliers," Connors said.

"You're not serious, are you?" Mooch asked.

"What the fuck would you use if you had a leech crawl up your ass while you were in the middle of a swamp?"

"I don't know," Mooch said sheepishly.

"Okay then, for Christ's sake." Connors drank some more beer. "We were in the middle of this swamp, and Charlie had us pinned down. There were bullets flying around everywhere, zinging right by us, and there were leeches everywhere. You'd pull one off, and two more would show up. It's getting dark and no one's sleeping or nothing and then this kid from Hyde Park gets the shits and he's running a fever and sweating like a pig. So, every time this kid craps, this oily shit oozes to the top of the water. Everyone's trying to keep away from it, so the best we could do was sweep it away with branches and anything else we could get our hands on as his greasy shit's floating all over the place. We can't let the fucking kid die, right? I mean, if he croaks, we're all gonna croak. So, everyone's going crazy, and it got really bad. A couple of kids made a run for it, and Charlie cut these poor fuckers down as soon as they took off. It was like shooting fish in a barrel. The first time it happened, we were able to drag this tall thin kid back in. We called him Philly because he was from Philadelphia. They got him good. We couldn't get the other kid and had to leave him there. He was dead, maybe ten or fifteen feet away, curled over. His eyes were wide open, staring at us. Every now and then, Charlie hit him, and a chunk of his head would spray all over the place."

"We had a few C-rats left, but not much," Connors said, lighting another cigarette. "We lost six kids that day." His voice started to crack as he welled up. "There was nothing we could do." Club Saigon walked away, leaving his beer on the table.

"Jesus Christ, what happened next?" Mooch asked.

"Well, we finally got a medic on the line, and he tells us we need to get the leech out 'no matter what it takes.' He tells us if we didn't get the leech out, this kid was gonna die. So, we told the medic we didn't have anything to use, and he said, 'Find something.' Well, shit, we ain't got no doctor stuff or nothing, and the medic says we got no choice. So, this medic asks us what we got. Half the guys got pocket knives, but that's not gonna work. So, we looked around, and all we got was a screwdriver and a pair of pliers."

"Do you mind if I ask, but how do you stick a pair of pliers up someone's ass without fucking him up?" Danny asked.

"Very carefully," Connors said, wiping his arm across his mouth. "So, we dragged him over to the edge of the swamp, and we bent him over and spread his legs apart, and the whole time, this poor motherfucker's screaming and fighting, and we still got bullets whizzing by. Once we got him down, we spread his butt cheeks open, and we could see the leech, but we couldn't grab it. The little fucking thing's wiggling around, like this," he said, waggling his little finger around. "They're slippery little motherfuckers."

"Sort of like your dick," Kevin said, wiggling his little finger around.

"So, once we got his asshole open, we stuck a piece of wood in his mouth 'cause he's screaming and yelling. So, all of a sudden, this guy, Levine, a Jew from Jersey, said his uncle was a rabbi, and he'd seen a lot of circumcisions and said he could do it. If you ask me, them Jews are kinda fucked up."

"No shit!" Bugsy said.

"So, we kept telling this kid to quit moving around, or we're gonna knock him out. Cuz he's moving all over the place, Levine doesn't want to do nothing. So one of the guys gets this great idea to use a deck of cards."

"A deck of cards?" Danny replied.

"Yeah, a deck of cards. Don't ask me how he figured that out or nothing."

"You're making this shit up now," Bugsy said.

"Believe what you want," Connors said.

"Go on," Danny said.

"So, we rolled a couple of them up, like a small tube, and stuck them up his ass. Once we got them up there, they kinda unfolded, you know what I mean?" Everyone nodded. "So, Levine works the pliers in, and he starts turning them around and around, and this kid, he's screaming. We get some lighters going so we can see, 'cause it's dark and everything. This fucking Jew, he's good. He's gonna make a great doctor. I mean, this guy was fucking good. This poor kid's thrashing around like a fucking flounder, and the Jew, he's wiggling the pliers around, real careful, and after a few minutes, he yells, 'Eureka,' and the next thing you know, he pulls the fucking leech out. It was fucking unbelievable."

"Fuck me!" Danny said breathlessly. "That's an amazing fucking story. So, what happened to the kid?"

"Yeah, what happened?" Mooch asked, sitting up and looking around, hoping he didn't sound too stupid.

"After we got out of there, like a day later, the first thing they did was get an IV in him and fly him out in a chopper."

"Did you ever see him again?" Danny asked.

"Yeah, a couple of months later," Connors said as his chest heaved. "After he got better, they sent him up north. He and a bunch of guys got in a firefight." Connors drained his beer. "He got his head blown off." Connors stared straight ahead, and for the first time since he'd started talking, he stopped. "I gotta take a piss," he said in a monotonous voice.

A couple of the older guys got up, and a few stayed. Danny stuck his hand over the table. "I'm Danny," he said. The guy across from him, a greaser with a cigarette stuck over each ear, stuck his hand out. "Jackie. Half my friends call me Jack-in-the-Box, and the rest call me Jack-off."

"Jack-in-the-Box?"

"Connors tells me it's 'cause I'm full of surprises."

"Hmm. Hey, I was wondering if I could ask you a question."

"No problem. What is it?"

"How long were you in Nam?"

"Thirteen months."

"That's a long time."

"It's a fucking eternity, man. Every week is like a fucking year."

"Would you do it again?"

"Fuck, yeah."

"Want one?" Danny asked, extending his cigarettes.

"Sure," Jackie said.

"Why didn't you go back in?"

"They won't let me," Jackie said.

"Why not?"

Jackie pulled his left pant leg up, revealing what was left of his calf, a mass of discolored purple meat veiled behind wafer-thin layers of skin. His bones and muscles, torn and twisted, were visible just beneath the skin. "I'm a fucking gimp."

"Is everything else okay, if you don't mind me asking?"

"Yeah, they didn't get the family jewels. I can still fuck like a race horse."

"What happened?"

Jackie shrugged. "I stepped on a mosquito mine."

"What's that?"

"Ahh, it's a small land mine. They make 'em over there, and you never know what they're gonna do. Most of the time, they'll blow a few toes off. This one totally fucked me up. Almost took my fucking leg off."

"Jesus Christ. I . . . I'm sorry," Danny said.

"No big deal. It is what it is. It's ancient history. I was lucky. I got out of there."

"Looks like it still hurts."

"It does. Sometimes worse than other times."

"Can they do anything?"

"Naw, not really. It's too fucked up. They said I gotta be careful, or I could lose it."

Danny made a quick sign of the cross. "Can you work?"

"Not really. I can't stand up for a long time. I'm on disability. They send me two hundred and sixty-eight dollars a month."

"That's not bad; I mean, all things considered."

"I suppose," Jackie said, rubbing his leg. "I sometimes wish I'd just lost it. It'd be a lot easier. It lights up and gets going sometimes, hurts like a motherfucker."

"I'll keep you in my prayers."

"So, you going in?" Jackie asked.

"Naw. I'm sort of like you. They won't take me."

"Why? You look okay to me."

Danny stood up and lifted his shirt. "What the fuck happened to you?" Jackie asked, leaning forward and looking closer.

"I got jumped by a bunch a niggers, and one of them stabbed me. I almost died."

"When'd that happen?" Jackie asked.

"A few months ago, on Washington Street, across from Mother's Rest. Me and my girlfriend got robbed."

"No shit. Just the two of you? Is she okay?"

"Yeah, she's fine. By the way, what were those pills Connors took? The little white ones."

"Speed."

"I never heard of it."

"They gave 'em to us to keep us awake whenever we were in a big fight. Some guys'd stay up for three or four days and never eat."

"Why's he taking them now?" Danny asked.

"He's hooked on them, like a lot of the guys. That motherfucker's gonna be up all night yacking, all fucking night long. Yacking"

"That's fucked up."

"It is. Take my word for it; it is. Me, I don't fuck with 'em anymore. I'm good with my beers and a highball now and then. You feel like you can conquer the world when you take 'em like he's been doing. It's when you stop that you're fucked. It's worse than any hangover you've ever had. They're bad shit; stay away from them."

"I gotta catch up with my friends. Want another smoke?"

"Sure."

"Take a couple. I got another pack."

"Thanks." Jackie nodded like he hadn't a worry in the world.

"I'll catch you later."

Jackie tossed a half salute.

# 53

After grabbing another rum and Coke, Danny strolled back into the cellar. The card game had ended, and the only light was from a row of windows covered with spiderwebs and dirt. He could make out silhouettes of people at the back of the room. He heard heavy breathing and moans, along with sloppy lips kissing. There was no place to sit, so he went back outside. The kids lounged beneath a leafy maple tree, while the older guys and their girlfriends sat at the picnic table. Danny walked over to the carriage house, leaned against the doorway, and listened to the Beach Boys on the radio, humming to himself and tapping his feet. When the song ended, he made another drink and paused when he heard a female voice call his name. He looked around but didn't see any familiar faces, and so he thought he must have been mistaken. Then, whoever it was called him again. A girl was walking toward him. She had straight hair, neatly bundled in a bright red ribbon, knotted at the nape of her neck. Her silver looped earrings hovered above a multi-colored silk scarf draped loosely around her neck and shoulders. Her slacks clung to her hips and accented the natural curves of her calves. Complimenting her ankles were a pair of low black pumps. A few steps more and Danny recognized her. It was Mrs. McPherson, the owner of the black '65 Mustang. He'd never seen her anywhere else but the gas station. When he did, she always wore sunglasses, a hat, a scarf, or a high-collared coat, dressing like she didn't want to be recognized. Her jacket was always buttoned up, and her chest was always covered. Now, her blouse was open at the collar; he caught a glimpse of a lacy bra, instantly arousing him. He swallowed to wet his dry throat and then stuttered when he spoke. "Mrs. McPherson." His voice cracked like a leaf on the first day of winter.

"It's Lindsey. I'm not that old," she said.

"Yeah, sure . . . sure, okay, Lindsey." He fumbled with his cup as he fidgeted. She reached for his drink and lifted it to her nose. "Rum and Coke?"

"Yeah! How did you know?" Danny sputtered. "I mean . . . how could you tell?"

She handed the drink back to him. "Rum doesn't do much for me. I'm not too fond of mixed drinks. They're usually too sweet for me. I like wine. So, what are you doing here? Do you know Kev?"

"I'm a friend of his little brother, Ricky. Me and my friend Bugsy have known him for a long time. Bugsy's my best friend. He's joined the army. Ricky invited us down for his going-away party." Danny took a sip of his drink, more out of nervousness than thirst.

Lindsey took a sip from her glass and spoke in a solemn voice that sent a chill up Danny's back. "You know, Danny, the war's not what they say it is." She glanced around the yard and removed a handkerchief from her back pocket. Her blue eyes, bright and cheery a minute ago, were now red and beginning to well.

"Are you okay?" he asked. "Want to take a walk?"

"Yes, that'd be nice." She wiped her eyes with her handkerchief and blushed ever so slightly. Danny placed his hand on her upper arm and led her down the driveway. He kept looking over his shoulder, expecting Bugsy, Mikey, or one of the older guys to say something, but they didn't. He turned to his left, walked to a low granite wall in front of the house next door, and sat down. She sat alongside him, still dabbing her eyes.

"I'm sorry," she said. "It's just that . . . God, I must look a mess." She glanced at her mascara-stained handkerchief and shook her head. She wiped her eyes again and lifted her glass. "Can you get me some more wine?"

"Sure, of course," Danny replied. "I don't know too much about wine. Is there any special kind you like?"

"Anything white," she replied. "Pinot Grigio would be nice."

"Peanut, what?"

She laughed. "You really don't know anything about wine, do you?"

Danny blushed. "Not really."

"There's a few bottles. You'll spot it."

"You want anything else?"

"No, thanks; thank you for asking."

"My pleasure."

When he entered the carriage house, a brunette wearing too much makeup and a too-small pair of jeans spoke. "Is she okay?"

"I think so," Danny said.

She reached her hand out. "I'm Kerry, a friend of Lindsey's."

"Danny," he said, placing his glass on the bench and extending his hand, expecting one of the older guys to say something. "Umm, pleased to meet you."

She turned to the girls next to her, lifting her glass as she introduced them. "This is Kathy," she said, "and Pam." He nodded at each in turn as her name was mentioned. "Nice to meet you all."

"How do you know Lindsey?" Kerry asked.

"She's one of my customers at the gas station. You know the Port Gas station at Neponset, next to the skating rink?"

"Sure, I know the place."

"She comes by a coupla times a week, and I got to know her. I've changed the oil on her car and put air in her tires. Stuff like that."

"That's nice."

"Yup," Danny replied. "She asked me to get her a glass of wine."

"You're sweet," she said. "How old are you?"

"Twenty-one," he lied.

"Where do you live?"

"Four Corners."

"If you need any help with Lindsey, let me know," Kerry said.

"I will."

"You know," Kerry said, sipping her glass, "Lindsey's still having a hard time, losing Tommy and everything, the poor thing. Ever since Tommy died, she stopped going out. Today's the first day most of us have seen her." She squeezed his wrist. "She's so sweet. Were you in the war?"

"Me? Nah," he replied, shaking his head for emphasis. "They wouldn't take me."

"How come?"

"Medical reasons," he said, hoping that would end that.

"Let me know if she needs anything. She's my best friend, and I'd do anything for her."

"I appreciate it. I'll let her know." He turned to the tabletop bar, studied the bottles, and lifted them, stopping when he spotted the Pinot Grigio. He refilled Lindsey's glass and made another rum and Coke, taking a long sip and topping it off with more rum. Then, he made his way down the driveway, pausing several times to sip his drink so it wouldn't splash around. "I got you the peanut butter drink you asked for," he said, handing the glass to her.

Her eyes turned blue again, and she laughed.

"How do you say it?' he asked.

"You need to put an accent in the second *G*. It's *jee. Gree-jee-oh*."

"Grigio," he repeated.

"Yes, that's it." She took a sip and patted Danny's upper thigh. As soon as her hand touched him, he felt his dick harden. "I haven't seen you in a while. Are you still working at the gas station?"

"Yeah," Danny replied, adjusting his legs so he was not so uncomfortable. "I've been out for a while. I was in the hospital."

"I'm sorry. What happened?"

"I got stabbed by a spook up on Washington Street. Me and my girlfriend got jumped."

"Was that a few months ago?"

"Yeah."

"I heard about that. Was that you?" she asked in a two-octave voice.

"Yeah."

"You almost died, didn't you?"

"Well," he said, drawing the word out like a rubber band. "It wasn't that bad. I'm getting better. I gotta take it easy for a while." He instinctively lifted his hand to his stomach, and as soon as he did, she gently touched his shirt where he had been stabbed. He thought he was going to faint.

"Does it hurt?" she asked.

Danny squirmed, hoping he could control himself. "Not really; not anymore." He stood up and stretched his legs out, focusing as best he could on anything but her.

"Jesus! I can't believe that was you. If I had known, I would have visited you." She took another sip and shook her head. "Well, you look good now."

"I'm getting better. My doctor told me to rest and take it slow—no horseplay or sports or nothing."

"Listen to your doctor," she said, playfully scolding him.

"Oh yeah, I saw a doctor when I went in for my physical, and he told me I couldn't enlist because of the stabbing. Umm, can you excuse me? I gotta go to the bathroom. I'll be right back."

"Sure."

As soon as he got inside, he stuck his hand down his pants, straightened himself out, and scratched until he started bleeding again. After a quick splash of cold water, he tucked his shirt in and returned outside, not bothering to stop or look around. She leaned over and kissed him on his cheek as soon as he sat down. "That's good news," she said.

Danny blushed. "Er, what is?" he asked.

"That you can't go in. It's wonderful!" She kissed him on the cheek again, and he blushed so hard he thought his eyeballs would fall out. "I lost my husband, Tommy, over there. He stepped on a landmine."

"I know," Danny said. "Mr. Erickson told me. He said he knows—I mean, knew him, your husband."

"He did."

"How do you know Kevin?".

"Tommy grew up with him. He's from the neighborhood. He grew up down the street. He lost both legs in that godforsaken place before he died. They couldn't save him." She took another swallow from her glass. "And for what? For what?" she cried, folding over into herself. "For what?"

He gave her a moment before placing his arm over her shoulder and holding her. He felt her tears run down his arm as she shivered and cried. They stayed that way until she stopped, kissed him on the cheek, and walked out into the middle of the street. He got up, snapped a small branch from one of the bushes, and swung it around. He walked toward her slowly and spoke. "So, where do you live now?" he asked.

"Savin Hill, near my family, in a two-family home on Auckland Street. I live on the second floor."

"Yeah, I know where that is. One of the guys I go to school with lives over there."

"It's a nice neighborhood."

"Yeah, it is. Say, what's your maiden name?"

"Sparks."

"Like in electricity?"

"Yeah, and get this. My father's an electrician."

"You're kidding."

"No, I'm serious. Well, he was one. He worked for the MBTA."

"That's wild."

"Yeah, it is. Dad's retired now."

"What about your ma?"

"She's not doing so well. She has cancer. It's been tough on her and my father, on all of us. I help when I can. That's the main reason we live there. I mean, lived there, Tommy and me."

"Do you mind if I ask you a question?" he asked.

"No, what is it?"

"It's personal and all . . . I hope you don't mind."

"It's okay."

"Why did you get married? If he was going off to war, weren't you worried that something could happen?"

"I was pregnant; we had to get married."

"Of course."

"We were in love; we'd been dating for a long time. We always talked about getting married. When I got pregnant, it moved things up. It would have killed my mother if I'd been pregnant and unmarried."

Danny nodded, all the while thinking of his sister Chrissy.

"It wasn't a big ceremony or anything, just the family, some relatives, and a few friends. You should have seen Tommy. He was so handsome." She looked back down the street again. "Kevin was our best man."

"So, where's the baby?" he said, suddenly wishing he hadn't said anything after he heard himself.

"I had a miscarriage. Three weeks after we were married." She pulled her handkerchief out and wiped her eyes. "It was a boy."

"I'm sorry."

"It's okay; it's in the past." Danny nodded. "Can we go for a walk?" she asked.

"Sure. Where to?"

"Down the street. I want to go by Tommy's old house."

As they passed by the next block, she stopped and pointed. "See that house over there?"

He followed her extended arm. It led him to a tall, gray house needing painting and repair. The windows were veiled with threadbare curtains, looking like an old Italian woman at a funeral. A tall wrought iron fence, moored in a low granite coping strip, surrounded the property. Beyond it, a rusted metal gate led to a long concrete walkway lined with small granite squares overrun with weeds. An expansive wooden deck and a massive oak doorway hovered between the windows. The front yard, marked by patches of uneven dirt, was covered with decaying leaves wedged between small stands of wiry weeds.

"It's haunted," she said with a tinge of excitement. "Tommy and his friends told me about this place. Look at it. It *must* be haunted."

Danny surveyed the gray slate roof and the copper gutters along the peeling fascia boards. He could almost smell the inside; dark, stuffy, and dusty. "What's the story?" he asked.

"They say that an old sea captain used to live there with his wife and three daughters. The youngest two were twins, Harriet and Melissa. They were little, eight or nine years old. The oldest was twelve, and her name was Mildred. The captain owned a ship down at the Port, and he used to leave town every few months to pick up things from the West Indies: rum, sugar, and other stuff. They say he came home from one of his trips and found the twins in the basement. They had been murdered and stuffed inside a coal bin. Can you imagine that?" Her eyes sparkled with every word. "They found the older girl in the attic, hanging," Lindsey said, pointing to the top floor. "They didn't know if she'd killed herself or someone else had done it. They found the captain's wife in the backyard, knitting, just knitting. When the captain came home, he went crazy, took off, disappeared, and never returned. He left his boat and wife behind."

Lindsey turned and walked backward, staring at the house while talking. "Some people think the mother did it, but I don't believe that. What kind of mother would do something like that?"

"What happened to her?"

"They say she moved away, back with her family, to the South somewhere."

"Wow, that's a heck of a story!" Danny said. "Do you believe it?"

"Of course. I mean, look at the place. If it wasn't true, don't you think someone would be living there?"

"I guess. I didn't think about that."

"It's true; it has to be."

"I heard of some haunted houses around town, but nothing like that. There's one on Claybourne Street, behind the Y. Have you heard of it?"

"No, I don't think so."

"I ain't never seen anyone go in or out. But at night, you can see some lights on. They're never the same. When we were little, we climbed the fence and looked inside, but we never got close enough. The curtains were always closed, and no one had the guts to get closer. We were too scared."

"When it's warm, or there's a full moon or something, you can hear the girls crying. It's a horrible sound. I've heard them myself. They wander through the halls in the middle of the night, banging the walls and making all kinds of noises. You can see them sometimes, looking out the window, crying. They say they do that because they're looking for their father, waiting for him to come home."

"I'll bet there's a lot of haunted houses around Dorchester," Danny said. "When you look at some of those old houses, it makes you wonder."

She stared at the house for another minute. "C'mon," she said, tugging on his arm. "This place still gives me the creeps."

A small pack of dogs ran by them as they neared the corner. "There!" she said, pointing. "That's Tommy's house!"

It was a massive home with a front porch big enough to play a basketball game on. The trees surrounding the house were broad, leafy, and neatly manicured. The windows were clean and bright. Colorful curtains hung from them, giving a look of happiness to the place. A long driveway led to a carriage house in the back. Danny spotted Lindsey's Mustang in the sideyard, shining in the afternoon sun.

"That's your car, isn't it?" he said, picking his stride up.

"It is; it was—Tommy's car . . . it's mine now, of course."

Danny bent over and looked down the hood like he was lining up a pool shot. "I love this car." He tilted his head to the side after spotting a water drop. He rubbed it off with his sleeve.

"You want to take it for a drive?" she asked.

"Are you serious?"

"Sure. It needs a run." She fished the keys from her back pocket and tossed them to Danny. "Go on, get in."

He walked around to the passenger's side and opened the door for her. After she slid in, he closed the door, went to the other side, climbed into the leather bucket seat, and started the car. He pumped the gas several times until the car came to life, and large round dials began spinning. He let out a deep breath, closed his eyes, and listened to the roar of the pistons pumping in the engine. He smiled so hard after opening his eyes that his teeth nearly fell out. He adjusted the rearview mirror and moved the seat. "Do you mind if I put the radio on?" he asked.

"Oh, no problem," she said.

He rolled the dial to WMEX and adjusted the volume so they could talk. "Where do you want to go?"

"I don't care. The tank's full."

"How about the Blue Hills? We can drive through Milton and out to Houghton's Pond."

"Sounds good." She turned the radio up, slid her seat back, and extended her legs onto the dashboard. "Tommy and I used to go to the Blue Hills to watch the submarine races," she laughed.

Danny glanced at her thighs, more visible by her shorts sliding higher. He struggled to keep his eyes on the road. He tried to think of something to say but failed. Finally, he managed to refocus on his driving as the tachometer spun. He pressed the clutch in and slipped the car into reverse. The gears clicked into place, and the engine hummed like the Boston Symphony Orchestra. He revved the engine and backed off the clutch, expecting the car to shudder, surprised at how smoothly it engaged. Instead, when he reached the street, he turned the wheel and shifted into first gear. The Beatles were on the radio singing "I want to hold your hand."

Danny cruised down Freeport Street, waiting until Gallivan Boulevard hit fourth gear. He coaxed the engine to take them toward the Blue Hills, passing through Mattapan and Milton, continuing onto Blue Hills Parkway, a broad, majestic street lined with tall brick homes accessed by wide concrete stairways. They crossed a busy intersection, past the skating rink, and drove through the winding tree-lined roadway. Lindsey rolled her window down and turned the radio up when "Yummy, Yummy, Yummy" came on. Danny downshifted as he leaned into a curve, double-clutching throughout, continually working the gears until he neared the State Police barracks, where he slowed down.

"You drive good," Lindsey said, pulling her legs up to her chest and hugging her knees, exposing her panties. "I can tell from the sound. Every time I drive, it sounds like I'm grinding coffee or something." She shook her head and ran her fingers through her hair. "I wish it was an automatic. I don't like driving a stick." Danny downshifted as they came into a long curve. "Besides, if I'm wearing high-heeled shoes, I have to bend my feet to push the clutch in. That's why I'm thinking of selling it."

"Selling it? Are you serious?"

"I'm thinking about it," she said.

"Heck, if I owned it, I'd sleep in it."

"You're funny," she said, pulling her legs closer and exposing more of her underwear. "Besides the clutch problems, it's a two-door. I have to take my parents to their doctors, and I need a four-door. And, besides, my father doesn't drive anymore." Danny nodded as she spoke. "I'm thinking of getting a station wagon," she said.

"A station wagon! Are you serious?"

"Don't get me wrong or anything; I like the Mustang and all." She took a deep breath and tilted her head back, sending her breasts high in the air, drawing the air out of Danny's chest. "I smell Tommy whenever I get in the car; it's his aftershave." Danny decided to say nothing, knowing she needed a moment. She finally spoke again. "It doesn't make sense anymore. I talked to my father-in-law about it, and he said he'd store it for me for as long as I wanted. That's sweet of him, but it's time to move on. Tommy's gone, and he's never coming back."

He drove some more until he stopped at an MDC parking lot and parked under a tall pine tree that had dropped some brown needles, creating a mat around the roots. "I've got to use the ladies' room," she said.

"Well," he said, smiling. "I'm gonna use the boys' room. I don't think I can use the ladies' room."

"You're funny," she said, a sprinkling of words that changed the color of his cheeks.

Danny swung his door open and trotted around the car to open hers. "And a gentleman," she said, accepting his extended hand. They walked silently to the restrooms and parted. Danny took a leak, then splashed several handfuls of cold water on his face, across the back of his neck, and on his itchy crotch. After patting his groin with a napkin, he washed his hands again and carefully zipped his pants up. When he came out, Lindsey was standing beneath a broad-leafed maple tree, staring at the water.

"All set?" she asked.

"Yup."

They strolled beneath the boughs of the tree-shaded path, shuffling through the leaves to the chestnut brown sand that ran alongside the edge of the pond. Danny picked up a small branch and stripped the leaves off. When they reached the shore, Lindsey removed her shoes and dangled them from her hands, making her walk look graceful.

"How much do you think your car's worth?" Danny asked, swatting the air with his branch.

She dragged her feet through the sand. "I don't know. I haven't thought about it much. Tommy had some work done on it. I'm not sure what for. The talcometer, I think that's what it's called, and the exhaust system."

Danny laughed. "The tachometer. It's the big dial in the middle of the dashboard. It looks like a clock."

"What's it do?"

"It shows how fast the engine's spinning."

"Tommy loved the sound of that engine. It was music to him. Sometimes, we'd be out for a ride, and he'd hum along with the engine. Can you believe that? It was almost like he was playing the car like a musical instrument or something."

"Oh, I can believe it." A breeze blew off the water and cooled them down. "If you're serious, would you consider selling it to me? I'd take care of it, and you could drive it anytime."

"Really?"

"Yeah, I'm as serious as I've ever been."

"I'd give you a good price, of course. But can you afford it? It's a lot of money."

"I think I can. I got a good job, and I'm working full-time. Mr. Erickson said he'd help me if I wanted to buy a car. He said he'd give me a loan if I needed one." Danny tossed the stick away and stuck his hands in his back pockets. "I run the gas station on weekends and sometimes at night."

"I didn't know that. That's wonderful. I know how much Mr. Erickson thinks of you. He's told me a lot of times."

"No kidding," Danny said.

"Oh yeah." She took a few steps into the water and resumed talking as she walked beside him. "I know the car will be safe with you. God knows you won't grind the gears up like I do. Tommy would have liked that, knowing someone like you had his car. And, he would've liked you, I'm sure of it. In the last letter I sent him, I mentioned the car and that we needed a bigger one. I told him we'd have a baby someday and need a station wagon." She splashed some water on her arms and kicked her feet around. "That was the last time I wrote to him. I don't think he ever got my letter."

Danny shuffled to the water's edge; picked up a small, flat rock; and threw it across the water, watching it skip across the surface, leaving a trail of undulating ripples behind it. "So, what's up with that guy, Connors?" he asked.

"Him." She harrumphed like she had indigestion. "He's an asshole."

"What do you know about those little white pills he was taking?"

"They're called Bennies. Some people call them Pep Pills. They're kind of like drinking a lot of coffee. They gave them to all the soldiers. They passed them out like candy to keep them awake. Tommy didn't like them. He said they gave him a stomachache."

"Where'd Connors get them?"

"Who knows? So many guys went over there. Coming back and forth, they bring 'em back. They're all over. They're not that hard to get."

"Is that why Connors talks so much? I mean, that guy never shut up. He reminds me of my Aunt Millie. She'd start talking, and you'd walk away and come back half an hour later, and she'd still be yacking away. I know some girls like that. They never shut up."

Lindsey chuckled. "I know a lot of girls like that too. Did you know some girls take them too to lose weight? If you take them, you have no appetite; you don't eat."

Danny pulled his smokes out. "Want one?' he asked, an offer she declined with a quick shake of her head. "I noticed the other guys weren't really telling stories or nothing, not like Connors."

"Most of them don't like to talk about what they saw and . . . and what they did. Most of them aren't proud of it."

"So why was Connors running off at the mouth like that?"

"It's the speed. Plus, he's an asshole, a first-class one. The only reason we were there, the other girls and me, was for Kevin and his brother. Kevin invited us." Lindsey picked up a small rock and tossed it in the water. "You know what's upsetting?" she said, not waiting for an answer. "That asshole wasn't even invited. I know because we asked beforehand; all the girls did. If we knew he was going to be there, we wouldn't have come. He's such a jerk." She threw another rock into the water, sending a large painted turtle scurrying. "And I can tell you, none of the guys wanted to hear any more of Connors' stories. They've had enough. Everyone's had enough. God forgive me, but why didn't that asshole Connors step on a mine?"

With that, she started crying. "Why did it have to happen to Tommy?"

Danny shrugged, saying, "I don't know."

"I'm sorry. I shouldn't have said that. It's just that, I don't know, it's unfair." Her chest and shoulders heaved in pain. "It was a horrible place, and it's not what people think. If you don't have to go there, you shouldn't. You should stay home and find a girlfriend and get married."

Danny thought about Patty, missing her.

"Don't go over there, Danny. It's horrible, just horrible."

She removed the handkerchief stuffed in her sleeve, dabbed her eyes, and strolled along the shore, dragging her toes behind her, running them through the sand. "I remember Tommy talking about this kid, Billy Halchuk. He was this cute kid from Saint Anne's Parish, maybe five ten or five eleven, blond. He had a little sister, Janie. She was a little cutie. He joined the marines at the same time Tommy and Connors did. He wasn't there more than a month before he got killed; he stepped on one of those god-awful land mines. Connors was there; he saw the whole thing." She took a deep breath and continued. "Well, that's all any of us needed to know. Billy Halchuk died. Isn't that enough?" Her chest heaved again. "No one needs to know anymore. It's horrible enough. But no, that wasn't enough for Connors! He had to tell everyone *exactly* how he died. Everything! He told that story to some of Billy's friends, and they asked him to stop, but he didn't. He kept it up until everyone, even some of the guys, started crying. A couple of the girls got sick."

She threw another rock in the water. "I've saved every letter Tommy sent me, every one of them. I read them every now and then, sometimes over and over. It's all I have left of him. That and the car."

"It must be hard," Danny said.

"It is," she said. She looked casually at her watch. "Oh God, we gotta get back! The party must be winding down. Let's go."

They turned and stepped onto the asphalt parking lot. He tapped his feet to dislodge the leaves and moist dirt stuck to the bottom of his shoes. She sat down on the asphalt curb and ran her fingers through her toes, removing little clumps of sand. After brushing her feet off, she put her shoes on and stood up. "Would you mind driving back?" she said.

"Sure, no problem. You won't have to ask me twice this time. Don't you like to drive?"

"Not really. I like being a passenger. I can relax and look at everything." A gentle breeze greeted them with the scent of pine trees and fallen needles. He slowed down to itch himself, doing his best to hide his efforts. He wobbled and caught up to her. "Is everything okay?" she asked.

"Yeah, no problem. I got a little stomachache."

"I'm sorry. Do you want to stop and get some Tums?"

"Naw, I'll be okay. It's not that bad."

Lindsey nodded, satisfied with his answer.

Danny took a different route back, passing through Milton and skimming along the edge of Quincy, heading back through Neponset Circle. He continued past the car dealers lined up along Gallivan Boulevard, turned up Freemont Street, and rewound his way to Ricky's house. When he turned the corner, he stopped. There were half a dozen cop cars scattered across the street.

"What's going on?" Lindsey asked, sitting up.

"I don't know."

The cops were patting kids down, cuffing them, and shoving them into a paddy wagon. An older cop with a pillowy belly walked over to the driver's side of the car. "You gotta keep moving," he said. Danny nodded politely and was about to clutch into gear when Lindsey spoke up.

"I live there," Lindsey said, pointing to Tommy's parents' house. "What's happening?"

"A bunch of kids got into a fight," he said, turning his head back to the police vans.

"Who did?" Lindsey asked.

"A bunch of punks. They aren't from around here."

"Fuck," Danny muttered to himself, loud enough for Lindsey to hear but not enough for the cop to.

"You can pull over there," the cop said, pointing to an open section of the street. "Keep out of the way."

"Thank you, Officer."

Danny pulled over to the open parking spot. "C'mon, let's see what happened," she said.

"Umm, okay. I don't want to get into any trouble or nothing."

"Don't worry. You didn't do anything wrong. If anyone asks, tell them you're my cousin."

"Okay," Danny replied, nervously looking around. "Between you and me, all these cops make me nervous. Those kids are my friends."

"I know," she said, turning in her seat and looking at him. "Don't you want to know what happened?"

"I already know what happened."

"What do you mean?"

Danny smiled and shrugged.

"Well, I don't," she said, opening her door. Danny shook his head, laughed, and followed her up the driveway. The lawn chairs in the backyard were overturned, and beer bottles were scattered everywhere. The older guys were sitting at the picnic table as if nothing had happened. Lindsey and Danny strolled into the garage. One of the girls wiggled her way over to Lindsey.

"My God, where have you been?"

"Out. I went for a ride," Lindsey said matter-of-factly. "What happened?"

"Have you met my cousin, Danny?" Lindsey asked.

Pam suddenly deflated at the word *cousin*. "Oh, yes, we met earlier," she said.

"Hi, again," Danny replied.

"So, what happened?" Lindsey asked, moving toward the workbench so she could pour a glass of wine. Danny followed and made a rum and Coke.

"A bunch of those kids from Geneva Ave. got into a fight with the kids from the park. It started in the cellar. We were here, in the garage, and the guys were outside. Suddenly, a bunch of the younger girls started screaming and running out of the cellar, saying the boys were fighting. Our guys broke the fight up, but it was too late. Someone had already called the cops."

Kathy, a blonde with her hair done up in a massive hive, joined the conversation. "One of the younger girls was pretty drunk. God, you should have seen her."

"They all were," another girl said. "They were flirting with some of the kids from Geneva. Then, they started screaming out of nowhere, like someone'd been killed. Kerry and I ran over to the guys and asked them to break it up."

Lindsey took a sip of wine and looked over at the house. "Who broke the windows?"

"That one over there," Kerry said, pointing at Billy. "He ran around the house, kicking all the windows out. What a fucking asshole. Kevin grabbed him, and then this other kid jumped in. I think his name was Bugger or something." Lindsey lifted her eyes above the rim of her glass and looked at Danny. "That didn't last very long. The other guys grabbed them and broke them up. I heard someone say they know his brothers or something."

"There's something wrong with that other kid that broke the windows," Kathy said. "He kept laughing the whole time like it was funny, like it was a joke or something." She shook her head.

Danny listened for a while, finished his drink, then strolled over to Lindsey. "Hey, I'm gonna take off," he said.

"Do you want a ride home?"

"Naw, I'm gonna walk."

"Are you sure?"

"Yeah. I'm gonna go by the station house and see who the cops locked up. If they let any of the kids go, I'll walk home with them."

He turned and headed down the driveway. "Danny, wait a minute," she called out. He watched her write something down on a piece of paper and then walk over to him. "Here," she said, handing him the note. "Call me so we can talk about the car."

"I will!" he said excitedly. "I'm gonna talk to Mr. Erickson as soon as I can."

"Sounds good," she said, kissing him on the cheek. "I'm gonna go too."

He pulled out his smokes, lit one, and watched Lindsey walk down the driveway, past the kids, the cops, and the squad cars, over to her car, where she got in and took off, backing down the street.

# 54

Danny got up early and stayed in bed, thinking about what Mr. Erickson had said; he needed to figure out how to sell more things like motor oil, wiper blades, antifreeze, and air fresheners. The best place to start was the motor oil. If the oil cans were more visible, people would buy more of them. He drew sketches of the office with the pump islands, racks, and storage areas and started planning where to move things. He planned to put the little pine-scented trees in the office, where they would make the place smell nice, hoping everyone that came in would buy one or maybe even a three-pack. "You can do pretty good," Mr. Erickson had said. "All you have to do is give the customers a reason to buy something." That, and the thought of a pocket full of folded bills and the Mustang, kept Danny thinking. When he was done, he shuffled into the kitchen. As soon as his mother saw him, she turned the stove on to reawaken the tea kettle.

"Morning, Ma," he said as he walked over to the window and looked outside. "How's Chrissy?"

"She seems okay."

"Has she been eating?"

"Yeah, probably too much. She's putting on a lot of weight."

"That's natural, right? I mean, she's gonna be okay, ain't she?"

"Sure. I put on almost forty pounds when you were born."

"Forty pounds!"

"Yep. Chrissy's put on thirty-two pounds so far. I've been trying to get her to eat better. Most of the time, she nibbles on toast and crackers and sometimes ice cream. When I'm not here, she eats sugar sandwiches with lots of butter." They both turned when the kettle whistled. Danny got up and filled the teacups with hot water. "Her friends come by every week, and they help her make clothes," Bridie said.

"I ain't never seen 'em."

"You're never around."

"I can't argue with that."

"She and her friends have tea and go through sewing patterns so they can make baby clothes. You should see them; they're so cute."

"I'm sure they are," Danny said. "I'm gonna stretch my legs out on the front porch."

"You want breakfast first?"

"Maybe later."

"Okay."

As soon as he stepped outside, a thick blanket of humidity suffocated him. He took a deep breath and thought about the cool waters beneath the Malibu bridge. He finished his tea, went back inside, grabbed some toast, and sat down with his mother and chatted some more about Chrissy. They spoke longer than he'd expected. Finally, exhausted, he said goodbye to his mother and left.

He stopped at Chuck's and grabbed a pepper steak sub, a bag of chips, and some cookies for lunch. He made it to work ten minutes early, just as he'd hoped. From a distance, he could see Mr. Erickson unlocking the pumps and pulling the racks of oil out. Danny wrapped his lunch sack up like a football and trotted over. As soon as Mr. Erickson saw him, he waved at him. Danny waved back and continued jogging down the street.

"Welcome back, son," Mr. Erickson said, pulling his mechanic's rag out to clean his hands so they could shake. "How do you feel?"

"Good, thanks," Danny said. "Looks like you got everything set up."

"Most of it. I wanted to get an early start; it's gonna be a hot one."

"No kidding. This humidity is murder. I tried to get here early to help you out."

"I appreciate that. Remember, you gotta take it slow. No need to kill yourself."

"I know, it's just . . . I don't know. I wanted to help out."

"You can. There's plenty to do." He placed his hand on Danny's shoulder. "Here, come with me." He led the way and opened the front door to the office, where a giant chocolate cake with *Welcome Back* inscribed in red-colored letters waited. "My wife made it. She wanted to be here, but she had a few things to do. Oh, and this is from her," he said, handing Danny a card.

He opened it, read it, then took a deep breath. Mr. Erickson waited a minute before patting Danny on the back and walking into the storeroom, giving him some time alone.

Danny popped his head into the backroom. "Thank you," he choked out.

"You're welcome. We're glad you're back. She still tells her friends the story about when you fixed her tire," Mr. Erickson said.

"Neat," Danny said. He stuck his lunch bag sub in the refrigerator and grabbed a clean rag. "Hey," he said, suddenly excited. "You'll never guess what happened."

"I dunno. I hope it's good."

"It is! I was at a party over the weekend with Lindsey McPherson."

"No kidding? Where was it?"

"At a friend's house over in Harrison Park. He's going in the service. Lindsey knows this kid's big brother. Her husband grew up with him at Harrison Park."

"She doing okay?"

"Yeah, really good. We talked about her husband and me getting stabbed. She didn't know about it, so I told her. We went down the street to the house where her husband grew up. That's where she parks the Mustang. Anyways, we got to talking, and she let me take it for a drive—with her, of course. She told me she's been taking care of her parents, and because they can't get around anymore, she's gonna sell the car. I couldn't believe it. I told her that I'd sleep in it if it was my car."

"Anything else?"

"Yeah, she said she's thinking of buying a station wagon because her parents can't get in and out of the Mustang, you know, because it's a two-door. And then, jeez—I couldn't believe it, she started complaining about the clutch, telling me that it's hard to push it in when she's wearing high heels. I mean, who would wear high heels when they're driving a stick?"

Mr. Erickson laughed some more. "There's a lot you have to learn about women."

"I guess."

"Believe me, you do."

"So, I ask her, if she's gonna get rid of the car, can I have first dibs on it, and she says yes!" Danny slapped his hands and did a quick spin on his left foot.

"That's wonderful, son. It's a great car."

"It sure is!"

"So, how much does she want for it?"

"Well, we didn't talk about it. I was going to ask you if you wouldn't mind figuring out a fair price. I mean, if you don't mind, of course. We both think you're the best person to do that, and we trust you."

"Are you sure you're okay with me doing that?"

"Oh yeah, sure. We both are."

"Well, it's pretty straightforward. The car companies publish resale books. They're called *Blue Books*. They list what a car is worth based on its age and other things, you know, like the size of the engine, mileage, wear and tear, that kind of stuff. I've got some in the back room."

"I don't think I've seen 'em before."

"Probably not. They're on the top shelf. I don't use them that much. Have you thought about how you're gonna pay for it?"

"I was hoping you could help me figure that out. You mentioned how important it is to establish my own—what did you call it? Credit?"

"Yes, that's right," Mr. Erickson said, gently nodding.

"My ma doesn't know much about credit and stuff like that."

"Don't worry. It's not that complicated. Say, have you ever gone to driving school?"

"Naw, I studied the book and passed the test. After that, I got my permit and then my license."

"Have you thought about insurance?"

"Naw, not really. Should I?"

"Well, even though you have your license, you should think about going to driving school. I'll bet you didn't know that you'll get a break on your driver's insurance if you go to driving school?"

"Is it expensive?"

"It can be. Most companies charge a lot of money for young guys like you, being high-risk and all."

"I never thought about it," Danny said awkwardly.

The pump bell rang, echoing through the garage. "I'm gonna grab that," Mr. Erickson said. "Do you know how many miles are on the Mustang?"

Danny reached into his pocket and removed the small piece of paper torn from the Globe. "Nineteen thousand, three hundred and eighty-two miles."

Mr. Erickson pulled a small pad of paper out of his back pocket and made some quick notes. "We'll talk later. We got some new inventory in. It's in the garage. Would you mind stocking the shelves?"

"Not at all."

"Welcome back, son."

# 55

The day wasn't as bad as Danny had thought it'd be. The humidity was gone by mid-morning, and the heat was tolerable. Danny was scheduled for nine radiator flushes, making for an otherwise long, sweaty day. Mr. Erickson had bought several cases of tonic for the customers who'd end up waiting in the office while their cars were being worked on. He'd placed a large ice chest on his office desk. Many of the regulars dropped by throughout the day. A couple of the ladies from Saint Anne's promised to return with cake or cookies after seeing Danny at work. He'd already eaten five pieces of Mrs. Erickson's cake. He decided to take the rest home.

Robby pulled up for his shift when Danny started stocking the oil racks. It was a quarter to five; Robby was always punctual. Danny grabbed a paper plate from the office, placed a slice of cake on it, and put it on the office desk as Robby swung the door open. "Good to see ya, man. How're ya feeling?" Robby asked.

"Like a million bucks!"

"You're full of shit."

"Yeah, I know. Could be better."

"I was worried about you. Everyone was."

"All in all, it could've been worse. I'm pretty lucky."

"No shit," Robby said. "Real lucky."

"As long as I take it slow, I should be okay. The doctor told me not to lift anything heavy."

"Yeah, well, that makes sense."

"Yup. I gotta take a piss." Danny grabbed his crotch and tugged on it. "Can you give me a hand?"

"Fuck you, fag," Robby sputtered, laughing, nearly coughing himself to death.

"I gotta finish a coupla things. Need anything?" Danny asked.

"Naw, I'm good." Danny put the money away, grabbed the rest of the cake, and headed out the door.

"Hey! How's your girlfriend? God, what's her name? She was with you that night, right?"

"Patty," Danny said. The sound of her name stabbed him straight through his heart. "Patty," he said again softly.

"Yeah, that's her. So, how's she doing?"

"Fine," Danny said. "I'll catch you later," he said, walking away from the conversation.

The afternoon sun hung high above the houses across the street. Danny unbuttoned his shirt, hoping to catch a breeze if one came by. He shifted the box from one side to the other, making sure to keep it level so the cake didn't get crushed. He stopped and sat down on the curb in front of Saint Anne's to catch his breath and to watch the world go by. After a smoke, he continued down Victory Road and stopped in front of a three-story apartment building built of beige-colored bricks where his old friend Ricky Hale used to live. When Danny was younger, his mother used to drop him off at Ricky's when she worked nights after Danny's father had left. Danny didn't have many fond memories of the place. The hallways smelled like piss, and the front door was never locked. On the weekends, a steady stream of housewives from Quincy and Milton, in need of a few bucks for a new pair of shoes, would scrape their knees in the hallways, giving blowjobs.

Danny headed down Gibson Street and found a buyer, a grizzled old guy shuffling around in pissed pants, talking to his shoes. After finishing the deal,

Danny walked around the corner; sat on the loading docks; opened a beer; took a long, slow swig; and thought about Patty. With each swig, he became surer of what to do; he just had to figure out when. He scratched his crotch and thought about Kat again. He took a sip and stretched his legs out, pressing them against the cool concrete as a thousand thoughts ransacked his head.

His thoughts suddenly stopped when he heard voices. He looked to his right and saw a Chevy with a bunch of kids inside hollering at him; they were from Upham's Corner. Danny sprang to his feet, ran along the top of the loading ramp, and jumped off onto the paved loading lot. The car followed him, and the kids got out and ran after him. Danny made it to the far end of the building, where he grabbed a large metal drainpipe bolted to the side of the building and pulled himself up. When he was halfway up the building, one of the kids started shimmying up below him. When the kid got closer, Danny kicked his hands, sending him to the ground. The other kids started throwing rocks at Danny, small ones, as that was all that was available.

A second kid came right behind the first one, making his way up the pipe. Danny climbed faster, and when he reached the top, he dragged himself over the edge, tearing the scar on his lower belly open. He grabbed a handful of roof pebbles and flakes of black pitch and threw the dusty debris into the kid's face, stopping him. "Get the fuck away," Danny yelled, throwing more pebbles in his face.

The kid coughed as he climbed down the pipe and tried to wipe the dirt out of his blackened eyes. Danny scrambled across the roof and gathered up whatever he could find: wood, shards of metal, cans, bottles, and balls. He ran back to the edge and threw everything at the kids below, sending them running in every direction. He ran to the other side of the roof, jumping over heating and air conditioning equipment, wires, cables, ventilation pipes, and whatever else was sticking up and in the way. He spotted some drainpipes on the edge of the building, grabbed them, and climbed down, hand over hand, until he reached the sidewalk below. He ran toward Dot Ave. and darted across the street, running through traffic, into Hi-Fi, where he dashed into the bathroom, locked the door behind him, and leaned against the wall, gasping to catch his breath. He looked down at the oozing mess of blood, dirt, and roofing tar covering his shirt and stomach. He pulled some toilet paper off the roll, wet it under a faucet of hot water, and tried to scrape everything off. He repeated the cleaning several times, and when he'd removed as much as he could, he wrapped some paper across his stomach and tucked his shirt in. He peeked through the door to make sure no one had followed him, and when he was sure they hadn't, he walked over to a young girl wearing a checkered red-and-white blouse and a red cotton skirt.

"Hi, do you have a dish towel I can use?" he said.

"Is there something you need to clean up?" she asked in a helpful-sounding voice.

"Naw, it's kind of personal," he said.

She looked at his bloodied shirt as she grabbed a couple of towels. "Are you all right?"

"Yeah," he said, wiping his sweat-soaked brow. "I had a little accident."

"I can see," she said. "Are you sure you're okay?"

"Yeah, I'm fine. I just need to clean up. It's no big deal."

"If you need anything, let me know."

"I will." He went back into the bathroom, locked the door, and ran the towels under the faucet. After working some suds out of a bar of soap cemented to the sink, he rubbed his stomach until he'd scraped most of the black stuff off as small streams of blood ran down his belly. He soaked the towels again and, after another pass, rinsed them, wrung them out, tucked his shirt in, and walked out the door.

"Thanks," he said, putting the towels on the countertop. He stepped outside. The late rays of the afternoon sun cast a warm feeling over him. He reached his hand inside his shirt; he was still bleeding.

The walk was slow, tedious, and painful. The blood soaked through his shirt, making a mess. He ran into Johnny Wilkinson and Gerry McDonald at Westville Street, standing in front of Charlie's Spa, talking about baseball.

"Are you okay?" Johnny asked as soon as he saw him.

Johnny and Gerry waited for an answer. "Yeah." He leaned against the wall and tried to hold himself up but couldn't. Danny's eyes rolled. He buckled over and fell on the sidewalk.

"Help!" Johnny yelled. They rolled Danny over. His stomach was covered in blood. Gerry lifted Danny's shirt. "I'll try and stop the bleeding," Johnny said. "Get some help! Hurry!"

Gerry sprinted around the corner to McCarthy's Tavern. He swung the door open and screamed. "HELP! My friend just passed out. He might be dead! Somebody call an ambulance. HURRY!"

Everyone stopped talking and looked at him.

"HURRY!"

The bartender grabbed the phone and started dialing. A tall man in a gray-colored work shirt with a whiffle cut got up. "Where is he?"

"Outside," Gerry said, holding the door open. "Over there. Hurry!" he said, pointing.

The man shuffled past him. Danny was lying on his back, blood oozing from his stomach. "Try and stop the bleeding," he said. He ran back into the bar. "Charley!" he yelled to the bartender. "Get me a couple of towels and bring them outside. And get some ice. Did you call an ambulance?"

"Yeah."

"I'm a fireman," he said, dropping to his knees at Danny's side. "What happened?"

"I dunno," Gerry said. "We were just hanging out, and he came down the street. He started talking and all of a sudden collapsed."

"He got stabbed a couple months ago," Johnny said, peering over the fireman's shoulder. "Is he gonna be okay?"

"I don't know. Go inside the bar and get some towels. The bartender should have them ready. Bring them out to me as fast as you can."

Johnny ran inside and met the bartender on his way out. He grabbed the towels and ran them over to the fireman. The bar emptied and the men, drinks in hand, formed a circle around Danny, mumbling their suggestions.

"Here," the fireman said to Johnny. "Put a couple under his head. You," he said to Gerry, "be careful; he might have injured his head." They slowly lifted Danny's head and slid the towels underneath his neck.

"Good. Make sure his head doesn't move around. He might try to get up, but you can't let him. Do you see any bleeding back there?"

"Naw, not that I can see," Gerry said.

"Me neither," Johnny said, kneeling and twisting his head to inspect Danny's neck.

"Good. Give me another towel," the fireman said, sticking his hand out.

"Here you go, Hugo," Charley said.

Hugo scrubbed Danny's stomach, drawing more blood as he scraped the tar and pebbles out of the wound. The sound of approaching sirens caught everyone's attention. Charley stepped forward and waved his arms in wide, broad strokes. "Give 'em room," he said. "C'mon, they're gonna need some room. Move back."

"What's his name?" Hugo asked.

"Danny—Danny McSweeney. He lives on Bowdoin, at the top of the hill," Johnny said.

"Okay, let the ambulance driver know."

"Sure," Johnny said, speaking in an important tone of voice.

"Yeah," Gerry added, just as significantly.

"How old is he?"

"Seventeen, eighteen maybe," Gerry said.

Hugo continued working, tossing the used towels aside, pressing the last one against Danny's stomach. He remained that way until the ambulance pulled up. Two medics in white uniforms jumped out. Hugo kept pressing the towel as he filled the medics in, staying until they took over. A squad car pulled up and blocked the intersection. A police officer swung his door open, hung his legs outside, and got on his radio. "Take him to the Carney," he said when he finished. "Follow me."

The medics placed Danny onto a stretcher and carried him into the back of the ambulance. "Anyone with him?" one of the medics asked.

Johnny and Gerry looked at each other. "We are," Johnny said.

"One of you want to come along?"

"I'll go," Johnny said. "That okay?" he asked Gerry, turning toward him.

"Yeah, sure."

"You gotta let his ma know what happened!"

"I will!"

"Tell her I'll stay with him and not to worry!" Johnny said.

"I'll go right now," Gerry said as he ran off.

The ambulance followed the squad car down Geneva Ave., a cavalcade of sirens and blue-and-red lights. The medics stuck a needle in Danny's arm and started pumping him with morphine. He felt the needle and then the medicine course through his veins. As soon as they arrived at the emergency room, one of the nurses waved a flashlight in front of him. "Where am I?" he asked.

"Carney Hospital. I'm your nurse, Evelyn. What happened?"

"I, umm, scraped my stomach," Danny said.

"Here, open," she said, sticking a thermometer in his mouth.

"I can see that. You scraped it pretty hard. What's all the black stuff? It looks like tar."

"It is," he mumbled around the glass stick rolling around under his tongue.

"Let's be quiet for a minute."

She stared at her watch, and when she was ready, she removed the thermometer. "You've got a pretty good temperature."

"What is it?"

"One-o-three. I'm going to increase your IV so we can get that down."

"Thanks."

"Okay, let's start all over again. What happened?"

"I was chased by a bunch of kids. I was down in Fields Corner. I climbed a roof to get away from them."

"So, what happened there?" she asked, nodding at his stomach.

"I got stabbed a couple of months ago."

"Let me take a look. We're gonna have to take your pants off."

"Are you a doctor?" he asked.

"No. I can get one if you'd like, but they're busy right now. If you want one, it will take a while. We were hoping to look at it as soon as possible since we're worried about you getting an infection. That will need cleaning, and if you got all that stuff from a rooftop, I'm sure there are a lot of very bad things in there that'll be a problem if they get into your wound."

"Okay," he said, resigned to the inevitable. A pair of scissors flashed as Evelyn clipped his underwear on both sides and slid it out from under him. She reached over to some alcohol and swabs and wiped them across his stomach, causing him to flinch.

"Does that hurt?"

"A little," Danny said, wincing.

"Need anything for the pain?"

"Naw, I'm okay."

She scraped and cleaned until the dirt and tar were gone. "How's it look?" he asked.

"Not bad. You'll need some time to heal. How long have you had the crabs?"

"The WHAT?" Danny replied, struggling to lift his head.

"The crabs."

He exhaled and rolled his eyes back into his head.

"You didn't know you had them? Didn't you know why you were scratching so much?"

"I thought I had a rash or something."

"No, it's the crabs. You've got a bunch of them."

"Jesus Christ. How do I get rid of them?"

"Well, the first thing we have to do is shave you."

"Shave? Down there?"

"Yes. They lay their eggs at the base of your pubic hairs. They'll never go away if you don't shave."

"Will that get rid of them?"

"No. You need to use some medicine: A-200 Pyrinate. It's a shampoo made for crabs and lice. We have some, but we can't use any right now, not while you have an open wound."

He rolled his head from side to side.

"Are you ready?"

"Not really."

"Well, the doctor's going to want the area clean. I can shave you now, or you can wait until a male nurse's available. If you want to wait, you could be here for a while."

"For how long?"

"We might not get to you until sometime tomorrow."

"Are you serious?"

"Look, it won't take long. I have to prep you anyway for the doctor to examine you. So, you might as well get it over with while we have the time. This place changes by the minute. If someone really hurt comes in, you're gonna get lost in the shuffle."

"Fuck, no. Let's get it over with. Can I ask you a question?"

"Of course."

"It's, um." He paused. "It's personal."

"I'm a nurse. I deal with a lot of personal things."

"What happens, you know, if I . . . well . . . you know . . . get excited or something?"

"You think yours is the first penis I've ever seen?"

"Well, no, of course not," he said sheepishly.

"I'm a nurse, and I can assure you, yours is nothing special. I've seen them all."

He nodded.

"I'll take a wet cloth and put it over you to keep everything out of the way. It will only take a few minutes."

"Will anyone else be here, watching or anything?"

"Oh no, unless the doctor comes in. I'll make sure the curtains are closed; it'll be private."

"Okay."

"Why don't you take a deep breath and relax? I'll be right back. I want to get that IV going before I start."

As soon as she left, he reached down and grabbed a handful of pubic hairs and tore them out. He held them up to the light and saw the tiny crabs and the eggs clinging to the follicles. "Goddamit!" he said, flicking the tainted hairs to the floor.

Evelyn returned with a metal tray filled with bandages, a razor, shaving soap, a brush, a couple of towels, and a small basin filled with hot water. She placed the basin on top of the table and put one of the towels in it to soak. "How're you feeling?" she asked.

"Like shit."

She hooked the glass bottle on the table beside her to the IV and adjusted everything.

"I'm going to place this on your groin before I start shaving you. It's gonna be warm, but it will help with the shaving."

As soon as she placed the towel on his crotch, he moaned. "Ahh, that feels better."

"Good," she said. "Let's give it a minute. I spoke to the doctor, and he'll be here in about half an hour."

"Great. Do you know if my ma's been contacted?"

"I don't know. I think one of your friends is in the waiting room."

"Can he come in, you know, after this?"

"Sorry, family only."

Danny nodded. "Okay."

"Ready?" she asked.

"Not really."

"Relax."

She removed the towel, grabbed the shaving cup, and spun the brush around until it was covered in suds. She placed the brush on his crotch and swirled it around, stopping when she'd worked up a thick white lather. Danny was surprised when he didn't get a hard-on, but there was nothing sexy about it, and it felt just like it looked—medical. He closed his eyes as she started shaving. He could hear the scraping and feel it as she shaved. She collected all the hair in one of the towels, rolled it up and placed it in the tray. "When you get home, rub a little A-200 over your anus if you have any hair back there. They don't usually go there, but you never know."

She grabbed another towel and wiped the suds away. "It's gonna be itchy when the hair starts growing back. So, whatever you do, don't itch it. Here's some cream to use," she said, handing him a small container of lotion. "It'll stop itching in about a week."

"Was it bad?" he asked.

"I've seen worse," she said, "but not by much."

"That's good."

"It is. So, are you still seeing the girl?"

"No, it was . . . you know . . . one of those things. I was drunk."

"Oh," she said, nodding. "You should stay away from her for a while."

"Yeah, I kinda figured."

"A rubber won't do any good against crabs."

"Yeah, I get it. Say, can you do me a favor?"

"Sure."

"Can you check with my friend? Let him know I'm okay and everything? And can you ask him if he's heard from my ma?"

"Sure, no problem."

"Oh! Don't say nothing about, you know, what you just did, the crabs and everything."

"Of course. I couldn't anyway," she said, picking the tray up. "Your medical condition is private."

"And don't tell my ma! If she found out, she'd kill me."

"Of course not. I'll be back with the doctor when he's ready."

"Thanks. You know, you're a good nurse."

"Thank you."

Danny lifted the towel off his stomach. His wound and groin were red, bloody, and clean. He put the towel back on and thought about Kat. She must have known she had the crabs. What would happen if Patty found out? He didn't know how long he'd been thinking about everything when Evelyn returned.

"Your friend, Johnny, said your ma's on her way down. He said Gerry, your other friend, went by your apartment. He didn't tell your ma too much—just that you weren't feeling well."

"Thanks. Did he say how she's getting here?"

"No."

"Okay. Thanks."

"I'll be back."

Danny closed his eyes as his head filled again with too many things to think about.

"Are you awake?" a voice spoke.

"Yeah," he said, opening his eyes.

"Are you okay?" Bridie asked.

"Yeah," he said. "I had an accident, climbing over a fence. Kinda messed up my stomach."

"Can I see?" she asked, stepping closer.

"Let me help you," Evelyn said, tactfully stepping in front of her. "We've prepped him for a few stitches." She lifted the upper half of the towel.

"Mother of Mary, that looks like it hurts," Bridie said. "What were you doing climbing a fence?"

"We were playing stickball, and one of the kids hit it over the fence."

"If you'll excuse me, the doctor is scheduled to come by shortly," Evelyn said, winking at Danny. "If you don't mind, can you wait in the lobby?"

Bridie leaned over and kissed Danny on the forehead. "Do you need anything, honey?"

"Naw, I'm okay. Evelyn here's taking good care of me."

"Thank you," Bridie said, turning to Evelyn. "Will he be able to come home with me?"

"We'll have to see what the doctor says. He'll want to run some antibiotics through him, and he might want to do that intravenously. If he does, he'll have to stay overnight. The doctor's worried about an infection."

"I see," said Bridie.

"Ma, can you do me a favor?"

"Of course, honey."

"Can you call Mr. Erickson and tell him I hurt my stomach? Can you tell him I was lifting some stuff at home?"

"Sure."

"Are you ready?" Evelyn asked Bridie.

"Yes, thank you. I'll see you in a while, honey."

"Okay." Danny closed his eyes and tried to rest.

"Danny," Evelyn said, gently shaking him. "The doctor's here."

He blinked his eyes and rolled his head.

"Hi, Danny, I'm Doctor Turner. How are you feeling?"

"Sore."

"Can you tell me what happened?"

"Yeah, I scraped myself climbing on a roof."

"What were you doing on a roof?"

"Some kids were chasing me."

"There was a lot of stuff in there—small pebbles and what looked like roofing tar."

Turner took the towel off, leaned forward, and inspected the wound. "I'm going to put a few stitches in; you tore your old scar open. There are still some raw areas that'll need some treatment, and, just to be safe, I want to get some antibiotics in you. You've got a pretty good temperature." He turned to Evelyn and spoke. "Let's give him twenty-five milligrams of chloramphenicol succinate every six hours for the next twenty-four hours and check his labs at the same time. I want some blood cultures every four hours."

"Yes, Doctor."

"Can you give him a local so I can get the stitches in?"

He turned to Danny. "I spoke to the doctors over at Mass General. You're lucky you're not in worse condition. If that residue had got into your wound, you'd be in the ER. Thankfully, the medics and your nurse did a good job of cleaning your wound."

"I know," he said, looking over to Evelyn.

# 56

Danny got home the next day, just in time for a supper of franks and beans, canned brown bread, and a stick of butter to slather on everything. Bridie, Frankie, and Chrissy were there, as was Chrissy's friend Edna, a tall, freckle-faced brunette who always dressed nicely, usually in skirts and white cotton blouses. She was skinny, and her hair was always coifed and kept in place with a barrette. She'd been married to her high school sweetheart, Eddie Curriden. He'd joined the marines and got shipped out to Vietnam and never come back. Four months later, Edna had received a four paragraph letter; he was MIA. Two days later, she'd had a miscarriage. Danny liked Edna. She was good to Chrissy and friendly to him.

After supper was over, Chrissy sat up. "I have an announcement," she said. "I've decided on a name for the baby.'

"How exciting," Bridie said. "Aren't you excited?" she asked Frankie. He shrugged. "Frankie?"

"Yeah," he responded, sounding like someone had died.

"If it's a boy, it'll be Martin, and if a girl, Maria."

"Why'd you pick those names?" Bridie asked. "We don't have any Martins in the family, and Maria? That sounds like a spic name." She turned to Danny. "Honey, do you know any Marias?"

Chrissy interrupted before Danny could answer. "Ma, it's from *West Side Story*. Maria. I love that name."

"Mother of Jesus, it's a Puerto Rican name, and . . . well, you're not married, and you don't have a boyfriend." Bridie fidgeted around and stirred some more sugar into her tea. "Well, you know, people are going to talk and . . . well . . . people can be cruel sometimes, and . . . well, I mean . . . it's bad enough you're having a Jew's baby, but Maria? My God, what will they think? A spic name and a kike for a father?"

"Ma, I don't care what people think or what they're going to say. If people ask, I'm going to tell them my boyfriend and I were going to get married, but he got killed in Vietnam."

Bridie continued dumping more sugar in her cup until her tea was nearly a paste.

"You know, I wouldn't be the only one that's happened to," Chrissy said. "Do you know how many guys have gone to Vietnam and never returned? I thought about it, Ma, a whole bunch, and I'm going to have to tell them something, right? If they ask, I'll tell them my boyfriend's mother was named Maria. It's no one's business but my own. Right? You agree, don't you, Danny?"

Danny glanced at her for a second and then into his teacup.

"Right, Danny, it's nobody's business. Right?" Chrissy said louder and more forcefully. He looked at the window, thinking about jumping out.

"Right?"

Danny lifted his head. "Yeah," he mumbled.

Bridie stirred her tea and spoke as if she was giving a eulogy. "Well, there's nothing we can do about it now. I wish things were different."

"I do too, Ma, but I can't change what happened."

"I know . . . I know," Bridie said, as her words lost air, like an old balloon after the party had ended. She stood up slowly. "I'm gonna lie down for a while," she said. "I need some rest."

"G'night, Ma," Danny said. Chrissy and Frankie joined in.

"Good night, Mrs. McSweeney. Thank you for dinner," Edna said.

"You're welcome, honey."

Chrissy got up, went to the sink, and ran some water to fill it. "Want anything?" she asked everyone.

"Can you get me a glass of milk?" Danny responded.

"Sure. Frankie? Edna?"

"No, I'm fine."

"I'm okay," Frankie said.

Chrissy handed the glass to Danny and sat down. He sipped it slowly, listening to the girls babble on. If it was Maria, she'd get married to a wealthy man, and they'd have lots of kids, and she'd drive a Cadillac. And, of course, she'd go to school for art and music. If it was Martin, he'd be a star athlete. He'd letter in baseball and football and track, go to Harvard, and be a successful businessman. He'd marry a beautiful girl from Milton, and they'd have half a dozen kids. The girls went on and on, picking names for Chrissy's grandchildren and Bridie's great-grandchildren; dozens of them. Danny listened until his head was filled with thoughts of diapers, baby clothes, and breastfeeding. There'd be crying, the smell of shit, and diapers everywhere. He grew exhausted thinking about it all.

"I'm gonna go to bed," Danny said, getting up.

"Me too," Frankie said, half asleep already.

"Goodnight," Edna said.

"Night," Danny replied.

"G'night," Chrissy said.

Frankie said nothing as he flopped his way into his bedroom.

---

Danny got up the next day, still tired. He read some old comic books, trying to distract himself from everything that filled his head, things he couldn't stop thinking about. Mr. Erickson had been patient, but how much more would he take? A business needed dependable people who showed up every day and were willing to work weekends and nights if needed. Danny called Bugsy and asked him to come by in the afternoon by himself.

Bugsy showed up, loud and noisy, with Mooch and Billy lugging a bagful of beers. As soon as Danny opened the door, he stopped them from coming in, half pushing them into the hallway. "Keep it down. My sister's sleeping."

"Sorry, man," Bugsy slurred.

"You guys gotta be quiet. I'm not fucking around. She'll be in a shitty mood if she wakes up; I don't need her shit."

"Okay, okay," Bugsy slushed.

"I'm fucking serious."

"Okay, okay. Don't have a conniption."

"So, when's she gonna pop?" Mooch asked as he followed Danny and Bugsy into the kitchen. Billy shuffled along, close behind.

"A couple of weeks if all goes well. She wants to have it natural, doesn't want them to cut it out, you know, a C-section," Danny said.

"What's a C-section?" Mooch asked.

"If the baby's too big or isn't pointed the right way, they'll cut it out. It's s'posed to come out head first. Sometimes the cord gets wrapped around something, so they have to take it out. They slice 'em across their belly. They call it a C-section. The *C* stands for something—Caesar, or something like that," Danny responded with an air of authority.

"That sounds fucked up," Bugsy said.

"It is," Danny replied.

"So what happened with those kids from Uppies."

They sat down, and Danny told them the whole story, including most of the stuff at the hospital, leaving out the part about the crabs.

"Was that little fucker there, the one with the sweater?" Mooch asked.

"Yeah, I'm pretty sure. It all happened so fast." The kids nodded. "Has anyone seen Patty?"

"I saw her friend Emily," Bugsy said. "She said Patty knows about everything and not to try and call her."

"Yeah, that's what I figured," Danny sighed.

"I heard from one of the girls she was looking at some colleges. It might have been New Hampshire or New York. New something," Mooch said.

"Hey, didja hear?" Billy asked, suddenly, out of nowhere. "Johnny O'Brien, T-Bone, Jimmy Dorsett, Headso Harrison, Roachie, and Ducky all signed up with the marines."

"Are you shitting me?" Danny replied.

"No. They figured they'd take their chances by signing up instead of getting drafted."

"What about you?" Danny asked Mooch.

"I talked to the recruiter a couple of times."

"That guy up at Codman Square?" Danny asked.

"Yeah."

"The same guy I talked to," Bugsy said.

"My Uncle Charley might have a job for me at the Fore River shipyard. My ma doesn't want me going in," Mooch said.

"So, what's happening with you?" Danny asked Bugsy.

"I'm shipping out in three weeks, and I got a lot to do. Mostly I gotta get laid."

"Are you gonna have a going-away party or anything?" Before Bugsy could answer, Danny threw another question down the middle of the strike zone. "How about your family? Are they gonna have a time for you?"

"No fucking way," Bugsy responded. "My ma's pissed."

"What about your old man?" Billy asked.

"Shit, he's okay. He told me he was proud of me but won't say anything more than that, not around my ma."

"You got your own time planned?"

"Yeah, down at Nantasket."

"When?"

"A couple of weeks. You think you'll be feeling good enough to go?"

"I hope so," Danny said. "Even if not, I'll go."

"I was thinking maybe we could get the pigs from Eastie to come. If we got them some of that dope they smoke, I bet they'll give us a blowjob on the Congo Cruise. Wouldn't that be wicked?" Bugsy said.

"Well, if it don't work out, you can give me a blowjob. We can sit in the last row of seats," Danny said.

"You're an asshole."

"Yeah, I know. So, are the other kids going, you know, the ones that signed up?"

"I think so. Everyone's invited. It's gonna be a huge fucking party. We're gonna hang out on the rocks at the end of the beach and cook some dogs, drink some beers, and go on the rides. The girls said they'd bring some sheets and blankets."

"Are you still seeing Karen?"

"Naw, I dumped her."

"How come?"

"Fuck, she started getting way too serious. She's a good fuck and all, and she gives great head, but other than that, she doesn't do nothing for me. She said we should get married when she found out I was going in. I mean, she has all this shit figured out, right. I mean, married? I can get my rocks off a lot easier with the chicks from Eastie or those jizz-sucking whores from Hingham, know what I mean?"

"I do, yeah, I do," Danny said.

"So, how's your sister doing?" Bugsy asked.

"She's okay. She's been nice to me lately. It's kinda fucked up, but I ain't complaining."

"The whole thing is fucked up. Shit! You're gonna be an uncle. Uncle Danny! That's gotta sound weird. Uncle Danny! Hey, Uncle Danny, change my diaper. It's full of shit."

"*You're* full of shit, dickhead. I never thought about it, not like that anyway," Danny retorted. "I hope it ain't like that."

"Good luck with that," Bugsy said.

"And fuck, my little brother Frankie's gonna be an uncle too," Danny spurted.

"Hey, one thing's for sure," Bugsy said, blowing the smoke from his cigarette through his nostrils. "We gotta put an end to this shit with those fucking punks from Uppies. We can't let them come into our neighborhood and fuck with us."

"Yeah, we'll get 'em back when I get better."

"You can bet your ass on that!" Bugsy said.

Chrissy banged on her bedroom wall and yelled, "Keep it down!"

"Keep it down, will ya? I gotta take a leak," Danny said. When he returned, the kids were on the back porch, looking out over the brick-faced buildings clustered around Four Corners. After everyone had had a smoke, Danny spoke. "Let's play some cards."

"Sounds good," Mooch said.

Danny grabbed a deck of cards, sat at the kitchen table, and started shuffling. "Poker. Nickel ante," he said. The kids stacked their change in front of them. "So, you ready to go?" Danny asked Bugsy.

"Yeah, I think so."

"You know it ain't like the arcades at Paragon Park," Danny said. "They're gonna shoot back." Bugsy shrugged. "Can I ask you something?" Danny said, pausing to look at his hand. "I'll raise you a nickel."

"You can't touch my dick, you know that, don't you?" Bugsy said.

"Fuck you. I ain't Fitzy."

"Blow me."

"Take a Dudley."

"Seriously, don't you wish you'd finished high school? If you had, you could have gone into the marines, or you could've gone to college. Shit, you could've gotten a decent job if you wanted. A real job, not packing shit or working at Seymour's, going in and out of that fucking freezer. If you do that enough, your dick could fall off. Fuck, do you remember Tommy Richardson, the kid from the Port? He got in that accident with the forklift. It tipped over, and he broke his arm; snapped it in half. The fucking thing still ain't right. And what about Kevin Nealy, the kid from Ashmont? He got burned by that fucking packing glue. That shit spilled all over his leg and burned right through his pants. He has a huge purple scar that runs down to his ankle. Have you ever seen it? He's lucky it didn't burn his balls. C'mon, man, you don't want to work there. You should stay in school so you can get a good job, one with insurance and everything."

"You know, I just want to get the fuck outta here. It don't matter to me if it's the army, the navy, or the fucking marines. I come home every night and watch my old man, and it's the same fucking thing every night. My ma cooks him dinner, and it's always the same: steak and potatoes or meatloaf and peas. Every now and then, it might be pork chops or something. And then, after he's done, he goes in the living room and watches TV, drinks a couple of beers, and after she's done doing the dishes, my ma sits down with him. That's it. They do it every night, day in, day out, and it's the same fucking shows. And then, they go to bed, and the next day, my old man gets up and does the same fucking thing all over again. Fuck! I can't do that! I can't. I'd go fucking nuts. So, tell me, what the fuck am I supposed to do, huh? Marry Karen and come home to her fat ass and a house full of kids and leftover meatloaf, and then, what, watch *Bonanza*? Give me a fuckin' break."

"I didn't mean to bust your balls," Danny said. "If anything ever happened to you, I don't know what I'd do. A lot of kids ain't coming back, and those that do are usually all fucked up." Bugsy pulled a smoke out and lit it. "Did you hear about the kid from Savin Hill? Ricky something or other?" Danny said. "He got drafted and ended up in Sailong, er, Sag Wong."

"Saigon," Bugsy corrected him.

"Yeah, that's it," Danny replied. "Anyways, he was out with some other guys, looking for a sniper who'd been picking off a bunch of guys. They sent this kid Ricky in to flush the sniper out, and he got separated from the rest of his platoon. They found him two days later, hanging from a tree upside down. Those slant-eyed motherfuckers had cut his head off and jammed it on a stake." Danny paused and took a deep breath. "When they found him, a pack of fucking rats were crawling all over him, eating him."

"That'll never happen to me," Bugsy said defiantly. "There's no fucking way that would happen to me! No fucking way! Not in a million fucking years!"

"Look, I know you're a tough bastard and all. But, you know, this kid Ricky played football at English High and Pop Warner football for the Town Field Tigers. You gotta remember him. He was a really tough kid, and he hit really hard. I saw him knock one of the Lyons brothers on his ass at one game. He hit him so hard, Lyons had to leave the game."

"I've been through a lot tougher shit than that," Bugsy said. "I mean, I fucked Karen once in the back of a train, going downtown to the movies. You know how hard it is to get laid on a moving train?"

"You're an asshole."

"Yeah, I know," Bugsy said. "I know what you're saying, and I 'preciate it. I do." Bugsy pursed his lips and nodded. "You're a good friend."

"There's some crazy shit going on over there."

"There's a lot of crazy shit going on over here," Bugsy said.

Mooch interrupted the conversation. "Hey, let's play some poker. I need some cigarette money."

# 57

Following another restless night of tossing and turning like he'd been thrown in a Laundromat washing machine, Danny called Mr. Erickson, knowing he'd be busy stocking the oil racks and checking the pumps. He could hear Mr. Erickson pausing to sip his coffee.

"It won't happen again, I promise," Danny said.

"I understand, son. Right now, all that matters is for you to get better. I'm going to put Robby on full-time, and for now, it'll be best if you work part-time until you're better. I need you back to full strength; you've been through a lot."

Danny replied, "Yeah, I know, you're right."

"You're still young, son, and you have your whole life ahead of you. You need to pace yourself, take these challenges in stride, and take things more slowly."

"Yes, sir, I know."

"I'd like you to take a couple of weeks off to rest up and get better, and then we'll try you on a few afternoons and see how that works out."

"Okay."

"I've got a couple of books I'd like you to take home and read if you're up to it."

Danny perked up like a water bubbler. "Sure! What are they about?"

"One's about managing a gas station. It's a training manual covering inventory, fuel consumption, storage, oil weights, markups, margins, and product sales."

"That sounds great."

"And the other's a basic business book. It's about cash flow, payroll, taxes, insurance, and employees. It's one of my old textbooks from when I went to college."

"I'll read them, promise."

"You have to read them both. All businesses deal with cash flow, payroll, taxes, insurance, customers, and things like that. Running a gas station is no different from running a Zayre's, movie theater, or liquor store. You deal with the same issues, no matter what kind of business you're in. A movie theater might need new seats and a popcorn machine, while a gas station might need a new gas pump or a compressor. There's no difference; it's all business."

"I didn't realize there's so much to it. It's pretty complicated."

"Son, if you can run a gas station, you can run almost any other business once you understand the basics."

"How 'bout I come and get the books today?"

"I'd rather have you stay home. How about I drop them off?"

"Really?"

"Sure, no problem. Son, I have to get back to work. Is there anything else?"

"No, that's good. I appreciate it. Tell Mrs. Erickson I said hello."

"Will do. I'll see you soon."

"Um, before you go, I want to tell you something."

"What's that, son?"

"Well, I . . . I want to thank you for what you're doing. No one's ever done anything like this for me before. You and your Mrs. Erickson, I just . . ."

"It's okay, son. You're a good worker, and you're earning your way. Don't ever forget that. Everything you earn is on your own merit, by your own hands and the sweat of your brow."

"Thank you, I understand . . . and I appreciate it."

"Take care of yourself, and get some rest."

"Will do," Danny said, hanging up.

He returned to his bedroom, lay down, fell asleep, and woke up a little after noon, hungry, awakened by the sound of voices and spoons tapping against teacups. There were several female voices, none of them distinct enough to recognize. He threw his pants on, grabbed a shirt from his closet, stopped in the bathroom, and ran water over his face. After running a comb through his hair, he strolled into the kitchen. The girls were sitting around the kitchen table, which was covered with magazines, pieces of cloth, and children's sewing patterns. If the girls noticed him, they didn't let on. He went to the refrigerator and poured a glass of milk, and after filling the tea kettle, he placed it on the stove and lit it. "Anyone want any tea?"

Two of the girls glanced at him before returning to studying the patterns. The others continued doing what they were doing without acknowledging him. He took his cup of tea out to the back porch and lit a smoke. A group of noisy little kids tossed a ball back and forth over a line scratched in the dirt in the yard below. The door behind him clicked. A girl younger than the others and a little shorter than he was stepped out. Curly blonde hair framed her freckled face. Her eyes were bright and as blue as the winter sky. She was wearing a white, loose-fitting cotton blouse tucked into a pair of pink jeans, held in place by a thin black belt trimmed with silver sequins.

"Hi, I'm Jennifer. My friends called me Jenny. Do you mind if I join you?"

"It's a free world." Danny stuck his hand out, stopping when he realized his cigarette was wedged between his fingers. He turned, flicked it over the wooden railing, rubbed his hands together, and wiped them on his pants before extending his hand and shaking hers. "I'm Danny. You look kinda familiar. Have we met before?"

"I don't think so," she said.

"How do you know Chrissy?"

"She's friends with my big sister Edna. They went to school together."

"Oh," he said, nodding. "Did you go to Dot High?"

"No, my sister did. My father wouldn't let me. He said there were too many Negroes there. I went to Cardinal Cushing, over in Southie."

"That's a good school. I was wondering if you—" He stopped mid-sentence and mumbled.

"What did you say?" she asked.

"Nothing. It's nothing. So, what parish are you from?" he asked.

"Saint Anne's."

"I know a bunch of kids from Saint Anne's."

"Like who?"

"The Donovans, the Zanes—you know, the Greek family—and then there's the Workmans, the Valentis—all fourteen of them, or is it fifteen? Heck, I can't remember. They're a big family."

"I went to school with one of the Workman boys. Arnie," she said. "He had a couple of brothers and a big sister, Cheryl. Arnie and I went through the fifth and sixth grades together. God, he was so cute. I had a big crush on him. Whenever my parents went out, we used to play spin the bottle in our basement."

"Yeah, that's him. He's a good kid."

"He was," she said.

"Did you say *was*?" Danny asked.

Jenny nodded, turned, and looked out over the rooftops. "He was killed in a car accident. Another kid was driving. He was drunk and ran into a seawall at Nantasket, and Arnie died at the scene." They both grew silent. The kids below continued chattering, and the ball kept bouncing as they yelled points back and forth.

"I didn't know. I hadn't heard," Danny said, placing his foot on the lower railing. "When did it happen?"

"Last year, after graduation."

"Did he go to Dot High?"

"No, he went to Christopher Columbus."

"If he'd gone to Dot, I would have heard about it." Danny looked down at the kids after one of them hollered something.

"Can I get you a cup of tea?" he asked.

She brushed her hair back, lifting it high in the air, and after fluffing it up, she tidied and tugged on her blouse. "Yes, please. That'd be nice. A little milk and two spoons of sugar."

Danny slapped his hands together in a quick clap, returned to the kitchen, and turned the stove on. After picking out one of his mother's favorite cups, he set it next to his and filled them both with boiling water after the pot whistled. "Anyone want any hot water or more tea?" he asked, turning.

"I'll have some water," Chrissy replied.

He walked around the kitchen table, topped off her cup, and glanced at everyone else. They shook their heads *no.*

"So, I see you met my little sister, Jenny," Edna chirped.

"Yeah. She's a nice kid," he said, walking away, making a point to end the conversation. He grabbed the cups and went outside. Jenny was sitting on a milk crate, leaning against the wall.

"So, how're you feeling?" she asked.

"Okay, I guess."

"Weren't you at the hospital?"

"Oh, this?" he said, touching his stomach. "Oh, I'm fine. My doctor said I should be back to normal in no time."

"That's good," she said. "If you don't mind me asking, what's normal?"

He laughed so hard that the kids below stopped playing and looked up at him.

"How did you know about my, ah, accident?"

"My best friend's sister is a nurse at the hospital. She says you're lucky to be alive. And if you were a cat, you'd only have six lives left."

"Ha ha, that's a good one."

"And my sister Edna mentioned you."

"Oh yeah? What'd she say?" he asked.

"She was worried about you and Chrissy, and she's glad you're both okay."

"Really?"

"Really." She got up, leaned over the porch railing, and looked down at the kids below running around and screaming.

"What are they playing?"

"I don't know. Whatever it is, they're having fun."

They watched for a few minutes, trying to figure out the game. "I gotta go to the ladies' room," she said. "I'll be right back." When she returned, Danny could see she had reapplied her makeup. "So, are you in school?" he asked.

"Not right now. I'm working this summer, and I start college in the fall."

"Where do you work?"

"I'm interning at a law firm."

"What's interning? Do you work at a hospital?"

"No, there's all kinds of intern jobs. An intern works at a place where you get to learn something. It's where you volunteer to work."

"Huh? You mean you work for nothing?"

"Well, I guess, sort of. It's one of the ways to learn about becoming a lawyer. If you're lucky and do a good job, the law firm will hire you after graduation."

"A lawyer, huh? God, you must be wicked smart." She blushed, and her freckles lit up like tiny cherries. "So, where do you go to school to learn how to be a lawyer?"

"Boston College."

"I don't know any lawyers. Can I ask why you want to be a lawyer? I never heard of anyone from Dorchester learning to be a lawyer."

"I want to help people."

"How?"

"I want to be a public defender."

"What's a public defender do?"

"Well, if someone gets arrested, say some kid from Dorchester, and they can't afford a lawyer, the court will assign one."

"I can see that now. You'll get to meet every kid from my Corner. Heck, you'll probably get to meet every kid in Dorchester. I know this kid whose big brother Tony came back from Vietnam. He married and moved into a three-decker near Shawmut Station on Center Street. He's got a really good job, works construction, so he fixed up this apartment really nicely. You should have seen it. He built a new kitchen with real tiles on the floor and counters and a new bathroom with one of those fancy showers, with the sliding doors, you can walk in."

"I like those. They're nice," Jenny replied.

"So, one day, the landlord came by to check on things, and when he saw all the work Tony had done, he raised his rent a hundred bucks a month! Can you believe that? A hundred bucks! Then he told him because the place was so beautiful, he could get more for it if he rented it to someone else."

"Are you kidding me?"

"No, I'm not. It's a real story."

"So, what did he do?"

"He told the landlord he wouldn't pay anything more, so he had him evicted. Tony found another place near Ashmont, somewhere behind the station. A couple of weeks later, he and some friends went back after they'd been drinking, and they trashed the place. They ripped everything out, the tiles, the kitchen, the bathroom, all the stuff he'd put in."

"When people get wronged like that, they want to get even, which usually creates more problems. What he did was wrong, no matter how you look at it. A good lawyer could have helped your friend."

"I know," Danny said. "Tony knew it was wrong. He's not an idiot or anything, but he felt he had to do it because his landlord was such a jerk."

"So, what happened after that?" she asked.

"The landlord filed some legal papers and paid this guy to find him. This idiot came around Tony's corner, asking about him. Can you believe that? He must have been stupid or something. So, when Tony found out this guy was looking for him, he figured out where he lived. He and a bunch of guys drove out and parked in front of his house. When this guy came home, he saw them. Tony got out and walked over to him. The guy was smart enough not to call the cops or nothing. He told Tony he didn't want the job, and Tony should forget everything. The landlord said he had insurance, and it would all get paid for anyways."

"Lucky no one got hurt."

Danny changed the conversation. "So, how long do you have to go to school to be an attorney?"

"Well, it depends. I'd be happy if I could get through it in four or five years. Half the problem is getting all the classes you need. It's not like high school. Most of the classes fill up fast."

"Five years! That's a long time. On the other hand, you'll graduate really fast if you're as smart as you're pretty."

She blushed, lighting her freckles up again. "I'm so lucky that I'm going. I earned a scholarship and qualified for a student loan because of my grades."

"Man, you are wicked smart."

"I don't know about that. I do know of a lot of smart people who went to BC."

"Oh yeah? Like who?"

"Have you heard of Kevin White, the secretary of state? He's a BC graduate who grew up in JP. He's going to be our next mayor. And there's William Bulger from Southie. He's a member of the House of Representatives. And there's Francis Bellotti from Quincy."

"Isn't he the president or something?"

She laughed at his response. "He was the lieutenant governor."

"How do you know all this stuff?"

"I read a lot."

"So, can I ask you a personal question?"

"Well, sure."

"Do you have a boyfriend or anything?"

"I just broke up with my boyfriend. We were going steady for almost six months. I was at the Braintree drive-in with some friends and caught him making out with this other girl."

"Man, he'd have to be an idiot to cheat on you."

"Well, it happens. Plus, he lied. He told me he was at a Red Sox game with some friends."

"What a jerk!"

"So, what about you? Do you have a girlfriend?"

"Me? Naw. I was dating this girl, but she's going to college. We weren't going steady or nothing."

"Oh. I see."

"I was wondering if we could go to the movies. It wouldn't be a date or nothing, just the movies."

"Gee, I'd love to. That'd be nice."

"Pissah. We could go downtown, maybe grab something to eat at Kresge's or Joe and Nemo's. There's a couple of good theaters downtown. The Paramount's a good one."

"Well, the movie sounds good, but I think I know a couple of better places to eat."

"What's wrong with Kresge's?"

"Nothing, really. I'd like to eat somewhere where we can sit down. You know, where we can be a little more comfortable."

"Kresge's got booths."

"How about I surprise you and pick the place?"

"Wicked. Let me grab a pencil and paper to write down your address and phone number." Danny stepped inside the kitchen and started rummaging through the junk drawer.

"So, how are you two doing out there?" Chrissy asked.

"We're doing good, really good."

"What're you looking for?" Chrissy asked.

"A pencil and paper."

"There's a pad over there," she said, pointing to the chair in the corner. "There should be a pencil too." He grabbed the pad and pencil. "What do you need that for?"

"None of your business."

The other girls looked at him as if he was on trial. "I want to get Jenny's number."

"Why?" Edna asked.

"Because I want to call her."

"Why?"

"We're going out to the movies."

Edna started to ask another question, but Danny didn't stick around to listen to it. He turned, strode out the door, and passed the pad and paper to Jenny. She added a little map with a mailbox and a couple of streetlights.

"So, did my sister say anything?" Jenny asked. "I heard her talking to you."

"Yeah, it was nothing. It was mostly my sister. She has to know everything."

"That's what sisters do best, don't they?"

"Yeah," Danny said.

The back door opened. "Are you ready?" Edna asked. "We gotta get going."

"Okay," Jenny said.

Danny took her cup from her. "I'll call you next week."

"That'd be nice."

"Bye."

"Bye."

# 58

Danny felt strong enough to walk down to the Corner. His sister was due any day now, and her friends were constantly dropping by. He had to make sure he was wearing pants and a shirt if he left his room. It was annoying to have no privacy, and he figured it would only worsen after Chrissy had the baby.

By the time he made it to Shur's, the cramps in his leg were gone. He bought a pack of gum and a Coke and continued walking, listening to barking dogs and mothers yelling for their kids to come home. He rounded the corner to the schoolyard, following the sound of voices and the smell of cigarettes.

"Hey! Danny. What's going on?" Pinhead, Mooch's little brother, was hanging out with some friends.

"Where's your brother?" Danny asked.

"Fuck, I don't know. I ain't his fuckin' babysitter." The other kids laughed. Danny shook his head and continued walking toward Mother's Rest. Voices came from the houses he passed, some from television sets, some from people laughing and talking. Some people sat on the wooden stoops of mottled three-deckers, talking or playing cards on small tables. On others, young couples held hands, whispering beneath the glow of a yellow porch light. He slid between a pair of fence posts and listened to the sounds of bats swooping overhead, catching buzzing insects from the sky.

He hiked along the chain-link fence that enclosed the park, where he spotted several couples sitting on wooden benches, holding hands and talking. He walked over to a bench at the end of the park to sit alone and look out at distant lights, trying to figure out which ones were cars and which were boats. A shooting star shot across the sky, arcing gracefully to the south. He closed his eyes and leaned back, spreading his arms behind him, listening to the sounds of the night, thinking about Jenny. She was one of the smartest girls he had ever met, and they were going on a date. He told himself not to mess it up.

He drifted off for a few minutes, listening to the sounds of the night. He stretched his arms and sat up, realizing it had fallen silent. The sounds of the night had stopped; the crickets, the birds, and the hand-holding couples were all gone. Then, he heard something—footsteps—and turned. A dark figure was standing behind him. Danny started to get up but froze when he saw a flash of steel and felt a knife slash across his face, opening his cheek. He ran his fingers across his face, feeling the open cut. Blood began flowing, dribbling initially, then gushing down his face, winding beneath his jaw and neck. He heard voices; the kid with the knife came closer. Danny saw the blade just as the kid thrust it into Danny's stomach, once, twice, and then a third time, in his chest, deeper.

Shadows moved back and forth, growing fuzzy. Danny looked down and watched his shirt darken. His mouth filled with the taste of metal. He felt the blade again. The air roared around his ears, and his eyes blurred and shuttered. He felt the knife again, and he heard laughter. The lights flickered before everything disappeared.

Another star shot across the sky.

# EPILOGUE

"**No American—white or black—can escape the consequences** of the continuing social and economic decay of our major cities. Only a commitment to national action on an unprecedented scale can shape a future compatible with the historic ideals of American society. The great productivity of our economy, and a federal revenue system which is highly responsive to economic growth, can provide the resources. The major need is to generate new will—the will to tax ourselves to the extent necessary to meet the vital needs of the nation."

The Kerner Commission
Report of the National Advisory Commission on Civil Disorders
February 29, 1968